# THE DOCTOR'S BUILDING

by

Robert Hendrick

WESTVIEW BOOK PUBLISHING, INC.
Nashville, Tennessee

© 2006 by Robert Hendrick

All Rights Reserved. No portion of this book may be copied; whether electronically, mechanically, or by any digital method, without the express written permission of the author. Short excerpts may be used for purposes of media reviews or discussion with the permission of the author or the publisher.

First Edition November 2006

Printed in the United States of America on acid-free paper

ISBN 1-933912-56-1

Cover design by Sarah Nelson, Elizabeth Nox, and Lemmie Stone

Typography by Westview Book Publishing, Inc.

WESTVIEW BOOK PUBLISHING, INC.
PO Box 210183
Nashville, TN 37221
www.westviewpublishing.com

To my parents.

Where we come from determines where we go.

# Acknowledgements

I believe that one's personality is made from small bits and pieces borrowed or copied from the people that surround them. The manuscript for The Doctor's Building follows that same recipe and owes its results to the small touches of the many people around it. To that end, I owe my thanks to the English instructors who instilled their grammatical style, Mrs. Bowen and Mrs. Mary Helen Lowry.

My initial editors, Sally Hendrick, Betsy Hendrick, Dr. A. Hugh Wright and Matt Foster provided me with input at the most critical time. Even though the novel was hardly ready for primetime when they got their hands on it, each of them plied me with equal part constructive criticism and encouragement, both of which I needed to continue forward. As I came down the home stretch, the efforts of editor Lori Fredeking further honed my style and polished the details as I tightened up the final manuscript.

In between, there were countless editors with comments. Some of them enjoyed The Doctor's Building enough to pass it along to a friend or family member. And while I made a concentrated effort to try and capture all of the names of those who got hold of the early versions, I know there are those that I missed. Those of you I have omitted inadvertently may be assured that your input is equally appreciated. In addition, there were many people who aided me along the way in the form of research or other assistance.

For their contributions as editors and/or researchers, I would like to acknowledge the following: The Book Ends Book Club of Nashville; John Connelly, Nashville Davidson County Historian; Ken Fieth, Metro Davidson County Archivist; Debbie Cox, Metropolitan Davidson County Archives; Gresha Allen; Rob and Fronda Alley; Amy Bennett; Kim Blanz; Claudine Brown; Todd Counter; Harlan Dodson; Hugh Daniel; Pat Dunlap; Bradford Gioia; Gretchen Horner; Lareada Johnson; Eloise Perry; Hobart Payne; Mike Slate; Ken and Mary Steverson; Janice Ward; Ridley Wills, Sr.; The Staff of the Metropolitan

Davidson County Archives and The Staff of the Metropolitan Nashville Davidson County Library

Additionally, there were countless books, newspaper articles and other sources that helped bring 1916 Nashville to life. Of those, The Nashville I Knew by Jack Norman, Sr. was a great source of detail.

And a special thanks to Cabedge.com – Chris Blanz and Lemmie Stone – for their graphic design efforts and for putting together the Addy Award Winning web site TheDoctorsBuilding.com

# THE DOCTOR'S BUILDING

# 1

Had I known the significance of meeting Miss Nancy Pettigrew, I might have paid more attention. Listened to her speak. Taken better note of her accent. Wondered at the summer cold causing her to sniffle and dab at her nose. Instead, I caught the tidbits that interested me and savored the soft details of her beauty. Her age approached my own, and I couldn't help but take interest.

She had the look of a china doll with delicate features and powdery white skin, striking, yet unremarkable, an admittedly odd combination. No one aspect defined her appearance more than a notably square jaw and a small mole on the right side of her chin that marred the image of perfection. Nothing is faultless, and that single identifiable flaw gave the impression of otherwise immaculate beauty.

She was in the company of a girl a few years her junior, someone I had been courting the past few months, one Miss Beatrice Rose. The prettiness of my Bea equaled that of her companion though, and even eclipsed it in some ways. But Bea's single flaw eluded me. Either I had found love, or I was blinded by it. Whatever the case, as I drank in the beauty of her friend, I found myself envying the man who, with the certain knowledge of Nancy's one flaw, possessed her heart. And I wondered why he would allow her to find her way home unescorted, as she was that evening.

Ever the outgoing one, my Bea spoke first, "This is Nancy Pettigrew, a fellow suffragist. She works in The Doctor's Building, on the second floor just below me." She then turned to the beautiful girl beside her, "Nancy, this is Mr. Nathan Black, the man I've been telling you about."

I tipped my hat at the introduction.

Nancy extended her hand. "It's a pleasure to make your acquaintance, Mr. Nathan Black."

I replaced my hat and delicately took the offered hand. "My pleasure, entirely. But I don't stand too much on formalities, please call me Nathan."

She allowed her hand to linger in mine. "I've heard quite a bit about the investigator and aspiring physician."

I cast a sidelong glance at Beatrice. "Hopefully most of what you have heard about me is good—and accurate. As for my medical career, I've chosen to set those intentions aside for the time and focus instead on investigative work."

Beatrice leapt into the conversation, "But he may practice, yet."

The comment went unheralded, and I released the woman's hand to face Beatrice. "And how are things among the working women and future voters of America?"

She giggled. "We are still downtrodden and unrecognized."

Nancy Pettigrew put a hand to her forehead to shield the sun from her eyes even though we stood beneath the awning. "A bit warm, too. The evenings are a bit cooler where I come from."

I saw an opportunity and turned to the woman. "I suppose I'm just used to it, since I grew up here." I looked into her eyes, and it caught me for a moment. "Where are you from?"

Nancy twirled a lock of her chestnut hair around her finger before she tucked the loose strand behind her ear. "Kentucky, just outside of Louisville. I've been here about a year." She had adopted the local dialect so well that the remnants of her small-town heritage were all but indistinguishable. She had her hair bundled on her head, so that no part of her face remained hidden, and she cut a slender, but not slight figure in a new store-bought dress. She seemed a suitably healthy girl, a viable candidate for marriage.

We stood talking at the entrance to The Doctor's Building where the awning provided us with a slight respite from the late afternoon heat. I had been waiting patiently for my Beatrice to finish for the day that I might have the honor of seeing her to her door that evening. The girls lingered in the entranceway and continued with their discussion that had started in the elevator on the way down from their offices. Not interested in their gossip, I struck up a conversation with a fellow who, like me, regularly loitered about at the entrance to wait for his girl at the end of the day. Our discussion that Tuesday inevitably turned to things more of interest to the men.

He waved a folded newspaper. "Did you see the sports page today?"

I nodded. "I couldn't believe that about Johnny."

He shook his head. "I saw him when the Gulls played at Sulphur Dell a few weeks ago. It makes you wonder what would've happened if the Vols had kept him on as third sacker."

I clucked my tongue. "He wasn't very consistent for us. But he'd found a good spot there in Mobile. And he was having a bang-up season for the Gulls. He had two of the four hits off of the Gallatin Gunner yesterday before he took that pitch. Poor Johnny Dodge. Dead. It's hard to believe—"

Nancy turned quickly to us. "Excuse me. Did you say Johnny Dodge had died?" Nancy added a tomboyish interest in sports to her intrigue. "The baseball player?"

"You know baseball?" I smiled, encouraged by her curiosity and anxious for an audience not already familiar with the tale.

"Of course," she stammered, "but what happened to him?"

"He got hit with a pitch," I said.

Nancy heaved a deep sigh. "Is that all?"

We men looked at one another, and I took the lead. "That's all, but it killed him."

Nancy drew her breath in sharply. "Are you sure?"

"Positive. Shotgun has quite an arm. That's who hit him."

"Shotgun?" asked Beatrice her mouth hanging open.

"Tommy Shotgun Rogers. The Gallatin Gunner. He's been having a pretty good season, too, but the rest of the team hasn't had the bats to back him up, if you know what I mean."

Nancy flapped her hands impatiently, "Yes. I know what you mean, but tell me how it happened!"

I pulled back my coat and stuck my thumbs in my galluses. "The Vols were playing the Gulls in Mobile yesterday. Johnny came to bat against the Gallatin Gunner in the seventh, and Tommy served up a fastball. That pitch has earned him quite a reputation in the Southern League," I said glancing from one girl's face to the other. "But Johnny didn't cull. That just wasn't his way. He was a full step ahead of the pitch before it had even left the Gun's hand. The problem was that instead of breaking away like fastballs sometimes do, it broke in, and Dodge realized it too late. The rawhide caught him full force in the center of the forehead and knocked him to the ground."

Beatrice gasped and put her hand to her mouth, but Nancy was intent on my every word, her green eyes wide in anticipation.

I bowed my head momentarily out of respect, and then looked both women in the eyes. "Two doctors attended him on the field, and he was removed to a sanitarium. The initial prognosis was good, but he died before dawn."

Already pale, the skin of each of the two women turned translucent with my detailed account. "How horrible! I just can't believe it!" Nancy said, revealing a squeamish feminine side to balance her boyish interest in sport.

"Exactly what I was saying," chimed in the other man looking to establish some rapport with the beauty.

Beatrice still had her hands covering her mouth, "Oh, my. That's simply gruesome," she said in a hushed tone.

"It certainly befits The Shotgun's moniker, but that's an awful way to have it confirmed," I said.

The girls turned and sidestepped politely away from us. "I can't imagine what the poor boy's family must be going through," Beatrice said, and they returned to their own conversation no longer interested in hearing more of what we men had to talk about.

After my counterpart's sweetheart arrived, I passed the time playing the role of attentive, yet disinterested beau while the women chatted. The remainder of their conversation lasted the sum total of five minutes, most of it about suffrage issues and gossip about the doctors in the building where they were employed. They spared me too much idle chatter before Nancy said, "Excuse me. I feel a bit of a headache coming on."

"We can escort you home if you aren't feeling well," I offered.

She put a lace handkerchief her nose again. "I don't want to burden you two love birds. Besides, I think I have some powders up in my office."

We took our leave, and started in the direction of Beatrice's home. "Well, if you weren't awfully fresh. You simply ogled her the entire time we were talking," she observed.

"I'm sorry. Did I?" Her response was the feminine manifestation of a grumble, and she affected an ill temper toward me for the duration of the stroll home. Jealousy is not a feature that she wears well, and I wondered to myself that it might be the one flaw that I sought. If so, it was a serious one.

The next few days were hot and humid as well. I met Beatrice each day, but she was never in the company of Miss Nancy Pettigrew at the end of the day, and I got not another glimpse of the lovely woman to remind me of her features.

That Friday, Beatrice eagerly awaited my arrival at the entrance of the building. High spirits replaced the specter of jealousy that had reared its ugly head days before, and taking my arm, she practically skipped along, dominating the conversation.

"How are things going?" she asked.

"Fair to middling," I replied.

"No new mysteries to solve? No robberies? No missing persons to find?"

"Not just yet."

"Are you working on an investigation?" she asked.

"You know I'm not." I replied.

"Good," she squeaked before realizing what she had said. "Well, I don't mean good that you're not working, but good because I've found a case for you to work on." And then she launched breathlessly into a description of the circumstances before I could backpedal from the situation. She left me no option to politely decline, laying out the details and binding my success to her own by associating all of the parties involved—hardly a feat in a town of sixty thousand people where it seemed that everyone knew one another.

I have a knack—a knack for happening upon unusual situations that require problem solving of a discrete nature. I do not go looking for them, but they come looking, and all too often, find me. It is that which has led me to my informal if involuntary calling as a private detective.

True to its nature, that propensity now surfaced itself in regards to the whereabouts of Miss Nancy Pettigrew, the same one over whom Beatrice had blown into a jealous rage only days before. The woman worked for an insurance company in the building, and she had gone missing the day after I had met her.

Beatrice saw Nancy's employer while on the way back from lunch, and she had inquired after the woman. "I told him that I'd hoped to catch Nancy today, but I hadn't seen her since Wednesday."

"He hasn't seen her in a few days himself." She drew a quick breath. "He had hoped that I might be able to shed some light on her whereabouts. He's becoming a bit concerned."

Flattered to be availed of her assistance and emboldened by her feminism, she pressed the conversation with the man. "She's been gone and he's had no word from her or of her. He's even checked up on her at her place of residence, but they know nothing either. So I told him that I know a private investigator, and perhaps he needed someone to help him track her down and find her."

She grinned at me.

I tried not to sound too eager at the prospect of going looking for Nancy Pettigrew. "And what did he say?"

"He asked what experience you had. I told him that you were quite good at what you do and had many a high-profile episode to your credit." Bea offered.

But when he had asked her to elaborate, she faltered, hindered by my tendency toward uncompromised discretion that limited her familiarity with my work. Having little idea of how I present myself to clients, I fear she did more harm than good with my professional reputation.

She looked away. "He suggested that we discuss the whole thing a bit more over a Cher-O Cola at the counter at Jennings there on the corner."

"Did you tell him that you and I are seeing one another?" I pressed.

"Not at first. I wanted to pique his interest, and I did," she said coyly. "He wants to discuss the matter with you over lunch on Monday—should Nancy not have returned by then."

"Is he handsome?"

She didn't answer. "I think he wants to hire you."

The remaining details of the conversation were not readily forthcoming from Beatrice. What little I did learn led me to believe that the entire exchange was about my Beatrice, and not about the business at hand.

Of course, she just waved off my concerns, told me not to be silly, and enjoyed my green-eyed display—thoroughly. But the tryst stuck in my craw, and I determined to keep the appointment in three days time if only to glimpse my rival and size up the competition with which I had now to contend.

I saw her to her door, and we confirmed our plans for the following day. I went home, but could not get to sleep. I was burdened by the recent events and the prospect of being employed to find Nancy Pettigrew.

I spent a restless night on the heels of our conversation. The heat kept me awake as much as my apprehension over a new suitor for Beatrice's attentions, and I vowed to do something about both issues.

# 2

The following day, Beatrice and I caught the No. 13 Fairfield trolley to the park. A good distance south of town, the early morning ride was pleasant and not terribly long. For five cents one could travel anywhere in the city, complete with transfers, so the park drew a respectable crowd. It was a beautiful day for courting a young woman, particularly this one I had been delicately pursuing since she had caught my eye almost six months before. Part of the attraction to Beatrice was that she saw more in me than I did—the net result being that she encouraged my every effort, no matter the frivolity of it, and I tried to show my appreciation without fawning over this girl, five years my junior, but more mature than most her age.

"Tell me a bit more about this man I'm to meet on Monday," I prompted as the trolley rolled out of town.

"Nothing much to tell," she said.

"Well is he tall or short? Fat or thin?" I encouraged.

"He's tall. Not fat. Fairly handsome actually. But don't fret over him. You just worry about finding Nancy," she said, and she refused to discuss the topic any further.

"Well don't bring it up in front of people today," I admonished her.

"Why not?"

"You know how I feel about discussing people's business, especially if there might be a case involved."

"Well, I can tell what little I know if I want, can't I?"

Grudgingly I allowed her that minimum of leeway in the hopes of hearing more of the meeting with the missing woman's employer in the process.

This lovely woman, precious in many ways, possesses a stubborn streak—a touch of tenacity to complement a sharp mind. Easy on the eye, she had coiffed her auburn hair and pinned it carefully in a bun on the crown of her head, very much in step with the style of the day. The high-waisted skirts she wore left the secrets of the figure beneath an enticing mystery, though with a modicum of imagination, one could easily envision that what she concealed beneath was equally as pleasing.

Out in the countryside, the grounds of Glendale Park were ample enough for a substantial gathering away from the crowds of the city. As we sat beneath the trees on a wooden bench, our picnic blanket under us, she flattered me with a kiss and a playful caress of her arms and neck. I felt her pulse quicken when my hand grazed the soft nape of her neck, and I tasted her lips. She exuded a faint musky aroma beneath the scent of fresh soap and a lingering hint of perfume, and the fragrances conspired in the betrayal of her longing.

We exercised restraint, however, for we were not alone in our indiscretions. It was a place where other young romantics went during the weekends to court under the guise of a public gathering place. Beyond the reach of the prying eyes of parents and guardians, no activity such as that in which we were engaged could have been imagined to occur—never mind the fact that our elders before us came here for exactly the same reason. The park had been serving up such opportunity for better than a generation.

Hoping that I had interpreted correctly, I chanced a peck on her neck, and she drew her breath in deeply. I stole a glance. Her eyes were closed and her head tilted back as if permitting more, a request that I obliged by tasting her neck where it curved to meet her shoulder.

She gripped my arm tightly to keep from falling. At that signal, my hand slid from her shoulder down to the ruffled blouse she wore, and I was rewarded with the opportunity to imagine the form of her body like a blind man who touches an object that he hopes one day to have the privilege of seeing.

"Beatrice!" cried the voice from afar and shattered the moment. Then again, but more insistent and closer at hand. Once more, it called loudly before the young blonde appeared around the base of the maple tree. Her long braided hair twirled about her face as she came to a halt in front of us.

Beatrice and I remained entwined atop the bench. The ill-timed appearance of my sweetheart's best friend with her beau, Jeff, close behind had caught us quite off guard. He alone had demonstrated a minimum of good judgment and held back a few steps.

"Beatrice, come on! I want to get a good spot to see the Indian princess and her diving horse!" she said, referring to one of the most popular attractions at the park. "Whatever have you two been doing over here all this time?" she exclaimed. The blanket had gathered awkwardly beneath us, and we had knocked the picnic basket over in our digression. "We've been looking all over for you—" she stopped short and blushed darkly enough to nearly conceal the wealth of freckles covering her face.

Beatrice brushed her dress, adjusted her collar, and checked her hair. She was flushed with a mixture of embarrassment and arousal. My state of excitement from the recent events rendered me unable to stand immediately, but the appearance of Caroline and Jeff had diminished any amorous intent. I struggled to my feet, coughed, and turned my back to them to hide my sense of urgency.

All of us were crimson-faced and unwilling to meet one another's gaze. I brushed at my sleeves and stared aimlessly around at the treetops, the sky, and the grassy rolling hills. Beatrice cleared her throat three times, before I realized that it was directed at me. Her forward thinking stance on women's rights did not extend to the vagaries of southern chivalry, and my delay in offering my hand had drawn a stern look.

We gathered our belongings and stowed them in the basket while the girls chattered and the men listened. It was all small talk, until Beatrice informed them, "Nathan has a *new case*."

The revelation elicited a squeal from Caroline, "Oh! Really? Do tell us about it!"

Bea cast a mildly resentful glance in my direction. "I can't say much. Nathan won't let me." And true to our understanding, Beatrice was prudent with what she told. Still, the premature announcement served to make me a bit uncomfortable.

"He's looking for a girl who's gone missing. She works in The Doctor's Building."

"Someone you know?" Caroline interrupted.

"Well, I really shouldn't say too much, but yes, she is an acquaintance," Bea admitted.

The basket packed, we headed toward the gates, stopping to survey the selection of horses and buggies arranged near the trolley stop. We noted the presence of a familiar carriage or two, anticipating seeing their owners also out for a day of leisure.

Slowing my pace, I gently separated Beatrice from the others "We don't know if there truly is a case, much less, if I shall be engaged on it."

"Oh, there is, and you will," she stated with absolute confidence as we approached the gates.

She skipped ahead and caught up with our companions for the day.

The sound of running water caught our ears as we walked. We stopped at its source, a fountain, to take a drink from the spring, cupping our hands beneath the faucet. None of us could stomach any more than a handful of the pungent sulfur-tainted liquid, but others had brought jugs with them to collect the bitter water.

At the entrance, the five-cent admission was a fair price for a day's entertainment, but once inside and at the full mercy of the trolley company profiteers, we were accosted by additional opportunities to be relieved of our earnings. The vendors came hawking their wares just beyond the gates and shouting, "Popcorn! Peanuts!" and they shamed Jeff and me into spending more before we could escape.

From there, we walked the short distance to the amphitheatre. People had already begun to gather by the time we arrived, and it was a sizeable crowd when one considers that we were all there to see a horse forced to jump into a pond.

A rotund little man gave an overwrought introduction that lasted a hundred times longer than the event we had come to witness. "This stunt is a perilous one that risks both life and limb of the Indian princess, Two Feathers, and the beast she rides." He proceeded to warn us about what we were about to see and prattled on longer than need be for his speech, intent on luring in those casually passing by.

After the buildup, Two Feathers appeared, leading her trusty mount. Both seemed calm and resigned to the fate that stood before them. Then the stout little man launched into another speech, "Two Feathers holds a position of great importance as the sole remaining member of her tribe and a direct descendent of many a famous chieftain." (Exactly which ones, he had failed to specify.) "Her steed is the result of a long lineage of proud stock, many of which are also part of Indian legend and folklore…"

And so on in such a manner for several minutes.

Mercifully, he concluded his spiel and directed our attentions to the princess and her equine companion. Two Feathers took her cue to mount the horse and ride him up onto the platform above the pool. There ensued a lengthy pause.

A long one.

Far too long and far too poorly scripted for anyone to believe that there was a moment of hesitation or concern from either the princess or her horse. They took a tentative step forward. She pulled hard on the reins, and he pranced a few steps backwards, agitated with the show of indecision. She allowed him forward once more to glimpse the water beyond the edge of the platform. And then, she permitted him a step, one more, then rapidly another, a trot, then a leap that propelled him out over the pool straining his neck forward with the Indian princess in tow. They plummeted to the depths of the pool erupting in an enormous wave before bobbing to the top in the frothing water. The princess remained mounted on the frantically paddling steed as he tried to keep his head above water and instinctively made his way toward a ramp that provided escape.

The crowd burst into applause for the daring feat; even the few drenched souls in the front row joined in. The Indian princess reached the safety of the platform and turned her mount to face the audience. She directed the horse to lower its head and forequarters in an equine bow. Water streamed endlessly from the saturated hide of the beast and the bottom fringe of the princess' dress as they acknowledged the crowd. The people clapped exhaustively, and the performers paused long enough to soak up the adulation.

The exhibition complete and there being little entertainment value in the smell or the sight of witnessing a wet horse as it dried, the crowd began to disperse. I took Beatrice by the elbow and lead our small procession away from the spectacle. We followed the well-trodden dirt paths through the park.

There were a wide variety of species populating the grounds. The collection of birds made for a most fantastic sight and the shows were beyond compare. We stopped to glimpse a few, never staying long enough to catch the entire performance, but anxious to try to experience as much as possible since we had gotten a late start. I tried to steal a word or two with Beatrice regarding Miss Nancy Pettigrew, and more specifically, the woman's bold employer.

"So what do you know of this man? Nancy's employer, I mean."

"His name is Samuels. He's nice enough," she said.

"Would you say he's handsome?" I asked.

She turned her head quickly, "So which animal in the park would you compare me to?"

Having learned that there are no innocent questions, I stalled. "I haven't thought of it really, but apparently you already have. What animal is it that you would compare me to?"

She hesitated only a second. "I think either the elk or the buffalo. Both are strong and smart." She glanced up and looked pensive for a moment, "Maybe more the buffalo. The elk seem too delicate." She smiled. "Now me. What animal do I remind you of?"

I closed my eyes in mock thought. "The alligators."
She furrowed her brow.
"The ostrich?"
"I'm serious," she said.
"Oh me too. The mountain lion!"
"Honestly! Why do I put up with you?"
"All right then." I tried hard to come up with a benign choice. "The horse. You dive into things just like it did, and you drag everyone along with you."
She squinted her eyes and smiled broadly before stooping down to play with a stray bear cub.

The steel bars mounted in the limestone cave were close enough to keep the adult bears at bay, but far enough apart that their young were able to slip out. Their thick black fur was soft to the touch, and since the cubs posed no danger, the park did nothing to confine them or discourage people from playing with them.

I overheard Caroline asking Beatrice, "Do you think we could take them home as pets?"

"Oh, Daddy wouldn't let me keep one," Beatrice said.

"Do you think it would get along with my cats?" said Caroline.

As for Jeff and I, we just shook our heads at the very idea.

At the middle of the park, we found the Casino and the band. Clad in white high-collared shirts with Buster Brown ties, galluses, and trolley caps, they were in full swing, and we decided to take advantage of some nearby benches to rest for the moment and enjoy their music.

"Look at the fiddle player," Beatrice smiled. "He looks like he's having more fun than the banjo, the drummer, the piano player, and the horn players all put together."

"He may even be having more fun than we are," I countered as the band played a rousing tune of Dixie and other popular songs, taking them up in rapid succession as if each musician knew what the others were thinking.

We spent most of the remainder of the day wandering the park waiting for evening. I tried to corner Beatrice for another private word about the case of the women's employer, but Jeff and Caroline remained our constant companions, and we never had another moment alone.

We stayed for the evening's band performance by Von Stechow, and the concert was quite good, but I failed to enjoy it. Instead, I was consumed with mixed emotions. I was jealous over Beatrice's new suitor and excited by the opportunity to learn more about the intriguing Miss Nancy Pettigrew. Beatrice's efforts were undoubtedly based on good intentions, but the circumstances gave me justifiable cause for concern. The situation was rife with pitfalls and warning signs that should have steered me clear from the entire affair. But rather than heed the cautionary signals, I barreled forward into the entire mess determined to pursue my own interests. In her innocence, Beatrice believed herself to be doing me a favor as she sought to further my career. In fact, she was drawing me into a volatile and dangerous situation that might cost far more than it would return.

# 3

In anticipation of my meeting that Monday, I searched the day's paper for signs of Nancy Pettigrew. When it involved a missing person, I began with the broadsheet because it required the least amount of footwork. In effect, it was like having the entire staff of the newspaper working on the case. Unfortunately, if it wound up in their reporting, it became difficult to justify my fee, so it was a double-edged sword.

For two cents, I received a sentinel record of a moment in time committed eternally to the printed page. It was the privilege of the news that I consider one of the greatest pleasures in life to be savored rather than consumed. The texture of the newsprint between my fingers, the rustle of the turning pages, and the smell of the freshly applied ink were a delicious combination. Blended with the aroma of a freshly percolated cup of coffee, the bitter taste made sweet, they marked the start of the day. That day's brew was superb—rich and warm, and it fought off the morning haze.

The day of the meeting arranged by Beatrice, the newspaper had little to offer in the wake of Sunday's tome of a journal carrying the news that subscription rates were being raised from ten cents per week to fifteen. The big news was that we had troops arriving at the local fairgrounds in anticipation of war with Mexico. In sports, the Vols kept their pennant hopes alive. They smashed the Gulls 9-2, but there was precious little else. For the remainder of the time between dawn and noon, nothing transpired to distract me from the pending confrontation with a man who was either my latest rival or my newest client. Or both.

Pilchard Samuels turned out to be a rangy sort. His height rendered him imposing enough to be noticeable in a crowd, but it did not make him stand out. While I am not a small man by any means, he was broad enough that only the more pugnacious or foolish would engage him in a round of fisticuffs, and I hoped that a common interest in Beatrice would not bring us to blows at some point. His thick black hair had a distinct wave subdued by the generous application of Dapper Dan and further concealed by a fashionable gray felt Panama. The tailored suit shadowed his frame perfectly. The dark-grey pinstripe accentuated his height and drew the eye up to a square cut jaw. Judging by his appearance, he began his day clean-shaven at the hands of a barber, but his midday beard had already begun to cast a shadow.

He arrived late for our noon appointment. "You must be Nathan Black." He extended his hand, but made no apology for keeping me waiting.

The coffee shop at the Maxwell House Hotel was already busy, and we were forced to wait for a seat. He passed the time by ignoring me and was preoccupied with scanning the morning's news, skipping the sports section. I am not overly biased, but am inherently distrustful of gentlemen who do not follow sports. You can tell a lot about a man by the team he roots for and what sports he prefers.

Our table, when we were finally shown to it, was wedged in a corner, and we shared it with two other businessmen. "Now about Nancy—

"Not, yet," he hissed and cut his eyes at the two men sharing our table.

A few moments later, the other two diners took their leave, and we were alone. He leaned forward and motioned me nearer, so that our noses nearly touched, and we were able to speak without being overheard by the other patrons.

His breath smelled of stale cigarettes. "I trust that all that is said will be kept in the greatest of confidence."

I offered my assurances with a nod and opened my mouth to speak.

But he held up a hand. "Good enough. I'll tell you what I know of things."

Over the course of the meal, I learned from him in hushed, quick tones about Miss Pettigrew. "Nancy is my office bookkeeper. She's gone missing. I last saw her on Wednesday as I left the office."

I noted that it had only been the day after I had first met the handsome brunette.

He continued, "I thought she might have simply taken off a few days without notice, so I decided to wait in the hope that she would return. But she still has not. And the books require tending. I've waited as long as I can, and now find myself in desperate need of someone to handle the accounts." He lowered his voice to a whisper. "I don't know what's become of the girl. When I spoke with Beatrice, it seemed a novel idea that we meet, so that I could inquire about your services."

I reiterated what I hoped Beatrice had already conveyed. "Discretion is my trademark. I have done my job well, if no public record of the affair exists." The latter was the hook with most of my clients, and Samuels proved to be as predictable as the rest, seeking to avoid any public embarrassment that might stem from the entire episode.

He pointed his fork at me in a most impolite manner. "Have you in fact met Miss Pettigrew as Beatrice says?"

"I have. But only to exchange pleasantries while the ladies spoke."

"Then you know her?" he insisted.

"I know her face and have made her acquaintance."

He smiled. "If you have met her but once, then you know her."

I swallowed uncomfortably. "Nevertheless, please describe her again. You know her and see her everyday, and I have met her but once socially."

Had I not met her already and arrived at many of the same conclusions, his assessment might have been of relatively little value. He described her in a wistful tone, detailing her features, and repeatedly echoing thoughts of her incomparable beauty, "She has the smoothest of skin. And beautiful hair. She tucks it behind her ears. Deep eyes. A bright-green color. And her scent, well it's very unique."

He consumed a few bites of food, and I held my tongue anticipating more to come. My patience rewarded me, and he lapsed back into his discourse.

"Her speech is gravelly. It serves her well. Gives an edge to her debates. It's a voice of authority even among men. It's quite alluring actually. That's probably what propelled her to a prominent role in the suffrage movement."

But he made no mention of her professional skills as his bookkeeper, focused as he was solely on her features.

I took a piece of meat and poised it before my mouth. "So tell me about the situation," and I stuck the bite in my mouth to chew while he spoke.

"She left without collecting her final week's worth of wages, and I doubt that she will return for them now." He put the fork on his plate suddenly and looked up as if an idea had freshly popped into his head, "Any expenses I may incur in the effort to find her can be deducted from what she's owed." Then he grinned at me.

The ethics of the situation did not sit well with me, but rather than quibble over the source of funds for a job yet to be landed, I did not object.

He then adopted a serious look of concern and newfound consideration. "Her intentions may not have been honorable in light of the manner in which she discontinued her services. Skipping out on a job is not unheard of. But skipping out on a week's worth of wages speaks of something wrong," he insisted.

With that issue, I tended to agree, and it piqued my interest. "How did she seem the past few weeks? Anything odd about her behavior?"

He grimaced. "Nothing out of the ordinary. She had headaches off and on. More so lately, I guess. Probably a female thing."

"But nothing serious?"

He shrugged. "Nothing that kept her from working. She did seem a bit sluggish at times, but I attribute that to the headaches."

He had momentarily satisfied my curiosity on that subject.

"Does she have any friends?" I asked.

He shook his head. "She's a bit of a loner. She may have simply blown out with the wind much as she appears to have blown in." His voice had become cool and his outward concern was well in check once more. "I do wish I'd had a chance to speak with her one more time about the books."

He gazed past me into the open air for a few seconds before jerking back to the moment and taking another bite of his food.

I held my fork for a moment and watched, before I asked, "What do you know of her social comings and goings?"

He shrugged his shoulders. "Her most fervent interest was the suffrage movement, as I mentioned before. That's something I know little about other than what I've heard through her."

"Did she have a beau?"

A grin split his face once more. "Not of which I am aware. Hard to believe of someone like her, isn't it?"

I ignored the remark and continued with my meal.

Finishing his lunch, he selected a toothpick from the holder on the table and began to unceremoniously probe his teeth and gums, his discourse completed for the moment.

I looked up from a bite. "Do you have a photo perchance?"

"No. I never had need for one. I saw her every day," he replied with a smirk.

"It might be more difficult to find her without a photograph."

"People would know her if she were about," he replied brusquely. "She creates a broad wake in her path, carrying herself with aplomb and confidence—the kind of woman you know not to cross simply by her posture and her countenance. She is exquisite—her beauty nonpareil. She is spirited and unattainable. She is mundane, yet uniquely dark and mysterious. But you know that. You've met her," he said eyeing me.

I squared my shoulders. "She has a talent for making an impression on men. Sounds like my Bea."

The toothpick he held snapped, and he pitched it on the table. "No. There are few like Nancy. I daresay none. She let no barrier stand in her path." He lowered his eyes in warning and glared at me, "No man either."

"Like Bea." I responded and waited.

He thought for a moment like a fish considering a lure, then took the bait, "By the way, how is the delightful Miss Rose?"

I wiped the corners of my mouth. "Fine. We spend a great deal of time together. It has developed into quite a serious courtship." I offered, slightly self-conscious that my words might be carried back to her on his tongue.

"Yes. So it would appear." A long pause followed his statement, and we glowered at one another for endless seconds.

I pushed back from the table. "Nothing else?"

To which he shook his head. "Not of any consequence."

"Does she have any family?"

"Not of which I am aware." He shook his head and spoke, "She claims to be from Kentucky, but I never paid it any attention. She mentioned family there, but I don't know any particulars."

Our meal finished. He then rose from the table and excused himself to the gentlemen's room, passing the waiter as he laid the check on the table and never breaking his stride to acknowledge the incurred tab. I waited a full five minutes for his return, but he was otherwise indisposed, and finally I was forced to pick up the check. Another five minutes passed, and I began to wonder that he hadn't skipped out on both the tab and me. Leaving the lunchroom, he joined me anew, and we strolled through the hotel lobby to the front door in silence.

The Maxwell House Hotel was located on the corner of Church Street and Fourth Avenue. The main entrance faced a collection of houses of ill repute, saloons, and gambling halls known as the Gentlemen's Quarter, an area where no respectable lady would be seen.

A few stalwart women graced the west side opposite the establishments during the day, but as evening approached, the street filled with those of lowly origin and crude manners. Most ladies used the side entrance on Church Street.

We were disgorged through the front doors onto Fourth. Samuels's momentum carried him to the edge of the sidewalk, and he narrowly caught himself to avoid stepping off the curb in pursuit of the worldly distractions to be had on the opposite side. Glancing wistfully in the direction of the Quarter, we made our way to Church Street.

He traveled quickly, his loping gait covering better than a yard at each step. When he slowed, it was to a stop with no sense of moderation in his pace. The way he held himself spoke of confidence. He was every bit a ladies' man, tipping his hat to each female passerby on the street and offering them a sly grin to which they returned delighted giggles and politely covered their mouths. "Good afternoon," he said to one. "Beautiful day," he said to another with his affected accent. He had adopted the local dialect, but something in his voice betrayed a different background.

Our timing at the corner was fortuitous. The officer waved us across in front of two carriages and a motorcar. The equestrians were made skittish by the presence of the puttering conveyance, and they fidgeted, nervously clattering their hooves on the pavement.

The drizzle that had fallen only minutes before thickened the air as we covered the short distance between our lunch and his office. Samuels vaulted the rain-slick tracks of the trolley in the middle of the street, skirted the filthy trickle of water in the gutter, and lighted on the curb with unexpected grace from such a large man.

He resumed, "Well at any rate, Miss Rose speaks highly of your problem-solving abilities and she mentioned your medical background which may be of use – one never knows. I am not convinced that it is necessary to go to the extreme of hiring a private detective. However, it does warrant a concentrated effort that I am simply unable to give it due to my other responsibilities." He paused long enough to catch his breath, but still maintained his rapid pace, "I could resolve the issues myself in a short time no doubt, but I recognize a need to have someone else with more time on his hands and whose time is not so expensive."

I ignored the blatantly condescending remark and the clumsy attempt to begin negotiating my fees. He stopped short, and I stumbled past him, forced to turn around in order to continue the conversation.

His ruddy cheeks puffed in and out, and he took a breather, the burden of his large frame forcing him to pause. The sun shook free of the clouds and glinted off the shiny surface of a silver cigarette case he had pulled from his inside breast pocket. Holding the case, he deftly flipped it open with one hand and produced a lighter in the other. Not bothering with a courtesy invitation to join him, he held the paper-wrapped tobacco tightly in his lips and brought the flame up, inhaling deeply and causing the fire to blaze. He drew and held a lungful of smoke, savoring the flavorful aroma and ashing a full half inch of the unfiltered tobacco before relaxing and releasing a plume of smoke into the air.

"Helps clear the lungs," he claimed.

"So I hear."

"Where is your office?" he inquired, identifying the single greatest weakness of my current disposition.

"I have none. No need."

"One must have a place to ply one's trade. And a place where I can find you when I need you." He turned to begin moving again, then stopped short, nearly causing me to run into him. "I have access to an office that you can use. Not one of mine, mind you—that would be too conspicuous. An extra one to which the company has access. Nearby. In the same building so that you can more easily conduct your...investigation." A smile split his face as he conjured the semantics of a new trade.

"I think you can do this." He stabbed the lit tobacco at me and pointed. "It may be a bit above you, but I do see something of that promise that Miss Rose sees." Overhead, the wires sang the announcement of an approaching trolley. The crackle of sparks and rattle of the car caught up to us and passed on the way to its next stop. Without looking, Samuels flicked the line of ash from his cigarette to the ground before stepping off again, leaving me to catch his distended pace.

"I'll subtract the rent for the office from your fee. Probably won't leave much for you, but it should suffice to keep you going."

I made a mental note to be sure to compensate for the imposition of the additional expense. His low opinion of my abilities was welcome. It indicated that his expectations could be easily exceeded and gave me a bit of an upper hand.

Even before the meeting, I had fingered him as a prime suspect in the event that a crime had occurred. His blatant disregard for my interest in Bea had me set against him from the word "go." His disdain was an added cause for concern. Oftentimes, a criminal sees themselves as too smart to get caught. An attitude such as his generally lands that person at the top of my list of suspects, and since I knew no one else involved in the case thus far, that was exactly where I placed Mr. Pilchard Samuels—a problem considering that he was my employer and thus my source of revenue.

He stood there on the street corner in front of The Doctor's Building, pondering some unknown issue, obviously not intending for me to follow him further.

"Try her boarding house," he said. "See if you can get a photo or any indication of her family there." He then pulled a beautiful fountain pen from his pocket, its ebony case striking and its nib a gleaming gold. Uncapping it, he searched for something on which to write, ultimately finding a scrap of paper with the phrase I.O.U. scratched out. He scribbled the address and did not wait for the ink to dry before folding it and smudging the writing, leaving it only marginally legible.

He warned me, "The lady runs the house since her husband passed away, and she's a piece of work. I haven't met her personally, but I've heard about her from one of my door-to-door insurance drummers whom I sent by to inquire about Miss Pettigrew. Be careful what you say to the woman. Don't tell her or even imply that you are conducting an investigation.

"My former bookkeeper traveled frequently by rail. I assume that a beau or a family member covered the expense. She went at least once a month if not more, but she always informed me in advance and was never gone more than a day, usually on the weekend. Someone must pay for the luxury of the constant passage. And she dresses nicely. That ready-to-wear clothing must originate from the same source. She could ill-afford such luxuries on the wages she earns. But her pay is commensurate with the position," he assured me.

"Your office is on the third floor. It will be unlocked, and the key will be on the desk. It's the door next to the men's room. You're a detective. You should be able to find it."

His cigarette completed, he tossed the butt into the gutter and exhaled the last breath of smoke before disappearing into the building.

# 4

The following day, I looked through the obituaries and daily scraps of news in search of the missing woman. Tuesday's edition brought no mention of anyone who might have been construed as Miss Pettigrew, but proved marginally more interesting than the day before. The Mexicans had destroyed our consulate in the ever-escalating tensions. Word of that had everyone convinced that war with Mexico was inevitable—probably the reason that we had distanced ourselves so much from the European War, although word of Italian advances against the Austrians had managed to make the front page.

The Vols dropped another game, 1-0 to the Gulls in a defensive struggle. Otherwise, it was a slow day. Satisfied that there was no mention of my quarry, I searched back through the previous week's worth of papers on the chance that Samuels had overlooked something. I sifted through the breaking stories that had been immortalized as part of the public record. I could have been easily distracted, but I kept myself on task.

Next I placed a handful of phone calls to the patently less pleasant options. The city directory listed roughly twenty hospitals that could easily be reached. There were half as many undertakers engaged in the business of transporting the injured and burying the dead. Many more were known in their neighborhoods and were not listed. Some were simply not available at the time, but I noted those so that I could call back later. In general, I was able to reach someone whom I had contacted in the past regarding other inquiries, and they were quickly able to eliminate those alternatives. As a consequence of past cases, I knew the city jailhouse number from memory. The approach was admittedly a bit haphazard, as it was impossible to touch everyone in those professions, but I had hoped that word of mouth would carry the message through to the appropriate persons.

Finished with my standard initial foray, the next step was to retry the more obvious places. My first stop was Samuels' office, the hour for morning break quickly approaching.

The trolley deposited me at the western corner of The Doctor's Building. From that vantage point, I could see the two public faces of the structure. I walked the final few steps admiring the beauty and elegance of the architecture. The irony of my taking an office in this building was not lost on me as I approached.

The cast concrete contrasted sharply with the brick structures of the other buildings along Church Street. Only just opened, the three-story Renaissance revival structure marked the gateway of the main business district. Its rows of double windows and concrete medallions nestled between cement columns were details befitting the building's tenants and their position as society's medicine men.

The primary entrance faced Church Street where a Federal Bakery and Universal Accessories Company complemented the druggist storefront at street level. I knew from Beatrice that there was a less public entrance on Polk Avenue running along the west side facing the Tulane Hotel. It provided access to the second floor by virtue of the change in elevation caused by the rolling hills of the city. Many of the tenants utilized that entrance as a private route by which to access their offices. Such an arrangement allowed the physicians to maintain a professional distance from their clients.

The yawning main entrance covered by its striped awning where I met Beatrice at the end of most days and into which I had watched Samuels disappear was intimidating. A shudder went up my back as I entered the mouth of the edifice. Inside, white marble covered the floor of the lobby, and the wainscoting was made of Tennessee pink marble. The stone amplified and echoed all noise in the corridor and drew attention to the step of even the softest sole.

Everywhere there was metal, it was brass—doorknobs, kick plates, mail slots, call buttons, and the mailbox. The elevator dials were semicircles of the gleaming metal alloy with the numbers bolted to the frame. From the top of the mailbox, a glass chute extended to the floors above and rose like a smokestack before it disappeared into the ceiling.

A brass hand traced the course of the elevator cars from floor to floor. The doors of one stood open, the ebony attendant patiently awaiting his next passenger. I stepped to the waiting car, and two pieces of mail came gliding down the chute to land unseen in the box with the crisp sound of paper on paper.

"Two, please," I said to the attendant. I received only a silent nod in response.

A few seconds later the doors opened and the attendant drew back the brass gate. He had a good touch with his machine. The car was perfectly level with the floor, and I stepped out.

I turned to him as he closed the gate. "Which direction is Pilchard Samuels's office?"

He pointed, but still said not a word to me.

In his office, a young woman at the reception desk answered my inquiry. "He's not in, yet," I was told at an hour I expected my new employer to be in his office. Within seconds, he came striding into the room, the smell of burnt tobacco wafting in with him.

"Where have you been?" he asked without any greeting.

"What do you mean?" I responded warily.

He threw his hands in the air with each phrase. "What have you been doing? Why are you here? Have you found anything out, yet, or am I simply paying you to sleep late?" His inference that I was sloughing off was not easily stomached in light of his own tardy arrival.

I lowered my voice and noticed the receptionist averting her eyes, but I knew Samuels's and my exchange would become fodder for gossip by the coming lunch hour. "Per our agreement, I began this morning, and to that end, I have already checked with a number of sources."

"Did you find anything yet?" he snapped, heedless of the girl's presence.

"Not yet," I replied, "But not wanting to overlook the obvious, I came by on my way to her boarding house to see if perchance she had appeared here making short work of my efforts."

He stood immobile, and looked at me from the corner of his eye. The skepticism on his face made me anxious about how pleasant the conditions might prove to be under his employ.

"She hasn't returned," he stated flatly.

"Of course," I answered. "But the confidence of your reply surprises me. Miss Winston just finished telling me that she had not seen you all morning long. I was merely curious since Miss Pettigrew may have been here earlier—to collect her check or turn in her notice or on some other incomplete piece of business."

He threw a sharp look in the direction of the young woman that I thought might reduce her to tears before he backed off. Then he brought his face close to mine, the smell of stale tobacco heavy on his breath, "She would be sitting right there." He pointed a stiff finger in the direction of the timid woman at the desk.

He motioned me to follow and walked around the counter through the waist-high swinging door. Our brief march ended at his office. "I do not care for your questioning," he emitted in a veritable growl.

I carefully turned the handle to secure the door.

What followed was a fairly pat speech that I have developed over the years, "Mister Samuels, I do apologize, but put things in perspective. Please. You have hired me to find someone. At this point, I am only beginning the investigation. I do not know anything significant about Miss Pettigrew. For that matter, I do not know that a crime has even been committed—"

"It has." He walked around to his side of the desk.

"In that case, then anyone who knows her is a suspect. Seeing as to how I know only you and Beatrice who have had any contact with Miss Pettigrew to this point, you are my only two suspects."

"You've forgotten to include yourself in that list, Mister Black."

"Agreed. I will consider myself a suspect." The concession made, I moved on. "In time, I will learn more about Miss Pettigrew and add to that list. In order to do that, I will exhaust all means and ask many questions—even some that may be uncomfortable at times. Please remember that I ask only because you may unknowingly hold some small bit of information that might aid in the investigation. So I ask. And I will continue to ask. Surely you understand that? After all, it is on *your* behalf that I am working."

The assault warded off, he took a seat and then circled back to attack on a different front. "Have you moved into your office, yet?"

"No. I have not, but I intend to do so, on the heels of this meeting."

He raised his eyebrows. "So you are headed there now?"

"Yes. In order to plan out the first few steps in the investigation. Not the least of which is my intention to visit Miss Pettigrew's place of residence today at noontime. Until then, you may expect to find me in my office for the better part of the next hour, but failing my presence, you can simply leave a note." I then reached for the door, which opened silently. Though he'd said nothing in reply, I had felt his stare on my back when I left in search of the office he had provided.

Not wanting to disturb the attendant for the luxury of an elevator ride up a single story, I took the stairs.

The floors and the wainscoting on the third floor were marble as well, a beautiful milky pink color with dark veining throughout. A series of identical doors outfitted with touches of brass interrupted the waist-high stone at regular intervals.

Mottled Mississippi Florentine glass lined the walls above the marble wainscoting and filled the top panel of each door. There were no external windows on the hallway to be seen, but sunlight seeped through the distorted glass behind which windows existed. Ambient light filtered through, but preserved the tenants' and their patients' privacy.

Each dark mahogany stained door had a glass panel that bore a three-digit gold-leafed number outlined in glossy black paint at the top of the pane. Below that, the same gold-leafed paint, shadowed in black, announced the name of the physician and their specialty—"Medical Practitioner," "Surgeon," or "Internist." A small flourish underneath the name set some of them apart, and one of the doors had an outline of a small hand painted in black with the phrase, "Next door, please."

Even in the subdued light, the brass hardware shone like muted gold. Everywhere I looked, the copper and zinc compound radiated – doorknobs, hinges, mail slots, kick plates, mail chutes, elevator dials, call buttons, and even the spring-loaded doorstops were of the counterfeit bullion, and the sheen was as bright as the day it was cast.

I stopped to notice the termination of the mail chute between the elevators. It capped out here on the top floor in a clearly labeled waist-high slot. I was inspecting the clever invention designed to convey the post from the upper floors when a young woman approached and dropped several pieces of mail in. They shot their way down for the mailman to pick up on his next rounds, which he made four times a day.

I set off exploring the floor with the sole knowledge that my office was next to the gentlemen's room. The slap of my leather shoes against the marble reverberated off of the stone and glass corridor. It made me self-conscious and caused me to lighten my step.

The passageway made a square with offices on both sides of the hallway. Those on the inside overlooked an enclosed courtyard.

I walked the corridor and turned the corner. A door opened behind me and the sounds of an office interior escaped into the echoing passageway. The automatic closer pulled it shut a little too rapidly, slammed the door and rattled the stippled glass in its frame.

At the end of that section of hallway, I was greeted by the same set of indistinguishable portals. A colored man was hunched over a doorknob polishing the brass, his frame permanently disfigured from constantly rubbing the paste on and off the metal. The presence of so much of the alloy required constant maintenance to keep it from turning green. In passing, I offered a greeting of, "Good morning," and caught him slightly off guard.

He recovered in time to return a, "Mornin', Suh," and a courteous nod in response.

A faint medicinal smell pervaded the passage. I continued along the door-lined path, and the smell of rubbing alcohol, ether, or some other medicinal compound became more intense, almost overwhelming before I had reached the end of the hall and the fumes had begun to dissipate.

My office was here, close to the stairwell, just on the fringes of the odor that had affected me so adversely. I knew because there was a minor anomaly, a solid wooden door, this one labeled, "Gentlemen."

The door to my office was slightly narrower. It held the glass like the others, but no light radiated from it; no gold-leafed paint indicated its number or its occupant; and no mail slot awaited correspondence. Instead of swinging into the office, the door was hinged to open into the hallway, and it was fitted with a smaller knob than its counterparts. Per Samuels's own acknowledgement, I knew it on sight.

With justified apprehension, I reached down to turn the handle. There was no key plate, and the wood around the hole where the key would have gone was already worn with use. The door unlatched, and though I had turned the handle, it held fast. I pulled harder, but nothing gave. With a violent jerk, I wrenched the door from its perch, and it emitted an ear-piercing screech. Stuck open less than ninety degrees, I noticed the markings where already the door already had scarred the stone floor.

In the same moment, a portly faced man exited the lavatory. "Someone has been fooled into renting this glorified broom closet, I see. Never rent sight unseen." He extended a hand. "Doctor Mortimeyer Breedlove. Mort to my friends. Awful name, but my parents did think it novel."

"A pleasure to meet you." I accepted the friendly offer of a handshake. "Black. Nathan Black. Guess I got the marginally better end of the deal with the names."

He had the hands of a bear and the laugh to match it, but he possessed the gentle grasp of the consummate medical professional. He roared at my frail attempt to be sociable. His white lab coat with the obligatory stains of the vocation made him seem more imposing than he actually was, and his Santa Claus white hair and beard lent him a genial air. In the absence of my own father, he presented the image of what I might have hoped for in a paternal figure, and I took an immediate liking to him.

"Most assuredly, my pleasure," he replied, "Especially seeing as to how you don't appear to be another of these hacks around here claiming to be a surgeon." His accent marked him as a native of the city, as well as educated and refined.

I stood up straight. "Actually, I did study medicine, but I chose not to practice."

He assessed me with his eyes. "Really? That is a shame—quite a loss for our profession. We could use more men like you."

He poked his head in and surveyed the office. There was little room for much else. "It's smallish, but at least it has a desk, even if it is facing the wrong way," he consoled me.

I could see that each end was wedged tight against the wall and kept the feet on one end from touching the ground. I took a step in. "It's sitting whoppyjawed. One end is higher than the other. How did it get in here like this?"

"I don't know. Not sure how you'll get it turned around either." He flicked the switch on the wall twice. "I'll send over my nurse with a light bulb for you."

"Thank you," I replied.

We stepped over a small pile of papers heaped at the door. Upon closer inspection, the desk did not sit unevenly on the floor, but was too wide for the room. It was wedged into place in a physically impossible manner with the right side slightly higher than the left. The blotter pad, a memo spike, and a dried fountain pen fought for space on the lower end.

"You have a chair for visitors. At least it has all of the amenities," he said to avoid being critical of the situation.

I climbed aboard the desk. It gave slightly under my weight, wedged itself down tighter, and left a fresh set of scars in the plaster wall. I dismounted to the opposite side and found that the previous occupant had been of the same notion. A castered wooden desk chair awaited me, and in my dismount, I tangled a foot, narrowly avoiding being thrown to the ground.

"Careful," the elderly physician cautioned me before making his departure. "I'm late for a procedure just now, and I don't have time to patch you up if you injure yourself just now." He glanced around the tightly cloistered interior. "I would keep this door open and allow the air to move some. Dreadfully unhealthy to stay cooped up in this room."

The lighter atmosphere generated by the doctor's welcoming was short-lived. My employer had made an appearance and stood impatiently awaiting the departure of my incidental guest. The physician was unperturbed by Samuels's lack of decorum and finished at his own pace. He bade me good day before vacating the doorway that he had blocked up until that point.

Samuels's dismay at the presence of a visitor engraved his face, one eyebrow raised as if he had caught someone trespassing. "Good," was all he had to say.

Satisfied that I was in place, Samuels excused himself. "I have other business to attend to now that you have *settled in*."

# 5

I retreated to the relative solitude of my office and began to try to piece together the next steps in my plan, but the distractions continued. The good doctor's nurse appeared five minutes later, bulb in hand. And then Beatrice dropped by with a message from her employer.

She was less than radiant that morning. She stared at the floor rather than meet my eyes. Her look was downcast as if she had been chastised which it turns out she had.

"Dr. O'Hare is not too pleased that your office is so close—on the same floor even. He's forbidden me to have any contact with you during the day."

My mouth hung open at the audacity of such a statement, but there was precious little I could do about it without jeopardizing Bea's position of which she was so doggedly proud.

"He sent me here to tell you that and to tell you to keep your door shut, so you don't disrupt the *professional atmosphere* of the offices. I'm sorry. I have to go. He'll be angry if I'm gone too long." She quickly turned for the door, and the downtrodden look on her face nearly cracked my heart. I consoled myself that it might actually be a blessing in disguise since it offered me an excuse to concentrate on my investigation.

With so little on which to go in the case, it was difficult to begin any real consideration of the possibilities, and as usual, getting started proved the hardest part. That fact, coupled with the mounting claustrophobic feeling brought on by the hole-in-the-wall office, forced me to search out a reason to again climb over the desk and escape the confinement of my cell.

As the lunchtime hour neared, I had determined to make my way to Nancy Pettigrew's place of residence. It was only blocks removed from the office, and I hoped to find her there. If she failed to present herself, I intended to make some casual inquiries of the other residents in my efforts to shed some light on her absence. If nothing else, I might occasion a free meal at the boarding house table in the process.

I decided to take the quick way out. I hit the stairwell and exited via the west side stairs to Polk Avenue. I met the sidewalk and a steady stream of people cluttered the concrete headed for their homes and for local restaurants in search of noontime sustenance. I reached the corner at Church and Polk, and the flow increased. The flood of people undulated in and around the wide-striped awnings and the black street lamps topped with frosted-white glass globes. The No. 7 Belmont Heights Line Trolley came to a halt at the front of the building, squealing its approach as the brakes brought the loaded car to a stop. A section of the crowd that had been fidgeting on the curb swarmed the car, to search for open seats, fully aware that most were gone since it was one of the last stops in the main business district. From there, it would head out into the fringes of the city where single-family homes had begun to sprout up like unchecked briars.

I'd crossed the street in front of the trolley, careful to avoid the horse droppings and the approaching motorcars. The latter of these, a relatively new introduction at the time, had begun to make the streets quite hazardous. The owners roared through crowds at breakneck speeds, and the beasts belched smoke and fumes, the likes of which caused the indelicacies of the horses to pale in comparison.

A grocer had his fruits and vegetables displayed, and I stopped to select an apple from among the mound of its ripened siblings. "Five cents," the owner's wife told me. I dropped the coin in her hand and noted that her simple working woman's dress was homemade and not store-bought like that of the missing bookkeeper. From where I stood, I could look up and see the windows of the office across the street where Nancy Pettigrew had worked. In this town, the degrees of separation between any two given people are few.

A passing stranger jostled me back into my surroundings and pardoned himself before he continued on his way. I moved on toward the corner of Seventh Avenue and paused long enough to exchange greetings with each passerby. No matter how fast the city grew, its denizens remained cordial and retained the small-town feeling that everyone knew one another. Granted, there were those groups that keep to themselves– the Negroes, Jews, Catholics, Italians, Germans, and so on. But for the most part, it has always been a tight-knit town where the men tipped their hats to the ladies as they passed on the street and where everyone knew a little something about other people's business. That fact made my investigations easier, but added to the difficulty of maintaining discretion.

At the corner of Seventh, I turned in search of the boarding house. The façade of the Jewish Synagogue dominated the street. Its onion-shaped dome and its round window bearing the Star of David offered a sharp contrast to the residences opposite the temple, and the remaining homes were beginning to show their age.

The sidewalk stretched out toward the main thoroughfare of town, the appropriately named Broadway, an avenue so domineering in its girth that we Nashvillians referred to it simply as Broad. It was unequalled in that feature in its sister cities across Dixie. Within sight of it, I'd arrived at the boarding house residence of Miss Pettigrew. The modest front garden was well-tended. Daylilies bloomed along the sidewalk in a burst of yellow and white and in front of a few small plants with wide blades in shades of deep green that grew near the porch. The vegetation drew attention away from the once grand home in the twilight of its existence. Formerly majestic Victorian homes like that one spotted the landscape of the city in increasingly fewer numbers. The city grew, and its voracious appetite consumed the stately structures to replace them with less ornate, but no less impressive edifices—more for business and less for habitation.

The slate roof was in poor repair with a handful of tiles missing and a few more askance. The round turret with its curved windows was in need of fresh paint, and the spindles of the porch railing were beginning to bow with the drying of the wood. Even the gable ornaments were fractured and needed repair.

Like the house, the wrought-iron fence adorning the edge of the property was beautifully ornate. The hoop and spear railing was *de rigueur* for its era, but was losing favor quickly in the newer, more simple homes. Thick arms of wisteria wove in and out of the fence and lent it an unkempt look. The spears, bent in places, had spots of rust beginning to show through where the black paint had worn off from horses being irreverently tied off and from the abusive handling of people passing by. When I put my hand on the gate to open it, I noticed that the latch no longer secured the entryway, but the hinges were well oiled and the gate swung open easily.

Anxiety produced a knot in my stomach. Discretion is my trademark, and I had composed a cover story to justify my inquisitiveness into the comings and goings of a single young lady living in the city. How well that story would stand up to the scrutiny of those who knew her better than I, was soon to be put to the test. My stride shortened as I rehearsed the lie—specific enough to be plausible, but vague enough to be pliable. At the top of the three steps up, there was no more time to hone the story. I crossed the porch, reached out, pulled the handle, and was greeted by the faint tingling of a bell. The paint on the door was weathered, and the knob well worn, but still up to the performing of its function. As I waited, I couldn't help but notice that some of the boards of the porch needed to be replaced.

Deliberate footsteps grew loud as someone approached unseen behind the door. The unevenly slow and heavy steps seemed to require considerable exertion to be placed in motion. The handle turned, and the door swung inward, to reveal a largish woman dressed in a flamboyant manner. Her collar was cut lower than the passing style, and her substantial arms were exposed from the elbows down. It gave her the appearance of a madam preparing for the Friday rush. My first impression was one of shock, then embarrassment, and I wondered if I had arrived at the wrong address and instead stumbled across a well-concealed brothel in the heart of the city.

"Good afternoon. How can I help you?" Her manner was cool, but did not dispel the impression of a house of ill repute. Her accent was thick, well ingrained. She might have been a native of the city, or she might simply have been here long enough to have adapted.

"Hello. My name is Nathan Black. I'm looking for my cousin, Miss Nancy Pettigrew, and am led to believe that I might find her here." I had hoped that the missing woman had shared less than her entire family history with her fellow lodgers and that in the event that it was a den of vice, my mention of being a relative would squash any offer to partake in illicit activity. I felt already inordinately uncomfortable, and the thought crossed my mind that Samuels had perhaps not known as much about Miss Pettigrew as he had thought, and that I had now blundered into a situation for which I was ill-prepared.

"Yes. This is the place. She's not in right now though," she said, offering nothing more.

I sensed a bit of a reprieve and heaved an audible sigh. "When do you expect her return, if I might inquire?"

Her eyes followed the activity of the passersby on the street. "I don't know. We haven't seen her in a few days."

I turned at the sound of the gate rattling when it failed to catch.

She looked over my shoulder and pointed with her chin. "There's Mr. Merriweather. He knows her quite well. He might have an idea where she is."

The man approached the porch and stopped to rest one foot on the lowest step and looked up at us. The madam launched into an informal introduction. "Good afternoon, Mr. Merriweather. This is

Miss Pettigrew's cousin. He's looking for her. I told him I haven't seen her around in the last few days, but that you know her fairly well."

Merriweather blushed slightly at the mention of his association with the missing woman. His bulky hands were hairy and soft; his grip yielding. A single word uttered was an unintelligible greeting before he denied any knowledge of Miss Pettigrew's whereabouts. "I've begun to wonder if something could be amiss. I haven't seen her in a few days— since midday Wednesday last week. She hasn't joined us for meals, nor has she been in the parlor. As a matter of fact, we had an appointment of sorts." He paused and waited for my next words. None prepared, he realized his advantage and astutely began to turn the tables on me. "Ah. But exactly what is your interest? She never made mention of a cousin, nor has she ever had any relatives come calling."

Emboldened by their admitted lack of familiarity with Nancy's Pettigrew's family, I jumped in. "Well, we are cousins, a bit distant, but still close. Second cousins. Quite close actually." Then I noticed his sales case, and I recklessly began to *ad lib.* "I believe she mentioned you though in writing. You're a drummer?" I said and pointed at the salesman's bag he carried.

"Yes," he responded, and his eyes narrowed. "I am," but he revealed no more.

The madam seemed a bit more wary and with good reason—her boarder had turned up missing for the better portion of the week, then a stranger, who claimed to be a distant cousin, had come looking for her. The guarded look that crossed her face alerted me to a need for a bit more coercion.

"She mentioned you as well, ma'am. Very fond of you as I recall."

The remark had its intended effect. She swept her massive arms toward the door. "Mr. Black, pardon my manners. Let me invite you in and offer you a glass of lemonade to cool us down on such a beautiful day before all of the others arrive. Mister Merriweather can put his sales case in his room and join us as soon as he gets his things put away." She stepped to the side of the transom and made room for me to open the screen door for her in the proper Southern tradition.

Mr. Merriweather, however, took it all in stride, humored somehow. He lumbered forward, "Yes, yes. Well, we had an appointment of sorts you see, and she didn't show. We were to go to a meeting together. We often engage in spirited intercourse, and this was just such an instance." He grasped me by the arm and guided me toward the open door from the porch. Once inside, he peeled off and toted the cumbersome leather case up the stairs.

The madam snorted, "Spirited? Huh!" and before the man was completely out of earshot, "They argue like a married couple. Pitiful lout chasing after a woman well beyond his means, if you ask me," she hissed. "They can clear the parlor in nothing flat. I've got one boarder who leaves the room anytime both are present."

In the parlor, the madam directed me to an elegant if timeworn chair next to an equally ragged couch. She disappeared into the kitchen and returned quickly with a middle-aged Negro woman in tow and carrying a tray complete with a pitcher of lemonade and three glasses.

The lady positioned herself atop a wooden stool located in front of an upright piano. She stretched her arms wide and wiggled her fingers. The action was more clumsy than it was delicate in its execution. Her back to me, she faced the keyboard and drew in a deep breath. Then she began to play.

Her timing was off. And her fingers, while steady and confident, exhibited terrible form. The first few notes were not encouraging, and overall, there seemed to be no redeeming quality in the piece. In fact, I was unable to identify the selection, though it had a nagging familiarity about it. She said nothing, and I was wary of interrupting.

The odd performance was punctuated by the return of the salesman. His look was different, his face freshly cleansed of its street grime, and the weight of the case lifted from him. Without his hat, the thinning hair atop his head aged him a few years. She turned to acknowledge him and it distracted her from the piece. As a result, she lost her concentration and yet another bar suffered at her hands. For his part, Merriweather took his place on the couch where he sighed and fidgeted like a schoolboy held after school to write definitions as punishment for an offense unworthy of such torture.

The liquid poured from the pitcher was enticing to the eye. The fresh ice recently chipped from the block had condensed thick beads of water on the outside of the glass, but the beverage was not potable. It was prepared with too much lemon and not enough sugar. My mouth puckered at the first sip.

To my right, Merriweather sat and nervously turned his refreshment in the napkin wrapped around the bottom of the glass. He did not take a sip. He winced at each note when it failed to strike properly, and I was forced to block them out myself.

"Please enjoy your drink," she said. The diversion of her attention from the keyboard resulted in the mercifully premature demise of the piece.

"Very nice," I complimented her.

"Yes. Isn't it?" Merriweather followed and earned a nod of appreciation from the landlady.

"So, Miss Pettigrew lives here? I am glad to learn that she hasn't moved in the interim since she last wrote." I had forgotten to drop the formalities when referring to my newfound first cousin, and I chided myself to stay in the role.

The madam twisted around and began playing anew, "Yes, she's been here for around a year." Her fingers flailed wildly. "She wouldn't move. My boarders tend to stick around for a while. Convenient location. Reasonable rates. Good food. Friendly people."

Merriweather's eyes rolled at the sales pitch that he obviously had been subject to all too often.

The madam's body swayed out of time to the music. "We serve meals promptly at quarter to six. If you're late, you are welcome at the table, but we clear it at six-thirty sharp, and I don't allow stragglers in the kitchen after dinner. I have a good deal of family recipes that I serve as an added amenity, and I don't intend on folks making off with them by snooping around in my kitchen as some have been known to do." The speech came off well rehearsed, and her performance improved marginally with the familiar subject. "I do have a room available, though I'm certain it shan't be for long." She turned her head to smile and completely lost control of the performance. It flustered her to reposition her fingering before she could resume.

"Really? Hard to believe." I thought that should my investigation go further, it might be necessary to avail myself of the room. Still I tried not to commit too quickly. Merriweather, on the other hand, seemed headed into a trance, in an attempt to calm himself and not contradict the lady of the house.

"Not everyone knows how to prepare a fine meal, you know, and these Yankees, like Mister Merriweather, have never had such Southern delicacies as we serve – cornbread, poke salat, turnip greens, okra, and the like. Everybody knows that a Northern woman can't cook like a Southern lady."

I nodded politely in agreement, but I had determined to change subjects. I turned to the little man next to me. "Mister Merriweather, refresh my memory. What is it that you sell?"

He looked up, somewhat taken aback like a schoolboy caught daydreaming, and he fumbled with his hands when he spoke. "Books."

"Books?" I repeated and turned to face him directly.

"The Word of the Lord," the madam broke in, and then turned to me. "If I've told him once, I've told him a hundred times, he needs to polish his pitch and not be so hesitant about it. Mister Merriweather has an honorable profession. He sells the Word of the Lord, the *written* Word of the Lord."

I was certain of her meaning, but somewhat perplexed. I raised an eyebrow to Merriweather in request of clarification. The landlady was alternately obtuse and overbearing in her communication.

"Bibles," he whispered, and the landlady continued her butchering of the current selection.

"Really. Most interesting." Nothing else forthcoming, I blundered forward, "So do either of you know when you expect my cousin back?"

"Miss Pettigrew? Why, no. I thought you might be bringing word of her. I haven't seen her in almost a week—since last Tuesday if I remember correctly."

"Wednesday," corrected the little man. He perked up and took interest in the conversation as if anticipating my response.

"No, Tuesday," she insisted, striking a discordant note.

"No. Wednesday. Noon. You served pork chops, unexpectedly breaking your routine."

The woman stopped playing and cocked her head to one side before conceding, "Yes. Yes. You're right, Mister Merriweather. My, but you do have a good memory for some things."

"Yes, well—" I stammered searching for my story, "We haven't heard from her either in a while." I stopped to clear my throat in an effort to stall and come up with more fabrication. "And to be quite honest, we were a bit concerned, or perhaps curious is a better word. Yes. Curious about her situation."

I tried to keep track of the lies I had told interspersed with truths so that I did not weave too tangled a web. "I went to see her employer, Mister Samuels at her office. Of course, I spoke with Mister Samuels earlier today, and he hasn't seen my cousin since around that same time. I came in earlier today on the train and had planned on catching her at work. When she wasn't there, I decided to make my way over here in hopes of seeing her." My confidence began to rise. "But it seems that no one has had word of her of late." I saw no hint of reaction, though I searched for some response "You do know where she was employed by Mister Samuels?" My speech slowed, and my voice grew weak. I feared that I had overplayed my fragile cover story.

"Yes, yes. Of course, we know where she works. We've never had the pleasure of the acquaintance of Mr. Samuels, but we do know where she works." She prated and usurped the short balding man. It obliged me to accept her response on both of their behalves.

She stopped playing, and Merriweather and I fumbled over each other complimenting the horrendous display of talent or the total lack thereof.

"Very nice playing," I offered.

Merriweather clapped softly. "Yes, indeed. Lovely, isn't it?"

I offered my applause as well following the little man's lead. "Quite a talent you have."

"Yes. It's a true amenity for us here. We are treated to it *quite* often. Though we wouldn't want her to wear herself out as she had been known to do," he said through gritted teeth.

The smell of cooking vegetables began to permeate the room, and another boarder entered. With a welcome break in the conversation, I thought that an ideal time to extract a free meal and perhaps learn more about the elusive Miss Pettigrew. I tried to promote the opportunity with a compliment, "Mmmm. Dinner smells wonderful."

"Mandy does a passable job filling in for me on those days when I don't cook. She has learned my recipes by watching me. Coloreds can't read a lick, so I don't have to worry about her stealing them." The landlady beamed without an offer to sample the product.

 No invitation was forthcoming. "I probably should be going, I did not mean to come calling right at dinnertime."

"Not at all. Not a problem. However, you are correct. It is dinnertime, and I have my boarders to tend to, so if you will excuse me." She stood to make her departure. Mindful of our manners, Merriweather and I both stood. "Mister Merriweather can show you out. If you would like to join us for dinner, you are more than welcome to do so."

"Well that would be—"

"There is always plenty of food, and it is reasonably priced at only ten cents for a nonboarder," she said squashing my aims.

Not wanting to part with the coinage, I declined.

However, to his credit, Merriweather tried to come to my aid. "Since Miss Pettigrew has not been here for the past week and likely not again today either, might he take her place? Her meals are already paid for. I mean to say that I suppose they are. Aren't they?"

The look from the madam seemed to freeze Merriweather where he stood, his sentence trailing off to a faintly audible whisper before he could complete it.

"You really must excuse Mister Merriweather," she said. "If I've told him once, I've told him a thousand times, never give away your best product. It cheapens it. It undermines the appreciation of the well-deserved price that it earns. It's no wonder that he has such trouble selling enough to make room and board. Mister Black, that room is available, if you are interested." She cast a vicious glance at the man beside me, "I might soon have two."

I bowed ever so slightly, "I already have that matter in hand for the time being, but I might return in the next few days, if it doesn't work out, and if, by some remote chance, the room has not been taken by then."

"A pleasure meeting you, Mr. Black." She passed through and allowed the swinging door to the kitchen to flop shut behind her.

The pudgy man shrugged his shoulders in defeat. I felt that I'd owed him an apology for sticking his neck out for me, but saw that the look on his face had hardened now that she was gone.

"Lucky for you actually. Awful rotten food if you ask me—or anyone else who's survived it. Mandy's is marginally better." His eyes took on a furtive narrowed look, and the tone of his voice was hushed yet sharp for a moment. "The woman needs to keep those recipes a secret. They need to die with her so that no one else has to live through the torture of those concoctions. We don't go in the kitchen looking for her recipes. We go there in hopes of finding something to eat before she's gotten her hands on it and rendered it inedible. When Mandy can keep her out of the kitchen long enough to prepare a meal, we eat quite well, but that doesn't happen often.

"Let me show you to the door, Mister Black." He gestured to the hallway through which we had entered.

I took a moment to try to build a bridge to him based on his distaste for the madam. "I'll bet you and my cousin get along famously when it comes to the landlady."

He snorted a sarcastic note of agreement.

I slowed my step and looked around at the cracked plaster. "It does seem like a nice house despite the proprietor. Looks like a good number of rooms. How many?"

"Five of us, plus her and the vacancy." He jerked his head back in the madam's general direction.

"Really? So now, where is your room?"

He motioned up the stairs. "The last one on the right, just next to the water closet."

"And my cousin's?" I finally got to one point of my visit.

"Corner room off of this main hall here." He volunteered a wistful look toward her room. I noted the general direction and tried to orient myself should it be necessary to return.

"Nice rooms?" I inquired.

"Not bad. Some better than others." Suddenly, he perked up. "Say, you're not thinking of moving in here are you?"

I tried to set the hook now that the bait seemed to have been taken, "Well, I was thinking about it. With my cousin here—"

"Oh no. Your cousin will tell you when you find her, lest she doesn't like you. You don't want to be living here. Not with that woman around."

"So why does my cousin stay?" I asked.

"She's got the best room in the house. Better than the lady's. Big, corner room. Two sets of windows and an outside door to the garden. She moved in that one when it became available. Costs a bit more. Don't know how she affords it, but she seems to do well."

He held the gate for me. I stepped through and turned back to ask him one last question "So why do you stay, Mister Merriweather?"

Embarrassment seeped into his voice, and he answered flatly, "Because of your cousin."

I was taken aback by the frankness of his reply. "Of course. I can understand that." Given the opening, I asked the burning question, "You say you had an appointment with her?"

He nodded in response, and a look of disappointment crossed his face, but only for a moment before he caught himself.

"For what exactly, if I might inquire?"

"We were to attend a meeting together."

"When?"

"Wednesday, a week gone now."

It was clear that he had become guarded again, so I decided to back off. Yet, when I looked him in the eye, he did not shy away from my gaze, "It's been a pleasure to make your acquaintance, Mr. Merriweather," I said and extended my hand.

He accepted my grip, "Good day to you, Mr. Black. And good luck finding your cousin. Do let me know if I can be of any assistance."

The short stroll back to the office was spent rolling the madam and her curious boarder over in my head. Neither stuck out as particularly suspect in their behavior, but they were both strangely eccentric. By the time I had reached the office, I'd decided to keep an eye on them and look a bit deeper into their backgrounds as discretion permitted.

The remainder of the day I'd spent in the office pondering what I had learned and plotting my next move. I already had some indication of a time line. No one had seen Nancy Pettigrew since the close of business last Wednesday. Merriweather's scheduled engagement with her was either an unfortunate coincidence or an indication of his involvement. However, only an idiot would have admitted to an appointed meeting during which the crime occurred, and Merriweather struck me as timid, but not foolish.

Proving that there actually was a case was my first objective. To do so, I gave in to setting aside my principles. I had determined to break into her apartment that evening and look for signs of any unfinished business that might indicate whether she had left unwillingly – receipts, a diary, anything that hinted at her daily routine. From there, my goal was to weave the flailed ends of her path into a plausible scenario that hopefully would lead me to the discovery of her whereabouts.

With a few spare moments of time, I grabbed some groceries at H.G. Hills, the grocer a couple of blocks down from my new office. A loaf of fresh baked bread and a sizeable piece of salami were to be my sustenance for the evening.

Beatrice dropped by the office at the end of her workday and lingered for a moment in the door. "I do believe that being in this building among your peers suits you well."

I looked up at her gentle smile and decided it best to allow the comment to pass without notice. "I apologize, but I am going to be working late this evening trying to gain a foothold on this case."

I offered to walk her home, but she adopted a stoic feminist stance and declined.

Intent on conducting my next step in the investigation under cover of the night, I was bored and looked for something to do before the time rolled around. The sun set late that time of year. An eight o'clock presentation at the Vendome for Jewish War Sufferers did not pique my attention enough to draw me in, and I bided my time and strolled the streets before heading to my target that evening.

# 6

In the darkness, the stately home where Pettigrew made her residence gave me pause. It was Merriweather's information regarding her private entrance that had put the act of larceny into my head, and I found myself unable to resist the temptation once presented. Walking along the deserted streets, the ruse I employed was to convince myself that I was helping someone in need. But it was difficult to ignore the objections of my conscience.

The home backs up to an alleyway, which made it simpler to approach. Between the alley and the homes lay the back gardens. At one o'clock in the morning, all was deserted except for the occasional cat or possum in search of a meal. Modest carriage houses and picket fences staggered along unevenly, offering ample options to conceal my approach should I have alerted a neighborhood hound to my presence. My heart pounded in my chest with the anxiety of being caught in my trespass, and every sound froze my blood.

Recognizing the house from the rear in the dark was difficult, but my attentiveness to detail earlier in the day had paid dividends in this regard, and the outline of this specific deteriorating Victorian was distinct among the other rooflines. Standing at the back of the property, I oiled the hinge of the gate as my first order of business to silence its warning. I scouted the yard for signs of dogs or any other surprise. Seeing no reason for concern, I eased the latch on the gate and shifted the entry a few times to encourage the oil to permeate. The gate swung open without a sound, and then shifted wildly in my hand – the pin in the top hinge missing. Once inside, I carefully repositioned the gate so that the latch again supported the entryway in its previous arrangement.

Based on the conversation with Merriweather, selecting Pettigrew's private entrance was easy – there were no other doors on that side of the house. Traversing the back garden, I almost fell headlong over a hosepipe coiled in the tall grass. Three makeshift wooden steps had settled unevenly, and there was no handrail. Miss Nancy Pettigrew exhibited better discretion than many in the city, securing her door where many might not have. The lock was a simple one easily picked by even my mildly experienced hand. However, past success had told me to look for a key in the more obvious places first. My good fortune continued. Finding a key atop the frame, the door opened with a whisper, and bright moonlight flooded the room. I crouched at the doorstep of her chambers, flushed with the thrill of my own impropriety in the name of justice.

Not quite ready to throw caution completely to the wind, I scanned the room for any signs of its occupant. Seeing none, I slipped in and secured the door behind me. I had come hoping that the moonlight would serve me well, and it illuminated the room, dusting it with a lunar glow. But I was soon disappointed as the clouds darkened the night sky. Flipping on the electric bulb was not an option lest it alert one of the other boarders or the lady of the house to my presence, so an almost spent book of matches had to suffice.

The first match revealed the room, simple but well kept, its elements minimal. The bed stood made awaiting the return of its owner. The omen of bad luck—a hat lay upon it. It was there either in defiance or in ignorance of the superstition.

To one side sat a modest dresser that had been painted once too often. Atop it was a mirror, the silvering beginning to show its age. As I stood there in the light of the match, my own face reflecting in the glass, the discomfiture of my actions settled on me. And for a brief moment, I imagined her face displayed there, not my own. The shape and features were as clear as if she had been in the room as she brushed her hair and checked her attire for the day. Her green eyes stopped and looked at me, a trick of the reflection. The match burned my fingers and plunged me into darkness once more.

A small writing table and an old slatted schoolhouse chair completed the furnishings of the room. The desk was plain, yet neatly kept as might be expected from someone who worked with figures on a daily basis. In the fleeting seconds of the life of the match, the contents of the tabletop were revealed. The desk was set up for writing. A ream of paper, an ink pen, and a pair of reading glasses were the most obvious items. Fear of discovery in this situation forced me to move hastily, putting me on edge and leaving room for error in my quick assessments.

Atop the bureau by the light of the final match were her sanitary needs – a bottle of perfume, the bouquet still familiar in the air of the room; a silver-handled hairbrush, a few single strands remained entwined in the stiff bristles; a toothbrush and tooth powder, the antiseptic smell still fresh; two buttons, each one made of polished bone – a luxury for someone of Pettigrew's position; and a hair fob, made of tortoise shell and looking as if it still sat on display in the store counter.

Without another match, I was left to depend on the light of the moon, which had been sliding in and out of the clouds. While I could see, I pulled open the drawers, finding petticoats, stockings, and the like, but nothing out of the ordinary. Clouds extinguished the light once more, leaving me disinclined to rummage the drawers in the dark lest I was unable to set them back as they had been.

There were two doors in the room, other than the one though which I entered—one with a latch that led to the hallway, the other with only an escutcheon that was her closet. Finding a single unexpected match in my vest pocket, I moved to the closet filled with clothing and shoes. On the shelf above the clothes sat her valise, an item that both confirmed my suspicions and made my heart sink. Its presence was a clear indication that Nancy Pettigrew had not left town. At least not of her own free will. Her failure to appear at work or home in nearly a week, and nothing to support the notion that she had departed the city, spoke loudly to me in the darkness.

I waited a few moments for the clouds to clear, but the night had gone pitch black. Frustrated, I looked out the window to the west in anticipation of seeing a clearing, but was disappointed by an endless sea of darkened sky.

Discouraged, but not to be so easily defeated, I resolved to return the following night with a lantern or a full box of matches at a minimum to facilitate my hunt. The ease of gaining entry and knowing I could return emboldened me. Leaving, I replaced the key in its spot above the door, and I crossed the yard in an imprecise game of blind man's bluff arriving an arm's length away from the back gate and reached to unlatch it.

In the darkness, I swear that I saw, heard of felt something move. Or breathe. I stopped dead in my tracks, but could see nothing in the utter darkness. I held my breath, and a sliver of the moon cast a faint glow about the yard. It was not enough to make out anything definite, until I caught the movement from the corner of my eye. But I was too late to do anything about it. The blow took me down swiftly, and I vaguely remember the dampness of the dew on my cheek as I met the ground, but nothing more.

# 7

I awakened with my head aching. Either the shades were drawn or dawn had not yet fully broken. The landlady hovered over me, her brow pinched in concern that turned quickly to disdain as my eyes began to focus. The cold rag on my forehead offered only a small degree of comfort from the pain. Behind her stood the salesman, Merriweather, grinning like a hound with a treed possum and practically bouncing with glee.

"Mister Merriweather said that he believed you to be up to no good," the madam spoke. "I guess for once, he is due credit for his perceptions."

I moved my hand to the bump on my head. It was tender to the touch, and I was having fierce difficulty clearing my thoughts, though the gears were turning to find an explanation. I had formulated one the night prior for just such an instance, but it failed me in my moment of need.

The madam stood, lording her position over me. From this angle she appeared even taller.

Buying time, I fired an indignant accusation at the stout little bald man, "Did you hit me?"

"I only wish I had," His grin spread.

The landlady, not to be relieved of control, raised her eyebrows and in a scornful voice said, "No. One of the city scavengers found you in the alleyway, half in and half out of our garden gateway entrance. He assumed you belonged to us and came knocking at the back door to inquire." Her hand to her breast, "Imagine my horror on finding one of them at my own back door. Why, I tried to shoo him off before he could tell me what it was that he wanted. Mind you, we will persevere in this neighborhood and not have Negroes and other ruffians loitering about as has been the trend in the area of late."

Not wanting to allow her to get on a roll, I interrupted with my own defense, "Yes, well, Miss Pettigrew…my cousin, that is…had written to me of the key above her door." I rubbed my head, playing for sympathy but receiving none. "She offered the favor of her room for a day or two if I were to come to town."

Receiving no response, the remainder of my hand was called. "I had no place to go last night. I know it was poor judgment on my part, but I remembered the key late and had so a desire to sleep in a warm bed after the long train ride that I simply made my way here with the intention of overnighting in her room."

"Then where is your bag?" said Merriweather, leaping on the most significant flaw in my cover story.

"My bag?"

"Yes, your bag. Don't tell me that you came all this way with only the clothes on your back. One can tell by the quality of them that you are no beggar. So where's your bag?" he insisted.

My head cleared and provided me with a few sweet seconds of clear thought, "By the back gate, I think. I set it down when I opened the gate if I remember correctly."

The two looked at each other before the madam replied, "There was no bag by the gate."

Not wanting to blow my story, I widened my eyes, "It's gone?"

"Gone if it was ever there," responded Merriweather.

"Oh my. Whoever mugged me must have pinched my bag as well." Then a better thought occurred to me, "Or maybe I checked it at the station. I simply don't remember truthfully. My head is killing me." I lay back on the bed, trying to envision the role and how it should be played. "This is a rough town. I'm beginning to regret having ever boarded that train."

Merriweather huffed and straightened up to a standing position from where he had been hunched over me. "What a story!"

The madam looked at him then back at me. "I think this young man has endured a sufficient amount of our fair city's less hospitable side. It's time we showed him the goodness of our hearts. You of all people must agree Mister Merriweather considering your profession and your familiarity with the good book."

She lifted her eyebrows at him daring him to contradict her. Merriweather stood firm and did not give in, but he did not say a word to the contrary.

The landlady's face softened and relaxed. "Since it's my house, I'll do as I see fit. We'll check to see if there is a key as he says, and if so, we'll put him in Miss Pettigrew's room."

Merriweather grew rigid.

She pulled her key ring from its place in her pocket and took me by the arm to help raise me from the sofa. "Lend me a hand, Mister Merriweather," she directed.

They placed me on the missing woman's bed. The landlady went to the outside door and reached above the doorframe to find the key. "You see, Mister Merriweather. All is exactly as he has said. You owe Mister Black an apology."

Merriweather watched as she replaced the key above the door before answering. Then he turned to where I sat on the edge of the bed. "My apologies. It does appear that things are as you claim."

She moved toward the door. "The matter of your indiscretion is not forgotten, but that is something to be addressed later on. Mandy will return with breakfast for you. After that, the noontime meal is served at noon sharp, and I shall expect you in Miss Pettigrew's stead, if you feel up to it by then. Should you need anything else, call for me." Turning to Merriweather, "Now shoo!" she said as she waved him out leaving the door ajar behind her.

Outside the door, I heard her getting onto the little man. "Must you always be so distrustful? Really, I believe you have the poorest sense of judgment I have ever seen when it comes to a person's character."

I slept for over three hours, slowly becoming semiconscious around nine. As I lingered on the edge of sleep, the fragrance of the previous occupant of the bed licked at my senses. The smell of Nancy along the pillow was intoxicating—the scent of her perfume and makeup arousing. As I pulled the quilted blanket tighter around my neck, the aroma reminded me of her face and the few moments in which I had to take it in.

My arousal was impossible to deny, the vision of the missing woman was fixed in my head as she had spoken with us the week before. Lost in the dream, the missing girl became my fantasy for an instant before the sounds of a ragged piano recital broke my stupor and returned me to the present. Suddenly aware of my surroundings, the stiffness slowly subsided as she repeatedly butchered the piece of music, the playing stuck between practice and performance, revisiting a bar on a three count, but rarely at the start of the phrase and even then only in order to further wound the composition.

While I slept, someone had brought in a breakfast plate for me as promised. The biscuits were hard and the sausage cold, the grease a frosty color where it had pooled on the top of the patty. The music continued, and I knew that as long as it did, I had no need to fear the sudden appearance of the landlady. The other boarders should have been off to their respective offices and jobs for the day by now, so the opportunity to explore the room was ripe.

My head cleared, and I set to the business at hand, a most fortuitous opportunity provided to me by the wicked turn of events the night before. Without leaving the bed, I began to scan the room, searching out the details forgone in the darkness.

The desktop was organized, but the arrangement unusual as I realized that it was set up for a left-handed writer. A true southpaw is a rare thing, the tendency harshly discouraged and generally corrected in grade school. A small tray for writing instruments contained a single lead pencil. An ink pen sat atop a sheath of writing paper on the left. To the right were a short stack of envelopes, a two-penny stamp and a handful of one-cent stamps. There were no photos in view on the desk, the dresser or anywhere in the room for that matter—a fact that had escaped me in the darkness of the previous hours, but now deprived the room of any personal connection.

In the desk was a small drawer that had eluded me under cover of the shadows. Rising, my head spun, and I was forced back to the edge of the bed. After a few seconds, it had cleared sufficiently for me to reach to the drawer and then quickly plop back onto the mattress.

I was treated to an unusual find; an envelope with the image of an eye stamped on the flap in red ink. Immediately more curious was that it was sent to a post office box in the Arcade. Inside the envelope were two letters – one to Miss Boo and one to Miss Bobo. Miss Bobo is an eccentric and a less-than-notable character of the local landscape. Miss Boo, I suspected was actually Miss Nancy Pettigrew, but I was unable to make a snap assessment without a definitive sample of her script.

The music stopped for a moment, apparently for the landlady to turn a page, and the offensive performance marched forward.

Miss Bobo's exact trade varied depending on the need of the individual. She was one of a crowd of con artists who extended themselves as everything from a clairvoyant to palmist: reading cards, mixing love potions, telling fortunes, and analyzing handwriting. It was the latter capacity in which Miss Pettigrew had engaged the charlatan. They plied the trade via boxes placed in drugstores around the city. Their clients enclosed a letter and a nickel in an envelope in return for their professional assessment and deposit it in the box.

The letter submitted for analysis was an original composition, its wording slightly cumbersome, yet aggressive just as Nancy Pettigrew had been described. The page was blank but for her brief message for use in the analysis. Written neatly, the ink smudged by the occasional brush of a left hand, was the following:

*Dear Miss Bobo:*

*I am curious, anxious and somehow relieved to write this. I have no one with whom I can share my thoughts without fear of scrutiny or more harsh reaction.*

*I find myself in an unimaginable set of circumstances. I have crossed the boundaries of acceptable society, but that may be an understatement of my position.*

*My [indescretion] will ultimately come to light. Simply stated, the odds are against me and there is no denying my guilt. It weighs on me, but ~~it is too late for me to turn back~~, I will not turn back now.*

*I often find myself the unwanting recipient of many a man's attentions. I suppose I should be flattered, but I am not. I have a love. My relationship is such that it does not permit disclosure. Our meetings are sometimes in the most ill-reputed of houses simply for the benefit of the [descretion] they offer.*

*Please excuse my use of you as a confessional. I do not mean to burden you. Accept the small sum enclosed as a token of my appreciation for your confidence in this matter.*

*The favor of a reply is requested. The rendering of your services is a curious itch that will be scratched.*

*Sincerely,
Miss Boo*

The analysis had the aura of a cold reading.

*Dear Miss Boo,
First of all, let me say that you have a beautiful script - an unusual quality in someone who is not right-handed. Yes, I see more than you think.
Based on the letter you have provided to me, your current personality is revealed. Just as your mood may change from day to day, so may your handwriting and your current disposition.
From the sample supplied, I can tell that you are a secretive person, keeping many of your thoughts to yourself and sharing them with only a select handful of confidants. You are outgoing, yet reserved, feeling that many do not understand the rationale or logic of your pursuits.
You plan well in advance, and manage your affairs well. You live within your financial means, but find yourself pushed on rare occasions to make ends meet.
You are punctual and tidy. You keep a clean home.*

*You are aggressive when it comes to making your point and press your opinions strongly on others.*

*In order to gain a more full understanding of yourself, it is best to engage in a series of analyses over a period of time to draw a more complete picture of the person that you are.*

*I have returned your letter as I do not want the burden of its knowledge should it by some means fall into the wrong hands.*

*Sincerely,*
*Miss Bobo*

At the bottom of the folded page, just below the flourish of a signature, there was more printing in the same vein as that on the outside of the envelope. Neatly imprinted in red ink with a rubber stamp, it was the sender's appeal to the reader.

**Miss Bobo–Clairvoyant–Mystic–Seer–Graphologist**
**Drop-ins welcome.**

    I slid the letter into my jacket pocket hanging from the iron bed post, and turned my attention to the chest of drawers. Ever mindful of the unlatched door, I longed to close it and continue my discoveries uninterrupted, but thought better of the potential repercussions should it have been found secured.

    Hindered by the black of night in my previous effort, I saw now that the drawers were filled with the usual feminine clothing, the top drawer with a small selection of accessories – a necklace and a small charm box, its contents missing. The middle drawer contained a collection of undergarments. Self-consciously I sifted through them, the soft articles thrilling to the touch, my other senses on alert with the prospect of discovery in such a compromising position. My curiosity was rewarded when I uncovered a heavy object at the rear of the drawer. Drawing it out, I found a small derringer of the type carried by some ladies in their handbag. As a single woman living in a boarding house in the city, caution would be understandable. Living in the rural south where guns are an everyday part of life would be as well. But such an item in the possession of this particular young woman awakened my instincts and reminded me that this may be a precarious situation into which I had stumbled.

Carefully replacing the weapon, I closed the drawer and moved on to the next. The bottom one was filled with winter weight clothing neatly folded and put away for the warmer seasons. A search of its contents divulged nothing as exciting as the one before, but the clothing seemed slightly less in volume and much of it more worn than that of her summer clothing.

It registered with me that the room was cold with its void of personal items, such as photos or letters from home. It was as if the room had been intentionally stripped of anything that might give any significant insight into the life of Miss Nancy Pettigrew. If it was she who had affected such a style, then it appeared that she did indeed have something to hide as Miss Bobo had intimated.

Across the room, the closet was filled with a robust collection of store-bought dresses, waists, skirts, and blouses. Pulling two or three from their wooden hangers, I was able to envision her again, as she had stood before me only a week removed. Her taste in fashion ran toward higher quality. It allowed me a slightly more intimate look into the life of Miss Nancy Pettigrew.

It was the valise on the upper shelf which ultimately slaked my thirst for intimacy. Within it was a cigar box filled with the souvenirs of her life – rail tickets, many of them, but a few longer ones for further destinations; tickets from the theatre; a small collection of pamphlets and flyers on the suffrage movement; a stack of penny postcards; a small collection of receipts from Castner's and Cain Sloan; an unlabeled key; and other reminders of the artifacts that comprise a person's life. The stash was far more than I'd hoped for considering the remainder of the boarding house room.

I flipped through the receipts and was shocked to learn what an exorbitant amount she spent on clothing. A claim check for a dress caught my eye. It was to be altered and ready a day or two after the last known sighting of Nancy Pettigrew. Also, there was a collection of receipts for a drug counter at the corner of the Arcade. The walk from either her office or her apartment would take her past many other closer drug counters, but I found no other receipts for any of those. In my exuberance, I nearly forgot my surroundings and had to stop myself from emptying the remainder of contents on the bed and trying to assemble it like a picture puzzle of her life. I pocketed the claim check and one of the drug counter receipts and proceeded with care.

As I crowded the door of the closet, the piano paused only long enough to turn a page or change the sheet music. The tickets and programs were from events about town and spanned back nearly a year – approximately the time Pettigrew had arrived in the city. The penny postcards were of places around the city, and within a half day's train ride of Nashville. Each of them bore a date and a brief cryptic message addressed to Miss Nancy Pettigrew from "Boo." The handwriting was identical to that in the single red-eye envelope from Miss Bobo, the wording lightly swept by the passage of a left hand over fresh ink. More than before, I was convinced that Pettigrew and Boo were one in the same.

The find was encouraging. The contents might allow me to reconstruct the missing woman's movements over the past several months in the hope that it would provide me with some indication of her intentions. At a minimum, I was optimistic about uncovering something that would lead me to her.

The remainder of the closet was empty except for a hamper in which a few pieces of unwashed clothing remained. The only other item in the room was a bathrobe hanging on the back of the room door. The cloth was soft, almost luxurious. I recognized the scent as the same soap that Beatrice used. In the pocket, I found a wad of fresh cotton—the kind typically utilized by women during their monthly cycle, but nothing else.

The music stopped and did not immediately begin again. Satisfied with the results of the morning's search, I was selective about what to take in the event that the room was not so freely accessible later. I pulled the envelope from my jacket, its red eye staring at me in admonishment for my petty thievery, and planned for a rendezvous with Miss Bobo the following day. I hoped she would remember the letter, and perhaps offer some enlightenment. I placed the penny postcards with their cryptic dates and inscriptions in my coat pocket along with the letter from Miss Bobo.

The remainder of the cigar box collection was awkward in its small wooden tomb with a brass hook latch. Surmising that the postcards contained the meat of the information required, I resolved to return for the other items selectively to see what further light those other tokens might shed on the subject.

I laid back down and fell once more asleep. I awoke some time later and looked at my watch lying on the table. As the noontime hour approached, I still felt somewhat dizzy though my condition was passable. My mental state was slightly hampered by an increasingly irrational concern that Miss Pettigrew might make an inopportune reappearance for lunch bringing me face to face with someone for whom I had no prepared answers.

However, she did not appear, but the result was still an interesting debacle. All of the other occupants of the boarding house were in attendance, mostly so that they might have a chance to view me. I glanced around the table as I entered and uttered a small sigh of relief. There was no one there who would know me or my profession and might have a different story to tell of my identity.

Merriweather sat on the opposite side of the table, cautiously eyeing me, like an animal waiting to pounce. He said not a word and remained hunched over his plate while he ate.

The only other male boarder was a quiet sort. His characteristics were unoriginal other than a single wandering eye that drifted even while the other stayed fixed. Combined with his silence, the effect was unnerving. The oleo passed around the table to each of us in turn, and then found its place back in front of him again. When someone else asked for it, they invariably took a portion, then passed the plate back to its position before him He appeared to be the custodian of the oleo, and his fixed eye seemed to keep watch over it. As such, I was disinclined to brave reaching for it for fear that it might upset some unspoken sense of balance among the group.

The other two boarders were female, more the giggling-girl type than the serious hard-charging female exemplified by Miss Pettigrew and my Beatrice. They were both brunettes, dressed very nearly alike, and with similar names and neither bearing a distinctive feature. I found it difficult to keep track of which one was Eloise and which was Eleanor.

"Pass the potatoes, Eleanor," someone would say, and Eloise would pick them up.

"Is the salt by you, Eloise?"

"Yes," Eleanor would answer, picking it up and passing the shaker.

"Is that a new dress, Eloise?"

"Yes, it is," replied Eleanor.

"I picked it out myself," said Eloise.

"I'm borrowing it from her," explained Eleanor.

"Are you two sisters?"

They absolutely giggled in response.

"We're no relation to each another," said one.

"People often think so, but we just don't understand why," the other said as they both picked up a fork and took a bit of mashed potatoes in perfect synchronization. By the meal's end, I could not remember which was which or tell one from the other.

The food left much to be desired. The tea was sweetened so much that it could only be called sugar water since it lacked even a hint of the taste of the leaves from which it had supposedly been brewed. The beef tips in gravy were more fat than meat making for wonderful gravy but a grisly texture. The potatoes were grossly underdone with hard chunks still unmashed in the mixture. The cornbread had too much meal in it, making the bread gritty and nearly choking me since I dared not touch the oleo under its watchful eye. And the cabbage was limp from being boiled too long and overeagerly salted.

Conversation was polite, and most declined to comment on the missing Miss Pettigrew. One of the girls called her a strong woman and said, "Her disappearance has left a bit of a void, but you fill it handsomely," her eyelashes fluttering at me.

Concern was a rare commodity among the group. I interpreted the limited interest as their assumption that nothing good could come of being missing for such a long period of time, and no one wanted to be the first to mention the less pleasant prospects in the presence of a relative of the missing woman.

Midway through the meal, the lady addressed me, "Mister Black, you haven't mentioned the food. I made it all myself today especially for you. One of my specialties."

I choked down a mouthful of the gristle laden meat, "Oh, it's excellent. You shouldn't have gone to the trouble, but it is most appreciated."

The remainder of the meal moved along with no incident. At the end as I helped clear away the dishes, the madam cornered me in the kitchen. "Mister Black, we *are* coming up on the end of the month."

"Yes. We are."

"Yes. We *are*."

"I'm afraid the knot on my head has made me a bit addle, and I'm not following you."

"It's the end of the month." She rubbed her forefinger and middle fingers eagerly against the thumb. "I collect my boarder's rent on the last day of the month for the upcoming month," she informed me. "If you wish to keep the room for your cousin, I shall require payment. You are welcome to use her room until such time as she returns, then you can work out your arrangements with her. Perhaps you will want my spare room."

"I'll bring you the money this evening. How much is it?"

"She does have a corner room. Nicest in the house as you've seen for yourself." She had attempted to soften the blow.

"And what is the going rate for such a fine amenity?"

"It's a fair price. Fair for such a nice room."

I nodded in cautious agreement.

She steeled herself, "Twenty dollars. Per month, that is." Once she had it out she was drew her head back in anticipation of a more reactionary response.

I tried not to look incredulous, but the rate seemed a bit high. "Okay. I'll bring it this evening." It stung to know that Nancy paid such a rate, and set me again to wondering about her circumstances. The money would have to come from Samuels, and I suddenly remembered my obligation and dreaded what my new employer might be thinking of me having not yet made an appearance at the office for the day.

The lady released me from the corner, and I rushed to the building knowing that by now I had doubtless incurred his wrath. I hurried through the doors of The Doctor's Building and past a waiting elevator to the stairs. I wanted to avoid a chance meeting in the event that the car stopped on the second floor.

Already on my employer's bad side, dragging into the office at an hour and fifteen minutes past noon the second day working for him did little to enhance the relationship. A note from Mr. Pilchard Samuels greeted me, the paper stuck in the doorjamb. Not feeling up to the fight, I unceremoniously tossed it down on the desktop unread.

I began to climb over the desk, but the exertion of the dash to the office had left me fatigued, and I found myself atop the desk with my head at the higher end, unable to complete the climb into the seat. To make matters worse, rolling my head to the side, I saw that the door was ajar.

At some point, I lost consciousness again. When I awakened, I was staring up into Samuels's face. He loomed over me, his mouth moving—making words I couldn't hear. However, the look of narrowly restrained anger that raged in his eyes was easy to discern. He was repeating something, and I gradually came to recognize it as my own name. Slowly he came into focus, and the volume of his voice increased to a head-splitting level that shook any vestige of sleep from my aching body.

Struggling to a sitting position, aided by the incline of the desk, he backed away as if confronting a derelict on the street in the Gentlemen's Quarter on a Sunday morning. Hand to my head, I waved at him. He crossed his arms and waited impatiently for an answer.

He stepped forward as if to hit me. "Where've you been?"

"I've been at her boarding house," I replied.

"Whose?"

"Miss Pettigrew's."

"All morning?" disbelief clouded his face.

"All last night, *and* all this morning." The answer put a temporary halt to his tirade and calmed him slightly.

"Really?" he sneered.

"Yes, really. I went there last night to take a look around." The term *break in* is a semantically offensive phrase that I consciously avoided. "While I was leaving, someone hit me over the head. I awakened this morning in the parlor of the house."

"Good God, my man. Do you think it was Miss Pettigrew?"

"No. I do not think it was she," the implication provoked me. "No woman could deliver a blow like that, but your concern for my well being is appreciated and duly noted."

"Of course," he muttered and looked at the floor. His comment was intended as a backhanded voice of concern. "I can see that you survived, and I can well imagine that you receive such blows on a regular basis considering the line of work you're in."

"No, you assume incorrectly. I am not accustomed to being beat about the head in the middle of the night," I lashed back and glared at him until he backed off.

He clasped his hands behind his back. "Well if not she, then who?"

"Either someone involved in her disappearance or a bungling thief. Whoever it was went through my pockets, but found nothing of interest and left it all intact—including my wallet."

"So what did you find?"

"Nothing by that point. It was too dark, so I had decided to leave and go back again tonight with a box of matches or a lantern. That plan was cut short by the unannounced visitor."

Ready to give me up for hopeless, he went on the offensive, "So you have nothing to show for all of your time other than a knot on your head. And do you propose that I pay you for your time spent sleeping?"

Having played him a bit, it was appropriate to spring the snare rather than enjoy the chase too much. "Between bouts of sleeping in Miss Pettigrew's room where the landlady so graciously put up her bruised and battered cousin, I did do quite a bit of investigating for which, yes, I think I shall be paid."

"Her room?" He asked shoving a hand in the general direction of the boarding house. "You should be out on the streets looking for her in hospitals and such places. She's not in her room."

The curious look I gave turned his remark on him and he backpedaled quickly, "Of course, you know that because you were there, I mean. Come now Mister Black, what do you really expect to find there?"

"I expect to find the details of her daily routine, what she did, what her interests were, where she frequented, any if by chance she were involved in anything which might pose a personal threat to her well-being. I have concluded that something is indeed wrong, and you were correct in deciding to engage me." The fog began to roll back in to my head "That reminds me. I need a sample of her handwriting from you. I assume that you have one."

"Yes. Of course."

Pulling the postcards from my jacket, I dropped them on the desk where they slid to the low end rapidly eluding Samuels' grasp.

He snatched them up and flipped quickly through the odd collection, before he gave me a perplexed look.

I cleared my throat. "I think it's her handwriting," I hinted.

"It appears to be. Is that it?" he asked.

"No. I need twenty dollars to pay her rent. Since it would have come from her paycheck anyway, you can subtract it from that amount. Not to worry, I'll get you a receipt."

Grudgingly, he extracted the bills from his wallet, leaving him with no paper currency. "Yes, please do get me a receipt, Mister Black," he scowled.

"Do you think those cards will lead you to solve the case?"

"I don't know yet. There are notes and dates on the back, but they currently mean nothing to me. They may mean something to you."

He turned them over and began to scan the cards. After the first two, his pace increased until he was looking only to confirm that each card followed the same general pattern. "This is nothing," he announced.

"So I can safely assume that her mysterious beau is not you?" I said, taunting him in my hindered state.

He smiled, or maybe he leered. One side of his lip curled up just a bit more than the other to give his face an unbalanced look. "Yes, Mister Black, you may safely assume that I am not in any way romantically involved with Miss Pettigrew."

"You'll pardon my asking, Mister Samuels, but this is how my business is conducted. It is always that which appears to be nothing that proves to be something, and it is usually someone close who is involved. Now if you don't mind, I have a lot to do, and I need to get on with it." The message was somewhat blunt, like the trauma to my head the night before, but served its purpose.

Throwing the cards back on the desk, they began immediately to slide and he admitted, "You're right. It's not so much that you find her, but rather that you find what became of her." He said. "Let me know if I can be of any assistance." He offered as he left, not waiting for a parting response from me.

# 8

My office had no windows. That was in spite of the fact that the building was a beautifully conceived structure with a courtyard that opens up even the center offices of the building. There were windows on the courtyard – numerous windows, but my office sat in a blind corner. A single bulb hanging from a cloth encased wire was the only illumination supplemented by what little light reflected around the hallway and through the open door.

Already well into the afternoon, I was only now able to sit down and consider the stack of postcards purloined from the boarding house. I was shuffling through them when the interruptions began anew.

Doctor Breedlove was passing by and had noticed that my door was cracked. He decided to peek in, not knowing what to expect. Seeing the collection of penny postcards spread out before me on my desk had aroused his interest, and he rapped on the door, rattling the glass in its frame.

Anticipating a forthcoming admonishment for having the door open or another visit from Samuels, my response was a terse, "Yes?"

"Hello," he responded pleasantly.

He stood in the doorway, a man of sixty or better years, yet still seemingly fit. His powerful, well-fed, but not obese, frame looked healthy for a man of his years. Still, he was somehow pitiful in his presentation, an older gentleman in search of company roaming the floor of the building talking with whoever would take the time.

Noticing the knot on my head where I had been struck, he affected a professional demeanor. "How did you come by that goose egg?"

As I explained the events of the previous night, he leaned over the desk to press his thumbs to the surrounding tenderness of the scalp offering a quiet apology when he caused me to wince in pain. I titled my head forward, appreciative of his professional concern.

He grasped me firmly just under the chin to look in my eyes. He shifted my head side to side as he compared one eye to the other.

"Well, you appear to have a fairly solid head about you," he pronounced. "Some slight signs of a concussion. Don't see anything to worry about. Any dizziness, headaches, or subsequent blackouts?

Remember your name? Where you live? Who the President is? All of that?"

"No blackouts. Nathan Black. Hayes Street. The president is…Woodrow Wilson." I managed the last with only a short delay.

"Good. Did you hit the back of your head when you fell?" He said, leaning a bit further over the awkward desk between us, but I assured him that I did not, having landed on the rain-sodden turf of the garden.

"Nathan, I am curious, and if I may be so bold as to ask, why is it that you discontinued your medical studies?" His hands lay in his lap while he awaited my response.

I leaned back in the chair. "I found that I simply lacked the passion for the mysteries of the body."

"Fair enough," he said and did not press the issue with me, earning a significant degree of respect from me in that he allowed me my own decisions.

We talked, and his visage relaxed. The professional detachment of his work began to fade, and I was left with a fatherly man forty years my senior. His professional bedside manner was second nature, and I found myself quickly opening up to him. I related my current undertaking, and he listened intently for a while. Then the ravages of time began to take their toll on him, and he motioned to the seat with a hand, his eyebrows raised in request.

I stood and made to pull the chair out for him by reaching over the desk between us. "My apologies for not offering it before," I said, but he waved off my embarrassment without a word.

"Not to worry. Please continue." He rolled a hand encouraging me to go on.

I stood until he was seated. I winced as the chair creaked at his every touch and movement. "That chair is quite ragged. You are taking a bit of a risk with it."

"I'll hazard it." He suspended himself over the chair and supported himself on each of the arms. He gently settled his girth to see if the construction would hold which it did.

He had to push back to the edge of the threshold just to make room for his legs between the desk and the door. His white hair was thick and slightly unruly, and his jowls hung loosely with the better part of a day's growth of beard. The wire frame spectacles perched on his nose appeared inadequate in their task. He constantly squinted his eyes in a futile effort to focus, their lenses smudged with careless fingerprints. His lab coat that day was like the day before, littered with the stains of past procedures. All of this lent to the overall impression of a somewhat unkempt yet sympathetic appearance, as if the feminine touch had long since departed from his life, if indeed there ever had been one.

As he sat with me, footsteps echoed in the marble hallway accelerating as they rounded the corner heading in the direction of my open office door. The voice began loudly and escalated to the point that the windows on the floor rattled before Doctor Jack O'Hare, Beatrice's unpleasant employer, came into view "Keep...this...door...shut...or...I'll..." but he stopped short, narrowly avoiding a collision with the chair in the doorway as he careened into the room.

Doctor Breedlove rested his elbows on the arms of the chair with his fingertips steepled in anticipation. A mischievous grin creased his face as he prepared for the impending blow. However, the impact was minimal, the intruder barely pulling up in time to avoid slamming into the senior physician. He delivered a slight bump as he struggled to avoid an outright crash.

Still far too loud for the confined office, O'Hare stuttered a greeting, "Who? Oh. Morti. Hello." His voice deflated quickly, "Didn't know you were in here."

In defiance of Southern decorum and professional courtesy, Breedlove did not turn to face the intruder, much less stand or extend a hand in greeting. "Hello, Jack. What were you saying? You'll what?"

Searching for a means by which to retain some dignity, the intruder stumbled on. And then, interpreting Breedlove's mission to be aligned with his own purpose, he resurrected his original intent, "I suppose you're here to complain about this door being left open as well – impeding movement and generally disrupting business along the entire floor."

Breedlove exerted a curiously unspoken air of authority over his colleague that thickened the atmosphere of the room, "No." the doctor contradicted, "I'm not." He turned to look at the man. "Now Jack. Is that any way to greet someone?" He continued at a slow and deliberate pace. Each word was clear, his native Southern accent suppressed. "I'm here visiting with our newest neighbor—getting to know him. The door is open, because I opened it. You know how small this office is— made up of the leftover space between your office and mine. As I suspected, it's stuffy in here with no windows and no ventilation. Not a healthy situation at all, mind you." He paused to phrase his next statement, "I was just informing Mr. Black that he needs to keep this door open when he is in." He turned and fixed his glare on the fuming surgeon. "For his health, I'm sure you agree."

Flustered at his aborted attempt to curb my subversive habit and left with no recourse in the presence of his colleague, he backed down. "Oh. Well. Of course. If you…"

"Good day, Jack," said Breedlove dismissing the incursion of his sheepish colleague with a wiggling of fingers.

"Ah, yes. Good day, Morti. Good day…"

"Black," the elder physician supplied. "Mister Black. The man is a professional, just like you and I, Jack. He deserves the same respect. He's a detective. Finds out things about people. Doesn't miss a trick."

"Really?" said O'Hare somewhat taken aback.

"Not a thing, Jack," Breedlove threatened.

"Of course. Well in that case, Good day, Mister Black," the pleasantries given grudgingly.

"Good day, Doctor O'Hare." That was the first time since meeting the man that I had been afforded peer or nearly peer status.

Breedlove cut his eyes following the path of the doctor behind him as he returned to his office. My companion did not speak until we heard the office door of the physician close.

Breedlove smiled an answer, but not to the question at hand. "Where were we? Oh yes, short for Mortimeyer. My colleagues call me Morti. You can call me Mort or Doc. My friends do. I haven't been called Mortimeyer since my mother passed away."

Breedlove's age had brought him patience, and he took the time to hear the brief of my investigation without interruption before he spoke. When he did interject, it was to restate my version of the events, yet again a trait of his career. "So this Miss Pettigrew has gone missing. I know the one. There aren't many women here who don't work for the doctors. Pretty girl. Dark Hair. Yes, that must be her." He brought his hands together steepling the fingertips and leaned his head back, "Now that you mention it, I haven't seen her either in the past several days that I can recall. But that's not unusual." His head came forward again and he met my gaze.

While he was patient and seemed to have a passing curiosity in my work, he gave the eccentric menagerie of postcards laid out before me no notice. I had arranged the cards in chronological order, creating note cards that echoed the information recorded on the backs of each. As I sat with Breedlove, the pictures were each face up covering all but a small section of the desk. The compilation of thirty-two cards presented an eclectic mix including portraits of U.S. presidents, an ancient Greek architectural reproduction, and an admirable collection of train stations all along the L&N line.

As we spoke, he picked up one of the cards, unbidden, and examined it before returning it to the desk, his interest not unwelcome, but only fleeting.

Our discussion went on for over an hour. His life was a fascinating story that I absorbed like the pages of a fine novel. It spanned an interesting section of time. As he spoke, he wistfully recalled the memories of his childhood cut short by the War Between the States.

"I was a drummer boy, conscripted into the Confederate Army. I saw the front line of a battlefield only once before a General took pity on me and reassigned me to a marginally better position viewing the results of the warfare from behind the lines where I assisted the surgeons.

"I lived and worked in makeshift operating rooms in abandoned farmhouses and once glorious mansions across the South. I helped the doctors tend to the wounded, interning among physicians who themselves were little more than children, ill-trained in many cases and ill-equipped in every case for treating the gangrenous wounds that ailed our comrades.

"I recognized that I had been spared, so I worked the long hard hours making myself indispensable in order to avoid the horrors of battle that inflicted the mutilations I tended daily. The work was always unpleasant, and as the war progressed and the tide began to turn, it had become increasingly so. Supplies had been low throughout the confrontation, and as the battles grew more pitched, and the sheer volume of injuries greater, the disparity between supply and demand increased steadily as did the need for qualified surgeons.

"There being no more supplies and no more medical personnel, my first hand experience had become the basis for my impromptu promotion to surgeon. I was tasked with the amputation of the mangled appendages of wounded soldiers, often without the benefit of an anesthetic. While their brothers in arms held them down, I wielded the hacksaw blade and cauterized the wound. The work was not pretty, and it had not been pleasant, but it was functional and it saved many a life while often costing an otherwise able-bodied man a limb and usually his livelihood.

"I was a poor student of geography and certain only that we had remained below the Mason-Dixon Line. I was unfamiliar with the names of the places where they waged their battles. The unit steadily declined in numbers, occasionally being combined with another weakened division in an attempt to bolster the flagging effort.

"I was tired and already personally defeated. I had resigned myself to never seeing home again. Then I began hearing the names of places that were long familiar to me, and a flicker of hope smoldered within me when we began preparations for the Battle of Nashville.

"I decided that I would rather live under the Yankees than under the nomadic conditions of the rebels, and I determined to make a break the way I had seen it done by another surgeon.

"As the battle had worn on into its second day, the telltale signs of defeat began to emerge. The wounded began piling up outside of the door of the small schoolhouse where we rendered service. The sounds of cannon fire and gunshots came closer. Then the smell of burning cordite mingled with the stench of the gangrenous soldiers and rotting pieces of decaying cut flesh.

"At any rate, I heard the call for retreat sounded and the groan of the wounded as they attempted to raise themselves from among the dead and dying to fall back with their comrades. I busied myself in my work tending to those so mortally wounded that they could not be moved for peril of losing what little life remained in their bodies.

"Another surgeon stayed along side me, until a Confederate officer arrived at the door ordering us to fall back with the rest. We continued on with our work despite the order. The officer stepped up beside the other surgeon who held a freshly severed limb in his hand and repeated the order. The man dropped the arm onto the pile, finished cauterizing the wound and walked out with the officer leaving me alone with the dying mass of men.

"It seemed an eternity, but it took less than an hour before the Union army arrived in hot pursuit of the rebel soldiers. Their shells landed near and around the house where I was, but none struck the building other than to rattle the glass out of most of the windows. When the first Union soldiers arrived, they looked in on what was then a young man tending the wounded and passed me by. Numerous morphine-free hours later, the Union medics arrived under escort. The wounded were taken away by wagons to the city. As the last wagon was loaded, I joined the bloody crew and headed for the safety of the Union stronghold.

"On the return, a lone Confederate sniper had mistaken the wagon or made an errant shot trying to dispatch his comrades' captors. The shot took me in the small of the back narrowly missing my spine, but causing immense pain. I was unable to assess the severity of the wound because it lay behind me, and unfamiliar with such pain, I feared for my life.

"On arriving in Nashville, I became another one of the wounded prisoners, and was given a low priority for my less than mortal injury. Early the next day, a surgeon relieved me of the bullet and stitched the incision. I complimented him on his work and detailed my own experiences on the battlefield. He took me under his wing and allowed me to continue in my capacity as a surgeon under the Union army.

"Though I wouldn't take the Hippocratic Oath until some years later, the trials of being a physician revealed themselves to me at that early stage of my career. The most perplexing decisions were those with no good answers: performing surgery on a man without the benefit of anesthetic or knowing that the high doses of morphine I administered might result in an addiction referred to as *soldier's disease*. All too often, the most humane thing to do seemed to provide the mortally wounded an additional dose that would end his suffering and allow him some degree of dignity in death.

"When the war ended, I found myself in a state of withdrawal from the operating room. My family had fared poorly in the fall of the South losing my father, mother, and two brothers. Only an older sister survived. She had scraped and saved even lowering herself to working as a maid for a carpetbagger in the hopes of giving me the chance to become the surgeon I felt I could become.

"My sister survived to see me attain the goal, but consumption took her less than two years later. During that short time, I tried to repay the kindness she had showed me, but I always came up short of my own expectations."

Breedlove's eyes moistened as he finished the tale. Then he sighed deeply and smiled at me. "Time to get back to work, I'm afraid." He hefted his solid frame from the chair and rose to his feet. Grabbing the lapels of his white lab coat, it parted to reveal the worn blue-black suit beneath before he pulled it together and fastened all but the topmost of its buttons. He extended a hand, and I grasped it appreciatively, "Don't worry about that blowhard next door. I'll drop a word with my nurse and she to his. If he gives you any horseshit about the door, just tell him I opened it.

"And put some ice on that head. Looks like it still has a bit of swelling. Get some headache powders, too. You'll be needing them if you don't already. If it gets too bad, let me know. I can give you something a little stronger for a short time to keep the pain down. But only if you need it."

"Thanks Doctor Breedlove," I replied.

"Doc or Mort," he admonished, giving me a wink.

"Thanks Doc," I smiled.

He was not yet completely out the door before he turned back. "And if you need any help from a medical standpoint for whatever the reason with this girl you're looking for, just call on me. I don't do much, but I still do house calls as need be, and I could use a little excitement every once in a while," he smiled.

# 9

The blow to the head had unwound my internal clock leaving me out of synch. Beatrice arrived at my office door bag in hand and looking for an escort home, her duties for the day complete.

I stood in acknowledgement and took a shameful glance at the disheveled state of my desk with the postcards strewn about. "I suppose all of this can wait for tomorrow." I closed and locked the door and we made for the stairs while I explained the events of the previous night.

She made terribly over the goose egg on my head. "I do wish you would be careful. It worries me that your work can be so dangerous," she said. "So who do you think that it was that hit you?" Her brow was furrowed in concern.

"My best guess is a bungling thief, but that would be too much coincidence. It could be someone involved in Nancy's disappearance – someone she may have known," I bit my lip and said no more, holding back on my theories.

"So what were you doing prowling around the alleyway at that time of night anyway?"

"Searching for leads. Looking for anything unusual," I answered and found something else to take my attention as I looked away.

"Such as a person who might knock you over the head?" She taunted.

"Exactly," I replied, looking her in the eyes.

In the interest of discretion, I disclosed little of the investigation to her. Most importantly, I did not tell her that I had wound up in Nancy's bed following the night's events. Even though it was not occupied by the missing woman, I suspected that Beatrice would not have been understanding in the matter.

"So what else can you tell me?" She looked down at the brick sidewalk avoiding my eyes.

"Not much. I mean there is a great deal of information, but at this point, it's impossible to say what is or isn't relevant. Besides, I'd hate to endanger you by burdening you with the details of the investigation."

"You don't have to tell me." She involuntarily stuck out her lower lip and pouted just a little.

"It's not that I don't want to. I've just learned that it's a bit ill-advised to go telling too much—"

"Ill-advised to tell me something?" Her eyes had narrowed and her mouth had turned down at the corners.

"That's not what I mean," I defended putting my hands out to her. "It's simply not wise to throw out all of these unsupported theories."

We reached her doorstep and stood for a moment, I fumbling with me hands, and she fidgeting with the strap of her handbag.

I put a hand to my head. "I'm sorry, I'm still not quite right after that blow to my head."

"Go on then. I'll see you tomorrow," she said quietly not meeting my eyes.

We said our goodbyes, and I wandered off looking back at the screen door from the street as it swung shut.

I returned to the boarding house intent on continuing the ruse that I had begun as Miss Pettigrew's cousin. The exchange with the lady of the house was brief, with her gladly accepting the payment that I had offered a full two days in advance of its required remittance for a room that was not my own.

The wound had left me drowsy, and I was forced to forgo the evening meal and took to the bed early that night. Awakening in an unfamiliar place had left me restless and confused in the first light of day, and I found myself unable to chase down sleep again.

Not an early riser by nature, I rolled out of the bed before dawn and determined to make my way into the office. If I happened on my current employer, my intent was to impress the man with my industriousness and enthusiasm for the case exhibited by my early rising and self-sacrifice of body.

Not wanting to alarm the house matron and intent on keeping my option to return to the room open, I scribbled a note to the lady of the house on the stationary of the missing Miss Pettigrew, intent on finding a suitable place to leave the message. Quietly, I unlatched the door and set foot into the hallway where I heard the cook already hard at work. Making enough noise to avoid startling her, I wandered into the kitchen, she showing only mild surprise at being disturbed at this early hour.

She had a side of bacon ready for the cast iron skillet and was making biscuits when I walked in. She was deferential in her treatment, accustomed to being seen and not heard and acknowledged my greeting with a quiet "Mornin.'" I searched my memory for her name, but it was a casualty of the assault the previous night. I delicately plucked a bowl from the cupboard and helped myself to a quick serving of Oat Toasties and a cup of the morning's first batch of coffee. She watched me from the corner of her eye without a word.

She watched my every move without ever looking directly at me.

I grabbed the chair and turned it so that I could look in her direction while she worked. "Looks like it might be a nice day."

She kneaded the dough and did not turn to face me. "Yes, Suh," was her only reply.

"Have you been out, yet? Is it warm?"

Without looking up from cutting biscuits, she replied, "I suppose 'tis."

I finished my bowl of cereal in silence and stood to go. "If it's not too much trouble," I began and handed her the note. "Could you pass this along to the lady of the house for me?" She wiped the flour from her hands and pocketed the folded page in her apron with a simple nod.

Concerned about alerting the household to my intentions, yet still yearning for more details on Miss Pettigrew, I asked "Did you know my cousin Nancy?"

"Yes, sir," She cast her eyes downward. "I don't have much to do with folks here other than cooking up their food." Her tone struck me as unusual, a timid, fearful ring to it as if fearing retribution for giving an incorrect response, but I let it pass. There is a social barrier, of which I am not proud, that impedes communication between the races. My attempts at bridging that gap have met with only varying degrees of success over the years.

I stepped quietly down the hall, past Nancy's room, and out the front door to the street. A hint of the throngs that are the daily population were making their appearance. A few early-morning laborers dotted the sidewalk on their way to their jobs. The first trolley of the day rumbled past, throwing off the morning paper at the local stand while a one-horse wagon made its way toward the market on Fourth Avenue, laden with its recent harvest of squash, beans and cabbage.

Up the street, a shop assistant cranked out a striped awning while a street grocer stocked his inventory of fruits and vegetables at the storefront, arranging them in a display for the passersby. A window cleaner wiped the last bit of fluid from a shop front window with the company name painted in bold capital letters.

Stopping to purchase the news and a map, the vendor was likewise still setting up shop, but was appreciative of the early morning chance to move his goods. I folded the map into the newspaper and tucked it under my arm. Stopping at the grocer, I convinced him to sell me an apple despite the early hour of the day. I polished it on my trousers as I walked noticing that the late-night rain had again washed the city clean as it had so many days already this month.

Reaching the office, the morning's work lay before me on the desk – newspaper, a handful of penny postcards and a map of the country. Feeling ahead of the game for the day, I sat down to my first task, reviewing the paper, looking for signs of Miss Pettigrew in the obituaries or as a Jane Doe.

Nashville lost 6-4 to the Gulls again, and there was an interesting tidbit in the ongoing saga of the Vols and specifically, Johnny Dodge's death. Alongside news of the defeat was printed an open letter to the Vol fans and our pitcher. The missive came from Dodge's sister, Elizabeth, in Memphis. In it, she expressed her appreciation for the condolences and the flowers sent for her brother's funeral. She was saddened by the loss, but bore no ill-will toward the pitcher or his team. She hoped that Tommy would be able to move forward without guilt and relieved him of any that he might have continued to bear. The letter might have been of some consolation, but time perhaps offered a greater promise of absolution.

Also of interest in the news was that a break with Mexico had been averted, and they intended to release our prisoners. The news was welcome, but unexpected given the anxious buildup of hostilities between our countries. As it was, we had begun to marshal our troops. At that point, we had set the wheels of war in motion, and we might have been inclined as a country to go looking for a fight. There was one still to be had in the European theatre in the event that the one close to home did not materialize, but whether we joined it or not remained to be seen.

Otherwise, Saint Bernard Coal Company had announced that its prices were going up as of July 1. In anticipation of the increase, everyone was being encouraged to stock up now. It seemed a thinly veiled attempt to rid themselves of the last of their coal for the season so that they were not left to store it and keep it dry, but rather allow their patrons to do so in coal cellars throughout the city.

There was no mention of my missing quarry.

Finished with the news, I moved on to the task at hand. The postcards covered the desk, arranged as they had been from the previous night, and I allowed them to guide me. Most investigations are merely busy work, looking at something in a number of different ways until its meaning finally clicks. The first thing that I noticed, other than the abundance of cards from Nashville, was the inordinately large number of cards depicting train stations. Of all the cards, these were typical:

Nashville
Church Street - East from 7th Avenue
5th Avenue Looking North
The Hermitage Hotel – Nashville
The Maxwell House – Old Zollicoffer Barracks
First Floor, Castner-Knott Dry Goods Co.
Lake Watauga and Parthenon, Centennial Park
Union Street
Union Station Nashville
Union Station Louisville
Union Station Indianapolis
Union Station Evansville
Union Station Chicago
Lookout Mountain Chattanooga
Suffrage Postcard – Susan B. Anthony
Chestnut Street – Louisville
Tobacco Road – Louisville
Courthouse – Louisville
Hotel – Louisville
Votes for Women

The last of these was the sole card without a photo on it. On one side, at the top it said, "USE THIS SIDE FOR MESSAGE," and with a light-yellow ink printed was the phrase "VOTES FOR WOMEN." Four polling boxes, one in each corner, showed a ballot being cast. Also unlike the others, it had a perforated top edge where it had been torn from another piece of paper, presumably another card or a piece of propaganda in support of the movement.

Reading the contents of the cards in their chronological order seemed a bit telling. The words and phrases equated to a chronicling of a courtship, one that, like any other, has its highs and lows.

Tacking the map to a cork board left in the office, I had stick pins radiating out from the city. They appeared random and haphazard, and I was unable to make a correlation between the contents and the locations on the front of the card.

To help ingrain the words on the cards in my head, I pulled the stack of blank note cards from the drawer and continued to copy the dates, words and phrases from the back of each unsent communication.

There were many postcards proclaiming the beauty of the city from which they are sent, and usually some mention of "Romeo" was made, but for the most part, they remained relatively similar.

I stared at the postcards, their brief missives providing an insight into the secret life of Miss Nancy "Boo" Pettigrew. With time, the cards began to swirl, the dates and times intermingling and the contents creating a mixture in my head that began to congeal into a picture of the events. My confusion was understandable. As often as not, the front of the postcard did not coincide with the contents on the back. If the postmarks are to be believed, then she had purchased some cards from her trips and saved them for later use.

The following are representative of the entire collection.

Church Street - East from 7th Avenue (postmarked March 1, 1910)

*Dear Nancy,*

*Walked this street one evening with Romeo near at hand to show him where I work. The office where I am employed is just to the left of where the photographer is standing. The moment gave me more than a bit of thrill.*

*Love, Boo*

The handwriting was a close match to that of the letter to Miss Bobo and the sample which I had requested from Samuels. The photo was taken as if standing directly in front of The Doctor's Building and looking down Church Street into town. From the handwriting and the reference to a building on Church Street card, I decided that the cards were without a doubt composed of the hand of Nancy Pettigrew.

Evansville, Indiana (postmarked March 10, 1916)

> *Dear Nancy,*
>
> *We had a wonderful day! Romeo is the consummate Southern gentleman. He walked beside me carrying my things as I shopped just as if we were a couple. It is difficult always having to hide our love for fear of discovery, especially here, but the sweetness of it makes it all the more worthwhile.*
>
> *Love, Boo*

I began quickly to draw the conclusion that she had a beau. I felt a slight twinge in my stomach at the thought of there being another man involved with her, but I resolved to stay with my investigation and see it to the bitter end. She referred to him as Romeo, an uncommon name, and likely an alias like her "Miss Boo" pseudonym.

Lookout Mountain – Chattanooga (postmarked March 31, 1916)

> *Dear Nancy,*
>
> *Loved the city, but it is too close to home. Saw people I knew and had to hide ourselves quickly lest we be seen. It was really more stress than we had wanted for and the place where we stayed was simply horrible. Can't wait to get back.*
>
> *Love, Boo*

Union Station – Chicago (postmarked April 7, 1916)

> *Dear Nancy,*
>
> *Finally, we don't have to sneak around! This is like heaven, and oh how I wish we could live here and leave the rest behind. We will one day soon, we both promise each*

*other, but for now, we must lead our separate lives until the time is right.*

*Love, Boo*

What was becoming evident was that the collection of one-cent postcards comprised a makeshift diary. It chronicled an illicit affair, and it appeared that the man was married or otherwise unable to publicly declare his love for her. That thought gnawed at me, but try as I could, I found no cards to dissuade me of that notion as I flipped through them.

Tobacco Row – Louisville (postmarked Nashville April 20, 1916)

*Dear Nancy,*
*Oh my but it was a close call last night! The lady of the house almost caught Romeo sneaking in the back gate to come to me. We swear we'll never try it again, but I know that we will.*

*Love, Boo*

The reason for her maintaining the corner room with an outside entrance became clear. It bothered me terribly to think that another man might have had knowledge of her. Still, it did little to dissuade me from my attraction to her. I might ask the landlady about the incident, but I was wary of raising her suspicions.

Union Station – Louisville (postmarked April 28, 1916)

*Dear Nancy,*
*We stole a kiss! Right in the train station behind a column where we could not be seen in public! I know there*

*were those from Nashville traveling as well, but sweet is the deception of those that would keep us apart!*

*Love, Boo*

I wondered if perhaps I had read too much into the earlier cards. She spoke of stealing a kiss in public, hardly a mortal sin, yet she treated it as some great incident were she to have been caught. It left me wondering and hoping that perhaps her virtue remained intact.

Courthouse – Chicago (postmarked May 18, 1916)

*Dear Nancy,*

*Romeo could not come tonight. A trusted friend came to tell me, but it does not lighten the anxiety. Our plan has been to run away and be together far from here and all of those who might keep us apart.*

*Love, Boo*

If this Romeo had sent a trusted friend, then someone else was aware of the relationship. It was unlikely that I might find that person, but it gave me hope that the affair had not been so well-concealed that it would make it impossible to uncover.

Glendale Park – Nashville (postmarked Nashville, Memorial Day, May 30, 1916)

*Dear Nancy,*

*It is scandalous, but admit it, I must. I spent the day naked in his arms and awakened to him softly breathing on my shoulder as he lay sleeping. I long for a time when every waking moment will be like this one. Someone came calling at my door to summon me to breakfast, and I thought my heart would stop.*

*Love, Boo*

My hopes of finding her to still be virtuous were dashed.

Suffrage Postcard (postmarked Nashville June 13, 1916)

*Dear Nancy,*
*The past few days have been anxious ones indeed. It is now five days gone and still no visit. Romeo is due to come tonight, and I long for him, but fear what is amiss.*
*Love, Boo*

Evansville – Courthouse (postmarked Nashville June 16, 1916)

*Dear Nancy,*
*One week! Oh, this is not like me to worry. I have not seen Romeo, and I am so worried.*
*Love, Boo*

In the end, he showed himself to be little more than a ruffian, a cad. He took her virtue, and then left her. It angered me that someone would treat her so poorly, yet at the same time, it gave me hope.

Hotel – Louisville (postmarked Nashville)

*Dear Nancy,*
*He is here, yet I am still alone. I must resign myself to this though he promised me it would not turn out this way.*

*He is here with me for now, but I know he must go soon and then I will be truly alone again.*

*Love, Boo*

This was the last card in the series. In the end, he left her, but he at least came back and faced her in doing so. The feeling of disappointment that she had loved someone else was mitigated by the fact that the cards told of a relationship that had run its course and met its end. It strengthened my resolve to find her and allow her to move forward – perhaps with me. My thoughts ran wild – heedless of my Bea. I romanticized like a schoolgirl. And for a moment, I imagined that a relationship with Nancy might actually result from this investigation. But first, I had to size up my rival for her affection.

Based on what I had learned so far, I composed a picture of her lover in my mind – older, well-to-do with the money to accommodate her needs. If he was not married, then most likely, he was a man of position and involved in such a way that he was unable to publicly declare his love for her. Based on the relative extravagances that she heaped upon herself, he was the most likely source of the finances which afforded Miss Pettigrew the luxury of so much clothing, the many scents and the full compliment of cosmetics that she enjoyed. Even if I did find her, it would have proven difficult for someone like me to maintain her interest with such relatively meager means of financial support.

From the tone of the cards, I inferred that the affair was at an end. When he did come to see her again, her tone was resigned to its ending. Love or the end of an affair is often a strong motive, allowing the heart to rule the mind, a situation that can lead to an unfortunate and violent conclusion.

There seemed a fairly pat set of options for motive. She might have run off with her illicit lover. Her love might have gone unrequited, and she might have left town in order to save her reputation. Her lover might have paid her off and sent her away. Or she might have refused to go quietly, and in an effort to resolve his indiscretions, she had fallen victim to foul play. My interest was solely in disproving all but the last of these were suppositions. But things are rarely so simple as that.

My investigation in the short term focused on the identity of her clandestine lover. And I would search for the clues of his identity, and any evidence that supported the notion that she had not taken her leave of her own free will.

Based on the postmarks, she saw him at regular intervals spending more time with him during the weekend and often out of town. They traveled, presumably to avoid being discovered, though it did appear that he frequented her place of residence since she mentioned almost being caught by the lady of the house. Since she didn't mention going to his house, I thought it most likely that he was married and therefore her presence there would have presented a problem.

The nature of her business put her in fairly regular contact with the drummers of the insurance company for which she worked. Knowing that the salesmen travel frequently, I made a note to check with Samuels and inquire as to whether he had men working for him who might have been calling on the areas depicted in the bright images of the postcards.

As far as determining her willingness to leave, it is difficult for someone to tie up all of the loose ends of one's business on such short notice. My job had then become to identify those threads and determine if they unraveled into nothing or wove together in a pattern of foul play.

As quickly as I pieced together a plausible scenario under which each observation might be justified, I chastised myself for the hasty judgment. It is a rare case indeed when the most obvious premise is in fact the truth.

As I searched for alternatives, I grew weary again. The suffering from the injury made my eyelids heavy and lulled me to unconsciousness. Putting my head down on the gently sloping desktop, I vowed to only take a quick catnap before returning to the task at hand of ferreting out alternate scenarios.

# 10

When I did awake, the sun was above the horizon casting light in the hallway and illuminating my office with its morning reflections. Rising from my desk, my limbs were still heavy with the sluggishness of sleep and the severity of the blow my head had sustained. With great effort, I managed to drag my body across the desktop just in time to avoid being caught sleeping by my employer for the second time.

That morning's exchange with Pilchard Samuels was more pleasant than usual. When he arrived, the postcards were spread across the desk, and the map of the United States was pinned to the corkboard. The map was at least four years old, with Arizona and New Mexico still depicted as territories not states.

On the map, stick pins marked each of the cities from which a postcard was sent. The pins each held a small strip of paper containing the postmark date on the card. Samuels walked in to find me staring at the layout on the wall. He was out of breath and his appearance less refined than the dapper self he usually affected.

"You're early today," he said drawing in deeply as he gasped the words.

"I am," I said nodding and raising an eyebrow at his condition.

"I came by your place this morning thinking you would still be there reading your paper."

"No. I stayed at the boarding house again last night. Got the paper from the newsstand on my way in as the trolley dropped it off," I said, hoping that he'd caught my subtle reference to the start of my day coinciding with the four o'clock trolley.

"Damned trolley passed me by this morning. Full up."

I stifled a smile and took a small dig at him, "One of the benefits of being an early riser. But don't you own a horse?"

He froze like a cornered animal trying to decide which way to run. "I do. But she's at the livery."

I didn't give the horse a second thought. Leaning over the desk to get a better view of the work in progress, he made a quick study of the map and its pins, "Looks like every major city on the L&N and N.C. & St. L. lines."

"It is. The postcards are mostly of the stations along the routes."

"I hope you're not planning to visit them on my dime," he said drawing in his breath sharply.

A mean streak tempted me to threaten it, but I refrained, "No, I have business in town today. There are leads to check on—places in town she frequents; personal business she left unfinished; a number of things worth looking into. As far as my bill goes, I'll drop it off to you by the end of the day."

"Good. Don't be going out and running up some huge tab for me to pay. I just want you to find out what happened to her—who she might have been running with and if they might have any reason to harm her."

My response was a closed-lip smile. He took my cue and departed the office without wishing me good day or Godspeed in my search.

I could ill afford the time or the expense of a full lunch, so I stopped in the corner drugstore to stave off my hunger. A Goo Goo Cluster filled with peanuts, chocolate, marshmallow, and caramel is a "nourishing lunch for a nickel" according to the confectioner who created it, and it calmed my stomach's rumblings. My next order of business was to visit the graphologist on the east side of town.

The trolley deposited me in the general vicinity of the place of business and home of the mysterious Miss Bobo, clairvoyant, mystic, palmist and handwriting analyst. Nearing the noontime hour, I heard the whistle of the nearby factories signal its arrival. I oriented myself finding a street number as a reference point and walked eastward in the direction of the address listed on the back of the envelope.

The sender posted her return address, not in deference to the postal service and her customers should the note not reach its intended recipient, but in the hopes that her clients would find the way to her for a more thorough fleecing. While it drew me into her den of iniquity, my intention was to get the information and be gone, avoiding the cold readings that she would foist upon the unsuspecting. As I walked, I steeled myself—ready for the onslaught—and wary of falling victim to the deception of the trades descended of gypsies and carnival side shows.

Miss Bobo had exceeded my expectations from the time her place of business and residence came into view. She was the consummate professional con artist. Staring down on the roadside from the front yard of her home stood a hand-painted sign. It included the red eye on the envelope and a variety of scripts touting her services. The continuity of the red mark on the white envelope and the whitewashed board bespoke an understanding of the powerful impression that symbols can have on people. In this larger version, the red pupil of the eye was a thick, incomplete circle to imply a reflection on the globe of the eye. The eyelashes were exaggerated ever so slightly to accent their existence without making them comical. And its placement on the sign, centered left to right and one third of the way down from the top of the sign, made it impossible to ignore its hypnotic gaze as it watched over the neighborhood.

Behind the distinctive sign, the house itself was nondescript, a small clapboard shelter built for the sole purpose of providing a roof to cover one's head when the strong rains came and the cold set in. Though small, it was reasonably well maintained serving as both residence and business. Despite the heat, the drapes on the front room were drawn discouraging the inquisitive while the windows on the side stood open allowing the breeze to pass through or to allow her spirit visitors easier access to and from the structure.

The front door was unlocked; a neatly hand-lettered sign directed clients to enter and solicitors to turn back. It opened with a tingle, striking a small brass bell mounted above the entryway. The ambience was set by the blackout drapes over the windows and a mantel filled with candles in an attempt to hide the mundane trappings of a traditional home. The living room was undersized, but gave the illusion of space by a lack of furnishings other than a table on which sat an object covered by a silk cloth, presumably a crystal ball. Two mismatched chairs were positioned opposite each another at the table—one for the audience and one for the performer. Another curtain covered the archway to the rest of the house.

Within a few seconds, first a hand and then a woman appeared from behind the curtain. She was clothed in long layers of lightweight cloaks and shawls with an indistinguishable pattern printed on them. They hung loosely about her body in overlapping folds and ever-shifting creases. A silken scarf about her head completed the outfit. As she further parted the drape and before it drew to a close behind her, I glimpsed the conveniences of a perfectly normal home, tidy and well-kept behind the curtain.

"Good day. Come in and have a seat. Let me hear how Miss Bobo can be of service," she said. Her voice was soft. A slightly rough edge, brought on by age, gave it character and a certain sense of charm. Her accent was faint, from the old world, but far enough removed by time to have made its exact source indistinguishable, and she had adopted the local dialect skillfully. Her words moved without haste, measured, well rehearsed and well considered in their selection and order.

I kept at least two paces between us. "I'll stand, thank you." My concern was that by sitting I had invoked the use of her services and was obligated to compensate her accordingly. Stiffly, I handed her the envelope. "I'm trying to locate the author of this letter," I said, but offered no other indication of my interest.

"Ah yes. I remember this one," she said opening the letter and squinting at the lettering on the page. She was patient with my standoffish behavior, but offered nothing more.

"I doubt that you can be of any assistance really. This letter just struck me as odd, somehow out of character for her, and the subject was somewhat unsettling."

"Every letter is interesting," she quipped, "Each one is a window into the mind of the author – a glimpse into their very soul, their very essence of being," she spieled like a sideshow barker luring passersby at the fair.

"Yes, I suppose," I said.

Remaining skeptical, I agreed with her, wary of the spin which she had placed on the missive.

Casting a sidelong glance at me and pulling the letter to her chest as if to protect its contents, she asked the inevitable, "Why do you have it, and what makes you think that I can tell you more than what is already contained in my response?"

Ready for the question, I picked up my adopted persona, "I am her cousin, not her suitor as I can well imagine is often the case when a young man brings a letter to you." I waited for a reaction.

She nodded in acknowledgement but said nothing and offered only a tight-lipped smile.

I turned my hat in my hands and continued. "She has gone missing, and I am trying to find her."

"Well, if you be her suitor, then you have by far given the best performance and tale that I have seen to date. As you might imagine, I can tell a liar – I can see it, like I see so many things." She maintained the constant pitch of her sweet-talk, the words rolling in a lilting sing-song pattern.

"Can you help me?" I asked, growing impatient with her avoidance of the subject.

In response, she wiggled her bony fingers at me, the empty palm facing upward like a beggar requesting alms. Distasteful as the fare was, I conceded to pay the price in hopes of learning something of interest. The nickel landed with a flat sound in the time-worn hand, and it vanished with the skill of a conjurer.

"Be critical if you want young man, but graphology is a science," she wagged a finger at me. "Even if you do not believe in the supernatural, a man with your obvious upbringing should believe in proven science." While she spoke, she produced a magnifying glass from a shelf near the curtain where she had made her entrance.

Quickly and methodically, before she'd even looked at the document, she laid out the briefest of histories on script interpretation as a discipline. She lent herself an air of credibility by touting it as having being developed by the Greeks and honed to a science in the previous century by the French. "European universities even offer a degree in graphology," she pointed out. "And the study is an integral part of the psychiatric fields."

"I'm schooled in the French genre of the science. Every statement made in my analysis is backed up by well supported research that has been tested over time—independent of language – independent of nationality." She raised her chin with pride and an air of authority that dismissed any objections that might be offered.

By her assessment, the letter began with a fair margin at the top and on both sides. But as the writing progressed down the page, the margins became increasingly cramped until the final words and signature pushed the boundaries of the page. From this, she inferred that the well-intentioned plans of the author often fell victim to the constraints of time and money. Her further assessment was that she believed the writer to plan well financially, but then find that they must scrape to get by at the end of the month.

"Each of the loops is fully closed. This person is private. Not prone to want to share the details of her life such as might be revealed in her handwriting." Reading into it, she implied that the writer had secrets that were kept closely and not shared – potentially ethical dilemmas of the "seven deadly sins," to use her words.

"She writes with a heavy hand. She has a strong personality. Probably a forceful nature."

The pace at which the composition was written varied from slow and methodical to rapid and impetuous paralleling the tendencies of the individual. The direction of the lettering was initially sloped to the left implying a certain aloofness, but changed as the transcription progressed until the final line where the lettering was almost perfectly vertical. In the presence of her clients, she termed it, "flightiness." Privately, she called them, "fickle."

"The i's and t's are dotted and crossed perfectly each time implying punctuality and exactitude. The author might be best suited to a profession involving numbers. If it were a man, which it isn't, I might have thought them an engineer," she said.

I chose not to disclose Pettigrew's profession to her, fascinated by her justifications, but still awaiting either a greater revelation or chance to deny her logic.

"Most interesting is the lack of continuity. The base line for the letter varies within each line. The same letter might be styled in two or more different ways." Her response to Pettigrew had not been so in depth, but her assessment to me was that the author wore many faces depending on the need at the moment.

"And she is left-handed."

"I know."

"It's the devil's hand. The Latin word for left is *sinister*. That is no mere coincidence of language," she breathed, but I ignored her and pressed on.

"So there is much more here than meets the eye?" I asked for confirmation.

"Much more than to the casual observer," she preened. "Enough so that I was fascinated to meet her."

"You met her?" I asked.

"Yes, and don't look so surprised, it's a normal progression of events. Most of my clients start with a handwriting analysis. That whets their appetite for hearing about themselves. Then they want to know more. Everyone's favorite subject is themselves. Or am I telling you something you don't already know?"

Being aware that one is being led often does little to diminish the desire to follow, as I found myself doing. The first step is to find a common ground where agreement can be had and begin building from there.

"She actually came to me for a reading just after I did this analysis for her." Miss Bobo pulled a cigarillo from her robes and scandalously put it to her lips lighting it and filling the room with the sweet smell of cigar tobacco. I had heard of women who smoked privately, but had never witnessed it personally.

"Why did she come to you?"

"I am a seer, a palmist, a visionary. I tell the future," she said, casually waving her hand to dismiss the frivolous question as if the statement of her purported skills was sufficient answer to the question posed.

An exasperated sigh belied my skepticism, "So you read for her as well?"

"She wanted to know her fate," she shrugged and drew again on the tobacco.

I leaned forward. "And you gave her a cold reading?"

Her response was a wounded look, "I am no P.T. Barnum young man, going around and selling people a generic tale that they can apply to anyone…I am truly gifted," she hissed and blew a stream of smoke from the cigarillo.

"Sounds like cold reading to me," I repeated. "So what did you tell her?"

She replied by extending her hand and wiggling the long bony fingers knotted at each knuckle.

Pulling a nickel from my trousers, I dropped it into her hand to avoid the touch of the leathery skin. She extended her right hand and placed it over my own to distract my attention while she pocketed the coin in the folds of her clothing with the other hand. The touch was soft and velvety in contradiction of the appearance.

"You know, I remember her. Strong, yet feminine. A powerful mix. A determined spirit. She needed it for the trials she was to endure. She has serious trials to endure."

"Such as?"

"I don't recall exactly."

Exasperated, I reached for another coin, but she stayed my hand, "No, I am not trying to take your money, young man. When I say that I don't remember, I truly don't remember." She paused and leaned back a bit in her chair drawing me forward. "I tell what I see, and I see in great detail, and I tell all to those who want to know. But, my memory is like a writing slate. It is wiped clean after every session. I am left with no recollection of what has been told, only a vague impression of the overall subject and theme. Like the erased chalk of a school lesson on the board – enough to tell if it was a math lesson or a grammar lesson, but unable to discern the formulas or phrases."

"What details can you offer me, if any at all?"

"Why should I answer your questions? Are you her boyfriend – I think not. Her employer – I doubt it. A concerned relative – maybe, but no matter, what business is it of yours?" she asked.

"Because I want to help her through these *trials* as you call them."

She drew back her hands and clasped them together in thought. Her eyes closed as if going into a trance. I suppose that having paid the fare twice over, I was entitled to the full show. "It is a blessing really. I see things that mortal persons are not meant to see. To carry those burdens would drive me insane." She stifled a snicker and opened one eye, "But you may think my sanity already gone."

Impressed with her spiel, I offered up the stack of postcards that I carried in my vest pocket addressed to Nancy from Boo. "What is your assessment of the handwriting in the letter to you and the handwriting on these cards?"

Using the magnifying glass to amplify the size of the cursive script, she looked first at the letter then at the first card in the stack. With the comfort of a magician, she slipped the top card of the deck to the bottom in a practiced slight of hand motion. Slowly, yet increasingly faster, she worked her way down through the deck shifting them from her left hand to her right until she had studied every one of the brief notes. Concealing any emotion, she returned the cards to the hand opposite the one with which I had given them to her.

Distracted, she appeared to forget that I awaited her assessment, so I prompted her to confirm my suspicion, "Is it the same?"

"If you mean are the letter and the cards written by the same hand, then yes, of course. The style is the same; the intricacies of the script are too similar for coincidence; the pressure is the same. You can see it for yourself with your professional eye, even if it is a layman's eye when it comes to graphology." She continued to flip through the cards, more slowly now to read what was written.

I craned my neck forward. "And?"

Warily meeting my eye, she looked for something there and found it acceptable. "Her words tell one tale. The script tells much more."

"Such as?" I was growing weary with the hide-and-seek game that she played.

She cast a slow sidelong glance then called me close, her index finger curling out to me and drawing me into her confidence. "Her hand betrays increasing anxiety—to a fevered pitch—nearly irrational it seems." She closed her eyes, "Remember that she has something to hide – maybe a lot. Be careful what you read into things. Never commit to anything which is not certain." It was hardly a whisper, and I thought that she had stopped breathing.

For a brief moment, I thought she might have expired before my very eyes. Elbows on my knees, I belatedly realized that I had taken the chair at the table across from her and was now pitched forward occupying only the edge of my seat. She had me entranced, bordering on hypnotized, and her charm captivated me. Looking in her placid face, the eyes opened slowly, and I looked directly in where there seem to be many answers, though they were answers to questions that were best left unasked, and they were answers that did not serve the purpose of my visit.

"You should take a reading yourself. You have already paid the price, why not take advantage of it?" she said.

Trepidation over the truths or half truths she might suggest gave me pause, and it required a concentrated effort, a monumental resolve tempered by skepticism, for me to pull away from the enchantment under which she had me spellbound. There was no ill intent—none that I detected, but there was a force there that defied description.

With resilience beyond my abilities, I stood—my knees weak and my head heavy. The room was darker than when I came in, and its features less distinct, but the spell broken.

"You know, I help people solve mysteries, too, not just affairs of the heart, though I specialize in those." My scrutinizing gaze did not offend or deter her, and she continued, "They come to me for all manner of things; lost items; business decisions; adulterous husbands and wives, and I provide them with guidance in resolving whatever vexes them."

Standing, I stumbled over the chair in which I had been sitting. She cackled loudly as she rose, floating toward me. Her apparition came nearer, levitating until her eyes came nearly level with mine. It was more than a mere parlor trick, or so it seemed.

Trying to fend her off, I searched for a means by which to distract, "Do you cast spells or throw curses?" My tone was condescending in a futile attempt to hide the fear that had begun to creep over me.

"I am no witch. Do not mock me," she warned.

"I do not mean—"

"Then be careful what you say," she cut me off.

My confidence slowly returning, I pried into her motivations, "I notice some of the traits that you find in her handwriting appear in yours—specifically the decreasing margins and the closed letters."

She waved her hands as if to shoo away my question. "My words are written with care and special attention to the details to deter any such analysis. Oftentimes, I find myself mimicking the handwriting of the person I am analyzing. Besides that, words and phrases taken out of context can have their meaning easily twisted and turned—much like bits and pieces of a photograph or drawing. They make no sense without the remainder of the picture," she smiled and I noticed that the cigarillo was gone though the smoke still lingered about the room.

Losing confidence, I turned to take my leave.

"How about that reading before you go? The cost is inconsequential at only a nickel, and for the heartache it spares you, it is a bargain at that."

Concerned that her words would taint my investigation and manipulate how I proceeded even if only subconsciously, I countered her offer, "You mentioned fate. Fate is inevitable. Knowing mine would only cause me suffering in the anticipation."

She smiled, "You are wiser than you know." She raised a bony finger to admonish, "But you should still be cautious." The thickness of her old-world accent seeped in as she extended her hand and returned Pettigrew's letter.

"I do so hope that you will come back. Not for the reading mind you, but I think there is more that I can help you with." She reached out and clasped my hands placing my own pocket watch in my palm. My eyes narrowed, "Do not be mad," she said, the accent thick with a Baltic influence. "I thought to keep it to make sure you came back. But if you come back, I want it to be of your own free will."

Returning the watch to its rightful place, I checked for the security of my wallet in my vest pocket. Placing the straw hat on my head and touching my fingers to the brim, I pushed the screen door wide and exited the den of the fakir without another word.

In the light of the day, I paused on her front porch as if emerging midday from a darkened theatre, surprised to find that the world had continued its pace and its course despite my absence. Momentarily blinded by the sun, my eyes watered with the assault, and it was only with the shrill blast of the postman's whistle announcing his deliveries that I was able to fully break away from the hold of the mysterious woman and make my return to a more normal world.

I wandered back to the trolley stop and boarded the first one that arrived. Luckily, it was headed for downtown, and I had to dig for the fare when the conductor came by, as I was lost in my thoughts.

As a passenger on the trolley, I was sluggish as if the very essence of my being had been stolen from my body. I transferred to the No. 7 Belmont Heights Line at the transfer station and arrived at the front of The Doctor's Building a few minutes later where I headed for the office. I remember precious little of the journey, and had I not made note of my meeting with Miss Bobo on my return, I might not be able to relate the events at all.

Reaching no ground-breaking conclusions as a result of the day's investigations, I welcomed the distraction of company given the chance. Doc presented me with just the right opportunity to shirk my responsibilities and delve deep into the memories of a man who has seen the hands of time turn the date on a century and all the excitement that surrounded either side of the arbitrary point in time.

He had expressed some concern over my injury, but I assured him that I was feeling considerably better and in fact had been quite busy. He found the meeting with Miss Bobo curious and attributed my lightheadedness at her hands to the injury, but I remain unsure to this day.

We sat in silence for a few moments. I believe he was observing me for any signs of further injury that I had gone unnoticed before. Then he spoke of things he remembered presumably to test my longer term memory. "Are you old enough to remember the granite cobblestones and mule-drawn trolleys?"

"I vaguely remember them as a child," I said.

He leaned back in the chair. "I remember them like it was yesterday. Sometimes it still startles me to look up and see that they are gone."

I supported myself on the desk. "Were you born here?"

"Oh, yes. I've lived through a lot. I was here during the War Between the States." His voice had a reverent tone in it.

He told me of his adventures as a young soldier. "The Union doctor took me under his wing. With ample supplies behind Yankee lines, I found myself learning a more refined approach to medicine.

"I wasn't allowed to tend the invading Union wounded, but rather only the Confederates out of concerns for the security of the soldiers. Still, I faced a moral and ethical dilemma. Having borne witness to the hardships and cruelty of amputations performed without benefit of anesthetic at the mercy of a heavily used and well-dulled hacksaw blade, I thought there was little else so cruel. However, with the morphine in sufficient supply, it had seemed worse to subject them to *soldier's disease.*"

Discussion of the war left him languid and depressed, so I shifted topics. So you were here for the Centennial Exhibition."

His face brightened, "Of course, like anyone who lived in the city at the time, I attended the Centenary. The replicas of the pyramid representing Memphis and the Parthenon representing Nashville stand out most strongly in my mind. The predictions about the power of machines have come to fruition. But the promises of easier lives that they guaranteed have not come to pass.

"I recall the Women's and the Negroes' Exhibits as well, and wonder what impact those displays had on driving those groups to solidarity in their pursuits. It's rather ironic that once the coloreds achieved suffrage, they no longer cared to support the right of the women," he sighed. "Still, it looks as if women are on their way to getting the vote as well."

His more traditional view of society stayed the line of the older population though he was somewhat less conservative than his contemporaries. Nevertheless, the attitude would not have held water with someone of my generation.

As our conversation headed into the late hours of the afternoon, my interest did not wane, but rather it increased. His perspective gave me hope that if a society could have experienced so much change in a single generation, the next might hope to accomplish at least as much.

"I'm sorry, but I have a bit of work left to do – finishing up my notes for the day and some bookkeeping," I said.

He took the cue and reluctantly rose to his feet. Age and a full life conspired to keep him constrained to the chair before he managed to rise once more and stagger to the door with a casual wave and a parting word.

Following Doc's departure, I composed my first bill for Pilchard Samuels being sure to include enough to cover the overhead for the office space. I dropped by his office and left it with Miss Winston when I found that he wasn't in.

I didn't wait for Bea to escort her home. The spate of hours since I had awakened that morning had begun to take their toll on me, and I longed for the comfort of my own home even if it were only for a few moments before dinner that evening at Beatrice's home. Arriving at my apartment around four, I reveled in the comfort of my own surroundings.

My real home was a snug room on Hayes Street. A corner apartment looking toward town from three stories up; it offered a commanding view of the city. The apartment is modest, a bedroom and a small kitchen area with a sitting area off to one side.

The kitchen had been neglected during my absence the past few days and could have used some attention, but I was unable to accommodate it. Falling into the bed, I slept until nearly the dinner hour when I was forced to rush if I was to keep my engagement for the evening.

# 11

I rushed into town narrowly catching the trolley on its way in. I had to return to the boarding house to retrieve my wallet. The day's investigations had depleted me of what small amount of cash I had on hand. The detour only caused me further delay.

Wishing to avoid the madam and the other boarders who might have been about and caused me even greater delay, I took the easy route approaching from the alley keeping watch for any hoodlums that might be lurking in broad daylight. Passing through the gate and traversing the yard, I reached for the key above the door. But it was gone. Perplexed, I racked my aching brain to recall if I had done something odd with the key after checking for it that morning. Standing at the door failing to remember, my ears detected the sounds of movement within the room. Trying the doorknob, I found it unlocked.

Moving with the stealth of a cat hunting a bird, I slowly eased the handle around and pressed on the door enough to see a sliver of the room. Merriweather stood at Pettigrew's closet picking through things in the bottom of it. He was searching for something, stopping every few seconds to carefully peruse an item, his thick frame blocking them from my view. He dropped to one knee, and I saw that he was digging in the clothes hamper. Having failed to search it personally, I held my position hoping to be led to something, anything that might help me in the pursuit of the case.

He shifted, and I saw him in profile as he dug deeply in the wicker basket. When his hand came up, it was holding a small piece of cloth. He sniffed lightly at the material bringing it close beneath his nostrils. Pure curiosity paralyzed me as he sampled the texture of the material between his thumb and forefinger before pressing the crotch of the garment to his nose and inhaling deeply.

The shock froze me in place. As he continued to sort through her clothing, he selected certain pieces, and gracefully raised them up on his fingertips burying his face in them inhaling the scent of the owner's most intimate regions. With other pieces, he rubbed their softness against his face cooing with the sounds of a pleasured beast.

When he raised a pair to his mouth, his lips parted as if to consume the lace fringed panty, the debauchery of what I was witnessing loosed my grasp on the handle of the door allowing it to swing wide in a slow silent arc. With his tongue protruding from his mouth to taste the decadence that the article might offer, the door thumped softly against the bed frame putting him on notice of the public nature of his exhibition.

Who was more embarrassed in the situation, him or me?

I took little solace in the fact that witnessing such a spectacle as that was mercifully reserved to few times in one's lifetime. I was kneeling at the door with my mouth ajar; he knelt at her closet door. The crimson-faced little man hastily stuffed the clothing back in the hamper. Articles draped over the edge of the basket as he slammed the lid down. With the pair of panties still held in one hand and the basket shut, he thrust the guilty evidence into his pocket as if nothing had happened. Then he strode to the door expecting me to make way for his departure.

By that time, having gathered enough of my wits about me to stand, I blocked the door, and I extended my open palm. "The key," I said.

He drew it out of his pocket and stared at his clenched fist. Slowly he moved his hand over mine, opened it, and allowed the key drop into my palm with a soft flat noise. It was almost hot from being held so tightly.

Unsure what to say, I simply gestured for the contents of the other pocket. Grudgingly, he retrieved the panties. He rubbed the material in his fingers once more, and I reached to take them from his grasp. He held onto them for a few more seconds reluctant to forfeit them, but he finally did before shoving past me and out the door.

I emptied the contents of the hamper onto the floor of the room and searched through each article of clothing. Looking in every pocket and leaving no article untouched, I found nothing, not even a forgotten scrap of paper.

Not wanting to leave myself open to reproach, I returned the contents of the hamper to their appropriate place. I stood there, horrified at what I had just witnessed, and wondering if the man was Pettigrew's lover or simply a deviant.

Unfamiliar with such an obsession as his, and hesitant to condemn a man without first-hand knowledge, I slowly brought the cotton garment to my nose. The smell was pungent and acrid like the smell of sweat, but with a musky taint to it. It was repulsive, yet at the same time possessed some type of allure, like the smell of alcohol in a saloon.

I did not bury my face in the cloth as Merriweather had done. But having stared the temptation down, I placed the dirty undergarment back in the basket and covered it with the wicker lid before shoving it back into its place.

Anxious to address the situation, I went in search of the intruder with the balding pate. Rapping lightly, I did not announce myself in the hope that he would open the door. Receiving no reply, and already late for dinner at Beatrice's house, I pulled a pen and a scrap of paper from my jacket pocket and scribbled down a note requesting that he meet with me on Sunday.

I tried to put the episode behind me and returned to the room to collect my wallet and take another quick look around wondering what it was that I might have missed. Unsure of Merriweather's intent, I decided to carry the key with me rather than leave it there for anyone who might intend to do me harm or pilfer Nancy's things with the intent of blaming the theft on me.

Stepping briskly, my strides carrying me as fast as possible in the direction of Bea's house, I remained astonished at what I had just witnessed, and it clouded proper consideration of the event. Merriweather made an illogical match to Pettigrew as her secret lover. I knew him to be single, and dating within a boarding house is not unusual. So there would have been little reason for the secrecy of such a relationship. In addition, he did not have a great deal of amenities, much less than would be required to support the lifestyle of Miss Nancy Pettigrew.

Going through the possible scenarios, I wondered if Pettigrew and Merriweather were actually a pair of con artists working a scam on the landlady or someone else. The plausibility of the situation seemed so far fetched as to be laughable, but the thought still nagged at me.

The walk produced no new conclusions, and I reminded myself that I should make a note of the episode and record it in the files in the event that charges would later be filed. What he might have been charged with is unclear, but the threat might have set him to talking.

When I finally arrived at Beatrice's home, the family was already gathered at the table, and I had to knock on the screen door to be admitted. Beatrice answered, the scowl on her face confirming that I had done myself no favors with her or with her father.

The advent of so many lunchtime restaurants and the expansion of the city had diminished the amount of time being spent with family anymore, but the evening meal remained a time when loved ones could gather to spend time together and share the news of the day. It is also the time when a young woman is expected to bring any serious suitor calling to meet her family.

But this was not my first trip to Beatrice's home to break bread with her family. However, this time had an air of consequence unlike any of the handful of times before. The seriousness of our courtship was becoming more obvious. That being the case, it was important that I establish a line of communication with her father. However, such a goal did not come easily.

Normally, I might have built a relationship with the rest of the family through her mother. However, Beatrice's mother had been taken by consumption some ten years ago. She had left the man with two daughters and a business for which to care. Beatrice had fared well, being old enough to care for herself. Her younger sister had grown up under the doting eye of her father who lavished all manner of attention on the spoiled child and shared every bit of knowledge with her in the hopes that she might one day grow up to take a man who would also take his business over.

As I passed my greetings, her father merely grunted and declined the offer of my hand. "We waited for you in order to bless the food. Have a seat and let us give thanks." His mouth was turned down, and he moved sluggishly as if tired from being inconvenienced to wait for me.

He motioned me to a chair at the side of the table. He sat at the head of the table. Beatrice took the opposing seat leaving me seated opposite her twelve-year-old sibling. The positioning must be their own custom in the absence of her mother, but it bothered me.

His distaste for me was evident from the start. During the blessing, he made no mention of me as a guest in his home, but instead offered a prayer that his daughters would grow up to choose suitable husbands. It was not clear at first if I was considered among those or not, but I was left later with the distinct impression that I remained outside of that group.

Asking all of this "in Christ's name," he reached immediately for the fried chicken strategically placed in front of him and helped himself to the largest and only breast on the plate before passing it on. I was left to choose between drumsticks and wings in an odd assortment of a partial chicken. Not wanting to be rude and deprive the girls of their dinner, I took a small wing at which the younger girl gave a heavy sigh much to my chagrin.

As we commenced to dine, conversation turned, as always in this situation, to my profession. It was not something her father understood, and therefore he had trouble taking me seriously. "It amazes me that people will pay you to do something that our taxes pay the police to do." He held his fork upright in his clenched fist. His jaw was set and his gaze fixed on me awaiting a response.

"My clients generally require an air of discretion not afforded by law enforcement officials. The police are generally overworked and their records are constantly sifted by the press for tidbits of information about people and their dealings about town," I defended.

He remained unconvinced and motionless. Then he snapped back to the business at hand, eating his meal, and resumed issuing general commands to the room. "Pass the mashed potatoes. Pass the green beans. Pass the fried chicken." His largest helping was of turnip greens seasoned with vinegar, which he shook on them generously.

Much to the consternation of her father, my Beatrice followed the trends of the day. She had engaged herself in her profession as a receptionist with a rather disagreeable physician. While her father did not approve, he had learned that she was of her own mind and after nearly twenty years of trying to tame her independent spirit had finally decided it might be easier to simply let her learn the hardships of the path she had chosen for herself.

But while he permitted her to ply her trade and express her views on suffrage freely, he had not cast her completely into the hardened world. He provided the roof over her head and the food on the table each night. Not foolish enough to allow his daughter the freedom of boarding-house life, he had her home each evening to his table for dinner to which I was invited on occasion, though my presence was not encouraged by anyone other than Bea.

Without looking up, the man stuffed a piece of meat into his mouth and addressed me, "My daughter tells me now that you are studying medicine."

I shifted uncomfortably in my chair and shot a glance at Beatrice who kept her gaze fixed on her own plate.

I laid my hand on the table still holding the fork. "I've concluded my studies."

"Oh?" He looked up.

"I chose not to complete them, but the basic skills come in quite useful at times in my investigations." I looked him directly in the eye, daring him to counter me.

His responded with a disgruntled "Harrumph," and turned his attention back to his plate of food.

For her part, Beatrice shot me an icy glare from the corner of her eye at my having undermined her effort to win some sort of approval with her father.

Mercifully, he shifted his focus to the rhetoric which he wished to deliver to Beatrice. She took it all in stride heeding the more prudent advice and ignoring the rest. She had learned to pick her battles wisely fighting only those with important ramifications.

One which he regularly revisited was that of her eventual engagement and marriage. "No man worth his salt allows his wife to work," he was fond of saying, knowing that one day he would be proven correct. "Look at the ladies in the accounting department at Union Station," he proclaimed. "When they marry, they leave the company," he said, gloating triumphantly. He looked weakly to me for support, and I nodded as a courtesy, not so much in agreement, and it drew a grim look from Bea.

Occasionally, he was his own folly in the argument, usually when he made the mistake of comparing his day and age to today with arguments like, "When I was a young man, the Board of Education would not even allow a married woman on staff. Women did the appropriate thing and resigned their position. Just like your mother did when we married. God rest her soul."

The result was as if he had set a match to a Chinese firecracker. It remained unclear if the passion of the response was fueled more by the statement itself or the reference to her mother. Bea declared "There is no comparison! The social structure has advanced far beyond that since you were young. In a short while, women will be able to vote, and when they can, we may just put one of our own in the White House."

That always evoked a smile from the widower.

Then Bea condemned his use of her dead mother's name which generally produced an awkward hush about the dinner table for the remainder of the meal by signaling an end to her willingness to further pursue the discussion.

"The pecan pie is delicious," I said to break the silence.

"I made it myself," Beatrice beamed, and I decided to limit myself to trying to please her and gave up on the remainder of our dinner party.

Leaving the table, we took our place in the swing on the front porch. The air had cooled considerably from the heat of the day, but the sun had yet to set bringing on dusk. We dangled our legs as we moved back and forth holding hands and sitting close to one another.

Once the rush to make it to dinner was past, we had a few moments before we had to take our leave of the household. We were to go to the Vendome that evening with Jeff and Caroline. Bidding her father and sister good evening, we headed off in the direction of the theatre.

Opting to enjoy the cool night air, we strolled to the theatre by foot rather than trying to catch the trolley. The added benefit of the walk was some additional time alone with Beatrice, less time spent with her father and the price of the trolley fare saved.

We walked in silence the length of a few houses, and I enjoyed the moment, not realizing that Beatrice was building up steam, "It just isn't right the way he simply dismisses my ideas," she fumed suddenly. "Women are people, too – created equal in the eyes of God – from the rib of man so we are neither the foot to be trod on nor the head to be above."

At a loss for something to say, I stumbled forward offering what I thought would have been a welcome concession. "He did have a valid point about married women quitting their jobs. It does make sense. Someone has to mind the home."

Her mouth agape, I belatedly realized the error of my words, "So you side with him?"

"No." I stammered, but the box was opened and now it could not be shut.

"Well, Mister Black, I thought I knew you a bit better."

As if the formal address did not suffice to put me on notice that I had strayed into dangerous territory, Beatrice stuck her chin out leading the way and reducing me to nothing more than her escort for the evening to any passerby. Heedless of all the warning signs, I plunged headlong into the fray attempting to defend an indefensible position. "I am only stating a fact, not subscribing myself to its moral appropriateness. The fact is women do not stay on after they marry."

Stopping abruptly, she turned to face me. "Name me a colored woman who stops working when she gets married."

Dumbstruck by the challenge, my retort was weak, and I rolled my hands. "Bea, I simply don't know that many negro women."

"But you know some," she insisted and nudged me with her elbow.

I shrugged my shoulders. "Yes, those in the employ of maintaining households, I suppose."

"And do they have husbands?" She looked forcefully at me widening her eyes and raising her eyebrows.

I looked at her. "I suppose they do. But Beatrice, that is a different matter entirely. *You* are not a colored woman. For that matter, how many Negro women do you include among your ranks?"

"I think you're missing the point," she said, glowering at me through narrowed eyes. "Women's rights have been following closely in the steps of the advances made by colored men. Why, they have more rights in many instances than women do. They have the vote already."

It would not have done well for me to point out the fact that the poll taxes kept most colored men from even being able to vote, so I tried to cut my losses and concede—though I knew that it was too late. She did not allow me to completely forfeit the position, as I was branded with it and would be forced to wear it in her presence until she deemed me once again worthy of being allowed back into the fold.

It took only a few moments for her mood to cool before she accepted my arm again. The crisis averted, we walked in silence. My thoughts turned to the investigation at hand, and I found myself mulling over the recent developments. When I spoke again, it was of my work.

"Do you know Nancy Pettigrew well?" I asked.

She gave a small sigh and shrugged her shoulders before responding, "Know her, yes. Know her well, I doubt it. I doubt anyone does."

"Well then how is it that you know her?"

She stared straight ahead and did not look at me. "She works in the same building. We had exchanged hellos on passing. Then I saw her one night at a suffrage meeting, and so I went over and introduced myself as a fellow working female fighting for the rights of the women of our country."

About that time a carriage rushed past, headed in the opposite direction splashing the gutter water onto the sidewalk and soiling my pants leg. "Damn!"

"You shouldn't use such words, you know."

The bait proved too much, and I took out my frustration at the soiled clothing on her. "So, if I understand this correctly, you want the right to vote, but you still want to be insulated from vulgarities? You want the man to walk on the outside and accept the spoiling of his garments over your own, and you want him to open the door for you, and stand up when you walk in the room? I suppose you expect the man to pay for you at the theatre as well?"

The look on her face dropped and I could see that I had stung her with my sarcastic tone. She replied, "I only meant that it wasn't very Christian to say such things."

Cowed by her statement and shamed by my own reaction, I apologized and she accepted, but we walked along in silence again.

"What do you know about her?" I asked after traveling wordlessly for a block.

"Who?" Her thoughts had wandered during the break in our conversation, and she genuinely had lost the thread.

"Nancy Pettigrew."

"Oh. She's right nice, sociable and all, but quiet. Keeps to herself. Doesn't talk a lot with the rest of us about the things we talk about."

"Such as?"

"Girl talk." She looked away and skirted the subject.

I determined to be more direct in my approach, "Did she mention a boyfriend?"

"No." Her lips were tightly pursed.

"None at all?"

She glanced at me sidelong with an accusatory look in her eye, "No. Like I said, she didn't talk much with us about social things. Mostly about suffrage. She is convinced that someday we will have the vote. Like the coloreds do."

Wary of setting off another tirade against the inequities of the American society toward women, I recast the inquiry using what little knowledge I had, "It appears she may have had a fancy for a man."

"Really?" she seemed mildly interested. "Who?"

"I don't know. I think he may have been seeing someone else." The comment caused her step to falter slightly and an accusatory look crossed her face.

"Not me," I defended.

"Then who?"

"As I said, I don't know."

"You must have some idea if you know so much already."

"No really, I have no clue. For that matter it may as well be me she was seeing." The offhand remark touched a raw nerve.

"You? I didn't even know you knew her?"

"I don't."

"Well, you say you don't, but to hear you talk, it makes me wonder."

Jealousy is initially flattering, but it quickly becomes frustrating when it begins to breed anger. Still, the unfounded suspicion of my having a relationship with Nancy Pettigrew and the absurdity of the idea gave me cause to smile. My expression served only to fan the flames with Beatrice setting her off again on a first-rate huff. We walked the remainder of the distance in silence, the specter of Miss Nancy Pettigrew's and my nonexistent relationship weighing heavily on us.

Thankfully, our destination was not too much further. The Vendome had recently reopened that year after its conversion from a traditional theatre to one suited to the moving pictures. At Beatrice's insistence, I had been forced to take her to the first show four months prior. It had been a three-hour ordeal, an entertaining evening I must admit, but expensive beyond compare. At four bits per person, I had just as soon she'd gone by herself and spared me the remainder of my dollar. But that would never have done. So I endured the Birth of a Nation complete with its thirty piece orchestra and insufficient intermissions. I had spent the entire performance consumed with determining how the orchestra had managed to keep the proper tempo with the moving pictures on the screen.

The night's fare was to be a bit more palatable in terms of the length of the performance and the price exacted for the privilege. Our pace was well timed as we arrived just in advance of the show and before a crowd had gathered. The excitement, generated simply by being in the presence of the recently renovated old theatre, soon distracted us from the petty argument of the evening.

The building was magnificently done in the rapidly disappearing style with three oversized arches at street level. Above the massive first floor sat two more rows of windows, the second floor complete with small arched windows echoing the main floor's architectural distinction. Stone turrets, capped in a pointed crown, bookended the building.

We stood on the sidewalk beneath the web of utility wires waiting for our friends with whom we were to attend the night's show. They arrived by trolley only seconds after we had set foot on the curb.

Standing in line together, we talked with Caroline and her beau, Jeff—our friends from the park the previous weekend. The girls rehashed the events of the past week, Jeff and I lingering on talk of Johnny Dodge, the conversation renewed by the letter from his sister that had appeared in the paper that day. It was sentimental talk, but we both agreed what a wonderful player he had been destined to be if his life had not been cut short by his untimely demise.

We arrived quickly at the window, and I procured our tickets for the show and tucked them into my pocket in a gentlemanly manner. The gesture did not go unnoticed, as Bea cleared her throat with a gentle cough and extended her gloved hand, palm up in requisition of the ticket that she might exert her independence. I feared that this was to be only the first of the fallout over our earlier spat.

Entering the theatre, the attendant ceremoniously ripped our tickets in half pausing for a moment to give me a quizzical look when Bea, her arm entwined in mine, handed her ticket to him.

"She's my sister," I said, just loud enough for her to hear, and I shrugged my shoulders and rolled my eyes for effect.

"Your sister?" she said, and I got yet another fiery look from her punctuated by a frown that was more than vaguely reminiscent of the look that I had received earlier that evening from her father.

The lobby was impressive. But with the influx of theatre goers, the hall began to fill and became cramped pushing us toward the theatre. The paneled wood and full length mirrored walls offset the tightness of the room, but the humid evening air made it claustrophobic still.

We all made our way to the obligatory refreshment stand for colas and popcorn. We stood in the lobby making idle chatter for a short while seeing some of our friends and acquaintances among the other curious theatre goers. Suddenly, Beatrice shuddered heavily and stumbled nearly falling to the floor, before I grasped her arm and steadied her. Concerned, I looked to her only to find her hand covering the lower part of her face.

"Are you okay? Do you feel ill?" I asked.

She looked at me as if noticing me for the first time that evening, her eyes wide. Her voice was muted by her hand when she spoke, "Yes, I suddenly feel quite peaked."

Caroline came to her aid at that point and began to make a bit of a fuss which Beatrice waved off. The two of them disappeared quickly into the ladies lounge to recover.

"Just a case of the vapors," said Jeff with a grin, and I had to smile myself at the thought of Beatrice allowing herself to offer up such an excuse and show any sign of weakness given the night's discussion.

A few moments later, the two returned. Beatrice's eyes darted side to side hoping that her frailty had not been observed and betrayed her as a person less than worthy of the right to vote. Satisfied that her spell had not been made the latest of public gossip, she deigned to enter the theatre.

We found our places, which were fine seats by any standard. The performance hall was a prime example of what the theatre was intended to be rather than the venue of a barn as our not-so-distant ancestors had been subjected to. Box seats lined either side of the theatre and were glamorous indeed, but not intended for the masses. The ornate trappings of each box framed by a rose-colored tapestry and thin faux columns topped by a diagonal lattice grid would accommodate at best four people. Situated as they were off to the side, their view could not have been superior to our own, but the price suggested that the amenities were substantial.

As we sat enjoying the ambience of the theatre, Bea's hand in mine, I felt a sudden shudder running down her arm. When I looked to her, she had slumped in the chair and her face was partially hidden by her hand once more. Pulling her hand from mine and without a word to me, she enlisted Caroline to accompany her once more.

Jeff and I sat for a few moments knowing that our presence in the lobby would only serve to aggravate an already delicate situation. Two folded seats between us, we leaned over and spoke in hushed tones, "Are we obliged to whisper and giggle for them in their absence?" he asked.

I laughed despite myself, but knew that there would be hell to pay if the comment ever reached Beatrice's ears.

Moments later, Caroline returned alone, her eyes darting side to side embarrassed at the spectacle which she seemed to think she was making of herself. Jeff and I both stood as she approached. "Beatrice needs to go home. She's not feeling well, and I'm going to take her."

"No. No. I'll take her. She's with me and the two of you should enjoy the evening together. Don't let us ruin it for you."

"No. I'm going with her. She asked me to."

"Really, it's all right. I don't care to sit here anyway," I said moving to slide past Jeff.

Caroline hissed at me, "It's a woman thing. You should mind your manners and be so kind as to desist in your behavior."

Publicly reprimanded, I deferred from further comment and watched her retreat back up the aisle. Then I returned to my seat and began anew with Jeff, "Do you think we can recoup the money spent on the tickets since the girls aren't going to be with us? We could spend it better a few streets down at the Turf."

"You sound bitter," he taunted me.

"Not bitter, just frustrated," I said wringing my hands.

"Stay calm," he reassured me, and clapped me lightly on the back.

But my outlay for the evening was not yet over though, as Caroline reappeared once more, "I need the fare for a hansom to take us back to Beatrice's house."

Abandoning our seats, Jeff and I returned to the lobby and helped to tuck Beatrice and her attendant into a hansom at curbside paying handsomely for the favor of couriering two young ladies safely to their respective destinations. Following the show, Caroline's beau and I, the odd couple for the night, called it an evening early and headed in our respective directions neither one of us feeling up for an extended night in the dens of vice on Fourth.

# 12

The closeness of the boarding house made for a tempting proposition, even though its amenities paled in comparison to my own apartment, so I took advantage of it following the aborted evening. The fact that it allowed me to stay in character as the temporarily homeless cousin of Miss Nancy Pettigrew played into my decision as well.

There was no sign of Merriweather at breakfast. According to Mandy, he had made off early that morning, the beneficiary of a cup of coffee, a buttered biscuit and a heaping plate of eggs. He had passed on the bacon she had prepared. Frustrated by his avoidance, I returned to Nancy's and my room and collected a few pieces of paper to aid in my investigations for the day.

At the office, I chanced a quick peek in on Beatrice. Her hasty wave told me that she was doing better this morning, but that she had no time for me due to fear of retribution from her employer. Respecting her concerns, I retreated to my office to catch up on the news of the Vols latest win over the Pelicans and plan my day sorting out the loose ends left by my missing quarry.

Samuels's morning visit was uneventful, little more than sticking his head in to check that I was available. A shake of the head told him that I had nothing new. He paused in the open doorway, "Oh, and we have the small matter of your bill to discuss. Perhaps we can do so over a game of billiards. I'll meet you at the Maxwell House at five to go over what you come up with today."

The invitation produced a feeling of dread in the pit of my stomach.

I spent the bulk of my morning in the main business district of the city along Church and down at the Arcade. My exploration began just across Seventh at one of the finer dry-good stores in town, Castner-Knott. One of the items I had found in Pettigrew's apartment was a receipt for a "white waist" and a "white summer dress" she had purchased two days before her disappearance. The receipt noted that she had paid to have them altered and that they were due to be ready for her to claim the day following her disappearance. If she were leaving town for good, it was doubtful that she would have forgone paid items so expensive as a six-dollar waisted and a twenty-dollar dress.

I entered the store and made my way to the ladies' department in search of the clerk whose signature graced the bottom of the slip. Uncomfortable among the women's clothing, I thought belatedly how opportune it might have been to have brought Beatrice along for this part of the investigation while I made my inquiries. As it was, I was forced to swallow my mannish pride and press forward, heedless of the stares from the women perusing the store's goods.

"Could you point me in the direction of the salesgirl who signed this receipt?" I asked.

She looked at the paper, "This is for a dress and a waist to be altered. That would be located in the adjoining section," she said holding a finger out in a direction even deeper into the unfamiliar department. My inquiry effectively redirected, I forged ahead with my intrusion and followed the indicated path.

In the department, I introduced myself as the cousin of the young lady for whom the articles had been altered. "She sent me to collect the articles, a dress and a waist." She looked at the slip of paper once more. "I'll get them."

She gave me an odd look at my next request.

"Could I speak with the young lady who signed the receipt?"

She raised her eyebrows and instructed me to, "Wait here for a moment," and she disappeared.

An aged woman returned a few minutes later, smelling heavily of cigarettes and perfume. "I was stocking some items in the back," she excused herself, "How can I help you?"

I reintroduced myself, but she was taken aback by my subsequent questioning.

"Did she seem to be in good spirits when she bought the dress?" I asked.

"She hasn't been feeling well." She cocked her head to one side.

The other woman returned trailing the items for which the claim check had been produced.

"I was to meet my cousin in town today, and she had asked that I pick this up for her." I indicated the items as the woman opened and examined them before releasing them to me. I tried to chat the women up regarding my cousin's condition. They turned to face each other and there ensued a casual bit of conversation that I tried to keep focused on Pettigrew but to little avail.

The older one put her hand to her chest and said in a hushed voice, "The poor girl is quite ill."

"Oh my, there's so much going around, you just don't know what it could be," the other one said shaking her head.

The elder one had her hands on her hips as she spoke. "You just have to watch your health these days. Take care of yourself."

Oblivious to my presence, the first one continued. "That's the truth."

I cleared my throat to interrupt. "We've been trying to figure out how far back the ailment might go."

Drawn in as part of a mystery of sorts, they were suddenly intent on my every word and became overly zealous in their attempts to recall Pettigrew's mood at the time.

"Yes, she was a bit pale," the elder said wagging her finger.

"But always a good customer," said the other with widening eyes.

"Never asks for credit. Pays everything in cash." She nodded.

"Always picks what she likes."

"Seemed able to afford what she wanted," they continued.

"Did she mention that she was going out of town?" I asked directly to the clerk who had completed the sale to Pettigrew.

"No. Not that I can recall, but my memory has not been too good of late," she said tainting her own statement with doubt.

"Was a man ever with her?" I tried. Both shook their head at the very idea a man would ever set foot in the ladies' department.

Their chatter went on incessantly for a few moments until another clerk strolled over and joined the conversation. At that point, the first two clerks began to bring the new one up to speed describing Pettigrew to her.

"Oh, you remember her, Grace. The pretty one with the dark hair. Good customer," the younger of the first two said.

"Mostly comes in the afternoon," said the older one matter-of-factly.

"Prefers the better quality goods," the first one said with a nod.

"She's ill." The elder clerk gave a grave look over the top of her glasses.

"Quite ill," the first clerk added.

"She may not make it." The elder one was shook her head.

From there, the exaggeration of gossip was fascinating to experience first hand as the story grew so that Pettigrew lay on her deathbed fighting the ravages of polio and Lord knew what else.

Needing to break from the prattle that I had instigated, I interjected, "Oh, I am sorry. I've forgotten that I have some other errands to run." Holding out the dress to the young woman who had retrieved it, "Could you hang onto this for an hour or so? I don't want to carry it about town with me." The older woman looked perturbed with me for the trouble I had put them through, but the one who had just joined the fray accepted the dress with a gracious smile.

Since the dress had not been picked up, it added to the indications that she had not disappeared of her own accord. With the women still chatting up a storm, I quietly took my leave of the gossip and made for the exit.

As I hit the street, the day was beginning to swelter. Following another receipt, the next stop was to be at a drugstore at the corner of the Arcade. The location was a curious choice since Jennings Pharmacy is far closer, sharing the same intersection as Castner's and the office block of The Doctor's Building.

The most direct path was straight down Church and then left on Fifth. Striped awnings adorned the storefront of many of the businesses along the route. In the rising heat of the day, they were almost all unfolded to shield the goods of the merchants from the direct rays of the sun and ward off the threatening skies that were perpetually at hand of late.

Sandwiched between the flow of pedestrians, the motorcars that were becoming increasingly popular competed furiously with the trolleys and carriages for the right of way. Staying on the north side of Church allowed me easier passage. The opposite side was an obstacle course of utility poles to support the overhead tangle of wires. But the people crowded my side of the street, and not wanting to be rude, I exchanged greetings with all who made eye contact, an obligation in this town.

On my side of the street, I passed the ladies' businesses in rapid succession, apparel shops and jewelers one after another: B.H. Stief Jewelry, the Blouse Shop, Louis Rosenheim Jewelry Company, La Mode, and Jensen Herzer & Jeck Jewelers. On the opposite side were the more mundane necessities of life: White Trunk and Bag, Hebrick & Lawrence men's clothiers, and the Nashville Railway and Light Offices. Shoe shine parlors and fruit stalls dotted the sidewalk between the other businesses as I went.

Seeing the Railway and Light Company reminded me of the need to stop in and place an order for a fan for the summer for my apartment. At the price of one dollar per month, the fee seemed bearable for the small respite it would offer from the blistering heat of the pending months. No doubt, the one dollar charge did not cover the costs of the machine, but the company made their real profit on the sale of the electricity to operate the fan over the course of the months. The ads claimed that the cost was only a penny per hour, but totaled up, that equaled three times the cost of the rental even if one used the fan only ten hours each day.

Crossing the street was slightly perilous. I stepped lively in order to avoid the motorcars zipping in and out between the trolleys as they rolled along their lines, sparking when they hit a junction. Inside the office, the line did not take terribly long, and in return for my dollar, I received a handwritten receipt and a promise that the fan would be delivered early the next week.

Back on my trek, I finished my route passing the Watkins Institute, H.G. Hill Grocery and Joy Floral Company. At Fourth, men's and women's needs reached a confluence, the flower shop on the mundane side and the United Cigar Store on the other. Just opposite, the sounds of a well-played instrument emanated from the O.K. Houck Piano Company.

Traffic permitted and I crossed at the intersection. A kind traffic officer waved me across allowing me to walk diagonally and avoid crossing twice. The next block began with the rising Hitchcock Building, home to one of my competitors, the Dixie State Detective Agency on the sixth floor. On the other side stood the Princess Theatre inside the Luck Building and opposite the Jackson Building. At Wright's Hat Store, I paused to stare in the window a moment at the new summer panama hats they had on display coveting for a moment a gray felt one with a sharp black banding, reminding me yet again that I must discuss the bill with Samuels for my services that evening.

The Cain Sloan Dry Goods Company stood at the corner of Fifth and Church on Saint Cloud's corner. Its opulent façade and corner entrance gave it the position of prominence at this main intersection, and I was reminded of a few other receipts among Miss Nancy Pettigrew's things for purchases made there.

Turning up Fifth, I arrived at the entrance to the Arcade, the backbone of retail trade in the city. It ran the entire block between the Fifth and Fourth Avenues with the lady's favorite department stores on one end and the Gentlemen's Quarter on the opposing ends of the spectrum. What took place between the two terminuses served the needs of each gender.

Entering the drugstore at the corner of the Arcade, it was like every other drug counter in the city. The wooden counter separated the customer from the shelves filled with vials and bottles stoppered with either a cork or a glass lid. The medicinal smell of rubbing alcohol was mixed with the chemical smell of the remedies and other products. A countertop display advertised the latest in popular elixirs for the relief of the common cold and anything that might ail a body.

As I sauntered in, the pharmacist was just completing a sale to a young woman. The drug counter was well stocked with large glass jars lined up on the shelves and labeled with their contents—camphor gum, tincture of iodine, senna leaves, arnica, and carbolic acid. To one side sat tin-lined wooden barrels filled with turpentine and linseed oil. And a full complement of ointments and salves was on display each named for their inventor – C. C. Pills, Dr. Caldwell's Syrup of Pepsin, Sloan's Liniment, Grove's Headache Powders and the less personalized quinine and ipecac. The ladies' counter was equally well stocked offering the full line of cosmetics – face paint, face powder, powder puffs, glycerin mixed with rose water, and witch hazel.

While I waited my turn for the gentleman in the white lab coat, I noticed a wooden box sitting on the counter with a slot cut in the top. An inexpensive hasp and small lock secured the lid. It attracted my attention only because of its advertisement. On the extended wooden back was pasted a piece of card stock. Meticulously scribed was the message in various black and red inks, the pencil guides still visible. I recognized the name of Miss Bobo and an offer in a carefully constructed and flourished script: "Have your handwriting analyzed by a Scientific Graphologist," for the sum of a nickel. The sell went on to describe the service as "Fascinating" and "Informative" and promised "Character Traits Revealed."

On the front of the box was a carefully scripted set of instructions telling the reader to, "Enclose at least two lines of text in an envelope. Deposit it in the box along with the coinage indicated for the service." The author could pick up their analysis two days later at the drugstore. For an additional two cents, the interpretation would be mailed to the writer. Finally, the instructions questioned the reader as to how well they knew their friends and encouraged them to have their friends' analyzed as well by depositing a sample of their writing, with the appropriate fee, of course. Next to the box was a small sheaf of paper, old outdated forms identical to the one used by Miss Pettigrew to construct her note.

The pharmacist's business with the lady concluded, he turned his attention to me. "Hello, how can I be of service?" he asked.

I presented him the bill, "Do you remember the young woman who made this purchase?" He looked at me suspiciously, his oath of confidentiality weighing on the response. I gave him the same story, "She's my cousin and she's quite ill. We're trying to determine what might be ailing her." He accepted the lame explanation and reviewed the document once again.

Thinking for a moment, he said, "I don't recall."

I prompted him. "She has beautiful auburn hair. Twirls it around her finger before she tucks it behind her ear."

He drew in a deep breath. "Oh, yes. Her. Of course." His face lit up as his eyes grew wide. "Yes, I remember her now. Gosh, how could I have forgotten? Striking young lady. Forgot that this was her." He paused before continuing, wondering if he had overstepped some boundary. "She comes in here fairly often. Haven't seen her in a few days though."

"So she frequents your establishment regularly?"

"Oh yes. Gets her beauty things and perfumes here. Seems to buy a lot of the perfume, but can't say as she lets herself get carried away with it." He pointed to a large glass bottle of perfume from which portions were decanted into smaller bottles for purchase.

"Are they expensive?" In the stores one is expected to ask the price, unlike the mail-order catalogs where the price is displayed in a rather crass manner.

"Can be. She doesn't buy the most expensive one. But for scented water, it's still pretty pricey if you ask me." The memory of the small collection of perfume decanters arranged on the top of her dresser reminded me of the vice.

Taking a few steps in the other direction, but remaining behind the counter, he pointed, "When she comes in, no matter what else she gets, she picks up some headache powders." He indicated the Grove's packages stacked neatly together. "Must have them something fierce. She stopped coming in here for a while, then started back just like usual. I guess she just stopped having them headaches for a while. Come to think of it, the last time I saw her, she didn't look so good.

Looked like she was having a bad spell—pale and shaky. Bought the powders again like before."

The bell above the door jingled and a young boy walked into the store. The druggist broke off our conversation just long enough to address him. "Hey Jeremy, don't know how much there is today," he called to the lad of around twelve years of age.

The boy nodded to acknowledge the greeting, but didn't say a word. He minded his manners and didn't interrupt his elders in conversation. He wore a newsboy cap pushed forward down over his eyes and a jacket one size too big for his frame passed down from an older sibling or otherwise acquired secondhand.

The boy placed a small stack of envelopes on the counter next to the handwriting analysis box and pulled a small key from his pocket and inserted it into the lock. Sticking his hand in, he pulled out the two or three envelopes inside. As the owner and I watched, he deposited the windows into the writer's souls into his jacket pocket and replaced the lock watching us from the corner of his eye the entire time. The druggist selected a piece of hard candy from a jar behind the counter and tossed it to the boy, his face smudged with a bit of dirt and flushed from running store to store to collect the scribbled missives. Giving the man behind the counter a nod and a smile, he never spoke a word and accepted the sugary treat eagerly.

I jerked my head in the direction of the box and asked, "Do a lot of customers send things out to Miss Bobo?" My familiarity with the woman was exposed by my mention of the fortune-teller's name.

"More than you'd like to think. I see almost as many women come in here and drop their husband's hard earned wages on that stuff as I see of gentlemen dropping their wages down at the Climax and the Turf," he said jerking a thumb back down the direction of the Gentlemen's Quarter at the other end of the Arcade.

"Do they seem to like the responses they get?" I asked.

"They must. Surprising how many drop in a letter and a nickel, then come back a week later and drop in another one that they bring in with them instead of writing here," he scoffed. "They think I don't notice. They try to do it when my back is turned, but I don't miss much in this shop. They're all of them wanting to check out their husband or their boyfriend and be sure he's the right one and that he's behaving himself."

"Interesting," I said, thanking him for the information. He continued about this business arranging items on the shelves and preparing a prescription. Delaying my exit, I went to the box, wrote a few words on the page and dropped the nickel in for Miss Bobo. He busied himself with some task while I scribbled, and I detected a slight shaking of his head as I dropped the envelope into the slot.

The Arcade was a full block long running east to west and almost as wide as a street. Shops lined both sides and an iron railing framed the open second floor filled primarily with offices such as those for Saint Bernard Coal Company. The arched steel frame and glass ceiling encased the mall shielding the pedestrian clientele from the elements.

On my way in, a young boy pressed a handbill into my palm. He pushed one into each unsuspecting passerby's free hand as he strode past. The leaflet was unremarkable in its advertisement for the Arcade optician, but it did remind me that Miss Pettigrew had left her reading glasses in her apartment. On a hunch, I decided to drop in on the optometrist and see if he was acquainted with the missing woman.

The office was easy enough to pick out – the unique pince-nez sign stood out among the other shingles posted outside of the vendors along the Arcade mall. Entering the shop, I plied the clerk with a story about my cousin having lost her eyeglasses. "She has forgotten the name of the place where she got them, but assured me that it was in the Arcade. Could you check your records for a Miss Nancy Pettigrew?"

I was rewarded with an accurate guess. Asking her if it were necessary that my cousin come in for an eye exam again, she told me, "That would hardly be necessary. She only just purchased the eyeglasses—less than two months ago." Thanking the lady, I told her that I would return the following day to place an order for the spectacles.

I attributed Nancy Pettigrew's headaches to the need for glasses and the subsequent problems to her failure to remember them on occasion. I had tried them on in her room, and while not strong, they were unequal, which might have exacerbated her discomfort.

I left the eyeglasses shop and crossed the walkway to the post office where Miss Boo sent her letters to Nancy. The post box Miss Pettigrew used to receive her mysterious postcards was just below waist height making it awkward to look directly in without bending or kneeling. The combination lock displayed the letters A through H, each of them assigned to one of the eight points of a star. In the center of the star was a small-ridged knob with an arrow like a single hand on a clock. Turning the dial in the right succession of letters from right to left and back again would open the box. Below the dial, a small window disclosed the contents of the mail slot, packed full with envelopes. It sat there in the shadows of the box taunting me, but there was not enough light to make out the information scribbled on the top envelope.

For a few moments, I contorted my body, first squatting, and then taking a knee in an effort to read the note. I turned my head to one side trying to defy the simple physics that afforded the post box users their privacy. The result was an awkward public display that attracted the unwanted attention of an elderly female patron opening her box down the row from me.

"Forgot my combination," I excused myself.

She turned her head not wanting anyone to infer an association between the two of us.

I tried a few times randomly selecting combinations of letters that spelled something, but the lock proved more secure than anticipated. Finally, I was forced to stand in the counter line for a few moments while the other patrons conducted their business. Arriving at the window, I informed the clerk that I was there for the mail by the box number.

"The name?" he asked.

"Nancy Pettigrew. She's my cousin," I replied casually. The postman disappeared for a few moments before returning.

"There's a package," he said holding a brown paper and twine-covered box.

"What about all of the letters?" I asked.

"No letters."

"But I can see them through the glass," I protested.

"Yes, there are letters in the box, but not for Miss Pettigrew."

"For whom then?" the inquiry tipped my hand and the clerk became immediately guarded.

"That's for the addressee of those letters to know. And since you obviously are not that person, I cannot hand them over to you," I started to protest before he continued, "And you don't appear to be Miss Pettigrew either. But since you know the name and asked for it, I suppose I can give it to you."

"Of course, I'm not Nancy Pettigrew. I'm her cousin. She's ill and has asked me to check her post box. I wrote down the combination, but seem to have lost the paper on which it was written," I said patting my pockets with my hands in a mock effort to locate the combination. "She *is* expecting a package, and there should be several letters."

"To whom?" The question was simple as should have been the answer.

"Boo."

The clerk screwed up his face taken suddenly aback by the exclamatory name.

"No, sir. Not the name on the other mail. Go back and ask her to give you the name, and I'll be glad to hand them over to you then." He handed me the package, its brown paper cover rough beneath my fingers as I headed for the door before he had a chance to change his mind, and before I had a chance to read the sender's return address.

As I exited, I checked the post box number on the small package and looked in the box once more. It was undoubtedly the same one. The post in it was freshly shuffled, but no more readable than before.

I fumbled with the package in my hands. It was from Sears and Roebuck, a large catalog company. Neatly stamped on the package was the return address in Chicago, Illinois. Curious, but not willing to open the box in public while I stood in the midst of the crowded Arcade wondering where to go next, I was inexplicably drawn to the eastern end of the mall by the allure of the Gentlemen's Quarter only steps from where I stood.

Taking solace in the fact that as a male member of society, I was able to cross over to the eastern side of Fourth Avenue without shame and only a moderate amount of embarrassment, I headed for the Southern Turf.

The condition of the street was fierce. The blacktop applied several days ago had not cured and proved to be sticky and thick in the heat. Cardboard was laid over the tar to allow people to cross without ruining their shoes, yet the constant street traffic across the cardboard tracked the black mess anyway. Distracted by the state of the roadway, I had failed to notice an oncoming trolley only to be nearly knocked flat by its approach despite the ringing of its bell.

Reaching the other side, I tried to clean my shoes on the curb and noticed others less fortunate than myself who had crossed the street without the benefit of the unfolded cartons and as a result had ruined their shoes. As I stood at the door of the Southern Turf along with one or two others, I was relieved to have a legitimate reason to loiter there before casually stealing in the doors. Just as I pivoted on my tar-encrusted heel, I was surprised to see none other than my employer, Pilchard Samuels stepping from the curb. He followed the same path as I had only moments before, and like me, he had found the tar a terrible inconvenience. It was a distraction which I'd welcomed eagerly and used to my advantage as I slipped in the front doors of the Southern Turf.

On reaching the east side of Fourth Avenue, he surveyed the street looking for someone. I drew my head back slightly lest it be me that he sought. Failing to find other direction, he turned and headed south where he made his way to a private entrance leading to the second floor of the Southern Turf.

Curiosity got the better of me as did my investigative instinct, and I followed. The other door was removed from the main entrance sandwiched between the Turf and the next building. It was not covered by the same awning that covered the main entrance, giving it the appearance of being dissociated from the vices fed within.

I pulled the door open and climbed the steep stairs. Here the keeper behind the peephole was not so eager to allow me admission as downstairs where I am well known. But still, they admitted me without much delay.

The space was smaller and the crowd was thinner. I spotted Samuels immediately and found an opposing corner to avoid being noticed. He was having a conversation with one of the men who managed the bar, and after a few moments, Samuels pulled a bill from his pocket and was admitted to another door that opened to a stairwell. From the reputation of the Turf, I knew this to be an area where as you climb the stairs, the girls wait at the top for your arrival, each one beckoning to you to select them for the next half hour so that you can satisfy your needs and have your wallet lightened in the process.

Sauntering to the bar, I decided to wait out Samuels's return in a half hour. The mail-order package nagged at me as I placed it in front of me on the bar. I ordered up a single glass of Jack Daniel's Old No. 7 thinking to myself how ironic it was that the state is dry, yet Lem Motlow and his crew were still allowed to advertise their spirits in the pages of the newspapers along with an address for ordering the elixir from Kentucky. The sour mash looked like a dark brew of tea and it gave off a wavy form in the glass as it melted the chipped ice over which it was poured. It went down smoothly – one sip at a time while I waited.

Three drinks and nearly an hour later, Samuels reappeared. I had about given up, thinking that he had slipped out yet another of the many different ways in and out of this building. Having decided that I was on my last drink, I was headed for the door when he came down.

The smile on his face and his disheveled hair told me that he had indeed been a busy man. The length of time told me that he had spent a fair sum of money satisfying that particular vice and provided for me a newfound understanding of his preoccupation with the ladies.

Without hitting the bar, he left by the same door through which he had entered. A few seconds behind him, I shadowed his every move ducking into the doorway of a store when he stopped at a bootblack to have his shoes shined.

He covered the distance fairly rapidly otherwise and returned directly to The Doctor's Building. Tailing him produced nothing of any interest, much to my disappointment, but it did cause me to wonder if he had been shadowing me up until then. The thought was curious, and I considered it confirmed when I met him in the hallway of the third floor leaving the direction of my office.

"Five o'clock. Maxwell House Billiards Room. Don't forget," he reeled off not slowing down.

"You have a bit of tar on your heel," I said to his back as he walked away.

He craned his neck to look at the shoe before halfway turning to me, "So, I do. Thank you," he said before he marched off.

I was convinced that Samuels knew more than he was letting on, and I was beginning to wonder if he was, in fact, following me as I went about the investigation. As such, I resolved to be even more cautious and watch my back more closely.

# 13

On the heels of Samuels' odd comings and goings, I'd made a quick trip back to Castner's retrieving Nancy Pettigrew's new clothes. My intention was to avoid having my story unravel with a chance comment at the wrong moment by the women in the ladies' department. By my return, the idle chatter of the clerks had yielded way to forced courtesy. Luckily, the garment bag veiled its contents allowing me to avoid the embarrassment of carrying a woman's clothes about town.

Back in my office, the clothes bag hung on the wall facing my desk like a specter of Nancy Pettigrew watching over me. The effect was unsettling at the least, and I'd determined to ferry the garments to their rightful place at her boarding house at the first opportunity.

Doc poked his head in and greeted me heading into the lunchtime hour. "I have some rounds to make. Otherwise I would invite you to lunch to see how your case is progressing."

"I haven't much progress to report," I said.

"A change of pace might be in order. Take a stroll and enjoy the fresh air. Don't continue to waste away in this pigeon hole of an office," he chided.

The advice was appreciated, but it went unheeded. Some dogged devotion to the task at hand compelled me to remain at my desk reading the postcards and reviewing the events of the past few days, searching for some type of news to provide to Samuels.

Ultimately, I did leave the desk, though not to go very far. What seemed evident was that Miss Pettigrew had last been seen at her office. No one could account for her whereabouts after work that day. The appointment with Merriweather that she'd failed to keep and my recent encounter with him pointed to a need for further investigation.

The garment bag flailed along behind me as I rushed the few blocks to the boarding house. I'd hoped to arrive in time for the noontime meal in order to catch a word with Pettigrew's stubby fellow boarder. The prospect of his not being there was particularly unpleasant since my presence would obligate me to the displeasure of the madam's cooking.

The smell of burnt pork chops greeted my nostrils, and I almost forwent my professional responsibility in favor of sparing my discriminating palette. The thought occurred to me that I might duck out the private entrance of the missing woman's room as I placed the clothing in her closet, but dutifully, I entered the room only to find that all were present and accounted for, except Merriweather and the perpetually absent Miss Pettigrew. The meal left me feeling quite rough and in search of antacid on my return to the office.

As I walked, the pain in my stomach gave me clarity of mind, and I turned over some unanswered issues. Nancy Pettigrew had last been seen at her office, and not since. Could she have exited the building without being seen? Or how could someone have entered without being seen? The side door offered one option, but I decided to investigate and see if there was another means of entry.

The front of the building on Church Street offered no other entryway other than those of retail establishments – doors certain to be locked after business hours. Rounding the corner of the building, I saw no entrance other than the side door. At the back of the building, steps led down to an alleyway of doors, the back entrances to the retail establishments, which were of no interest for the reasons previously stated. A service elevator accessing street level and the subterranean alleyway proved inconsequential as well.

Confounded, I retraced my steps to the front of the building and was almost to the corner before I'd realized that it would be closer to go in the side door. As I turned back, the sound of my footsteps changed when I stepped on a pair of steel plates in the sidewalk. The pieces were not sealed tightly enough to be permanently closed, but the sheer weight of the metal kept them shuttered. Tapping my heel, the sound reverberated in the hollow area beneath. If there was any entryway associated with the building using these plates, it was accessible only from within.

Back within the main lobby, there was a stairwell that led down below street level to the maintenance and mechanical areas. There was nothing to stop me—no gate or door—so I strolled down into the inner workings of the building. At the bottom of the steps, there was a maintenance shop directly in front of me. The doors to one of the main lobby elevators stood to my left. To my right was a long stone-lined corridor hewn from the limestone foundation of the city. If I held my bearings properly, the corridor led back in the direction of the mysterious steel plates in the sidewalk. As I traveled the corridor, the atmosphere was thick with the musty smell of dirt and mold found underground. Bright light bulbs hung from a single electrical wire overhead every ten feet illuminating sections of the darkened tunnel and leaving black shadows in between. Utility supply lines ran overhead creating a ceiling of painted pipes of all sizes.

I passed a set of closed wooden double doors on the left, and forged ahead. Nearing the end of the passageway, I saw the focus of my investigation. There stood a set of double doors with a hasp securing them together in the center. To the right was a control box with two buttons simply labeled *up* and *down*. The platform itself had a steel arch that stretched from one side of the car to the other, but no other walls or containment. From where I stood, there was an unlit corridor on one side and the boiler room on the other, from which came the sound of the operating machinery that fed the floors above.

Opening the doors, I stepped onto the platform. Looking up, I was greeted by the sight of the underside of the two steel plates. Someone stepped on them, raining grit down into my face and momentarily blinding me.

At the far end, the elevator doors opened and a gurney was wheeled into the stone-walled corridor. Its passenger was shrouded by a white sheet. Minor surgeries in the comfort of a doctor's office rarely resulted as had this one, but death is part of the profession that will not be denied its due.

The service elevator where I stood was not only for the removal of trash, and inloading of materials, but also for occasions such as this to avoid taking the body through the lobby or having to manhandle a cadaver out the side door.

There was no place for me to stand other than the doorway to the great boilers in the belly of the building. The attending physician, his nurse and an undertaker rolled the gurney onto the platform. They paid me no heed and failed to even acknowledge my presence. The mortician rode to the top with the body, while the doctor pressed the buttons to raise and lower the lift. The arch over the platform pushed the steel doors up and open, the metal on metal screeching as it went. Bright sunlight streaked into the underground cavern before being blotted out as the platform sealed the void once more.

Once the man and his cargo were clear, the doctor dutifully lowered the elevator back to the basement and turned to leave. Behind me the sound of a generator kicking on startled me and prickled the hair on the back of my neck.

A series of seven or eight gauges, including a clock, stood mounted on a board to the right of the door. The two furnace doors were huge. They were more than six feet off of the ground, but of sufficient size to allow a body to pass through. The mere thought sent a shiver up my spine.

The equipment was fascinating and the nooks and crannies abounded. Behind the boilers was a small cubby hewn in the limestone foundation. It hid a small cot and a set of lockers. The area was neatly kept, but tightly confined and no doubt warm during the colder months. Far removed as it was and small as the quarters were, it must have served as the locker room for the colored employees that worked for the building manager.

Soon I found that I had consumed the afternoon and was now due at the Maxwell House for my appointment with Samuels. Not wanting to be late, I departed allowing myself twenty minutes for the short walk.

I arrived at the Maxwell House seven or eight minutes ahead of schedule. As I traversed the vestibule, a hotel call boy entered and moved about the room paging someone in a discrete, yet clear voice, audible to within ten or twelve feet of where he had taken up his position. The interruption passed unnoticed by the patrons of the hotel.

Entering the billiard parlor, Pilchard was already there waiting for me at an open table. Dispensing with the formalities, he ordered a drink for me before launching into an assessment of the bill that I had painstakingly prepared for him.

"I cannot believe that you would stoop to charging me for your newspaper and your trolley fare. And you've even pawned off your entertainment expenses under the guise of a graphologist."

He laid the bill on the edge of the table and pointed at each line item as he called them off. "One week's service is $27 as we discussed. 15¢ for your newspapers? Surely you don't expect me to pay that?"

"Actually—"

"No let me go on. 35¢ for phone calls. Then there's 5¢ for note cards. But here's the best part. 25¢ for trolley fares and 15¢ for a graphologist?" That comes to a total of $27.95 plus the $20 I've already paid out for her apartment.

"Everything is justified. What would you have me not do?" I asked with outstretched palms.

But he had already turned away and reached for a billiard cue.

My approach is to bill for every last shred of expense under the theory that what I do not invoice for at first, I cannot bill for later without being conspicuous and undermining the trust I hope to build with my clients. By adopting such a policy, I always begin at the high end and have room to bargain down as necessary allowing the client to feel that they have in turn received some reduced fee.

He chalked the stick. "I'll accept the charges, but I think you're taking advantage of me. I'll deduct a fee of five dollars as a week's rent for the office."

That was roughly the amount I had planned on for the office he had forced upon me.

Then his motivation became clear.

In the same voice that he had used to reproach me, he invited me to a game of eight ball. "Double or nothing on just your expenses, not the fees." he said, "We'll round it up to a dollar to make it easy calculating."

He proved a worthy opponent on the pool table taking the first game handily and reducing my bill by a dollar. The next round was closer still, but in the end I prevailed, sinking the eight ball in a side pocket on a fine bank shot off of two rails. "We're even," I said inciting Samuels to begin wagering on the outcome more aggressively having lost the gains of the first round.

"Double the stakes. Two dollars a game," he said.

Not eager to be parted from my money, I demurred. "One dollar."

As with the other games, it was again close, the two of us running several balls on each of our turns. The black eight ball sat on the table, its position relative to the cue ball making it a delicate, but not terribly difficult attempt for me.

As I lined up the shot, Samuels forcefully placed a note on the rail, "This dollar says you don't make it."

Without straightening up, I raised an eyebrow to better see the look of frustration painted on his face and nod in acknowledgement. The ball bounced cleanly off of the rail and sliced in without grazing the edge of the side pocket.

I moved to collect my winnings, and Samuels put a hand down on the dollar, the enmity palpable in his voice, "Double or nothing."

He was already down two dollars; nevertheless, I foolishly allowed my ego to take charge forgetting that he was my employer.

I tore into the game with the intent not of parting him from his money, but of putting him in his place and sending him home chastised for mixing business with pleasure.

This time, the game was not a competition. My eyes never left the table and I never heard any other noise or noticed who might have come and gone from the room. I sank one shot after another, nearly running the table, before being forced to yield a shot to him. When all was said and done, my opponent still had five striped ivory spheres remaining.

Another hotel call boy made his way politely through the room paging for someone just as we finished.

Samuels turned to me and through gritted teeth said, "Put it on my tab," before walking away leaving my invoice and his lone dollar on the corner of the table.

# 14

Still somewhat taken aback by the confrontation with Samuels at the billiards table, I found myself once more rushing to keep my evening date with Beatrice. I had asked her about the suffrage movement and their meetings without sharing the reason for my interest, and she had agreed eagerly to take me to the next meeting which happened to be that night.

When we arrived, the reason for her exuberance had become immediately clear. A collection of almost exclusively older ladies, precious few of them under escort, filled the room. The matrons of the movement, they dominated the meetings on Friday evenings since the younger crowd was all out courting. I was one of the few men lulled into the gathering, but I took solace in being assured that I was not the first. My interest was defensible with my investigation, but the inability to disclose the association made for awkward conversation as I tried to mingle with the true supporters of the movement.

My attendance proved worthwhile when I spotted someone who stuck out like a sore thumb even more than I. To the side of the room, combing the gathering crowd stood the man I had been wanting to see, Pettigrew's fellow boarder — Merriweather. The man appeared nervous—as he should have—unescorted and entering the den of his aspiring peers. As I lightly touched her hand to let her know that I was leaving her side, Beatrice gave no reaction.

Working my way across the room, I was able to get within spitting distance of the man before he noticed my approach. On registering my identity, he blushed deeply, and he made a futile attempt at an exit before I could catch hold of him, clasping his elbow. He resigned himself to acknowledging me and fashioned a sheepish smile of guilt as I greeted him, "Mister Merriweather, how do you do?"

"Mister Black," he replied offering nothing more.

"I haven't seen you in a while. Let's see since—"

"Since we last saw one another, Mister Black," he filled in.

"Yes, since then," I affably agreed enjoying having the upper hand in the situation. "I've been meaning to follow up on that conversation, but you seem to have been avoiding me, you old duffer you."

"No, just busy," He denied, but the remark hit home, and he squared his shoulders to me.

"Yes. Aren't we all?" I agreed still holding fast to his arm lest he attempt to leave.

Before I could continue with my questioning, he set to his own cheeky inquiry, "Do you have your lovely cousin with you?" He leaned to either side to peer behind me for signs of a companion.

"No. No. I haven't been able to track her down just yet. As a matter of fact, I have become quite worried and had hoped that you might have had some word of her," I prompted and finally released my grip.

His little mouth drew up even tighter, and he put his hands in his pockets to jingle some coins, "No, I haven't seen her either." I waited, and he continued, "I have a few things to discuss with her when she does appear though," he managed through his teeth, barred like a threatened animal.

"Mister Merriweather, might I inquire as to the nature of your relationship with my cousin?" I pried, hoping for some response.

"No. You may not," he defended with a steely eyed stare.

"Perhaps we could continue our discussion in private. Say over breakfast in the morning at the boarding house?" I doubted that he would honor any such commitment, but his verbal agreement was almost secured when our discourse was interrupted by the appearance of Beatrice at my side. She delicately clasped my arm with both of her hands to garner my attention.

Her presence was not unwanted, but it was terribly inopportune. I had not accounted for her in my cover story and had not briefed her on my role as Pettigrew's cousin.

"Introduce me to your friend," she said.

"Mister Merriweather, this is Miss Beatrice Rose. Miss Rose, Mister Merriweather," I stammered being intentionally remiss in providing any context to either relationship lest the weave of my story might unravel.

Beatrice gave me a small poke in the ribs which I ignored. She didn't understand my sudden lack of etiquette.

Merriweather seemed less fazed by the broach of protocol. He crossed his arms and put one finger to the corner of his mouth. "So Nathan, what do you think has become of your cousin?"

I jumped quickly to an explanatory answer, hoping that Beatrice would follow my lead and not contradict me this one time, "My cousin,

Miss Pettigrew," I began, carefully turning to Beatrice and pausing lest she missed my lead, "has simply vanished. I don't know what has happened to her." Feeling a need to fill the space, I stumbled onward hoping to keep Bea out of the conversation, "I have checked with her office again repeatedly since I arrived in town only a week ago, but have had no word of her yet."

Beatrice raised an eyebrow having caught my cue. Against her nature, she held her tongue.

"Too bad. I had hoped to see her here this evening. I think I mentioned that we engage in quite some lively debates, and we were to attend a related event together. The appointment was for one of these meetings, and I had hoped to catch up with her tonight."

"Yes, I had hoped the same," I said. Beatrice remained quiet, looking for a chance to jump into the conversation, so I tried to cut the encounter short.

He rubbed his chin when he sensed something amiss. "By the way, I haven't seen you of late. You seem to be coming and going at some very odd hours. I honestly don't think I've seen you since you paid the rent on Nancy's room out of your own pocket,"

Beatrice's brow furrowed in response. "You paid her rent?" she repeated.

"I did, but—"

"Well wasn't that noble of you?" she said, her remark caustic in the private way that can be interpreted only between couples,

Merriweather's genial comment touched the terribly sensitive nerve for which it was intended, "Well until she returns, he has the benefit of the room, if you don't mind sleeping in someone else's bed."

"Yes, I suppose so," she said, removing her hands from my arm. "Oh look. There's Betty. Excuse me, I must go say hello. Pleasure meeting you, Mister Merriweather."

I hastily took my leave as well, while the man's cat-bird grin widened in triumph. Unable to spare the time to wipe it from his face, I rushed to catch Beatrice before she engaged herself elsewhere.

She was still in motion when I caught up to her, "All part of the investigation," I blurted out.

"Sleeping in her bed is more than an investigation," she fired back.

"It's not as if she's in it," I protested.

Her eyes widened in anger, "So you *are* sleeping in her bed! And claiming to be her cousin! And Lord knows what else! But you have yet to tell me anything about it! Do I look a fool to you?" she spat and strutted haughtily leaving me struggling to keep up with her. It would have been best if I had simply let her leave, but in my frenzied state, I forgot myself and stopped her short of the door.

"No. You do not look a fool," I pleaded, as I held her hand.

"Then why are you sleeping in her bed like that odd little man said?" She stomped her foot and looked directly in my eyes.

"I'm not sleeping in her bed!" My denial was a little bit too loud drawing the stares of a handful of people in close proximity. Beatrice turned and walked away, further incensed by her public humiliation.

Following in her wake, I continued to plead my situation, but my pleas fell on deaf ears. The organizer pounded a gavel to call the meeting to order and begin the program. As Beatrice sidestepped her way to a seat, I followed, forced to discontinue my entreaties while she positioned herself in a chair with her back to me. She stopped, and I gave her my best pleading look. She replied by casting her eyes down to the seat in which she had intended that I sit. Aware that the battle was lost, I refused to take the indicated chair like an obedient dog. Locked in a stare, the anger and fear mixed in a most unsettling display. Determined not to be looked down upon by me, she refused etiquette, and we sat at the same time, rather than my waiting for her.

After the program, we made our way back to her home in silence. The measure of ire that I had stirred in her seemed out of proportion. And while I searched for things to say, finding nothing only further indicted me of the grievance of which I was accused. In my own defense, my infatuation with finding Nancy Pettigrew was of a professional origin. It was admittedly tempered by the allure of a strangely mysterious and strong woman of whom I knew very little, and would gladly have learned more, but not at the cost of the woman I had chosen to love.

I was forced to watch her simply glide through the door and lock it with a final anguished look at me. I swear that a tear, a hint of regret lay there on her face, but my glimpse was too short to be certain. And rather than be forced to knock upon the door, I opted to make my way home for the evening to resolve how I might overcome the predicament.

As I plodded along in contemplation, Beatrice's reaction bemused me further. It was she who had introduced me to Nancy Pettigrew. It was she who so quickly had identified that the woman was missing. And it was she who had introduced me to this case. A thought crossed my mind, but I dismissed it as preposterous.

I traveled almost a block in the wrong direction, heading automatically for my own home, before it occurred to me that Merriweather had seen me, and that I would be expected at the boarding house. Reluctantly, I turned and retraced my steps heading in the direction of the room that could then only create more problems than solutions.

# 15

When courting a young lady, especially one such as my Beatrice, leaving things to the last minute can always be a dangerous proposition. In light of our disagreement, that was all the more true. It is a lesson that I had learned before, but one that I would be inclined to repeat again that day.

With no set agenda for the Saturday, but an understanding that the day was reserved for one another, it became imperative that I set out early in order to recover from my error.

I racked my brain en route but could come up with nothing better than the proposal of a stroll about Centennial Park. The idea was relatively dull, but with any luck, it would afford us some time to talk things over. As I made her street, I still had nothing better in mind and decided to go with it.

On my arrival at Beatrice's home, I was greeted by her younger sister, the one on whom her father doted so heavily. The girl sat idly on the front porch swing, her legs dangling slowly back and forth with the pitch of the swing. She had the look of a brat, a smug smile on her face and dressed in her Sunday finest on a Saturday morning.

I tried to go past with a simple greeting, but was forced to engage her more in depth when she initiated the conversation.

"Where ya' been?" she smacked, the smell of her spearmint gum annoying in the early morn.

"Well, I've been working," I responded vaguely, trying to end the conversation before it gained momentum.

"Whatcha been workin' on?" she asked.

"Looking for someone."

"Who?" she persisted.

"A friend of your sister's?" I replied and moved for the door, but she detained me once again.

"Which one?" she pressed.

I put a foot up on a step and rested an elbow on that knee. My reply was somewhat terse, "Someone you don't know."

Undeterred, she kept on, "Maybe I do. I know a lot of her friends. Maybe I know where she is," she stated matter-of-factly. The site of a twelve-year-old child sitting on a swing paying me little attention yet saying just what I want to hear was unsettling. I must confess that the thought did cross my mind that maybe she did know where to find the elusive Miss Pettigrew. Perhaps she was somehow involved in this affair along with her sister. The absurdity that she might be an accomplice in some deception made it all the more plausible.

But looking at the child in front of me, it was obvious that she was simply responding in a manner that any child would, mimicking the conversation of the adults who surrounded her on a daily basis.

Hoping either to dissuade her from pursuing the conversation or to allay my professional suspicions, I told her the name. Nancy. Nancy Pettigrew. Someone you know, I'm sure.

She screwed up her nose at me. "Don't know her. Where'd ja' look fer her?"

Sensing that the conversation was going to be more involved than I had planned, I decided to make the best of it and try to earn back some of the ground with Miss Beatrice Rose that I might have lost the previous evening, so I settled down to the edge of the porch beside her and struck up a conversation with the child.

"I've looked lots of places – hospitals, her boarding house, places like that," I responded.

"That sounds like only two places," she said.

"It does, but there are lots of hospitals, and there are other places that I have checked as well," I defended. "So what have you been doing?"

"Playing with my new doll," she said pointing to a replica of herself, its china doll face framed by hair made from a horse's tail and dyed black.

"Nice." I commented noting that her father seemed rarely to buy anything for Beatrice, but left that responsibility entirely to me. "What's her name?"

"Rascal."

"Nice name."

"No, it's not. She's a naughty rascal," she snapped back at me.

For the next few minutes I was instructed and admittedly amused about the intricacies of the fantasies on which she had built her play world with the doll. Already within the span of a couple of hours this morning, they had gone to tea, taken a trip, married, and a long list of other activities.

"Did you know that if a girl can kiss her elbow she can find the right husband?" she asked.

Sensing an opportunity to continue on in my initial purpose for being there, I took the bait and turned to look at her. "No, I didn't know that. Say, can your sister kiss her elbow?"

Susan gave an audible grunt and shook her head, "I don't know. Pa sure don't think so." She swung her legs and left it at that.

My pride wounded by being one-upped by a twelve-year-old, I rose from the front steps making for the door to call on Beatrice, wondering why she hadn't heard my plight and come to save me yet. Perhaps she was letting me earn my redemption with her by serving my time with her child sister.

As I reached for the screen door, the twelve-year-old announced, "She's not here."

Puzzled, I turned to her in disbelief. "She's not?"

"Nope," her attention was more on the new doll than me.

I felt more than a little foolish standing there with one hand on the handle of the screen door. I was too far into the action to deny my intentions, but still searched for a means by which to save face in the situation, "Right. My mistake," I hesitated for a moment. "So where did she go?"

The child put her fingers to her pursed lips and twisted them miming the act of turning a key. Flummoxed by the childish gesture, I determined to pick the mimed lock. "Did she leave a message for me or anything?"

"Nope." She stroked the doll's hair and went silent.

"Say where she was going?" I squatted down to get at eye level with her.

"Nope." She shook her head and grinned.

The line of questioning taking me nowhere, I decided on a change of tactics. "So what do you know?" I asked dreading the response before it came.

"Belinda Nichols got a pony for her birthday."

Before I could make a retreat, she provided me with a plethora of useful information about her schoolmates and neighbors, but made no mention of her older sister who had disappeared for the day, no doubt in an effort to teach me a lesson.

As I headed for the front gate, she suddenly took an interest again. "Did you bring me anything?" she asked.

Empty handed, I reached into my pocket searching for a coin. When I did produce it, it was a slightly tarnished Indian Head Buffalo nickel. "Are you sure you don't know where your sister went?" I asked holding the coin up for her to see. "I'll bet you haven't seen one of these, yet." The U.S. coins have always been terribly boring, and a variation in size provides the only distinction. The newly minted Indian Head was something to behold.

She played it cool and plucked the coin gently from my fingers, smiling the entire time. Pocketing the nickel, she stroked her new doll's hair as she informed me, "I've seen it. Besides, Beatrice gave me a new Mercury head dime."

Only released that year, I had not yet seen the newly issued ten-cent piece myself. It caused me to momentarily forget my objective. My curiosity to see the new coinage gnawed at me knowing that she likely held it in her pocket, but I refused to allow her to bait me.

Satisfied that she had beaten me at that game, she picked up her doll and headed for the door leaving me on the steps wondering where to go next. A sudden fear overtook me that I might run into Beatrice wherever I went and lose what little remained of my dignity. So in order to retain that sliver of pride, I spent the remainder of the day in solitude reading my newspapers and reviewing the postcards for more clues while I wondered where Beatrice had gone, and why she would outbid me to keep her whereabouts for the day a secret.

# 16

Sunday tippling at the Southern Turf is one of the great male pastimes in the city. Despite state prohibition having been in effect seven years already, the Turf had managed to stay afloat serving twenty-five-cent glasses of liquor and a free meal. The alcohol was imported via the Hoptown Special from Kentucky that made deliveries on a weekly basis.

No respectable woman was to be seen in the Men's Quarter in the evening. The occasional brave suffragette might have been seen walking the west side, away from the saloons and gambling houses on their way to the Maxwell House Hotel, but those of stern enough character were few and far between. Even Beatrice could be expected to avoid the area making it a safe haven for me that evening.

I was able to mingle with the entire range of society from those of lowly origin and crude manners to those born of money and heeled in its ways. They all mixed freely at the bar and at the gaming tables in defiance of the Committee of 100 and the other Bible-thumping reformists. The same ones who were critical of what took place along Fourth Avenue appeared often enough at the doors asking for and receiving a charitable donation while condemning the activity within from the pulpit on Sundays.

My feet tapped loudly on the marble floor as I pushed through the glass doors from the street. Making an obligatory stop to sate one vice at the cigar counter, it was through the door to my right that I satisfied the others. Knocking once, a peephole slid open through which the sounds and smells of the saloon drifted. Recognizing me as neither a magistrate nor member of the police, the peephole closed and the door swung wide enough to admit me.

The room was already beginning to fill up. As the numbers increased, the crowd pulled in tighter to allow the latecomers enough room to slake their thirsts. The gaming tables in the back were in the early stages of a day's thriving business taking all they could from the honest wage earners' pockets. Normally they would have closed at five in the evening on a Friday, the result of a deal made with the mayor to keep the hall from siphoning off all of the wages, but the upcoming Independence Day had them working overtime.

Sidling up to the oak bar, I rested my foot on the brass foot rail and ordered a glass of bathtub gin, the day's special and the first of a handful of drinks for the evening. Then I worked my way back to the food bar where a cold ham and cheese sandwich, along with a hardboiled egg, dispatched my hunger.

Scanning the gaming tables I saw the usual suspects and a handful of the not so dedicated. Spying a friendly face among the crowd, I meandered toward the senator. He was an acquaintance, an ambiguous friendship made at some point, though I do not remember exactly when or how. He was not the sharpest tool in the shed. Nevertheless, he made for good company. The man hailed from some small community in either the east or west part of the state. Which one I had never been able to pin him down to. I could make the connection simply by picking up a list of the legislators, but I preferred the ambiguity. I did not want to prejudice myself against the constituents who would send him to represent their community.

My approach went unheralded until I was upon him at which time his reception was a bit boisterous even in the surroundings of the saloon. "Blackie!" he slung my name the only way he seemed to be able to recall it. The shout turned many a head at the bar as he staggered a step or two in my direction and waved me over. The small crowd where he had been holding court dispersed when he turned his back on them and they realized that a new victim had fallen prey to his political colloquy.

"How are you?" he said, slightly more subdued than his initial greeting as he shook my hand vigorously.

"Fair to middling, Senator," I said using the formal title that seems obligatory among those in the know when addressing a member of the state legislature.

"Oh, come on. It must be better than that. I for one am glad to see you out and about this evening. Have a drink for what ails you."

"Women problems," I sighed.

"Ah, yes. Nothing I can do about that. If you needed help getting the bid on some construction work or something, I could help you there. But women…"

"Yes, women."

"Women," he said sympathetically.

He wrung his hands. "They want the vote, you know."

I gave a sneer. "To hear them talk, you'd think they already have it."

He turned on the stool and spoke out to the room in general. "Suffrage is a perilous road my friend." He gazed around as he spoke and looked a number of nearby patrons in the eye. "They are well organized."

He spoke to the small crowd gathering around where we sat and he took to his feet. "They are organized at the national level. Why, they hold rallies in every major city around the country. They'll stop at nothing to get the vote." He winked at one of the men standing about. "Nothing, I tell you."

Hoisting a glass in the air, he ranted, "Let us hope that the Great State of Tennessee is not left to be the deciding vote on that issue. Why, we would be the laughing stock of the country if we gave up the ghost on that one!"

He received a vigorous round of cheers and slaps on the back before everyone scattered once more and he took his seat beside me once more. His ability to conjure a crowd out of thin air gave evidence to the source of his popularity back home.

Later, our conversation turned to the pending war with Mexico, and he was all too glad to venture the topic.

"We're going to war with them all right," he stated.

"You're certain, Senator?" I asked.

"That's what I hear."

"From whom?"

He was taken aback at not having someone simply take his message at face value and had obvious difficulty nailing down a reliable source.

He stuck his chest out and wrapped his thumbs inside his galluses under his jacket. "Well, I am constantly talking with the other senators and representatives of course as well as those who represent us in D.C. We are privy to all of the information. It's a chain that goes up to the President himself and the Secretaries of State and Defense. Indication from all sides is that we are going to war. Besides that, we are calling up the National Guard in light of all this business with Carranza."

We sat quiet for a few moments sipping our drinks and allowing my melancholy over Beatrice to set in once more.

"What is it that women want?" I said and pounded a fist on the bar. "If I could just figure that out, I'd be in good shape."

"They want the vote," the Senator said and laid a finger beside his nose.

"I mean what is it that drives them?"

"The desire to vote," he sighed.

"No, what do they want from men? I wish I knew."

"Wouldn't we all like to know?" He turned the short glass on top of the napkin on the bar. "But I know one thing they want."

"What?"

"The vote."

"You're drunk,"

"S'matter of opinion."

We had lost track of the time at the bar and the gaming tables. All at once, the room was emptying, and the good senator and I were gently shooed out by the barkeeper.

At that late hour, we were among the other tipplers who missed the line-up for the last trolley of the evening. I had only myself to blame for the indiscretion. Too many favors of the Hoptown Special had distorted my perception of time, though I was still able to stagger about without too much difficulty.

My political friend had one foot in the stirrup and was struggling to mount his steed. "I'll give you a ride on my horse."

"Thanks, but I'll walk. That mare doesn't look quite up to the task of both of us," I said noticing the sway in the mare's back became more pronounced with the addition of his weight.

"I insist."

"I'm not one of your constituents," I said, patting the horse on the neck to steady her and momentarily dissuading him.

He looked at me, bobbing his head forward and back trying to get me in focus by adjusting the distance instead of trying to control his ocular sense, "No matter. I'll make you an honorary member. You can vote for me anyway. Folks from the cemetery do it for me all of the time." He gave me a wink and a nod that nearly upset him from his mount.

"No worry that they'll come back to haunt you for using their names like that, is there?" I used a hand to steady him in the saddle lest he meet the pavement.

In his deeply inebriated state, he sat straight in the saddle and looked around wide-eyed as if expecting to see the ghost of his dead voters. "Oh you're pulling my leg now. You are a funny one," he said as he smiled and wagged a finger at me.

Not wanting to offend the man, I climbed on the horse, knowing that given the chance, I could bail out at the first opportunity, the bareback rump of his mare offering a less appealing conveyance than my own feet. As I mounted, I couldn't help but feel the eyes of someone upon me. Turning to look in either direction on the street, I spied no one that I immediately recognized and no one who paid me any attention. However, I must admit to being plagued by tunnel vision as a result of the evening's excesses.

We plodded off, he holding the reigns lightly, allowing the horse to find its own pace. By the time we'd reached the end of the block, he was passed out slumped in the saddle with his head resting on the mane of the horse while he snored loudly. Unbidden, his steed headed for the Hermitage Hotel, his home when the legislature was in session, and I quietly dismounted sliding off of the hindquarters of the horse, the leather of my shoes slapping lightly as I met the pavement.

Relieved of the extra passenger, the swaybacked beast continued on its path, and I quickened my pace to keep up for a moment and be certain that my friend was properly situated on his mount. It was one of the single greatest advantages of the horse over motor cars that they always watched the road and carried their rider to their home even if their owner happens to imbibe a bit too freely.

I parted with them at the next intersection stopping to watch as the horse walked slowly into the thickening fog. The clopping of the hooves assured me that the horse carried its human consignment to its destination. Mine was the longer journey to my apartment on Hayes Street as I opted for the comfort of my own bed rather than that of the woman I was employed to find.

The wee hours of the morning were desolate on the streets. As I moved further from the confines of the city, the isolation became even more acute. At times like these, the mind begins to play tricks on a man, especially one who has been partaking of the devil's elixirs, and the feeling of being followed returned shortly after I'd lost sight of my soundly sleeping friend.

My graveyard joke meant to taunt the senator now in turn began to burden me. As I traveled, my imagination amplified every sound leaving me jumping at the scuff of a shoe close behind me.

I turned to scour the street for signs of a shadow, but found nothing other than my own in pursuit as I passed the occasional odd street lamp still burning. The light fog caused by the constant rain of the past few days made me jittery. My route from here was fairly straight out Church until I cut over to Hayes on the other side of the viaduct. My options were few. Either I could continue straight, the shortest route possible to my home, or I could duck down a side street and double back on my pursuer. Neither option held much appeal over simply being safely home. The way was lined by trees offering a pursuer easy cover and ample opportunity to waylay me *en route*.

I opted for the fastest way home. Glancing nervously back, I could hear the footsteps of someone, but remained unsure if they were my own echoing off of the surrounding brick buildings or the sound of someone on my trail. Fueled by the imported liquid courage, I stopped and secreted myself at the wrought-iron gate of a residence. My ears detected the sound of a leather-soled shoe scraping to a halt.

Searching the shadows cast in the fog, I looked for the form of a person intermingled with those of the trees, but the dense haze and thick foliage darkened each trunk providing any pursuer easy concealment along either side of the roadway.

Losing my nerve now that my bluff had been called, I broke into a run. My pursuer started not long behind me, but I was close to home. Heedless of my course, I ran smack into another late-night reveler. It turned out to be a neighbor who shared a flat in the same building. The blow knocked him to the ground, and I stopped to help him to his feet. I was relieved for the company, yet loath to slow my step, he being less motivated than I. Still I held up and took his pace as mine. Much to my relief, when the pursuer realized that I had acquired a companion, he remained back refusing to show himself in the presence of another person.

Gradually emboldened by the safety of numbers, I entertained the thought of turning back on the pursuer to force his exposure. However, my newfound companion had taken more drink upon himself than had I, and my courage quickly waned.

"I believe someone is following me," I told him.

"Friend of yours?"

"No. I think they may mean me harm," I said.

His eyes widened. "You in trouble? Win big at the tables tonight or something?" he slurred as he looked at me. His head bobbed forward and back as he tried to focus on me.

"No, no. Something to do with a young woman."

"You been fooling with another man's wife?"

Realizing that this line of questioning might only further endanger us as we slowed, I resorted to a rather cruel tactic, "No, I think it might be a ghost."

The man's face blanched and he found sudden sobriety and a surefooted step. He outpaced me, and I was hard pressed to keep up as all manner of questioning came to a halt.

We pressed forward arriving safely at the apartment building and let ourselves in. With the door still ajar, but safely in the foyer of the building, I listened for the approach.

My neighbor peered over my shoulder as I looked through the gap in the door, "You shouldn't go messin' in the spirit world, boy. It'll get you in trouble faster than runnin' around with another man's woman," he advised me before stumbling off to climb the stairs to his apartment. I waited a few moments for my tail to show his face, but the stalker remained in the shadows, just beyond sight.

I heard the slap, or I think I heard it, walk away in the fog. I waited a few more seconds, then closed the door and climbed the stairs. My hand shook as I pulled the key from my pocket. Bending to insert it, the door swung wide at my touch. The light was on in the room, and I entered, my heart still pounding from the recent pursuit. I heard the slow heavy creak of my rocking chair, its runners the source of the noise.

"Come on in," the voice called, the old world timbre of it slightly enhanced by the lateness of the hour. "Got your letter. Been waiting on you. Finally had to let myself in." Miss Bobo sat nimbly perched in the rocker, her shawl pulled tight around her flowing clothes.

My initial reaction was to denounce the intrusion, but she waved off my protests before they could be given voice. "You don't need to apologize for keeping an old lady waiting for so long. I came as soon as I knew you needed me. It's my own fault for not listening to my instincts telling me to wait until morning, but what are you doing out so late on such a night?" She moved to the small kitchen and pulled a pot from the burner pouring boiling water over two cups with teabags that she must have brought with her. "Sit," she said, waving to my own chair, her back to me as she sweetened the hot drink. I did as she bade me in my own home.

She brought the cup and saucer to me, "I would have made it a hot toddy, but you got no white lightning or Jack Daniel's or nothing here for that. Besides, it looks as if you've had enough of that already."

Stupefied, out of breath from the run, and still mildly intoxicated, I could only stare at the liquid in the cup.

"Drink," she commanded. "We got a lot to talk about if we gonna figure this out."

I can't say exactly how long Miss Bobo remained. Her tea made a wicked brew that opened my eyes and forced me to stay awake despite the hour.

She had received the note I'd dropped in the box including my address, but not my name. Still she had known it was me, and that I was in need of assistance though my letter had not specifically asked for it.

I fed her the details of the past few days as regarded the case. When I pressed her for an assessment, and for the first time, I saw her hesitate. "I'll give you the nickel," I snarled, my mood a bit callous on account of the liquor.

"It's not that," she said, ignoring the remark, "It's that there is so little to work with. I can't get a feel for the situation. There are too many people involved." She sighed.

I slumped in the chair. "That's no help." Her response was a shrug of the layered cloth shoulders.

I turned to the aged face. "So you came all this way to tell me that?"

"And to tell you to be careful. You're putting yourself in danger and things are not always as they first appear."

"I know." I responded, pointing to the knot on my head that endured.

"No. More than that. Don't ask me how I know, but I do."

"You've *seen* it."

"No. I feel it. It's a woman's intuition. That reading is all baloney anyway. You know that," she said, cutting her eyes to me without turning to look. She halfway hoped that I had actually believed her shtick. "Anyway, whoever is behind all of this is being very careful. They know you, but you don't know them, at least not as they really are. Don't you let your guard down. Not for one second."

"I know. Don't worry; I won't go counting hacks in a funeral procession or anything."

"Good. That's really bad luck," she admonished me.

We sat in silence for a few moments. The tea kept me from falling asleep and my thoughts began to wander back to Beatrice. She had determined to torture me for the events of the past few days from the offhand remark about Pettigrew to the disastrous disclosure from Merriweather. Lost in my thoughts, I failed to notice the old woman silently contemplating my expression.

Finally breaking my self-absorbed trance, I reached for the lukewarm tea. The last swallow was cold and overly sweet, the sugar collecting in the bottom making the last few drops the best by far— probably how President Teddy Roosevelt had come up with his quote for Maxwell House Coffee: "Good to the last drop." Returning the cup to the saucer, a small ring of colored water sat in the saucer where the liquid had escaped down the side of the mug. My gypsy companion held her own cup as if prepared to clear the dishes. "Are you finished?" she asked.

"Yes."

"Good." She lifted the noggin from the saucer and peered down into it. "You drink too slow." She studied for a moment, then tilted it toward the light for a better look and furrowed her brow before announcing what it was she saw in the tea leaves. "I can see that you're chasing two women." She raised an eyebrow, "That's no good. Stick with one." Squinting into the china cup again, "The one you really love. Don't worry. Her heart belongs to you. One day she'll be yours. Just be patient."

A little sympathetic magic goes a long way with even the nonbeliever. Miss Bobo noted the small grin on my face.

"Smile, laugh at me even, if you want. But deep down, you know I tell the truth," she said, pointing a gnarled finger at her chest.

"Deep down I know you tell me what I want to hear."

She shrugged her shoulders again, "Sometimes it helps to believe in something—anything. She's a good girl, yes?" she asked, her European accent getting the better of her at the late hour.

"Yes. She is."

"You should go to her, tell her you sorry," she took the lack of response as an indictment against me, "You don't talk to her, she don't talk to you. Nobody talking, then nobody happy."

"Wise words."

"You listen. The future I maybe don't know. But love. Love, I know," she said nodding and winking at me.

A short time later, I fell asleep. I don't know whether it was mid-conversation, or if she hypnotized me into slumber. Either way, when I awoke at four o'clock to crawl into my bed, she was gone.

# 17

At five o'clock in the morning, I was awakened by an insistent rapping at my door. It was all I could manage to drag myself to it, still suffering from the previous night's excesses. When at last I did, Pilchard Samuels stood before me, his hat still on his head. Determined not to be outdone or shortchanged, he had arrived with the day's newspaper in hand. His look was cleaner than when I had last seen him, but his eyes were bleary with sleep, the corners of his eyelids crusty as he invited himself into my apartment.

Still in my clothes from the night before, he cocked an eyebrow at my appearance. "Tough night? Getting a late start this week or still not finished with the last one?"

"So it would seem," I mumbled as I staggered back to the bed.

He followed me in surveying the room as he went. "Or are you off this week as a result of the upcoming holiday?"

I let the comment pass.

He made his way into my kitchen and put on a pot of water to boil while pulling the tin of coffee from the cupboard. Once he'd finished preparing the brew, he fixed a cup for himself neglecting to attend to my need at this hour. He sweetened his drink with three cubes of sugar and the balance of the milk remaining in my icebox.

Not sure how to respond, I sat quietly on my bed, wondering what had precipitated the incursion.

He downed the thick, brown liquid in seconds, the chill of the milk having cooled the coffee enough to allow him to swallow without being burned. As he sat, the collar of his jacket pushed up around his neck having not bothered to remove or even so much as unbutton it. After five or six large gulps, he sat the empty cup down in the saucer on the table next to the rocking chair and with a disgusted look on his face said, "You should either tend your kitchen or hire someone to do it for you." He made no move to add his china to the dishes piled up to overflowing in the sink.

"This investigation has taken away from the time required for personal matters," I said. I had hoped to gain a short reprieve that morning but his appearance on my doorstep cut short my intentions.

He snatched up his straw hat that he had carelessly thrown in the rocker where Miss Bobo had sat only hours before. He smacked the rim in a vain attempt to remove some grime, before he placed it on his head. It was starting to show its age. The brim had lost a bit of its form, and it was dirty from handling.

"There is no mention of her in the day's paper. That should save you some time and allow you to pursue this case more aggressively. I expect you to show some progress quickly," he said before turning to leave.

I nodded in acquiescence as he closed the door. Mondays have never been my specialty and this one held true to form.

Despite being rousted from my bed at the crack of dawn, I'd managed to fall back into it and find sleep once again. When I finally did rise for the day, I suspected that I was late from the start, but my clock had stopped during my absence. My pocket watch lay on the table in Pettigrew's room, an oversight of mine from the previous day, and I was forced to impose upon a neighbor for the time after which I'd found myself hurrying in order to make a respectable showing with my employer.

My tardiness left me scanning the paper as I rode the trolley, thankfully not too full to pass me by at that belated hour of the morning. A notice that the poll tax must be paid by the third of the month in order to vote in August reminded me that I should pay mine. Ironically, even if women did get the vote, they might be hindered in their ability to participate if their husbands denied them the fee.

Putting a hand to my face, I realized that I had failed to clean the growth of my beard for the day. As a result, I was forced to expend my wages with the barber in advance of the day's schedule. I selected a shop close to the office and was in and out within a few minutes and sitting at my desk looking through the postcards, the receipts, and the map that formed the basis of my investigation.

Two hours later, I found myself still staring at the map looking like a voodoo doll with its collection of stickpins. I was fully engrossed by the puzzle at hand, but I was finding nothing new, attributable in part to the hangover that had set in. I wandered down the hall to see Beatrice. I was able to see her by poking my head in the door before being run off by the approach of her physician employer. Her look was one of regret, something on which I hoped to build with the aid of my apology at the first opportunity.

As I sat and pondered the evidence, it troubled me that I had not yet found Nancy Pettigrew's love interest of which she wrote. She offered virtually nothing to go on and no one seemed aware of his existence. I had yet to find him if he truly did exist and was not merely an element of fiction contrived solely for her personal entertainment. Or more accurately perhaps, he had not yet found me.

My focus was so intent that when I finally noticed the colored man standing at my open door slowly polishing the brass handle and escutcheon of the lock, he had already been there for at least two or three minutes.

He was as intent on his work as I on mine, but I stopped – mesmerized by his well-practiced motions. I saw him every day polishing the metal of the building on this floor and knew that he would repeat this activity on each door as he went down the hall.

But he had spent far too long on mine already.

He carried a heavily stained cloth so blackened with tarnish and polish that the original color was no longer discernible. I dare say it was once white, but it no longer classified as anything less than chocolate. He applied the polish in small circular motions being sure to catch every small nook on the fixture. Returning the blackened cloth to his rear pocket, he then took a marginally cleaner red cloth and began to buff the paste from the surface revealing the gleaming brass fixture underneath.

He seemed overly industrious in his cleaning, going over the same portions increasingly slower without lifting his head from the hunched position to which he seemed eternally confined. He raised his eyes to me questioningly and reached around the edge of the door with a hand to point at the brass faceplate of the light switch inside the door.

I nodded, and he gingerly stepped in, pushing the door nearly all of the way to, and I began to wonder what was amiss. As he vigorously polished the rectangular plate, occasionally using his fingernail covered by the cloth to reach the small crevices, he finally spoke, "It ain't no big deal to me. If'n you don' want me to clean it while you here, I kin come back."

Having never pondered the thought that he might speak, I was taken aback. He was one of around ten Negroes employed in the building solely for the purpose of polishing and maintaining the brass fixtures and marble floors. With some degree of embarrassment, I realized that I did not know even one of their names. To expect him to go about his daily job without benefit of a word or even knowledge of his name was uncharitable. But that is exactly how it was. Society had taught me to expect him to go mutely and invisibly about carrying out his daily wage earning in silence. The notion that I simply accepted that fact stung me, and I felt compelled to deny my ingrained prejudice.

"No, no. you go ahead. You aren't bothering me at all," and I continued to stare, entranced as he performed his function.

He never looked up and kept his eyes on his work. "You Mister Black, ain't ya'?" he asked, breaking his silence once more.

I laid down the pencil I had been holding. "I am. However, I am sorry to say that I don't know your name."

"It's not important," he replied trying to fade into the background again after stepping out.

"But it is to me. I'd like to know. It's difficult to carry on a conversation with a man not knowing his name." The chair creaked, as I leaned forward and put my elbows on the desk.

The silence hung in the air for a few unbearable seconds as he continued to work the polish in small circles. When he spoke, it was a single word, "John."

"John," I repeated for confirmation and to help make it stick in my mind, but he gave no signal of affirmation. He kept rubbing. "Pleased to make your acquaintance, John."

"Thank you, Suh," he said nodding, "Likewise, I'm sure." There was no other sound than that of the light friction of the rubbing compound on brass.

When he finished the switch plate cover, it was extraordinarily bright bearing the resemblance to gold that brass is intended to mimic. Replacing the dirty rag in his back pocket, he wiped his hands on one of the rags and reached to his breast pocket withdrawing a single sheet of paper, neatly folded and pristine, unblemished by the tarnish that covered the cotton rags he used in carrying out his daily job. He placed the page on my desk careful to stabilize it against the blotter so that it did not slide to the end of the desk. "Man said to give this to you, Suh."

Stunned, I looked at the folded note not knowing what to make of it. My slowed reaction allowed him to make an exit unhindered and unnoticed, much as he went about his day. Picking up the stock, I unfolded it to reveal a handwritten note in an even and well-practiced hand. I consumed the note quickly.

> *Mr. Black,*
>
> *I would like to request the favor of a word with you. Take the noon No. 13 Fairfield trolley from the terminal today, July 3ʳᵈ. I have some important things to tell you about Miss Pettigrew. Please come alone and sit at the back of the car. I will approach you.*
>
> *R.*

I read and reread the note a few times trying to make sense of it and reading between the lines even catching myself doing an impromptu layman's analysis of the script. Then I realized that my best chance at interpretation had just walked out the door. I climbed over the desk, knocking the calendar off and spilling a few pages onto that day's floor.

Afraid that John would disappear, I peered around the door frame looking in the direction I knew him to have gone. He had not traveled far, having finished the following door and moved on to the next one. Stepping out of the office into the hallway, I approached him without receiving any acknowledgement of my advance. As I stood over him hunched over in his work, my words were still forming with phrases coming and going. While I search for the right thing, the most obvious escaped my lips, "Did you write this?"

He rubbed the polish on the door knob. "No, Suh."

"Who did?" I shook the note at him one time, and then chastised myself for being so rude, but I failed to apologize to him.

He pulled out the red cloth to buff the door hardware. "Don't know, sir. 'S'pose it wuz the man what give it to me."

"How did you come by it?" I asked being careful to contain my haste lest I were to drive him away.

"Man asked me if I know who you is. I said, yes. He axt me to give you that note."

"What man? When?" I stayed my hand from smacking the note, but I could feel my face beginning to flush.

"Man on the street. Give it to me this morning on my way in to work," He used his fingernail and the cloth to remove the past stuck between where the pieces joined together.

"Do you know what it says?" I asked.

He stopped. Only for a second, but long enough for me to tell that the question had hit a nerve. The answer came heavy, "No, Suh. I caint write much atall, an' sho' caint write so good as dat," he said, pointing in the direction of the note in my hand.

John turned to me from his hunched-over position cleaning the doorknob and focused his eyes on me, brown pupils floating unblinking on a sea of white. For the first time, I realized that he was not an older man, but roughly my own number of years. His age was disguised by the hunched position that he adopted while he went about his daily tasks.

I extended my hand to him in gratitude, "Thank you." I had broken his routine sufficiently now that he had ceased to clean the brass for which he cared. He looked at my hand, and I shoved it forward a few more inches now unsure myself if I should have offered it.

He straightened up, and for the first time, I realized that his posture was not a deformity, but the result of the position he was forced to constantly endure in carrying out his work. That bias kept him hunched to one side, a permanent feature slightly retained even when he was upright.

"Yes, Suh, Mister Black. You welcome," he responded tentatively taking my hand before returning his attention to the brass, its shine beginning to break through the polish once more.

I put a hand on his shoulder. "Have you got a moment to talk with me? I have a couple of questions for you."

He stopped polishing again, his reply a furtive slow glance up and down the corridor. When he was certain that the hallway was empty, he said nervously to me, "Suh, I's jes' passin' along a note fer a man what axt me to. I don't know him or his bizness." His lower lip trembled as he spoke.

Out of frustration, I sighed. "No, you don't understand. I don't want to get you in trouble. I just want to—"

"You don' understand.' Standin' in this hallway talkin' to a white man is a good way fer me to git in trouble," he interrupted.

Exasperated I turned to go, and then spun on my heel to face him once more.

"John, you only did the outside of my door. I need the inside done as well. Maybe you could come back and finish, when you get a second." I pointed in the direction of my office as if he didn't know where it was, and then flushed at my own embarrassment.

He looked up. "Yes, Suh. Be right there soon as I finish this here do'." He gestured to the door and waited for me to walk off.

I turned and went to my office to wait.

The area behind my desk is small. Still, as I waited, I found a way to pace, twice striking my shin on the arm of the chair when I turned too quickly.

John arrived and nodded as he came in the door. "You still got that sittin' in here like that?" he said indicating the desk that occupied the space between us.

"I don't know how it got in here like this. Honestly it looks physically impossible to me, but I didn't put it here, so I don't know."

John smiled, his white teeth contrasting starkly with his dark skin, "Then I know something you don't." He seemed pleased to have some upper hand on me even if it was in so inconsequential a manner as this.

"How long have you been working here, John?" I held a pencil poised above a note pad on the desk.

"Since day one. I helped most the folks movin' in here." He watched the pencil, as I scratched on the paper.

"And what do you do all day besides polish brass?" I said putting the pencil down on the desk.

"That's it, Suh. I polishes the brass on this flo'." He held the red cloth in his left hand and switched it to his right.

"That's all? All day long?"

"Yes, Suh. Sometimes, I helps wid polishin' the flo' too," He waded up the red cloth with his hands. "Mistuh Black, Suh, I really cain't be outta sight too long."

"Do you know Miss Pettigrew from the second floor?" I asked.

"Don' think so." His eyes widened, and he shook his head.

"She's a pretty girl. Dark hair. Works for the insurance company."

"Maybe I does. Why you askin'?" He suddenly became wary of my intentions and gripped the red cloth tightly in his hands.

"I'm looking for her. She's gone missing, but that's just between you and me."

"Well, I'll help ya' out any ways I kin," he said.

"I appreciate that, John. I may take you up on that offer."

He shifted from one foot to the other. "I needs to be gettin' back to work now."

"Please," I said holding a hand out toward the door. "How can I get some more of your time, if I need your help?"

"Jes' axt fo' me real quiet. Like you done jes' now. That'd be fine," he said.

Not wanting to jeopardize a potential source of information, I took what I had gotten and ended the conversation, thanking him for his time and letting him return to his work and I to mine. He went without a word and silently returned to his invisible position in the world.

The walk from The Doctor's Building to the transfer station is not a long one. It would have been easy enough to take a streetcar over, but the walk did me well. Approaching from the Fifth Avenue side, I deposited my coin into the turnstile and entered the terminal. The crush was less the day before a holiday. The usual horde preferred the comforts of their homes for a longer weekend. Still, a fair number of people crowded the terminal changing over from one line to another headed out in a different direction. The city streets and the trolleys that run along them are in a hub-and-spoke pattern, and I stood now at the center of it all.

The ride I was seeking came through the open doorway jumping the lines as it entered. The attendants at the door, positioned there especially for this task, handily assisted it back onto the cables inside the building. There was a mild rush to get a seat, but luckily the No. 13 Fairfield Line on which I had been instructed to embark was not full.

The seats are slatted wooden benches well-worn with use, but tended regularly to keep them in good repair. The backs have long wooden legs that pivot at the floor so that the seats can be positioned to face forward no matter which direction the trolley travels. This way the conductor can drive the conveyance to the termination of the line, then switch ends and drive the trolley back to its original departure point without turning the car around.

A large brass wheel used for the brake stands at the top of the platform, its edges polished brightly by the constant rubbing of hands across it surface. Passing the motorman as I boarded the streetcar, I made my way to the back, per the instructions, and positioned myself next to a window on the left side in the final row of the car. It was no wonder that my appointment had selected this seat for me. It was vacant, and it was isolated.

As we departed the station, a few employees of the Nashville Railway and Light Company stood ready by the entryways to replace the car should it have jumped the tracks again as we made the switch from the lines inside to the street. But our launch was successful, leaving the eager young men without a chance to render their services again.

The backs of the benches in the row behind me were the sole seats in the car facing the wrong direction –the demarcation line between the whites and the coloreds. The Jim Crow law protests of a decade ago had gained Negroes the concession to ride in the same car with the whites, but not in the same seats.

Four rows of empty benches separated me from any of my other fair-skinned travelers. The looks from those individuals were less curious and more incensed at my choice of seating. Had the letter not specified it so, I would not have selected this spot and incurred the unwanted social scorn to which I was now subjected. If my contact was to be Pettigrew's suitor as I hoped, he was proving to be an admirable adversary. He already had managed to intimidate me and throw me off my game without yet showing his face.

I surveyed the occupants of the car, but found no one willing to meet my gaze or make an approach – little wonder considering my apparent reckless abandonment of social ideals. The thick glass of the window distorted the view of the street. With the air growing stuffy in the rising heat, I went to raise the sash. It stuck at first, but then slid open to allow a fresh breeze across my face. As we rolled along, I passed the time by reading the advertisements above the windows, anything to avert my attention from the ire of my traveling companions. The billets were from the usual businesses, a local area law firm, Maxwell House Coffee, Castner Knott and a shaving cream of which I had never heard.

No one who boarded the trolley at the next stop on Fourth Avenue took a seat with me, so I continued to sit alone. As we restarted our journey, the conductor made his way back through the car collecting fares. Reaching my seat, he shot me a baleful glance for which I had no reply. I was not beyond the boundaries of society, but on the very edge.

For an interminable two more stops, no one joined me. I watched the faces as they boarded via the open vestibules, and then selected a bench. I looked for an indication of my appointment's identity, but all I received were the hardened looks of surprised travelers still separated from me by two empty rows of space. In between stops, I stared at the sign that read, "Five dollar fine for spitting on the floor," rather than look in the hardened faces that accompanied me.

As we rolled away, I gazed out the window anticipating the embarking of a new set of passengers including my contact. Further from downtown, the thinning crowds offered an increasingly better view of the boarding riders. A horse, spooked by the approach of the electric monster, broke away and made a run for the adjoining alleyway in a calico streak, its owner in a mad sprint to catch her as we rumbled past.

At the next stop, one man chose to stand and take hold of the hanging leather strap rather than take the seat beside me. I considered that this might be my contact, but the quick look from him under a furrowed brow quickly dissuaded me from that notion.

I was developing a great regard for the psychology of my opponent. Realizing that I had underestimated him, I tried to anticipate his next move. It occurred to me that he might not show. That could have been the ultimate in this psychological game that he played, leading me to distraction through the ostracism of my peers. Feeling somewhat foolish, I gave him credit for anticipating my course of investigation and dissuading me from it. While I sat there riding the trolley to Lord knows what end, he might in fact be out perpetrating more injustices on our society. The thought of it began to gnaw at me until I felt the urge to stand and disembark at the next stop, but I knew not where to go otherwise, nor where to continue my search that might bear comparable fruit. As such, I remained in my seat, red-faced at having been so easily bested.

The car sang with the sound of the electric wires overhead and the low bass rumble of the wagon along the rails. It was difficult to hear clearly except when the car made its intermittent pauses to gather more pedestrians at each trolley stop. Our departure was delayed by a wagon stuck in the trolley line tracks just ahead. The conductor collected the fares from the new passengers and returned to the front of the car where he took his place to watch like everyone else.

A handful of concerned bystanders lent a shoulder to the wagon owner, and each of them sported a fresh dark line across their shoulders where they contacted the body of the carriage. We rolled by, and I watched as they surveyed the wooden wheel, each one in turn giving his opinion. One man turned his head spat a wad of tobacco juice away from the wagon, "She'll be good. Takes more than gettin' it wedged in a trolley track to ruin a wheel sturdy as that one."

They got clear of the track, and as we all peered out the window at the spectacle, the trolley eased forward. I turned to watch as we passed, not anxious to resume avoiding the angry glances from my fellow passengers.

From the seat behind me, a voice spoke softly. I was preoccupied with the wagon, and at first, I ignored it thinking they were speaking to someone else. It was not directed at me, or so I perceived. When it addresses me by name, my eyes dilated and fixed.

"Mister Black?" It asked quietly almost directly in my ear.

Completely off guard, I nodded my head a single time and turned to face forward once more. My face had undoubtedly gone white as a sheet, but none of the passengers in the front paid me any attention.

"Mister Black, Please don't turn around." The warning coming just as my head began to pivot and then stopped at the directive. Stark realization swept over me. While I had carefully scrutinized the whites boarding the trolley, I had failed to even recognize or notice the Negroes as they boarded. There had been no less than a dozen. Of that, I was certain. Among them my contact had passed right by me like all of the others—eyes downcast avoiding acknowledgement the entire time, simultaneously conspicuous and anonymous in the crowd of my other traveling companions who had either avoided my gaze or outright glared at me.

"I see that you're alone. Thank you for trusting me that much," it began.

I desperately searched out the details of the voice. The tenor reverberated off of the trolley window behind me and was largely drowned out by the ambient sounds of the trolley in motion and the light rush of air through my open window. The dialect was of a more northerly flavor, like Indiana or maybe Illinois, but I was unable to place it precisely. "I didn't know if you would come or not. I'm the person who sent the note. I'm Nancy Pettigrew's boyfriend."

Unable to respond, I merely sat, my mind racing to fit together the known pieces to determine how I could have missed the small fact that her boyfriend was colored.

His breath was hot on the back of my neck. "I know you can't talk, so I will." His familiarity with the social constraints of the situation exceeded my own, and he was right, I could not speak now had I wanted.

"Mister Black, I know you think that I had something to do with Nancy's disappearing, but I didn't," he said. "But I know who did. I saw everything," I heard him swivel to face backwards as the trolley stopped and a handful of other patrons both black and white entered the car. The voice had an educated ring to it with well-constructed sentences; the colloquialisms banished or suppressed – an unusual occurrence in the colored population and a characteristic generally associated with the likes of Preston Taylor, a Negro Nashville millionaire, or those who are in the service of whites on a regular basis.

"Her boss, Mister Samuels, did it. I saw him." The confirmation of my initial suspicions of my employer did little to persuade me. In fact, his accusation had the reverse effect giving more credence to my newer theory that Pettigrew's lover, Romeo, was somehow involved. "I know you don't believe me, but it's true. I saw him carry her out of an elevator in the sidewalk on Polk Avenue. He was carrying her like a big sack of potatoes, and he put her in his carriage and drove off. Just left the elevator sitting there and everything like he was in a big hurry."

Unable to contain my curiosity any longer, I whispered in a stage voice, "Well if you saw him, why not just come forward and say so? We could end all of this easily today. Why this clandestine meeting?"

I waited a few seconds, but no answer was given, I became concerned that my quarry had fled and could not resist the temptation to turn back and view him. All I saw was the back of his head and his plaid work shirt, a red bandana tied about his neck. As the trolley lurched forward, I turned forward again and heard his voice soft next to the window.

"Ain't you never heard of Julius Morgan?" He said referring to the West Tennessee Negro convicted of raping a white woman and sentenced to die in the electric chair for his crime.

I whispered hoarsely, "Are you saying you forcibly had relations with her?"

The response was quick and pointed, "No! But what do you think they'll say about a black man and a white woman when that white woman turns up dead?" he spat.

"Dead?" I exclaimed a little bit too loudly drawing some unwanted attention from other passengers and almost turning around before I restrained myself.

"Yes, dead. Ain't you found her yet? I saw Mister Samuels take her away. I ought to go kill him myself, but then there'd be no proof he did it. Then I'd wind up electrocuted."

"So you saw him kill her?" My agitated mumbling was beginning to attract the unwanted attention of my fellow commuters.

"I saw him carry the body out and put it in his hansom. I don't need to see anything else. He killed her and then rode off to get rid of her. I tried to follow him, but a black man running through the streets in the middle of the night tends to have problems, and I don't need any more."

"Mister...Mister...what is your name?" I asked.

"Don't be worrying about my name. You can call me Romeo."

Stunned at the Shakespearean reference coinciding with the name mentioned in Boo's letters to Nancy Pettigrew, I stumbled forward, "So, Mister Romeo...ah...well, how do you know she was dead?" I asked attempting to apply logic.

"Dead is dead. You can tell the way a body looks, and I've seen enough dead people to know. Besides I haven't seen her since, you haven't seen her yet, and nobody else has seen her since. Mister Black, I may be black, but I'm no fool. What is she if she isn't dead?" A logical conclusion based on a simple rationalizing of the facts.

"Maybe she's ill or incapacitated. Maybe she left town. Maybe she left town and took ill and was unable to let anyone know."

"Mister Black, if she left town, I'd know. If she was ill, you'd have found her by now or you ain't no count, and I know better than that."

"Listen. There are lots of explanations. Maybe you broke the courtship off, or she thought you were going to."

"I didn't break it off with her. I wouldn't do that to her, Mister Black. And don't go feeding me lines. You don't believe it, and I just told you enough that you ought to know what's going on."

"Well, I think the police need to hear what you have to say and judge it for themselves," I tried.

"Julius Morgan, Mister Black, Julius Morgan. Black man and a white woman – ain't nothing good going to come of my going to the police. You know that," he said flatly.

"Let me be your liaison."

His response was a muffled protest, and I know that his skepticism was well founded. In the Northern states, Romeo might have been able to get a fair hearing out of the situation. Here in the new South, the mantra is "separate but equal," but the mathematics of the equation do not hold true. A black man in his situation would receive no consideration of innocence. He would have been held up to the general public as a prime example of the danger Negroes posed to whites. For that matter, he would have been lucky to avoid a lynching and Pettigrew, if she were alive, would have been susceptible to the same sort of retribution for the betrayal of her own race.

Julius Morgan knew that first hand. He was due to die for his crime in the coming days. The great irony of it was the discrepancy of the standards. As a black man, he was allowed to vote; the white woman was not. The black man received capital punishment for raping the woman. A white man would not have. Admittedly, the laws, somehow seemed out of whack, but that's how they were. There was no sense in trying to convince Romeo to believe or behave any differently. But an idealistic viewpoint offered little comfort in the face of reality.

As we bided our time at the next stop, the crowd at the back of the car continued to increase and the atmosphere was increasingly festive, the result of the shortened workday on the eve of the Fourth of July. Despite a number of vacant seats in the front of the car, many of the mob to the rear were forced to stand, there being no more seats available for them. Pettigrew's lover had gone silent for the moment.

The houses were sizeable and well maintained along Troost, Lindsley and the other streets that we traveled while confined to the moving capsule. These were the homes of the well to do near Vanderbilt University and on the outskirts of town before we reached the farms just far enough removed from the city to be out of reach of its grasp. The limestone foundations of the homes here rose up from the ground, an extension of the bedrock that lies beneath the entire city. The stone was neatly cut and laced together creating the strong underpinning of the expansive homes that rested upon the rock. The thought occurred to me suddenly to disembark and force the man to follow, but I knew that he would not in this neighborhood, and to suggest such a move might endanger the opportunity to learn more, so I waited.

As the car moved, he began again, "That Mister Samuels did it. And he knows about me. He done it and he's figuring on letting me hang for it." His agitation had a calm quality to it filled with determination and rational thought. He actually lured me into believing his story at some level and almost had me conceding his self-professed innocence. The quiver in his voice was undoubtedly fear—the fear of being falsely accused and being made to pay for it.

I put both hands on the window sill. "Samuels knows about you? He didn't mention you."

"Yes, he knows. I won't go into how, but he knows. Knows more than a decent human being ought to know. Probably didn't tell you because he wants to keep himself clean. Wants you to find me and pin it on me," he spat.

"Does he know you as Romeo?"

"You're fishing now Mister Black. He knows. How many black men do you think a Southern woman is involved with? He knows exactly who I am."

"But how does he know, Mister Romeo?"

"No sir. I've been through too much and risked too much to get to where I am. White folks are not going to take it from me." His speech calmed, "No offense to you of course, sir," he paused and took a deep breath as he built up courage, "You want to help me? You can help me. Catch that man Samuels and give him his just due." He paused long enough to catch a breath, "I can pay you to help me out. It isn't much. Probably not enough to convince a white man to help out a black man. Kind of presumptuous of me to even think that."

Responding in a tone equally respectful to his own, I tried to connect with him as a gentleman rather than the confessionary he had made me, "Mister Romeo, sir, it's not a matter of social prejudice. It is a matter of ethics, I'm afraid."

I felt him draw in closer.

"You see, someone else has employed me to find Miss Pettigrew, and it would be unethical for me to accept payment from you for the same services. However, you have provided me with some most interesting information that I do feel compelled to follow up on and investigate to its fullest extent."

I sensed him pulling away.

"Please listen to me. Let's sit down and talk more. Tell me what you know, exactly what you saw. Let me help you. More importantly let me help Miss Pettigrew if you truly love her."

His breath was hot on my ear, "Don't you understand. She doesn't need your help anymore. She's dead. I saw her. I saw him take her away. Now I told you everything I know. No use sitting down to talk about it either. If you want to help me, then get that Mister Samuels and make him pay for what he did."

The trolley lunged to a halt. I stared out the window waiting for the commotion of the arriving and departing passengers to subside. With a jerk, I realized that I had missed the call for the last stop. Everyone was disembarking, and as I turned to seek the man, I found only an empty bench and the backs of the crowd. I hastily made my way to the front of the trolley chancing to catch my quarry as he departed, but was hindered by an elderly man feebly dismounting the steps to the crushed gravel roadway.

As I pushed past the gentleman almost knocking him to the ground, I realized my folly. A series of party wagons bound for Greenwood Park stood at the ready near the trolley stop. He had managed to make his way into one of the first wagons already pulling away. Removing his hat and holding it in his hands between his legs, he looked away denying me the opportunity to see his face. I watched as his plaid work shirt disappeared along with a crowd of other black, weekend-merriment seekers. The single, brown horse moved none too quick, but faster than I could have hoped to cover. Only then did I understand that he had accounted for every detail including anticipating that I would disembark using the front door, the only socially *acceptable* option.

Whether it was Romeo's intent or not, I do not know, but he had taught me a valuable lesson and opened my eyes to things that had been there in plain sight all along. As I stood on the steps preparing to reboard the trolley, the conductor was finishing his lunch and returned the shoebox that was his makeshift lunch pail to its place beneath his seat. I waited for him while he wiped his mouth and stood in the aisle. Then he proceeded back through the car reversing the seats so that they faced forward going back into town. Noting the seat Pettigrew's lover had occupied before the conductor changed them, I selected his former position for my return journey. It was the same seat, but it was far harder and lonelier now. As we prepared to leave, the conductor, remembered me from the trip out. He took my dime and jammed his finger down on his money changer to release a nickel. The coin he tossed at me and with it a look of disgust. I had only pity in return for him.

The trolley was nearly empty and the outgoing ones were filling up with people headed home early for tomorrow's holiday. The return trip to the transfer station and subsequently The Doctor's Building seemed quicker as I rolled the conversation over in my head. I was confounded at how I had missed something so obvious. Now that I knew, certain aspects suddenly made sense while others begged questions. The clandestine meetings were understandable in the circumstances. The repercussions had they been seen together as a couple would have been horrific. The travel was an issue though. How they managed to afford such luxury as that led me to wonder if there might be yet another man involved or if the postcards had been pure fantasy. Yet, the cards bore the postmark of cities far removed.

It was only as I stepped from the elevator to the third floor, and I caught sight of John that I realized how delicate his situation truly had been and how much had put himself at risk by approaching me. He stood polishing the handle of a door, and I could not turn and go the other way. He had seen me already, so I marched forward. He didn't acknowledge my approach, but he was aware of my presence in the corridor. Painted on him was the fear of reprisal for his being party to the knowledge of the tryst between Romeo and Pettigrew. As I drew near, his anxiety was evidenced by the beads of sweat forming on his brow in the coolness of the cold pink marble hallway.

Shame constricted my heart and tried to steer me from my course. But his concerns had to be allayed regardless of my disgrace. The final uncertain steps of my advance caused the fear to swell in him such that he noticeably shook as he rubbed the brass fixture on the door.

Unable to speak, I thrust my open hand into his line of site where he had no choice but to acknowledge me – an action which he would not be able to afford himself. His eyes rose up, the brown pupils searching my face as he stooped below me. He straightened to look me in the eye and accepted my hand.

"When you get a moment…" I prompted him leaving the statement unfinished, myself unwilling to continue to deny his existence and his importance.

"Yes, Suh," he nodded.

L heard his steps behind me even before I had unlocked my office.

We stood just inside the door, both of us on the near side of the desk in that cramped space, and I cut quickly to the chase.

"Did you know Miss Pettigrew was seeing a colored man?"

"No, Suh," he replied flatly. "If'n I'd known, I'd a tol' ya. I don' keep secrets an' don' tell no tales neitha'."

"Anything else you know about her?"

"Not much. She wuz in and 'round dis buildin' a lot. On all the flo's like she had friends ev'where."

"Thanks, John. You're a good man. I might could use your help. When are you done for the day?"

"Jes' about finish now. Boss man done give us mos' the afternoon off fo' the Fourth."

"Going to spend it with family?"

"'Less you got something need doin.'"

"Maybe. Where do you live?"

"Lives in Hell's Half Acre, Suh. It's a sight better'n Black Bottoms where we used to live." These were two of the predominantly black and rundown neighborhoods central to the city that house most of the working-class-Negroes

"Check back with me when you're done for the day, "I said, allowing him to return to his work.

I glanced at my watch and realized the lateness of the hour in the shadow of the coming holiday. I rushed down the Polk Avenue stairs to the second floor in an attempt to intercept Beatrice on her way out.

But my trolley ride had delayed me too long, and she had already made for home unescorted yet again. Having not as of yet made plans for the Fourth of July other than to assume that we would be together, there was some imperative in my need to see her soon lest she be hurt by the lack of time spent with her of late. Still I found myself unable to swallow my mannish pride just yet and chase her to her doorstep.

# 18

I wandered the halls of the office building preoccupied with the meeting with Romeo and its implications. I was uncertain just who could be trusted, and that insecurity had me thinking while I hoped to find someone with whom I could discuss the day's events.

I didn't foresee finding Samuels still in his office though the afternoon had not progressed too far as of yet. Still, I preferred to gather my thoughts and obtain an unbiased perspective.

John did not satisfy my need for serious discussion, but I was indebted to him and he seemed trustworthy. Beatrice was gone for the day, but it was just as well, since I did not feel able to bring myself to trust her with the information. Doc offered the most convenient alternative, and I was pleased to find him still lingering about his office just finishing up with a final patient for the day and eager for the company for the evening, a tired lonely man with little else to do.

"Let me finish up with this patient, and I'll be right over," he told me.

While I waited for him in my office, John appeared, his work for the day complete. Doc came as promised, and I dove immediately into telling of the trolley ride and how it had come to pass. As I recalled the events, including my own feelings and my resulting theories, they listened closely taking in all of the detail.

After I finished, the two sat pensive for a few moments. Doc's hands were steepled in his thinking mode. He stared at the ceiling, his eyes darting back and forth as he watched a scenario play out in his head.

"What do you think?" I asked.

Without leveling his head, he turned sideways to look at me. "I was simply going to listen. I didn't want to interrupt your train of thought and cause you to omit anything important," he said.

Then he leveled his head and turned to John to play the role of patient instructor to struggling students. "What do you think?" He asked of the man.

John cut his eyes to me not having anticipated being asked for his assessment. But he had been giving the matter serious thought, and I had to listen closely to catch everything that he said.

He cleared his throat before he spoke. "It make sense that Mista' Samuels hired you. Even tho' he don't seem so smart, he jes' might be smart enough to do it to make you think it ain't him. But the fella' on the trolley may not be tellin' the truth neither. Might be wantin' to get off the hook. Without looking 'em direct in the eye, it's hard to say who tellin' the truth and who not."

John was right. I hadn't looked Romeo in the eye. Had not seen his expressions. Had not watched to see when he cut his eyes away from me in a lie or held them fast in a genuine declaration of fact. And I needed the benefit of more than the sound of his voice to evaluate his testimony.

"If'n this Romeo killed Miss Pettigrew, sounds like he might a' been jealous," he continued, "But Romeo don't have the kind of money you talkin' about to take care of her like that. Unless of course she wuz seein' Mister Samuels, too."

"Or not," suggested Doc, countering the idea. His view, though that of a layman, was a well-educated and experienced one that I had come to respect. "You assume that Miss Pettigrew is dead and while that may be a safe assumption, you lack a body. And you lack any indication that a crime has been committed. You have hearsay from someone who you know only as Romeo and who suggests that a crime has been perpetrated. For all you know, she may have been inebriated, or otherwise incapacitated or any other of a number of explanations, and that, my friend, is not much on which to build a case."

His blunt rebuttal of the theory deflated me completely, yet the entire set of circumstances did not sit well with me. They were like a pyre of dry kindling ready to burst into flame, so I determined to set the match to them.

Planning as I spoke, Doc and John helped me refine my approach to see if I could touch off Samuels with the small spark of knowledge that I had gained.

Doc drummed his fingers on the desktop. "I'll recheck the hospitals for you."

"John, if you'd wait here for me, I may need your help after I talk with Samuels," I said, and headed for the Polk Avenue stairs that would take me to my employer's office.

I found no one at the front desk in the insurance agency, and receiving no service, I meandered through the office seeking out my employer. A light shone behind only one of the doors and through its mottled glass.

He was seated behind his desk, Miss Winston speaking animatedly to him from her place in a chair opposite him. Her hands lay perfectly still in her lap. Not yet seen, I did not interrupt and took a seat positioned near the door where I picked up the thread of the conversation.

The woman's voice, confident yet flustered, was methodically addressing an issue. Her hands flailed as she spoke. "Yes, sir. But do you understand what I am saying? You see this receipt dated here? There is no corresponding journal entry for the receipt. There are some discrepancies. The drummers are upset with me. They think I'm shorting them on their commission checks, and some of them are getting very angry."

"Well if you shorted them, then they should be. Why don't you just pay them what they ask and be done with it and enjoy the upcoming holiday?"

"Because I can't, sir. I can't figure out how much each one should get. I have the figures for last month, but they don't reconcile correctly with the balances in the ledger," she paused for a split second to catch her breath and steady herself before repeating, "There are some discrepancies, sir."

"Such as?"

"Accounting, sir. Like I described." Her assuredness waned as she was forced to back up her claim, but her resolve to see the matter through was no less diminished. "You see, the numbers just don't add up."

"Miss Winston, you have just made a very broad statement. I'm afraid that I don't understand what you mean when you say that they don't add up." His voice was calm and confident, unruffled by the accusation of improper management of funds that she presented.

"Well, sir as I said before, reconciling the general journal entries made here over the past several months with the sales numbers that the drummers have in their receipts books, well, sir, they just don't add up. Our debits should be far greater than what they appear to be."

"Miss Winston, could you put it in plain English for me?" he said, clearly unable to fathom the elementary mathematics of accounting. "Very simply now. What are you trying to say?"

"Sir, I am trying to say that someone has not been recording the sales properly in the books, but has been making the payment to the salesmen as if the sales were properly recorded. Sir, I am saying that it appears that someone has embezzled a sizable chunk of money from the company—most likely my predecessor." At the outright accusation, I jumped from my seat in the hallway and moved to just outside the door.

"Miss Winston, are you accusing Miss Pettigrew of stealing?" Samuels' tone was even and measured, no hint of surprise in the tone.

"No, sir. I would never imply such a thing, but what I am saying is that something isn't right."

Aware that the woman was being baited like a mouse at the mercy of a cat, I stepped to the doorway ready to deliver my own blow cautiously, lest I offend and lose my employer. The events witnessed in those few minutes presented me with information that I had not yet had the time to properly consider, so I moved with the utmost caution. Pushing the door open the rest of the way, I rapped lightly on the frame before entering the room. Samuels acknowledged me by raising a hand to silence his employee.

"Mister Black. So nice to see you. You seem to have arrived at an opportune moment. I trust you have the gist of the conversation," to which I nodded my head in reply. Turning to his sheepish bookkeeper, he bravely asked the first question of her that comes to mind in such a conversation, "How much?" He glanced in my direction to be sure that I noted his lack of surprise.

"Around $2,700 is my initial estimate, but there may be more." She said, no pride of discovery in her voice.

Samuels gave a dismissing wave of the hand and disrespectful shake of his head. "My dear woman, you must be mistaken. By my own accounting, there is a disparity of no more than $2,000. Of that I am certain."

"No, sir. Not to contradict you, but I'm quite certain of the figure. The unrecorded sales are one issue, but another error appears in the payments made to the home office. They seem to be short on a fairly regular basis."

"Not possible. Go back and double-check your figures, please."

"I already have."

"Then do it again." Waving a hand at her, he gave the woman a curt dismissal informing her that they would complete their conversation later.

The bookkeeper was unable to pass without my moving. I was hesitant to allow her departure wanting to hear more, but thought better of pressing the situation.

Pilchard Samuels' look of confidence had changed to one of concern as he spoke, "I'm sorry that you had to overhear that. It seems you've stumbled in upon the dirty little secret about Miss Pettigrew that I had hoped to keep quiet." He paused and shook a cigarette free of its package pulling it out with his lips and striking a wooden matchstick to light the end.

"She was stealing from you?"

"Misappropriation of funds from the company." His manner was calm and subdued. "Seems that it was going on for quite some time. Six or eight months, apparently." He puffed deeply on the smoldering tobacco causing it to glow as he drew the air past the tip and into his mouth. "I am partly to blame for allowing her so quickly into my confidence and allowing her such access to the business issues."

I raised my eyebrows in feigned surprise at his admission of inadequacy.

He cut his eyes and spoke under his breath. "Looks to have been almost $2,000 over the course of that period," he paused. "Or maybe more. It seems that my initial inquiry may have overlooked something." His brow furrowed. "That's a fair sum."

I nodded my head and waited, but none was forthcoming as he had gone mute in the absence of more to say.

"Have you already reported it to your home office?" I inquired.

"Yes, of course," he said waving his hand as if to dismiss my question or disperse the smoke, exactly which was not clear. "They've put me in charge of the investigation, of course. But first things first, they want her back here to answer some questions," he smiled. "That's where you come in. I'm afraid she may have gotten wind of the whole thing a bit early." He drew on the cigarette once more. "Appears she may have flown the coop on me. Of course with that kind of cash in hand, she could be anywhere by now. As a matter of fact, each day she's gone, the farther away I think she gets."

I studied his face for a moment, dozens of questions crossing my mind, but having not had the time to mull over the new information, I asked the question that curiosity provoked, "So why not fix the books? Why leave them for the new bookkeeper to find?"

His answer was unsatisfactory, but it was all he had to offer, "Several reasons actually. First, we aren't sure just what discrepancies there are, as is evidenced by the scene you just witnessed. So we may still be finding more. Secondly, it provides a good test for Miss

Winston. And besides that, someone is already working on this at the main office trying to reconcile all of the issues."

"And I was hired simply to locate Miss Pettigrew?"

"Yes, of course. Why else?"

"Well, it just seems that you would have informed me better of the situation. After all, I would search for an embezzler differently than I would a missing person. Look for places to which she might have fled. Check out her bank account. Things like that." I tapped on his desk with two fingers as I said the last. "So why not tell me of the misappropriation?"

He drew a lungful of smoke from the cigarette and expelled it into the room. "I can't see how that would have changed how you go about locating someone, but that's your profession, not mine. At any rate, you still haven't found her, I assume."

"No, I haven't found her, yet, and you haven't answered my question either. Why not tell me of the embezzlement?"

"For the same reason that I hired you in the first place Mister Black. My employers want this handled with the utmost discretion." A leer split his face.

My own words used against me, I bowed my head in defeat vowing to be better prepared for the next battle, and I fired the first shot. "Mister Samuels, which livery do you frequent?"

"The Derby, of course." He was indignant that there would be any doubt that he would use the premier stables in town.

"Did you rent a horse that Wednesday, the last day that you recall seeing Miss Pettigrew?" The question was innocuous in its approach.

However, it gave him pause before he responded, "I'm really not sure."

I let the answer ripen on the vine for a moment, and it did so quickly.

He continued, "Why do you ask, Mister Black? I assume that you have a reason."

"Mister Samuels, per our earlier conversation, I'm simply evaluating all of my leads, and you may have the one piece of information that allows me to resolve this case. I should think that you would be more than willing to give me a few moments of your time in order to save me countless hours spent trying to dredge up the information elsewhere."

"Well as your employer, I suppose that is a noble offer from you, however, I can assure you that I know nothing of her demise."

Unwilling to confront him outright with the knowledge supplied by Romeo without having some means to confirm it, even if it was simply to look into the colored man's eyes, I continued the stab and parry routine with him. "As I said, you may unknowingly have the piece of the puzzle which I require in order to resolve this affair. So I repeat my question, and please try to give me an answer. Or I can simply go to the livery and ask them. I imagine that they keep a record."

The large man shifted uneasily in his chair before responding, "Let me think then." He put a heavy finger to of his chin for a moment before he answered, "Yes. Yes, I do believe that I did rent a mount that evening."

"A hansom as well?"

His jaw ground back and forth, and his teeth grated audibly in the silence of the room, "Yes. And a hansom as well."

I pulled a chair forward and sat down. "That seems a bit of an extravagance."

"I had a good evening at the poker table that night. Felt that I had earned the luxury." He drew on his cigarette and released a stream of smoke.

"At which house would that have been Mister Samuels?"

"The Turf," he said without blinking.

"I don't recollect seeing you there before," I lied.

"I spend most of my time on the second floor. I have a reputation to uphold and the better clientele are invited to a more exclusive area. No doubt it is unfamiliar to you, Mister Black." He pulled at the cuffs of his shirt.

"And you drove the hansom to your office?"

He took another drag from the nearly spent tobacco. "Yes. Some of us are dedicated to our work, not that you would understand that."

"Perhaps not," I smiled sensing victory, "But still, it is something that you might remember fairly clearly, especially given its timing in relation to Miss Pettigrew's disappearance."

"Mister Black, I don't like what you are implying," he said stubbing out his cigarette in the ashtray on his desk.

"I'm not implying anything. I'm just trying to verify some facts about the evening your employee vanished."

"And have you found her yet?" he insisted.

Overanxious to land a finishing blow, I offered more, "Not yet. But I found someone who had an interesting story to tell. Not that I believe it, mind you, but interesting nevertheless."

He turned his head slightly to the side looking at me out of the corner of his eyes, so that I was unable to see directly into them for some indication of the inner workings of his thoughts, "And what story is that?"

"This person claims to have seen you leaving here with Miss Pettigrew in a hansom the night she went missing." I deliberately omitted the fact that she had appeared dead in an overt attempt to draw him out. "On top of that, they even claim that you know them, or at least know of them – yet another small detail that you *overlooked* letting me in on."

With effort, he remained stone-faced giving me nothing with which to work. Interminable seconds pass before the façade fell away, "Anonymous accusations are cheap to come by. If you would like something to look into, try her boyfriend."

"Do you know him?"

"Know him? I wouldn't say that I know him. I've heard of him, but have never had a face-to-face meeting, so I consider his existence to be a matter of pure, how shall I say it, hearsay from Miss Pettigrew whom I now know to be a thief. As for the story about seeing me with her that night, I can only say that it appears that someone may be trying to create their own version of events to conceal their involvement in the misappropriation and the disappearance of Miss Pettigrew." Hardly breaking for breath, he rose from his chair and leaned over the table at me. "Knowing the dishonest nature of Miss Pettigrew, I can easily envision that she might surround herself with the more disagreeable dregs of society who might malign a reputable citizen such as myself in the process of trying to hide behind their own cowardly deeds." His face was thoroughly flushed before he finished.

"Guilt by association," I offered.

"Exactly!"

"That's not a prosecutable offense," I said.

"It's not? Well it should be."

"I can see some different ways it might be applied in this investigation," I said before moving on. "So you did rent a hansom, and you did drive it to your office, but Miss Pettigrew was never in the hansom?"

"No, she wasn't."

"Please accept my apology, I do not mean to imply that you were involved, but simply wanted to corroborate some other information.

Your word is worth its weight in gold," I said sarcastically, the disdain in the remark lost on him.

He greedily sucked in a breath of air. "Excuse me. It is simply that such an accusation is offensive beyond belief. It's out of character for me to lose my composure as you have just experienced. Forgive me."

For a moment we sat in deadlocked silence. Each studied the other while he attempted to recover his breath, and I remained the calm observer.

His nostrils flared still and he collapsed back into the chair. From that slumped position, he continued, and his next words were as expected, "Might I suggest that this boyfriend may be involved, and that we may be well served in identifying and bringing his presence to bear on the issues?"

I nodded, waiting for more, but none forthcoming, prompted the logical next step, "What do you know of him?" I asked. "Any idea where I might find him?"

The idea was cold, but he warmed to it quickly offering that he seemed to remember Pettigrew mentioning that he worked for the railroad on one of the regular runs between Nashville and Louisville. He suggested that the man was probably employed by the L&N.

"Did she ever mention that he's colored?" I asked.

Either the delay in his response was a tad too long or his reaction a little too disingenuous, of which I am not quite sure. "I'm shocked."

But as he placed a hand to his chest in reaction, I knew the answer, though it conflicted with his words. He had far more information than I, and in order to solve this affair, I would have to find that information from someplace other than his lips.

He stood and walked around the desk. "Mister Black, you have brought quite a revelation this evening. It appears that I may have underestimated you."

I rose with him. "Give me time. I'll have more."

He gave a quick smile. "Yes, I'm sure you will. And I'd love to hear about it when you do." He put a hand on my shoulder and directed me to the door. "But I am quite busy at the moment, so you'll have to excuse me."

I was in the hallway and his office door shut behind me before I realized his intent to part with me there and not see me to the front door of the offices. I lacked any direct evidence to outright accuse him and further pressing the man with out such justification seemed to offer little at that point. So I returned to the third floor to plot with my counterparts and determine how we might best go about getting the proof we needed.

John was waiting for me in my office, as I had asked of him.

"Try the railway station. See if you can locate the man who gave you the letter there. He works on the trains," I said, dispatching him to Union Station in search of our Romeo.

I, on the other hand, had Samuels' story to check out and that required a trip to Fourth Avenue. "We'll meet back here this evening after we've both checked things out," I said rushing out the door.

The walk to the Gentlemen's Quarter on Fourth wasn't a long one. The pending holiday had cleared the early afternoon streets of the usual throng of people, and I made good time from my office.

The stone structure of the Southern Turf Hotel sets it apart from all of the other buildings on the street. Positioned on the corner of an alleyway, a cylindrical two-story turret stretches from the second floor to the third and is capped off with its own small dome similar to the Vendome. An ornate cast-iron awning with SOUTHERN TURF written in large capital letters announces the business to the public passersby.

There are multiple ways in. The main entrance which I normally use leads into the lobby with its gray-and-white inlaid marble floor tiles; cigar counter; big saloon; and gaming tables. Another entrance at the back, off of the alleyway, is for the colored, teamsters and other downtrodden of society. That doorway offers them access to a separate facility in the basement of the building.

For the more discerning observer, there is another entrance, a second door on Fourth, the one that Samuels used the day I stumbled upon him. That doorway led directly to the second floor. It was expressly for those who didn't wish to advertise their presence in such an establishment. It was through that door that I went in search of the owners in order to conduct my business on this occasion.

The proprietors at the Southern Turf are not your typical saloon-and-gambling-house types. Around town, they are well known among the masses for their generosity and their honesty. Still, the prying of a private investigator goes a long way in chilling their otherwise reputedly warm hearts.

There were already two individuals there to request a moment of the owner's time when I arrived. He was a handsome man, though on in years. His dark mustache tipped with grey gave him a distinguished appearance that no doubt played well with the ladies he employed on the third floor. His accent was that of a native of the city, the tone thick with the Southern dialect, not slow like in the more rural areas, but rapid, synchronized with the pace of city life and his profession in particular.

As I waited, I was witness to the wailing pleas of a woman. Her husband had come in the establishment and proceeded to gamble and drink away his entire paycheck – holiday bonus and all.

The owner was gracious, listening patiently to the woman as she cried pitifully. "I've got children to feed. They need shoes, too. The eldest has outgrown all of his clothes, and he's a good boy. He deserves better than a father that spends his time drinking and gambling."

His arm about her shoulders, he tried to console her, but to no avail. During the course of his reassurances, he twice looked over at the other man and myself and rolled his eyes in apology. He was slowly, but methodically moving her toward the door through which I had just come. As they reached the door, he pulled a large wad of bills from his pocket and proceeded to reimburse her for the entire sum she had named. The tears stopped. She extended him her hand and even a kiss on the cheek for his understanding and generosity.

"Thank you," he said, fumbling for her name, which she readily supplied, and he assured her that she need not worry about that happening again.

As the door closed, he turned to two of his henchmen, "OK, boys. Go downstairs and if he's down there, throw him out and don't let that son of a bitch back in. He's blacklisted here. Let him go down the street to the Climax and see if they give him his money back," he halted briefly, then turning back to the two of us remaining there. Each of us stood with our hats in hand. The proprietor eyed us as he sized up his next victim. "Who's next?" He growled.

I pointed to the other man who warily stepped forward, his black jacket and starched collar betraying his profession.

"Hello, Reverend," the owner purred.

"Hello. Yes, sir. I'm Reverend Jonas. Oh my, I'm not sure that I should even be here, but I've been told to come to you by some of my colleagues. You see, we're in the process of trying to build a new church for our flock, and well, we're a pious group, very giving. But, you see, we're a small congregation. And well, we're going about soliciting donations for our new place of worship, and well, to be honest sir, I've been told that you're a very philanthropic man—"

"Yes, and a busy one as well, Reverend. Get to your point," he said, still purring in the manner of a wild panther sizing up its prey before it pounces.

"Well, if you could make a small charitable donation, it would be gratefully received, and we would offer the blessings of the Lord upon you. At the day of reckoning when Saint Peter calls your name, we would be amongst those there in your defense, sir."

The reverend continued his groveling for a few more minutes, the proprietor maliciously enjoying the nervous humility of the man as he begged for the funds. After a few moments, the predator grew tired of the game and capitulated. "Just don't tell them where you got it, Reverend," the man said pulling a ten-dollar bill from the same roll of cash that he'd produced to pay the woman.

The holy man's eyes opened wide, and he accepted the bill carefully between thumb and forefinger, afraid of being corrupted by its touch, though he was already tainted by his mere presence in the establishment.

"Thank you. Thank you. Oh, the Lord's blessings upon you, sir." He tripped over the rug as he backed away from the proprictor. The reverend held the bill in his hand and did not place it in his pocket until he had reached the door.

At that point, the voice growled one last time, "Now I don't expect to be seein' you or your parishioners around here for quite some time, if you understand what I mean."

The reverend smiled a weak agreement before hastily opening the door and disappearing through it.

Without moving his body his eyes turned to me and his head slowly followed as he stalked me across the room. "It's those same sons of bitches that come down here during the week to beg for money that get up in the pulpits on their soapboxes on Sundays and complain to the mayor, the chief of police, the magistrates and anyone else who'll listen. Then they come down here with their Committee of 100 and try to shut me down. He'll be back again to raise hell about my business before his church even gets built." He stopped now that he had my attention, "Now what do you want? You're not a preacher, and you damn sure ain't a woman." He glanced at his henchmen for a muffled laugh of approval at the joke. "So what do you want?"

"Just some information." From the response, one would have thought that I had announced myself to be the devil himself come to see if that good preacher would actually stand by the promise he had just made.

"What information?" he asked warily, the snarl creeping back into his voice.

"Information on one of your clientele, a Mister Pilchard Samuels," I asked.

He averted his eyes immediately betraying the forthcoming lie, "Don't think I know a Pilchard Samuels. What do you want with him anyways?"

"I'm looking into a matter," I said softly and swallowed almost as loudly as I had spoken.

"And what matter would that be?" he asked with a rolling purr.

"An employee of his has gone missing. I'm trying to locate her."

Lurching forward in his chair, he quickly asked, "Are you the police?"

"No, I am not. I'm—"

"Then what are you bothering with it for?"

"He hired me to do so," I informed him.

"I'm confused." The large man looked at me from the corners of his eyes.

"If you'll excuse my saying so, I find myself equally confused about the entire matter as well. I'm simply trying to clear up what Mister Samuels has told me and corroborate his story. It's become quite complex. He claims to have frequented your establishment the night she went missing. I'm only trying to find out if he did come here."

"You tellin' me he's bringing dirty money in here?"

"No, sir. I don't know anything at all right now. All I'm trying to determine is whether he frequented your establishment and if so, what the nature of his business here is."

"I'll tell you this, you see the charity I give out. You see how I take care of a woman who's got a lout for a man. My people are well paid and cared for. Hell, my dealers even get a share of the winnings they take for the house each night."

"It has nothing to do with you or the Turf. It has only to do with him, and I will not drag your name into it."

"Damned right you won't bring me into it." He considered silently for a few interminable seconds, "So it has nothing to do with the money he's been losing?"

"Not that I'm aware of," I assured him.

"Nothing to do with the girls he so enjoys?"

I returned his confidence with a somber shake of my head.

He paused for a few seconds that hung heavily above me before he continued, "What night are you wantin' to know about?" he said, "And I don't want you goin' around asking other folks, my dealers and what not. Don't want you making them nervous. Just give me the day and I'll check and let you know."

Giving him the date that Pettigrew was last seen, he withdrew a ledger from the desk drawer. The book was large and well used. He crisply flipped through the pages snapping each one as it turned. Stopping, he scanned the page using his forefinger and lingered on a portion of the page.

When he returned his gaze to me, it was guarded. "He was here."

"He was?"

"Oh, yes," he repeated.

"Good night for him?" I pressed.

"To start with."

"At the end of the night?"

"Not so good," he offered. "Not even enough to pay the girl. We threw him out early. Long before closing. That's it."

Sensing the end of the conversation, I turned to make my leave, but his snarling voice stopped me cold when it called out my name that I had purposely withheld. "Mister Black," it said. "Do not drag this business in here and leave it at my doorstep. You're not welcome to return with regard to this matter, and you're not to talk to my people about it." The voice stopped. "Do I make myself clear?"

Without turning to face him for fear of turning to a pillar of salt as Lot's wife had at Sodom and Gomorrah, I nodded and continued for the door.

A parting statement caught me before I could escape, "Come back and see me, Mister Black. On the second floor. We'll have a drink." It was a demand, not a request.

"It would be my pleasure," I said.

"And one more thing." I turned to look at him, and he tossed me a package wrapped in brown paper, the unopened parcel retrieved from Nancy's post office box. I had forgotten it on the bar in my haste to follow Samuels. "I think you left this last time you were on the second floor."

I looked at the package. If it had been opened, it was not obvious. "Thank you."

"Think nothing of it. Glad I could be of so much help to you today," he smiled.

I traversed the stairs back to Fourth Avenue and stumbled through the door into the sunlight. I stood for a moment, and then looked quickly about before I turned on my heels and made down Fourth for Church Street to take me back to my office.

When I arrived, I placed the package on the desk and was poised to open it with a pocket knife I carried when John returned. Absentmindedly, I put the package in the drawer while he gave me an account of his afternoon.

He shifted from foot to foot as he spoke, clearly pleased with what he had been able to find out. "It sho' weren't easy. Nobody wanna talk wid me. Mos' folks jes' look pas' me. Some gimme dirty looks. Even da' colored folk what work on da railroad don' wanna talk wid me. But I find 'im."

Those who work the rails for a living have a bond that transcends society outside of it. They do not share information and they do not trust those outside of their own ranks. While some division of the races is maintained even in that society, the coloreds and whites are bound by a unique brotherhood.

John had entered through the coloreds' entrance. He knew the man's face having received the note from him. That made the task easier for him though slightly more challenging since Romeo knew his as well.

Further complicating matters for him, he was searching at the confluence of social circles – white and black, male and female, rich and poor—many of which were not particularly accepting of him and his questions.

A mass of human bodies, male and female, adult and child, were crammed into the hot waiting room for blacks. He quickly threaded his way through the mass of humanity making his way down to the platform from street level on Broadway to where the trains come into the gulch well below street level.

The high cover of the train is almost even with the streets above and keeps the sun and drizzling rain off of the passengers. Open on all sides, it allows a light breeze to blow through, but the breeze is tainted by the smell of the coal-fired engines, the smell of the huge machines in use and the grit and grime that fall to the lower point in the surrounding landscape. The shed does little to dissipate the mounting heat of the advancing summer and traps the pungent smells of the railroad instead of allowing them to waft freely into the skies.

He asked a few well-considered questions in his effort to locate Romeo. What he asked, he asked only of the other coloreds on the platform. And what he asked would not have aroused suspicions unless the person were directly involved in the case, but still they remained wary of him.

One assembly of cars was on the tracks being laden with goods, luggage and passengers bound for Louisville and other points north. The crowd along the platform was thick, impeding him as he tried to move graciously. Luggage was piled in oversized carts high off the ground so as to be almost level with the train cars into which they were to be loaded. A number of Negro red caps followed along behind white families toting their baggage for them to their accommodations for the trip.

He reached the end of the cover provided by the shed, where he spied the sleeper cars. With each step he took beyond the shelter, the crowd thinned a bit more, some of them finding their places in the closer cars, others not wanting to brave the fading light of the skies just yet.

John moved cautiously staying on the side of the platform opposite the departing train in order to stay out of the way of the other travelers and to remain beyond the focus of his intended quarry.

On the first pass, he did not spot the porter he sought. There were a few there, but he did not see the man for whom he had couriered the message. Reaching the end of the train, he turned back to search the sleeper cars again in hopes of catching the porter between assisting passengers. During the second pass, he spotted him helping a white couple into the third sleeper car laden with their bags for the trip.

Taking up a spot on a bench, he sat waiting for the man who was Pettigrew's lover and watched in silence. The man was courteous. He was professional. He was at ease in that meeting of worlds.

John waited patiently as the seemingly endless and steady stream of travelers turned to a trickle. Then the last few boarded. Pettigrew's lover came to the door of the car and looked back to the station not noticing the man seated motionless on the bench and partially obscured by the tall luggage cart. He reached down and picked up the small stool which each of the passengers had used to board the car pulling a rag from a compartment beneath it to wipe the top clean.

When John did move, the man turned to face him. It took a moment to place the face, but when he did, their eyes locked. John stood and moved toward the train. A whistle blew.

"When you gonna be back?" John asked.

"Every day but Sunday," he replied.

"Mistah Black want a word witcha," he said.

"I figured. I'll be here again, the day after tomorrow. Same schedule. I ride the overnight to Chicago tonight and the overnight back tomorrow night. I'm here every other day. It's my final stop."

Doc was almost an hour behind John arriving back at the office. He had called on the few hospitals close by and then returned to his office and placed phone calls to the others. His efforts were fruitless, but he remained hopeful that there might be some chance of finding Miss Pettigrew alive. Neither John nor I shared his optimism. Perhaps it was a relic of the profession in which he engaged to remain always optimistic as regarded a prognosis.

Aware of my situation with Beatrice and the upcoming holiday, Doc conspired to find a way to give me the following day off with a bit of assistance from John and a young colored boy that he intended to enlist to help him in the matter. That night and the following day, they would take turns tailing Samuels as he went about town to see what they might find out, but more importantly to make sure that he did not make a run for it in light of the new evidence I had on him from Pettigrew's lover.

"What will you do if Samuels makes a run for it?" I asked.

"Don't worry about it. John and I can handle it," he assured me. "For now, I think you should concentrate on that young lady you've been courting," Doc suggested.

# 19

By the time we had finished, it was too late for me to call on Beatrice, so I made it a point to be ready early in the morning. I wanted to have the entire day with her, as long as it took, to straighten out the entire mess I had gotten the relationship into. In the interest of remaining true to my intent, I opted to stay the night in my own bed rather than that of Nancy Pettigrew.

Up early the morning of the Fourth, I was able to enjoy the newspapers. Unable to completely forsake my professional calling, I searched, but there was no news of Miss Pettigrew. I found some news of advances for the allies in France and learning that the Vols were rained out yesterday against our other opponent from Alabama, the Birmingham Barons. The recent wet weather had cancelled and rescheduled more games than I cared to consider. As a painful reminder of the week's events, I noticed that the National Suffrage Rally date had been set for September, two to three months earlier than usual according to the report.

The hour with my morning coffee and the news, I spent going over the things that I intended to say to Beatrice. Composing numerous messages in my head and even committing a few to the written page against my better judgment, I realized that it all boiled down to telling her I was sorry. Sorry for the thoughts in my head to which she had not been privy, but which she had read and interpreted all too well. And ultimately, rather than provide too much information that might confirm her concerns, I decided to stick with a simple, heartfelt apology.

I arrived early at Beatrice's doorstep rapping gently on the screen door. She was already dressed for the day and was at first glad to see me.

Immediately after "Hello," I took her hand, "Beatrice, I'm sorry. I could go on and apologize for things specifically, but I'd just foul it up and wind up apologizing for my apology. So I'll leave it at 'I'm sorry.'"

She smiled and squeezed my hand. "Thank you. But it is I who need apologize. I'm afraid that my unfounded jealousy has done me far more harm than good. In the end, it may be our downfall."

"Nonsense. In the future, we will simply have to be up-front with each another and do our best to overcome whatever might come between us."

Her wan smile conveyed sadness and a beauty that pierced me through to the heart. The subject addressed, I felt we were well on the way to mending, but knew there was more to be done. The suggestion of an impromptu day at the park met with an unenthusiastic response, but agreement nonetheless.

While all around us was festive on the streetcar, she remained preoccupied, staring out the window uninterested in the revelry about us. Children and adults alike chattered in excited anticipation of the day's picnics and the evening's fireworks, but Bea's languid mood stifled my own.

My first inclination was to draw her into the rest of the crowd encouraging her to join the celebration, but my efforts met with no recognizable success eliciting only an abbreviated and saddened smile from her as if the luster of our togetherness had tarnished with the disagreements of the past few days.

She assured me that my actions the night of the suffrage meeting were forgiven and forgotten. She even went so far as to apologize for her behavior and her admittedly indefensible display of jealousy. My next thought was that the day itself had taken on an especially bitter meaning for her. The fight for suffrage in which she so devoutly believed served merely to commemorate the birth of a nation that refused her the privilege of casting her vote for the candidate of her choice.

Feeling noble and admittedly indifferent about the pending elections, I offered her something she could not otherwise have had. "Allow me to cast my vote in the upcoming elections as if it were yours. I'll allow you to choose among the candidates regardless of my own preferences. You just tell me who it is you want."

"That's sweet," she said with a smile, "But I need to be able to put my ballot in the box myself. Until I can, and every other woman can, this issue will rage on." The net result was that it did little to improve her mood over the course of the trolley ride.

"You don't appear to feel very well today. Perhaps it's whatever ailed you the other night at the theatre." Her reply was a resigned nod.

The return trolley ride was almost vacant except for a few people headed into town to make a transfer. Seeing her home, she embraced me unashamedly on the front porch before caressing my cheek and giving me a polite kiss that theretofore she had never had the nerve to do on her doorstep for fear of upsetting her father. With a simple, "bye" she disappeared through the screen door.

Head down, I slowly traced the familiar path to The Doctor's Building and returned to the office to pore over the collection of cards and receipts looking for what they had to tell me. The door ajar, Doc sauntered into my office surprised to find me in.

"Your Mister Samuels spent last night frequenting the Gentlemen's Quarter establishments as expected. He kept John up quite late as he tried to keep track of him. It wasn't too hard though. Seems he did a good job of being refused at the door or tossed out on his ear at any of the more reputable establishments. John sent a young boy he has helping over this morning to let me know that Samuels was down there again first thing this afternoon to pick up where he left off. I'm just on my way down there to relieve John. He had a long night of it."

His counsel on Beatrice was to remain patient with her. "She'll come back around," he assured me echoing what I had interpreted from Miss Bobo's late night visit. But my Beatrice wasn't a woman of patience. Still I heeded the advice suppressing my inclination to rush to her side and declare my undying love for her and ask her hand in marriage regardless of what her father might think.

As the afternoon turned to evening, it became increasingly difficult to weather the darkness without benefit of her company. With Doc's departure, the stillness of the empty building yielded no sound. Buried within its confines, I heard nothing of the happenings on the street, and even the familiar echoes of shoes and voices resounding off of the marble halls was lacking.

Still I stood fast on Doc's advice, determined to persevere. But in the absence of the warmth of her touch, I found myself in need of comfort. And as evening came, I was drawn to seek out some consolation. I went in search of it back at the boarding house and the familiar room of the missing woman who had driven us apart.

# 20

Rather than go to the office the following morning, I went directly home to pack a few things for my trip that evening. My intent was to follow Pettigrew's lover all the way to the end of the line if required in order to get what was needed. The ride out to my apartment on the trolley was pleasant. The day following the holiday and traveling against the incoming traffic made for a light turnout at the trolley stop.

Back at home, the newspaper offered no sign of the missing or simply evasive Miss Nancy Pettigrew. Instead it offered a full-page explanation, not an apology, of why the paper felt justified in raising its rates from ten cents for a weekly subscription to fifteen cents. The propaganda statement provided a long string of reasons including the need for more space to cover all of the current events in the world from, "the Great European War, Our Difficulties with Mexico and the Coming Presidential, Gubernatorial and Other Elections." The cant went on to detail all of the materials used and compared last year's and this year's pricing and noted the percentage increase in each item right down to the twine and wrapping paper used to bundle all that they considered news. Then they continued their effort to invoke our pity for them by noting that their increase in price represented a far lower percentage than that of the combined materials. Missing from the argument was any mention of the rise in rates to their advertisers who absorbed the vast majority of the costs and who produced the profits for them.

Still despite the sour taste left in my mouth, when the paper boy informed me that he would be collecting an additional nickel from me each week, I agreed to pay it. It's indispensable in my work, and keeps me abreast of the inconsistent play of the Vols who managed to make up for their rainout of the previous day by splitting a doubleheader with the Barons on the Fourth in Birmingham. Finding no news of the missing woman, I prepared for another day of employment at the discretion of Pilchard Samuels and took the trolley into the office.

The return trip back into town was almost as pleasant; the lateness of my commute that morning thinned the crowd even more. It was a relief that the electric monster deemed the small group worthy and stopped to pick us up instead of passing by packed to the open vestibules as it so often does during the early morning commute. I could have gone by foot, but was relieved to be spared the effort with my luggage in hand.

John was already hard at work upon my arrival and made to help me with my suitcase when I appeared.

"No, I've got it. Thank you, John." I waved him off.

He gave a courteous nod. "Yes, Suh. If'n you say so."

Five minutes after settling into my office, he appeared at the door pulling up hard on the handle to close the door without it scraping across the floor.

He filled me in on the events of the previous day and Samuels' night on the town. "We followed that man to more'n five diff'rent houses. He ain't no good. Ever' time, he wuz at the gambling tables or chasin' the ladies. He had had a awful run a' luck from 'fore he hit a short winnin' streak. He wound up blowin' it upstairs in the Climax with the ladies. But it didn' las'. Luck turn on him and he got throwed outta couple of places mo'."

Thanking John, I handed him two dollars for the day's work, which he refused. The look on his face told me that he had never seen two dollars paid for a day's work in his life. I insisted and finally he relented, accepting only one of the large coins from my hand as he exited the door.

A few moments later, Doc came through and reconfirmed John's relation of the night's events. When I mentioned to Doc that I had paid John, he said "Don't insult our friendship by attempting to pay for my time. Besides that, I experienced a brief lapse in judgment while trying to blend into the crowd. I placed a few bets. Call it beginner's luck if you like, but it made the evening a mildly profitable venture for me, and I don't intend to take anything that you might try to give me.

"I'm convinced that something is amiss with Samuels, but he represents only part of the picture. I'm curious about what you hope to learn from Romeo. I don't believe him to be involved, but do be careful just in case. I think there may be yet someone else associated with this who has yet to come to light." Echoing my own sentiments, he reminded me, "It's a wonderful city we live in, but it's tightly woven. The connections between people are very short. Be careful. You don't know who might be involved."

About that time, John stuck his head in the open door. "Jes' got word that Romeo arrived dis mornin' like he said. He headin' back out tonight on the eight o'clock."

Doc looked at me. "You be careful. We'll hold things down until your return."

John bobbed his head. "Yes, Suh. You be careful. It's a long ways to Chicago, and I don' wanna be lookin' fer you all along dem tracks."

"I'll try."

John and Doc turned to go back to their work, but I stopped them.

"Thank you both for all of your help. It's good to have people I know I can trust."

John nodded. "Yes, Suh." And he ducked out the door.

Doc coughed. "That's a high compliment being given someone's trust. I take it seriously." He stuck his hands in the pocket of his white lab coat and stepped out.

I left the office early to get to the station to buy my ticket for the overnight journey to Chicago. I took the trolley to save me carrying the valise the five and a half block walk.

Union Station has no peers among the other structures in the city. Oft referred to as the Castle in the Air, it seems to float alongside the roadway rising from the gulch. But it does touch the ground, consecrating the earth on which it stands.

The gulch is a low spot in the area just west of town where the elevation of the land deepens—a prime spot for the passage of the railway into the city. Traversing the many rails had long proved to be a perilous task until the viaduct was built over them. The suspended structure is long and has a fair amount of play in it, enough that "Old Shaky" vibrates with the passage of the engines beneath it and the wagons and automobiles upon it. A heavy gauge wire fence restrains the passerby from casting themselves into the gulch below.

A massive stone arch fronts Broadway bearing the name of the station. It's bounded by two smaller arches on each side. From there, the structure rises impressively in oversized floors, the arches repeated in a smaller scale in the windows above.

The clock spire extends heavenwards announcing the station afar. It's capped by the mythological god, Mercury, one foot in the air giving him charge over the land.

Though I have seen the station many a time, it's no less impressive with each approach. So much so that as I crossed the bricked roadway, I failed to heed the clanging warnings of an oncoming trolley and almost fell victim to it as I crossed its path.

I passed through the arch and paused at the wrought-iron railing, its ornate ironwork comprised of flowers within circles and nautilus shapes of all sizes nested among and beside one another. I looked over the balustrade and down upon the alligators in their refuge below. The day was warm, and they were content to pass the time lying idly in the pool of water provided by their keepers. They are but one of the many unique sights greeting those using this portal to the city.

While the outside of the station is impressive, it does not sufficiently prepare the casual witness for the spectacle of the interior. Entering the main lobby, the roof soars up to an arched ceiling equivalent of four stories in any ordinary building. It ends in a glorious stained-glass roof shielding its interior from the ravages of the weather outside. Gold-leaf, painted medallions adorn the walls. A single walkway enclosed by ornate wood and wrought iron railing runs around the second floor of the cavernous room where the arches of the exterior repeat themselves in the business offices overlooking the main room. The catwalk around the second floor was infrequently occupied in the wake of the holiday, and the shades were drawn on many of the offices, but a few industrious souls still had made their way in to keep the trains running and on time.

I walked through the main entrance and into the cavernous lobby. At each end, there were two clocks flanked by beautiful maidens said to represent the cities of Louisville and Nashville from which the L&N railroad took its name. Below each of these on the first floor stood a fireplace, each one large enough for a man to lie down in.

I stepped across the marble tile and terrazzo floor interrupting the light streaking through the stained glass skylight and walked past the wooden benches stained the color of dark molasses, where the waiting passengers sat. The benches were like pews with arms for each seat lined up back to back allowing their occupants to talk face to face. A handful of men sat waiting for their trains. The women along with their children remain sequestered in their special waiting area to the right as one enters the building and apart from the bustle of the main terminal. No Negroes were in sight being banished to a small waiting area in the southwest corner of the station. Even those coloreds engaged in the maintenance of the facility constantly sweeping the floor, polishing the massive wooden stair rails and benches were not visible.

As always, the building was spotless and immaculately cared for. The absence of filth fueled the mystique. The railroad was all smoke, cinders and ash, and the maintenance of such a large facility in proximity to the conducting of such a dirty business was impressive.

That it was done without being able to identify a single caretaker, is astounding.

Joining the short queue at the counter, I was third in line. A gentleman stood in front of me in his shirt sleeves, galluses exposed, his jacket draped over his arm and his straw hat in his hand. Despite the temperature, it's simply ill-mannered for a man to go about in a public place in his shirt sleeves, but there is no accounting for how some folks are raised. The heat of the day and the humidity of the recent rains contributed to the dark stain beginning to emerge between his shoulder blades soaking through his undergarment and adown his dress shirt. His pear shape betrayed a healthy-sized man, and his naked crown told of a life of worry. He reminded me of Merriweather and the fact that I had not been able to track him down for our discussion.

Looking past him to the large board mounted on the wall behind the counter, the schedule announced the disposition of the station. Among the various destinations, the Louisville-Chicago painted in white was bright against the jet-black slate.

The man in front of me stepped to the counter, his turn having arrived, and ordered a single, first-class, round-trip ticket to Louisville. His money clip in hand, the clerk told him the amount due and pulled the coupon from the drawer while the gentleman counted out payment. The clerk tore off the ticket removing all of the stops beyond Louisville and leaving the portion that listed those between here and there. Finished with his transaction, the man with the shiny pate shuffled to the side.

"A single, round-trip ticket for Chicago with a sleeping berth," I told the man, stepping up to the counter. Even if I were not in Romeo's wagon, I would still be able to move freely about the sleeping area searching for him if needed. The clerk pronounced the fee and drew the ticket from the drawer. Confirming that I had the appropriate funds, he gave me the entire ticket and a supplemental one for the Pullman car permitting me passage and a berth for the Windy City.

Double doors led from the terminal to the platform. Crossing the threshold, the station expanded into a single-span gabled roof of steel wrought-iron and wood that shields the ten platforms and rails from the elements. It was the largest structure of its kind in the world and it stretched out for what seemed an eternity. The roof was vented along the top to disperse the smoke and fumes, but still trapped a sufficient supply of the dirt despite the constant flow of air. The ventilation also allowed flocks of pigeons free access to the structure nesting, flying, breeding, and scavenging among the tracks for castoff delicacies and crumbs.

The cut limestone wall of the luggage house was to my left. The station bounded the north side of the shed, and the balcony where I stood overlooked the scene of parallel incoming tracks. Watching as the conductor guided the engineer, a train backed into place in the FILO station. He signaled the engineer deftly indicating the rate of the approach and stopped the train releasing a loud hiss of steam.

The wrought-iron railing of the stairwell goes down and plateaus, repeating the same pattern once more in order to reach the platforms where the trains arrive.

The crowds were thin following the Fourth of July, and making my way through the crowd was easy. Most of those who departed the city for a summer retreat at Kinston Springs, Estill Springs or the like were already long since gone. Likewise, those coming into the city had already arrived.

Outgoing shipments stacked on the platforms were minimal since the area manufacturers had shut down for the holiday and not geared back up. The hall was populated with travelers, Red Caps in their crimson pillbox hats with black, patent-leather bills and carrying baggage, and well-wishers, some toting the accoutrements of their friends and relatives. There were wooden wagons filled with the mail and luggage to be loaded into baggage cars waiting for the handlers to place them appropriately. The carts obscured the view making it difficult to pick Romeo out of the crowd. He still had the advantage of me, but the odds would even quickly enough once I spotted him based on John's description.

The train was shorter than its usual length leaving me to wonder if perhaps John had been mistaken in his information and my appointment had forgotten a holiday furlough. As I made my way down the platform, I was able to pick out the sleeping cars from a distance with their larger windows and the white curtains adorning them.

Romeo stood anticipating my arrival. He was distinguished in his pillbox hat with two decorative ropes across the front and a brass plate that proudly displayed the title "Pullman Porter." His familiarity with me gave him the advantage, and he picked me out of the crowd before I had him, his stiffly starched white jacket setting him apart from the rest of the people on the platform. As I approached, he removed himself without a word compelling me to follow him into the waiting car.

The wagon accommodates a water closet and a small cabin for the porter at one the end of the car. Romeo was not in the porter's area, so I followed as the corridor wound around to a hallway on one side of the train. Not immediately spotting him and thinking that he might have ditched me by ducking into the train and out the other side or some other trick of which I was unaware, I was ready to turn back when I noticed the motion in the compartment next to me. He was bent over busying himself preparing an empty berth for travel.

"You're not an easy man to find Mister Romeo," I declared stepping into the cabin.

"No, I don't aim to be," he replied without turning to acknowledge the greeting. He continued to fold and refold the linens for the car tucking them neatly into their place where they were to remain until his charge decided to turn in for the night. His jacket was pristinely clean and unwrinkled as is required of the service class. His eyes were dark brown and his hair closely cropped. If he was nervous, he hid it well. Despite the heat, he was cool and the red bandana that he used to wipe his forehead came away dry.

"It seems that I am two cars up. I had hoped to be able to share a car with you that we might pick up where we left off talking about Miss Pettigrew."

"This berth isn't taken," he said. "I've got it made up for you. I'll fix it with the porter and the conductor." His voice carried no emotion. The passion which he had displayed so intently only days before had been washed from him and he stood there now, plain and lifeless. "That your bag?" He pointed to my modest valise and looked at me for the first time giving me the opportunity to finally drink in his details.

"I'm traveling light. Up tonight and return tomorrow." His eyes narrowed in suspicion of my intent. "It's a matter of convenience for me, not a matter of keeping up with you," I assured him.

"If you say so," he said as he picked up the case and moved it to the luggage rack up out of the way.

"Mister Romeo, have no fear. I'm alone in my passage, and I'm here solely for the purpose of listening to your story," I assured him.

"Yes, sir." He patted the bed, and then put a hand on my shoulder as he squeezed past me to the door. "Go ahead and settle in. I have other passengers to tend to, but I'll be back with you after we get moving. I'll be pretty busy until everyone gets settled in, but I'll come. Don't you worry."

When he left, I quickly surveyed the room. The back of the bench where I sat pulled down to make a twin bed. A door concealed the upper berth in the wall above. A small toilet stood opposite the bench, the sign over it reading "Please do not use while in station or stopped." Pressing the handle, the trap in the bottom fell away to the tracks below limiting the need for sanitary plumbing.

A short time later, the massive iron beast pulled away from the station with a jolt. As the procession of wagons filed out and switched to the main line, the entire string of cars was jostled about.

Once we were underway, Romeo passed by several times fetching items for passengers and attending their every need. The conductor came through, and as promised, Romeo had taken care of my assignment.

He took my ticket and punched it officiously. "Yes, Trinidad told me you had been moved."

"Trinidad?" I asked.

"The porter. Says he knows you. You've traveled with him before, I thought." He squinted at me.

Now I had Romeo's name. Or at least his first name. "Of course. I didn't know his name. Just recognized him from before."

He gave me a small wave. "Good then. Enjoy your trip." And he left the cabin.

I contented myself watching the small towns roll by as we left Tennessee headed into Kentucky. I wondered that Nancy Pettigrew might have taken this same train at some point in her travels.

Almost two hours later, it had grown dark before Romeo returned. His look was not as crisp as before, the shirt a bit wrinkled, but still clean, and his cap slightly askew. His movements were slower, not as brisk as before, yet he still entered with authority and pride in his work and proceeded to prepare the cabin for the evening. "I saved you for last, so we can talk like you wanted."

Leaning against the small sink watching him as he went about the well-rehearsed task of preparing the room, I waited and was rewarded when he spoke again, "I forgot when we met before to offer you an apology."

"You needn't apologize." I said, curious to see where he would take the conversation.

"No, sir, I do owe you an apology," he persisted, "That night in the alleyway behind her house, I dealt you a serious blow 'cause I thought you were that man she worked for. When I saw that you were somebody else, it 'bout scared me to death. I couldn't see much of anything that night, and I felt a mite bit foolish when I saw how different you look from the man."

"So you're the one who hit me as I was leaving her room?" He continued with his task at hand not wanting to look me in the eye, "Actually, I owe you a bit of thanks. That incident got me better access to her room than I got by sneaking around."

He unfastened the top button of his tunic and allowed himself a brief moment of relief in my presence. His guilt assuaged slightly, he clarified, "Some nights I stay over in town. I was there looking for her that night again to see if she had come back. Guess I was just hoping that she was still alive," he paused. "I never have believed in ghosts, but I had to wonder when I saw that light creeping around in her room. Guess I just didn't want to believe that she was really gone." For the first time, he stopped in his work. Taking a bandana from his pocket, he wiped at his eyes, this time moisture coming away with the rag.

"Go on," I encouraged.

He shuffled and took a deep breath before continuing, "When I saw you coming out and putting the key back in its place, I thought you were him, like I said. When I looked at you on the ground, I figured you for a thief. I searched your pockets, but I didn't find anything, so I just left you there." Finishing the statement, he straightened up from where he had been bent over the bed and struggled for something to do with his hands finally finding the folding key used to lock the doors in the coaches. He flipped it open and closed as we talked. "Mister Black, I've told you the truth. I don't know how to make you believe it, but it's the God's honest truth. If I die tonight, I'll go to heaven with a clean conscience and a pure soul."

"Mister Romeo, I believe you." The statement was simple, and his expression lightened, but he held his breath in disbelief. "That's why I'm here. Alone." He stood unmoving afraid of breaking the spell that he had successfully cast, "Everything you have told me I have been able to verify. The only thing is, I cannot find her." I admitted.

"I can't help you with that." He pulled the hat from his head and ran his fingers through his wavy hair. "All I know is that he drove off with her in that carriage."

I sat on the bed. "What time was it?"

"About midnight. I was supposed to meet her, but our train was late that night. She knew I was coming, and she always waited on me. When she didn't show up, I knew something was wrong. I waited at her house for a while, but that woman she rents from saw me." He looked me in the eye, his eyes narrowed. "Guess black skin ain't got no business bein' in the alley behind respectable folks' home." He waited for a moment before he continued. "Anyway, I went downtown and wandered around down by her office for a while. Around midnight, I heard the sound of hooves on the pavement drawin' a carriage. That Mister Samuels drove right up to the door on Polk and went in. I thought that was strange, so I decided to wait and watch. I saw the lights come on in the office. Quarter hour or so later, they went out. A few minutes after that, something comes up out of the ground with him on it. In the dark of the night, seein' a man rise up out of the sidewalk scared me to death. I froze in my tracks until I realized what he was doin'. He had a lady over his shoulder. Threw her in the carriage and took off. Left the elevator sticking up out of the ground and everythin'. I tried to follow, but a black man running through the streets of the city at night draws a lot of attention, and I don't need more than my fair share. He turned onto Church Street then turned again goin' north up one of the avenues. That's when I lost him goin' over one of the rises; I couldn't keep up with the gait of that horse."

His statement rang true as I waited for him to finish, but I needed clarification on the details, "You said 'a lady.' Are you sure it was Nancy?" I wondered. Given his reputation with the ladies at the Southern Turf and the Climax, it might well have been some lady of the evening who had consumed more than her fair share of the drink, but the coincidence would have been uncanny.

When I asked him to repeat his recounting of the evening, it was almost verbatim the same statement. The third iteration was even more akin to the first lending his account the credibility of consistency. It contrasted starkly with Samuels' repeated errors of omission and the misgivings they bred.

He still stood leaning against the wall of the cabin while I looked up at him from the made bed.

I undid my collar and loosened my tie. "Romeo, I appreciate your honesty. I do think you're being truthful with me. Now it's up to me to try and figure all of this out."

He rocked back and forth with the rolling of the train. "So long as you keep me out of it, I hope you do figure it out."

I stood and took his hand. "I'll do my best. Now, I'm not going to keep you any longer. I'm awfully tired, and I'm going to turn in for the night."

He opened the cabin door and looked back at me. "If you want your shoes shined, just leave them outside the door. If you'd like anything else, like a pitcher of water or anything, let me know and I'll get it for you."

"No, I'm fine. Thank you. I'm just going to sleep."

Once he had gone, I pondered his story while I lay chasing sleep. The rhythmic clack of the wheels caught me quickly, and before I knew it, I was lost I sleep.

I awakened to the light shaking of my shoulder by Romeo. He stood next to the berth, a pot of coffee and a single cup on a tray.

"My apologies," I said. "Haven't gotten much sleep lately and the rumble of this beast put me under like nothing since I don't know when." Without thinking and in my early waking state, I made a faux pas, "For that matter you could have done me in, and I would have been none the wiser." I fumbled for an apology, but the man was far more experienced at letting the insults roll off of his back than I was at pulling them back once voiced. He set the coffee down and tidied the few things in the room as if I hadn't even spoken.

As he prepared to leave, he tossed a small barb back. "A dead white man in my wagon would be terrible difficult to explain."

# 21

We arrived early in Chicago, and I took my leave of Romeo for the day to wander the streets. There was a nice enough coffee shop near the station, and I enjoyed the bitter brew in the more moderate temperatures. Chicago's paper was a poor substitute for the news of home. There was no mention of the Vols, only the familiar drums of war in Mexico and Europe where the French had made some gains against the invading German forces.

With a day to spend and literally nothing to do, it seemed appropriate to search out a small gift for Beatrice. I tried a few stores, but found nothing that fit either my taste or my budget. As the morning wore on, the paths I chose funneled toward the finer shopping district of the city where the glint of gold and diamonds in a shop window caught my eye.

My mind and body separated and moments later, I found myself inspecting the quality and style of a yellow-golden band graced by a single precious stone. Such a purchase would not have been impulsive, nor would it have been in reaction to the distressed times we had been experiencing of late. Rather, it was the regret that we were not yet together as one. It was there in her eyes, and only now did I recognize what was so apparent when we had last parted.

Arranging for payment would not have been so difficult. I easily could have had the funds wired, but I opted to wait and buy the ring at one of the fine jewelers back home right there on Church Street. On my return, I would have to focus solely on the lifting of the burden of Miss Nancy Pettigrew from my mind and the resolution of the investigation before I could approach Beatrice unencumbered and with the confidence required. The choice was made, and I determined to make it so at the earliest opportunity.

The afterglow of my resolution warmed me in the light breeze. The noontime hour was long gone and hunger gnawed at me, but I fought the urge until I arrived back at the train station. I feared that to pause would give me chance to reconsider my recent decision. As it was, when I sat down to a late lunch in the station, the reality of the situation began to wash over me. The order I placed wasn't what I wished, but what I felt I could afford in light of the financial sacrifice to be made in the name of my love for Beatrice. I finished the meal right down to the parsley on the side, and depended on that love to fill the remaining void.

There was still some time left before my train was to depart, and I pondered what I could do to spare myself any additional expense. My return fare was already paid for and something that I would be reimbursed by Samuels as part of the investigation. However, my recent spendthrift intentions required balance. I found it by exchanging the sleeping compartment ticket for a coach seat. Admittedly, the move was part of a growing concern that Samuels might skip out on some—if not all—of my expenses and fees.

Arriving at the station, I strolled down to the sleeping wagons at the end of the platform. The cars were only lightly occupied making Romeo's job easier today than it was the night before, their presence simply a matter of maintaining the proper logistics for the railway.

He spotted me and gave an affable smile as if greeting an old friend. I wandered forward. He took the valise from my hand, and motioned me inside the car directing me to an available berth.

"I'm afraid that my ticket is for coach and not a sleeping berth on the return," I told him.

He waved off my protestations. "Your ticket is good in *my* wagon."

"I suppose that's better since it would be more difficult for you to explain a dead white man in your car than in coach." The grin on his face and accompanying laughter told me more than the entire conversation from the night before. I settled in and a short time later, the train began to pull away.

On the way back, we talked more and sat up late into the night. I sat on the bed, and he stood, as the previous night.

I motioned to the far end of the bed. "Have a seat, please. It makes me nervous to see you standing all of the time."

He shook his head. "Thank you, Mister Black, but I'd best not. It wouldn't do for me to be caught sitting down in one of the cabins with a guest."

I felt my face flush with my own embarrassment and I stood to look out the window at the passing landscape as we rode on. "Of course. I understand."

"No, sir, I don't suspect that you do. But I appreciate you saying so just the same."

I wasn't sure how to respond because I knew he was right.

We rode a few moments in silence, the clacking of the wheels the only sound. Then I turned to ask a question that had long plagued me in this investigation. "Where did the name Romeo come from?"

As I looked at him, a smile spread across his face, "She wanted a nickname for me. I was reading Shakespeare at one point and Romeo was the only character she could think of. It just stuck between us."

I leaned back against the wall. "So how did you meet Nancy?"

He looked at me and closed his eyes as he recalled. "She was a passenger on a train from Louisville. She wasn't able to sleep, and I just started talking with her. We talked all night long. When I left, she gave me a small kiss on the cheek. I asked if we might see each other again some time."

He took his hat off and held it in one hand. "She told me, 'We certainly will.' The next weekend, she had a ticket for my car. We talked the whole night up to Chicago. We did the same on the trip back."

He shook his head. "I was dog-tired, being awake all of that time."

My curiosity had been piqued. "So how did evolve into a relationship?"

He cut his eyes to the door, and then leaned closer to me. "Pretty soon she was traveling every weekend on the night train. On occasion, she'd go see her family, but most the time, she spent with me. After the first few times, I taught her the tricks of the rail, and she traveled all she wanted with me. She never paid the full fare.

"Before long, we were sharing a vacant drawing room on the train ride whenever it was available, traveling out on the Friday or Saturday train depending on my schedule and coming back the following night. On a long weekend when I worked, she might ride to and from Chicago or one of the other destinations twice."

"I would shuffle passengers to get an available compartment, and then a fellow porter would cover my station. On the rail, loyalty runs deep." He ran a finger around the top of his hat that he held in his hands. "People don't betray trust within the railroader family, and we protect each other from those outside. That degree of commitment runs even deeper with the darkening of the skin."

"I think I understand now. But tell me. How did you two get about in public?"

His shoulders relaxed. "She traveled in a sleeping car. I traveled as an employee of the railroad either working a shift or riding on a discounted fare. We secretly shared the berth like I told you."

"On arriving in our destination city, she would leave the station and carefully select a hansom with a colored driver, and then direct him to pilot around to the colored entranceway of the station to pick me up. I stayed out of sight in the carriage. From there, we paid the driver handsomely to carry us to one of the local houses of ill repute where we could be together in the city. That was how we arranged our trysts locally as well, at least until she got the corner room with an outside entrance. The key on the top of the doorjamb is mine. I came and went under cover of the night to share her bed."

I put my elbows on my knees. "So how did Samuels find out about you? How did he know?"

He ran a hand over his face. "He was on the train one night and saw me coming out of her room. We didn't know he was on the train, and I never saw him. He told Boo he wouldn't tell."

"Does anyone else know?"

He shook his head. "Two people I can trust on the railroad and Mandy, the colored girls who works at Boo's boarding house."

"How does she know?"

He smiled at me. "Mister Black, colored folks don't miss a thing that goes on in their household. She comes in early in the morning, and she caught me sneaking out one day. But she already knew. She does the laundry and everything at the house, and she knew something was going on."

Romeo straightened up and stood to put the pillbox hat back on his head. "If you'll excuse me. I need to get to taking care of things. Shoes to polish and all. Do you need anything else?"

I shook my head. "No I'm going to turn in for the night. Thank you."

"Thank you, Mister Black. I'm counting on you to make things right. If anybody finds out about Nancy and me, I might not live too long down in your part of the country. At the very least, I could lose my job, and this is about the best job a colored man can have."

"I'll do my absolute best to keep your confidence while I try to set things right. But at the very least, I aim to make sure that we figure out what's happened to Nancy and make whoever's responsible pay for it."

He nodded and left the cabin.

I lay awake longer that night listening to the sound of the wheels as they hit each joint in the rail between Chicago and Nashville. Romeo's story still rang true. Now I had to put the rest of the pieces of the puzzle in place around it.

I stared at the ceiling for an hour or better before I found sleep. Foremost on my mind was how to approach Samuels with the information without outright accusing him and jeopardizing Romeo's fragile situation.

I passed out with the issue of confronting Samuels still unresolved in my mind.

# 22

When I awoke, we were passing through Guthrie, Kentucky on our way into Nashville. I packed my things, and we arrived a short time later in the rail yards in Nashville, where we passed Union Station. Its stone foundation walls rose higher from this perspective in the bottom of the gulch, distorting the impression of the monument's grandeur. The parade of cars passed beyond the limestone monolith and then the equally impressive shed before gliding under the Demonbreun Street bridge, our long file of cars now barely in motion.

The train came to a stop with a jolt, and stood idle for a few moments while the switch was thrown redirecting us to the platform. Without warning, the procession nudged back. As we approached, I felt the cabin shift with the change in direction precipitated by the railway switch. The massive shed cast a shadow over the cabin and all activity on the platform stopped in deference to the iron beast.

With another light bump and an audible release of steam, the succession of wagons came to a halt. Anxious to address two immediate tasks at hand, I had made my way to the vestibule and stood ready to be among the first off of the train. With my single suitcase, the relatively small number of passengers allowed me rapid egress. The door was open in anticipation of the all-clear whistle, which came quickly, and Romeo was out the door, the stool placed at the foot of the stairs.

As I put foot to the concrete, the attendants were already at their job of washing the windows of the newly arrived train preparing it for departure. Further out the platform, the mail wagon doors slid open wide and belched forth white canvas bags of mail.

Pausing, I received that same unsettling sensation that had plagued me throughout the investigation, the feeling that I was not alone. In a minor display of paranoia, I scanned the platform for anyone following me, but found only Romeo, whose attention was focused solely on his departing passengers, particularly a rather heavyset woman in full dress and parasol who was balking at taking the proffered stool.

The platform was a fair walk from the terminal, and I began to make my way. Doing so, I recognized a familiar look in the crowd ahead of me. The strides were long, and the tall figure sparked some memory as I tried to keep pace. The straw hat was common, but the condition of this one had a familiar air to it. Hastening my step I repositioned myself to the side of the platform, away from the recently arrived train. The gait of my mark made it difficult to keep pace forcing me into a trot as I tried to avoid the obstacles of luggage and benches that crowded the unused side of the platform.

Reaching the staircase, I was only paces behind, but the painfully slow plod of an elderly woman slowed me. By the time I reached the top of the stairs, the man was no longer in sight. Hoping to regain him, I raced for the front of the station on Broadway where the carriages stood. A small group of people awaiting a hack clued me in that he was either on foot or had been picked up by someone.

My deductions were rewarded when I reacquired him on the other side of the street. He was a taller man, and he vaulted over the gutter to the curb before he disappeared up Tenth. Dodging the departing hacks and the oncoming trolleys, I rushed for the place of the last sighting, and I reached the corner just in time to see him turn onto Payne Street.

Racing to the intersection, I saw him once again turn north on Ninth and across to Commerce Street heading in a zigzag pattern back in the general direction of the main business district. My curiosity having the better of me, I hastened again through the next few intersections to Church Street and was rewarded with a glimpse of him entering The Doctor's Building.

When I reached Samuels' office, he was just hanging his coat and hat on the rack. He was unable to disguise his shortness of breath from the exertion between the station and his office, and he didn't speak in greeting or in defense. I stared at him in anticipation of some effort at dismissing the incident.

"Why?" I asked finally.

He remained mute, his nostrils flaring as he took on breath like a horse after a heavy run.

"Why?" I repeated. His glare was tainted by the look of fear mixed with desperation in his eyes.

He grabbed me by the arm and dragged me back to his office where he slammed the door behind us. He roared loud enough to shake the glass. "She was blackmailing me. Haven't you figured it all out by now? You've looked into my affairs. You know about the gambling. You know about the embezzling. You know everything. Haven't you figured it out, yet?"

"No," I admitted, ashamed at being so thickheaded.

He ground his fist in the palm of his hand. "She knew about my gambling. She started to take money from the company, then came to me and told me she had done it. She said to keep quiet about it – that she would pin it on me and my gambling."

I put my hand to my head. "So you killed her?"

"No," he paced the room gesturing wildly with his hands. "That's where everything is so confused. I didn't kill her. She was here in the office. Dead. I found her like that. When I did, I panicked. I didn't know what to do. I knew I would wind up accused of it, and that the embezzlement would come out, and I would get the blame for it."

"Wait," I said holding up my hands to stop his erratic steps. "So you're saying that Romeo actually did see you take her out the service elevator that night?"

"Romeo?"

"Her boyfriend."

He leaned over and put both hands palms down on the desk. "Yes. Of course he did. He saw me because he was here. He killed her and left her for me to find. I'll bet he found out about the stolen money and plotted to take it for himself or tried to force her to give it to him. Then he waited for me after he killed her in the office."

I took a deep breath. "How do you know he did it?"

"Because there is no one else who could have. I didn't. No matter what you may think of me, I did not. So if not me, then who?"

"There are other suspects," but my delivery was less than convincing even to myself.

"Like who?"

Ignoring the question, I backtracked having him repeat his claims looking for any manner of discrepancy or errors of omission that I knew him to be prone to commit.

We moved to the front office as he retold the tale. We were the only ones in the office.

I pointed down at the floor where I stood near the front door. "So you arrived in the office that evening – late on a Wednesday night – and found her here?"

"Actually, there," he said indicating an area obscured from the line of sight of the front door behind the receptionist's desk. "It did occur to me that it was rather an odd place for her to be, but truthfully, I didn't make much of it. The discovery of a dead body in my office was quite disturbing as you can well imagine."

"Her desk is there," I said indicating a desk in the opposite corner of the office.

"Yes."

"Was that all that was odd?"

"Not really," He sat down and his irregular breathing calmed. He seemed genuinely to recall more of the details of that night. "Her ledger was out—the one she fixed with the accounts as she wanted them to appear. The accurate ledger with all of her embezzlements is nowhere to be found," he claimed. "That's why Miss Winston was working from the flawed books." He shook his head and muttered. "It doesn't make sense."

I took a seat opposite him, "What doesn't?"

His eyes darted back and forth across the floor. "I thought both sets of books were here. I didn't even think to look for the real ledger until the following day."

"You seem fairly intimate with the details of which books she was cooking."

"It's my job," he defended.

"So what did you do with the body?" I ventured.

Shaken back to the real gravity of the situation, he responded with his eyes fixed, focused on nothing, "Went to the dump and threw her out." He used his hands to hide his eyes as well as any insight into his true emotions that might have been discernible.

Sarcastically, I remarked "You would have done better to have thrown her into the river."

"Do you think so?" he responded bringing me to the stark realization of the self-centered mentality of the man.

We moved back to his office where he took a seat behind his desk.

I stood and fought to keep my voice even. "So tell me the rest."

He sighed and sat straight in the chair to steel himself. I found her here, and I got scared. I went and rented the hansom, as you suspected, and drove her body to the dump. I threw her out there."

Sweat began to bead on his forehead. "I kept waiting for word in the newspaper of her being found. When nothing appeared for three days, I went back to the dump. I found no sign of her – no indentation in the soil, or any remnant of her existence. Granted I didn't tarry long for fear of discovery. The association between us as employer and employee would have been made easily."

He threw his upper body on the desk and extended his arms to me. "Please, Mister Black, help me. This is why I hired you. Help me figure out who killed the poor girl and left her here in my office for my unfortunate discovery."

I stood and moved away from his reach. "Yes. You did hire me, but under a different pretext altogether." I gave him more honesty than I had yet to receive from him, "I simply cannot trust you."

"Black, I have told you everything now. You have it all – enough even to prosecute me possibly." he dropped his head to the desktop.

"If I am to help you, you must answer my questions without reservation," he nodded in agreement.

I gathered my thoughts quickly and made a passing observation. "Where is Miss Winston?"

He drug himself upright and sat rigid in the chair. "Oh. Her? Well, it turns out that she was completely unable to perform even the most basic of math skills." He paused, hunting more excuse, "I wound up letting her go that day when you overheard our conversation. The poor nit was a complete loss, and I'm afraid she has set me back terribly in my own internal investigation of the books. I may never recover."

In my haste, I accepted the explanation without question.

"Tell me about Miss Pettigrew when you found her. Did she show any signs of trauma or did anything strike you as odd about her appearance?"

"No. She was pale as she always is, but nothing other than that."

My other questions met with equally useless responses that proved how unreliable the layperson witness is in the investigation of a crime. The responses seemed genuine, but still something was lacking.

Suddenly pensive, he offered one interesting bit of information, "She could not have been dead long when I arrived. Her body was still somewhat warm, and when I picked her up, she had not yet stiffened as I have always heard that a corpse does." My urging led to more, "She seemed almost to be asleep, not dead, but I found no pulse, and I couldn't feel her breath."

"You're no doctor. Do you think that she might've been alive and you simply misjudged her condition?" My suggestion startled him.

"I contemplated such a scenario, especially after I saw no word of her in the paper and then found her body missing. Perhaps she had simply stood up and walked off. It has caused me sleepless nights and left me looking over my shoulder constantly in fear of finding her behind me. But if she was alive, and I cast her off at the dump, then I may have killed her after all – purely unintentionally, but all the same..." The look of horror that spread across his face convinced me that he was ill capable of murder.

This left me with a potential murder, no body, and now no lead suspect outside of a man who, if guilty of murder, was one of the coolest characters I had run across in the form of a Pullman Porter.

I reached for the door and opened it. "Then our next step is to look for the body."

It was early in the day and the noontime heat would bring the smell of the dump to its pinnacle. I was hesitant to go to the police and divulge the story just yet, still wishing to retain some modicum of discretion considering the reputation of the insurance company which Samuels represented and the delicate nature of the handling of Pettigrew's illicit lover.

I felt the need to bring someone else into the mix lest Samuels be tempted to do away with me in order to ensure my silence. John would have been a good companion, suitably strong in the event that Samuels attempted to overpower me in any way. However, his testimony as a Negro might have proved to be less than adequate—an unfortunate fact—and parting him from his job might not have been possible during the day. Under the circumstances, Beatrice made for a poor choice and her boss was not likely to tolerate my borrowing her for the time. Doc was located only one flight of stairs up from Samuels's office. It was unlikely that his medical skills could be brought to bear, since Nancy had been left to die over two weeks ago at that point. But Doc's inclusion was more for the companionship, and the reassurance that he provided me.

Accompanying me up the stairwell, Samuels was resigned in his movements shuffling along as if he were already a shackled prisoner. His normally rapid gait had slowed to a crawl, and it seemed an eternity reaching the third floor.

We found Doc in his office his receptionist allowed us in as she pulled on her sweater to leave for an early lunch. In front of Doc, Samuels echoed his story with the physician as a witness.

I sat at Doc's desk to take notes with his ink pen. Samuels sat in one of the chairs opposite, and Doc sat in the other one beside him.

Samuels spoke reservedly, his voice soft and broken into phrases, until he mentioned Romeo. Then his fists clenched as he sat in the chair. "That boy she'd been gallivanting about with must've killed her, and then taken the money she had stolen and left me to take all of the blame."

Doc patted him on the arm. "Please, Pilchard. Stick with the known facts. Nathan will draw his own conclusions."

His admonition reminded me to do the same, and I struck the few words of speculation that I had already committed to the page.

When Samuels was done, his head hung so that his chin rested on his chest like a condemned man.

"We should each witness the statement," I said and stood to hand the pen to each man in turn.

Doc took the signed document and placed it along with a small pile of other papers in a locked pharmaceutical cabinet filled with vials of various medications. He secured it with a key from his ring.

Outside of Doc's office, he and I conferred while Samuels waited sequestered in the room.

"The statements are consistent," I began. "It lends him an air of credibility heretofore lacking in dealing with the man."

Doc was visibly shaking. "I agree. Give me a moment to wrap some things up here, and we'll all go together to search for her." He stopped and held a finger in mid-air. "You know, Nathan, perhaps medical forensics is the thing for you given your interests and your training. At the very least, you might want to consider it." Then he smiled and turned toward the front desk to relieve his nurse for the day, and I returned to the room.

Samuels's head was still down, when I walked in.

I put a hand on his shoulder. "I've decided that you are marginally credible, and I intend to humor you by going to the dump to look for Nancy's body."

I squeezed his shoulder tightly. "But I caution you; while I believe your story to some degree, there are many questions which remain to be answered, many of which might come with a study of Nancy's body. If those answers came back as anticipated, you might be cleared of the greater wrongdoing before we might take the matter to the police."

Samuels and I stood to exit the room and allow Doc a few moments to bring his business for the day to a close. We waited only a few moments before he reappeared looking fresher and more relaxed than he had before.

Doc pulled his hat from the brass coat rack. "We can take my hansom. It'll be a tight squeeze, but I think we'll all fit."

I did not refuse his generosity, and we were soon on our way.

The clop of the horse's hooves, along with the sobering nature of the business at hand numbered our senses. Doc whistled a soft tune as we went, but stopped after a block or two. Otherwise, he gave an occasional greeting and a wave to a passing traveler, but said nothing else.

Samuels kept entirely to himself during the ride, and the questions built in anticipation of what we might or might not find. The trip was mildly soggy, the ground moist and the air thick from the numerous rainy days of late. Combined with the warm temperature, the result was a fairly humid afternoon that announced the presence of the piles of refuse in advance as we rode north out of town.

The stench was becoming increasingly overbearing when Samuels stopped us short of achieving the dump. He reached his arm across my chest and pointed at a nondescript point on the roadside. "Here. Here. It was right along here someplace."

When we finally saw the spot where he claimed to have dumped her, I was appalled once more by the callousness of the man.

Miss Nancy Pettigrew's final resting place as intended by Samuels was a puddle of muddy water at the bottom of a steep embankment alongside the road.

We all peered over the edge of the roadway. "I didn't want her found," He looked from one of us to the other hoping to elicit some degree of support for his decision, but neither Doc nor I had any to offer.

I surveyed the muddy embankment. "How did you get down there to look for her?"

Samuels stared at his feet. "I've been no closer than where we stand right now. In fact, not even this close. I drove by to see if she were still there."

Doc raised an eyebrow. "So you could not have discerned any details about what might have happened to the body or make any insightful observation at all, could you?"

Samuels stared straight ahead. "Not really."

I clenched a fist and prepared to strike the man.

Doc caught my look and shook his head to discourage me.

"Well, someone has to look for her. I suppose it will have to be me." I pulled my jacket off.

Samuels remained at street level with Doc, and I slid down into the trench in search of signs of the missing woman. There was no body anywhere near the point indicated by Samuels. There were no signs of there having ever been one there—hardly surprising since a full two weeks had passed since the night of the crime. Looking back up to the roadside, I was unable to discern which of the men was which, the bright sun hiding both of their faces in shadow. Shrugging my shoulders, I continued the search.

The mud was soft and dark, and it dampened my feet as I waded in the drainage, thick with the stench of the runoff. Small bits of paper, broken pieces of glass and a wooden crate littered the ground along with the occasional bit of rotten food– eggshell, brown-leafed cabbage and other indecipherable bits once intended for human consumption.

The foul smell was not something to which one easily becomes accustomed. Hoping that my senses would adjust to the affront, I continued to search, sloshing through the muck and even boldly thrusting my hand down to pluck an item from the standing putrid liquid that swirled around my feet. For my effort, I claimed nothing other than a soiled hand and sleeve which I wiped on my pants leg.

As I surveyed the brush and the muck of the area, I was rewarded with a small scrap of torn cloth, similar to a particular petticoat that I had recalled seeing in the hands of Merriweather. There was nothing that made me certain that the cloth was related to the missing woman, but the find sparked an idea that I determined to follow up.

Turning back into the wind to return in the direction from which I originally had come, I was greeted by a new wafting of the fumes from the refuse that nearly rendered me unconscious. How anyone could grow comfortable enough to work in or near the smell was beyond me. With each new breeze came a new assault that caused me to water at the eyes and break into a cold sweat despite the heat of the day.

I reached the point where I had come down. My companions had disappeared from view, and I clawed my way back to the top of the embankment where I found them waiting in the comfort of the hansom. Samuels had a cloth pressed to his face and nose to fend off the stench.

Doc had likewise pulled a handkerchief from his pocket, and he alone dropped it long enough to inquire, "Find anything?"

"No. No need for you to venture down there. Your expertise is not required."

Reaching the carriage, I extended my hand to Samuels. Let me borrow that handkerchief."

He drew back from me.

I barred my teeth. "I'll take you to the police posthaste unless you give me that cloth!"

He reluctantly handed it over, and I cleaned the remainder of the filth from my hands and then my shoes now filled with fetid water.

I offered it back to him, but he withdrew from it as if I was passing him a poisonous snake.

I cast the cloth into the floor of the carriage, and we began our return to the city.

Doc encouraged the horse into a fast gait as we beat our retreat from the stench of the city dump.

Once the smell of the refuse began to fade a little, I shared my find of the cloth with my companions.

Doc was encouraging. "It might actually be a sign of her."

Samuels offered no opinion only looking at the cloth as if it were a scrap of a shroud.

With Samuels in company, I was reluctant to share my musings on my other suspects and opted instead to bide my time and make the investigation without Samuels's knowledge. Doc kindly drove me back to my apartment so that I could clean myself and don some fresh attire.

He tied the horse off at the curb and stepped a few feet away from the hansom. "John and I will watch Pilchard for the evening. You get some rest and clean up."

"Thanks, Doc. I'll try." I pointed at the carriage. "If he tries to escape, does us all a favor and shoot him."

He put a hand on my shoulder. "I think he might be telling us the truth, Nathan."

"It would be the first time," I spat.

Doc pushed his glasses back up his nose. "Nathan, I just don't think he has the gumption to commit a murder."

"He might not, but I could sure contemplate it right now."

Doc waited a few seconds for me to calm down before he spoke again. "Nathan, is it possible that you've gotten a bit too close to this investigation?"

I stopped and looked him in the eye. "Could be."

He tapped me lightly on the chest. "You've developed an interest in this girl beyond your professional responsibility, haven't you?"

I shook my head. "I don't know, Doc. I just don't know."

I did not wait to see them off, but made for the relief of a warm bath and the comfort of my apartment where I laid down only to sleep away the remainder of the day.

# 23

The following morning's paper brought no news of Pettigrew. Armed with the knowledge that Samuels had possessed for the past few weeks, I too developed the inescapable feeling that Nancy might reappear right behind me at any moment.

Early, I headed for the office with the intention of being at the boarding house in search of Merriweather over lunch. Samuels was dejected and bleary-eyed having not slept the night before, but he was in his office dutifully as Doc and I had instructed lest we go directly to the police with his signed confession.

"I should like to be paid for my services to date," I said.

"Of course." He pulled a check ledger from the drawer and began to make out the draft. "$27.95 was it?"

"Plus the billiards game. But perhaps that had best come from your own pocket." I did not blink.

He stopped writing for a moment, his pen poised above the page. "Quite right. It should," he said and put the pen to the check once more to finish the task. He handed me the check and leaned back to reach into his pocket. He extracted two silver dollars and handed them to me.

I pocketed them myself. "Thank you. Now I have other things to tend to, if you'll excuse me."

He waved a hand and did not delay me as I left the office headed straight for the boarding house.

I anticipated that Merriweather might try to avoid me, so I arrived early enough at the boarding house to catch his appearance. As he ambled up the walkway to the house, I intercepted him at the front porch and redirected him back out ignoring his protestations.

"It's nigh time we had that little talk which we keep meaning to get around to, but never seemed to be able to have," I said. Marching him into a local restaurant, I pointed him to a table in the back of the room where our conversation was less likely to be overheard.

As we seated ourselves, I ordered up a meal of pork roast for the each of us.

He protested, and grabbed the waiter by the arm. "I'll have the roast beef."

I took his hand from the man's sleeve. "No. I'm buying. He'll have the pork," and I rushed the server off.

We sat in silence for several seconds, staring each other down. Neither of us moved. His lips pursed indicating that he had no intention of speaking unless I made the first move. Since it was my confrontation, I obliged him that much.

I took the napkin and placed it in my lap. "So what is the nature of your relationship with Miss Pettigrew?"

"Our relationship is hardly your business," he replied and took his own napkin following my lead.

Aggressively, I responded, "Oh but it is, Mister Merriweather. You see, as you may have figured out, or perhaps not, all is not exactly as it seems. I'm employed to determine exactly what has happened to her and where she is."

His look was immediate distrust as his brow furrowed, "So you're not her cousin?"

I shook my head in reply.

He pounded a fist on the table. "Ha! I knew it! I told that idiot woman that you were no relation to her. But she bought your story, oh yes she did, hook, line and sinker." He began to rise.

I motioned forcefully for him to remain seated. "Neither of us is what we seem to appear," I cautioned. "Or need I remind you of our little run in the other day?"

The bluntness of the remark dropped him back to his seat, but he quickly gathered himself and sat erect to offer a rebuttal. "Nancy and I are, involved, you might say."

It was difficult to conceal the smile that crept across my face. "No, you're not," I responded. "You see, I know her boyfriend. And you are not he." I pointed at him with a toothpick taken from the holder on the tabletop.

His expression was blank, devoid of any emotion, then suddenly very serious. "So you know her boyfriend, do you?"

I sat back in the chair. "I do. But tell me what you know of him." I crossed my arms.

He smoothed the tablecloth in front of him. "Tit for tat. You tell me what you know of him. I have seen him creeping across the yard to her door at night. You should be able to tell me at least one distinguishing characteristic about him if you know him."

"Are you referring to the fact that he has a spine, unlike you, or the fact that the color of his skin is not the same as yours and mine?"

His lack of response confirmed that he knew.

"Tell me about your relationship to Miss Nancy Pettigrew and stick purely to the truth."

"Fair enough." His disposition visibly changed, and he dropped his guard to come clean, "She and I had an agreement that I wouldn't tell the landlady about her *gross* indiscretion."

"And what did she offer you in return?"

He stuck a finger into his collar and pulled to loosen its stranglehold on the sweaty roll of fat that protruded above the starched cloth. "Payment."

At that point, the meal arrived and was placed in front of us. Neither of us moved immediately engaged as we were in another locked stare.

The server arranged our settings and went out of his way to stay clear of Merriweather's grasp. The waiter glanced nervously from one of us to the other, "Anything else?"

We each shook our heads, and the server disappeared.

I raised my eyebrows. "The payment?"

He belligerently shook his head in defiance and picked up a fork.

We ate the meal in silence. He consumed every morsel of the vegetables and spuds. The pork, he cut up and stacked neatly to one side of the plate giving the impression that it was a smaller amount than that with which he had begun.

"Eat." I ordered and pointed with my fork at his meat.

"I'm quite satisfied," he claimed, but his growling stomach told me otherwise.

When I pressured him once again, he turned his head like a child refusing to eat his vegetables.

"Try the pork," I insisted, pointing at the pile of meat on his plate.

Once again, he claimed to have no hunger, but I persisted.

"It doesn't appeal to me. Mine has a bad flavor to it," he claimed.

"I watched you. You didn't put a piece near your lips. Now eat. Take a piece and put it in your mouth," I demanded.

I could see him grinding his teeth in his closed mouth, and the look on his face was growing increasingly troubled.

"As I said, Mister Merriweather, everything is not what it appears to be," I shoved a piece of the meat in my mouth and chewed. "Tell me, sir. How does a Jew become a Bible salesman?"

The curtain pulled aside, he was left without a defense and forced to deal directly with me.

"Tell me about the payment, or I share your denomination with your landlady and your employer, not to mention your predilection for women's undergarments!" It was a malicious threat below the standards of most respectable people, but my patience with the lies and deceit in this affair had worn thin. I wanted simply to be rid of the entire case and find the missing woman's assailant and her body.

A defeated man, he slumped in the chair and divulged all, "Five dollars each month. And I needed it. It is difficult to sell something in which one does not believe—no offense, to you or your religion, Mister Black."

I assured him that there was none.

He threw his hands about as he spoke. "I don't know where she got that kind of money and how she lived the way she did – nice clothes, fancy perfume, trips out of town and everything else." He paused to catch his shallow breathing. "She came up short last month, and it made my life difficult. We argued about it one day out in the garden. She had her laundry with her. She was hanging it out to dry. While we argued, I picked up a pair of her undergarments. She watched while I felt of them—the softness, the delicate lace of a woman."

With his undersized hands, he pulled out a handkerchief and patted the moisture on his shiny forehead. "She watched and did not rebuke me or deny me the pleasure that I derived from them. Our arguing had subsided. So I took the clothing still damp from the wash, placed it in my pocket and told her that those would cover the interest on the debt, but that she owed me the five dollars still."

He replaced the handkerchief in his inside pocket. "Mister Black, she's a wicked person. She then tempted me in a way that I couldn't have imagined. That night a large envelope was shoved under my door. In it was a note and another pair of her underwear, but these had not been washed. They still carried the scent of her. And the note inside it read, "Consider one-half of the debt paid." It was unsigned, and I threw the page out with the next day's trash. The temptation was intoxicating for me, you understand, or perhaps you don't. I'm not a handsome man, Mister Black, as you've no doubt noticed." His face reddened at the admission. "The arguments over suffrage and other issues with Miss Pettigrew were simply a pretext to be around a woman whom I so desired, but had no chance of ever attaining. Mister Black, I believe women to be equal to men in every way. Miss Pettigrew was far superior to many a man that I know. Suffrage did not concern me. Only the proximity to the woman who so desired it. My solidarity with her stance on the matter would have brought me nothing, but my defiance brought me interaction even if it was to hypocritically counter her opinions."

His chin was on his chest. "Alas, she would have nothing to do with me. No woman would. And I don't make enough money to pay a woman to lie down with me and comfort my needs."

For the first time, I noticed how truly unappealing he would have been to a woman. His poor physique and disproportionate featured made him very uninviting.

Wearied by the confession, I supplied the next piece of the puzzle, "So the night she disappeared, you killed her and took her body to her office for her employer to find."

His look was immediately quizzical notifying me that I had offered information to which he was not privy. "What?" he exclaimed.

I reiterated my statement in the rush of the adamant shaking of his head and his muttered denials. "No. No. No. Mister Black, I did no such thing. I could never hurt her." He looked at me with tears welling in his eyes, "She was my master. Without her, I would be lost as I am now."

The pitiful beast in front of me was crushed by the proposition of her death. In seconds, he was reduced to a sobbing mass drawing unwanted attention from around the room. Motioning to the waiter, I quickly settled our tab and escorted the devastated fool out.

As we walked the streets back to the boarding house, I extracted the last bits of information that I needed. The night Pettigrew went missing and turned up dead at her own office, Merriweather was at the boarding house in the parlor. With no money to go anywhere, he was left to entertain himself among the other boarders and waited in anticipation of Nancy's arrival. They could confirm his alibi. Arriving at the gate of the decaying property, we reached an agreement. I was not to disclose his indiscretions, and he was to continue to work with me as if I were Pettigrew's cousin to confirm his story and help me find her murderer.

Entering the house, Merriweather and I were greeted by the lady of the house, his reddened eyes drawing the scrutiny of the woman. "I'm afraid you're both too late for lunch. We have already cleared the table and I won't be paying Mandy extra simply to suit your comings and goings," she began.

Undaunted and with a sense of urgency, he delved into questioning her, "Do you remember the night we were all gathered in the parlor, and we kept saying how odd it was that we were all present and accounted for with the exception of Nancy?"

A frown still creased her face over our late arrival for the noontime meal as she put a finger to her chin in thought.

Merriweather prompted more before I could place a hand on his forearm to still his tongue, "It was the night you played that wonderful new piece you'd just purchased. I believe it was called *Come on to Nashville*," he fawned, causing her expression to soften.

His reminder sparked her memory, "Yes, yes. We kept waiting for her to show up figuring she would fairly soon, but she didn't. Of course, I remember that well," she paused, and then gave him a quizzical look, "But why do you ask?"

Wary that Merriweather had already said too much, I jumped in, "We were just trying to recall when Mister Merriweather here last saw my cousin. He was saying that he hadn't seen her that day, but the night before maybe."

She looked from one of us to the other. "Would you like for me to play that piece again? I think it was enjoyed by all. Not my best piece being new to it and all, but a fair rendition, I think Mister Merriweather would agree."

Offering my regrets, I cruelly declined the offer and committed Merriweather to the mercy of the landlady and her piano playing in the middle of the day. I made the front door, and I heard the first few notes of a naggingly familiar tune as the landlady abused the composition and with it, her pitiful boarder.

I stepped lively as I went, looking to complete one more errand for the day. This one involved Beatrice. I went to the office of her father. And though I waited the better part of the afternoon held at bay by his secretary, he didn't take my meeting. By the end of the day, thoroughly angered at the man's lack of manners, I determined to ask his daughter's hand in marriage—with or without his blessing.

By the time I arrived back at my office, Beatrice was gone for the day. Frustrated with the missed opportunity and poor treatment at the hands of her father, I slumped in my office comforted solely by the presence of a note from Beatrice:

My Dearest Nathan,

You know that I love you with all my heart. My deepest desire is for us to be together. I have come looking for you the past few days only to find you gone away in pursuit of this silly investigation. Your friends have led me to believe that you are in Chicago. If so, I wish you well and hope you find that for which you are looking. I must travel with father this evening and will not be back until next week. It is my sincerest hope that we can have some time that I may explain to you my situation, and why I have behaved as I have. May you find it in your heart to understand.

Yours,
Beatrice

# 24

After perusing the morning's news on British advances against the Germans and a particularly hopeful bit of news regarding a conference to avert the war with Mexico, I made the obligatory search for news of the missing bookkeeper, but there was nothing to be had.

Once more, John had committed to keep tabs on my employer, this time with Samuels's knowledge. The man sat under our own form of house arrest watched carefully for the day by the trusted man who maintains The Doctor's Building. Doc and I also poked our heads in on occasion to be sure that John was well, and to bring him something to eat. The idea of white men bringing food to him embarrassed John, but he adjusted gracefully and never faltered from his job of watching the insurance office manager.

There are few better ways to distract oneself on a Saturday afternoon than within the confines of a ballpark eating roasted goobers and washing them down with a near beer while yelling for the home team. And that was exactly what I determined to do. I hoped the afternoon respite would clear my head and allow me to put together the pieces of the puzzle.

The visit to Athletic Field at Sulphur Dell was a difficult one to justify to my client, so I adopted the philosophy of "act now and ask forgiveness later." I went by way of the Southern Turf for a bite of lunch prior to the game at 2:30.

I opted for a lunch plate and a glass of Jack Daniel's Sour Mash to wash it down. Finishing, I headed back to Fifth Avenue and turned north. The brick sidewalk beneath my feet in this area was passable if a little uneven in spots due to the settling that took place in the marshy area the Dell calls home. I followed the brickwork patterns absentmindedly turning the facts over in my head as I had been doing since the afternoon before.

The ballpark is located atop Sulphur Spring where all manner of animals would come to drink the waters. As a result, the field is really part of a bog and wet weather has its implications. Going my way was one of the mule-drawn carts headed for the dump. In the opposite direction, a lone man walked carrying two jugs full of the foul-smelling liquid from the adjoining Morgan Park.

Game time had arrived, and almost from the moment I crested Fifth at Union Street, I was able to see the wooden skeleton of the Dell. There was movement atop the stadium as the high dignitaries of the ballgame settled into the makeshift press box built on the bleacher roof. The game scheduled for Friday had been rained out and moved to that day making for the first showing of our Vols in a while. The crowd was gathering slowly in anticipation of the doubleheader. Many would arrive late like me to catch the last of the first game and most of the second game against the Crackers from Atlanta; some might never show with the weather threatening as it was.

From the outside, the stadium was an average sporting arena like any other city, but inside, the Dell made the most of the home field advantage. One of the first things you noticed was the irregularities in the field of play. To look at the first-base line, the distance to the fence was a bit shorter than the average ballpark at only 262 feet from home plate.

Even more disconcerting was the lay of the land. As the right-field line stretched out beyond the first-base bag, the chalk began a distinct upward movement around twenty feet from the wall, and it curved up to meet the fence at a point around ten feet higher than at home plate. If the right fielder wanted to play the wall, he did it at the top of the sloping hill called "the dump." If he played in and had to chase a ball back, he had to run up the dump.

The minor inconveniences were one thing. On top of that, when the Vols were in the hunt for the pennant, the crowds got larger. And the owners did not turn folks away. They opened up the outfield slope as seating for the spectators. It was truly a site to behold when the field was offering its fullest advantages to the home team.

That day promised to be one of those more interesting games where our tenth man was literally on the field. Our Nashville Vols were leading the pennant race, ahead in the standings by two games. And on the mound for us was none other than the lethal Tommy "Machine Gun" Rogers. In addition to the usual distractions, the field was wet, bordering on swampy with the rainy weather of the previous days and weeks.

Sitting down to my place on a wooden bench, I surveyed the gathering scene. It was straw hat time in the stands, and my fellow spectators' heads were covered to ward off any threat of heat. Blinkey Horn, the sportswriter for the morning paper sat along the high rows with the other journalists who rated a free pass for the day's entertainment. A popcorn vendor strolled by touting the qualities of his product—hot, fresh, crunchy—and I was an easy mark for the price of a nickel. Soon thereafter in a well-timed, one-two punch, his cohort appeared to relieve me of another coin in exchange for a near beer, the bitter option in the wake of statewide prohibition.

The game began under threatening skies. I pulled the paper from beneath my jacket where I had tucked it into my galluses. There was nothing of too much interest, but the news offered something to do to pass the time between exciting moments in the game.

Shortly it began to rain, the heavy pounding driving many of the spectators to seek shelter. Some of those under the roof decided to make a day of it as well as the thunder rolled on.

The Saturday shot; I sat in the humid air of the afternoon rather than brave the downpour that the heavens decided to bestow upon us.

Alone in a crowd at a baseball game waiting for the rain to stop allowed me to organize my thoughts and retrace all of the events of the past three weeks – the case, my relationship with Beatrice, and even my chosen career.

The monotonous tone of the downpour pounding on the tin roof of the stands numbed my mind. It made me pensive—depressive almost. After a while, all of my thoughts were washed away, cleansed by the falling rain, and then I picked my worries back up again, setting their order as I collected them.

My first priority was the missing woman for whom I had been searching for three weeks. She deserved justice. Knowing what I knew at that point, where would I have begun this investigation? That question haunted me, aware as I was of the information that had been known to my employer all along, and that I might have been able to resolve the case or even aid its guilty victim with those small scraps of knowledge.

My next priority was to declare my love for Beatrice and propose to her as soon as I resolved the case. If I was not finished with it soon, then I would abandon it purely for the sake of our relationship. Beyond that, little else mattered.

On the third matter, that of my career, I debated the merits of returning to the formalities of the medical field—the financial advantages decidedly outweighed the personal reasons—but I could not reconcile the image of myself in that profession. It seemed as if a career had chosen me and followed me around despite a few admittedly weak attempts to shake it in favor of a more palatable means of earning a living. I deferred making any decision regarding my career until I had resolved the first two matters, but I knew that procrastinating on that issue would drag along further than intended.

The game was delayed almost an hour, squashing any hope of getting in a double header. When the rain finally abated, I had already had my fill of the wooden seats and the wet weather. As I made for the exit to go check on John and my employer, a half dozen men in blue suits loitered in the open gates, the trolley conductors waiting for the game to conclude so that they could return their passengers to the main terminal, and from there, disperse them to their destinations throughout the city.

I went by foot merely passing by the window of The Doctor's Building to note that a light burned on that overcast afternoon. It illuminated the office where Samuels sat under our house arrest, but I kept my course, fed up with the case and how it was coming to pass.

I forsook the boarding house for my own home, where I continued to mull over the facts well into the night. Still, some pieces escaped me—not the least of which was the fact that Nancy Pettigrew's body was yet to be discovered. Those missing parts of the puzzle vexed me terribly as I lay on the bed, still fully clothed, and that was how I fell asleep.

# 25

The morning following the ballgame, I made my way through one of the less desirable parts of town. I was in search of John and hoped to have him accompany me on a return trip to the dump. My thought was that the young man might offer a more willing attitude than that of my previous counterparts when it came to digging about in the muck and mud.

Hell's Half Acre is a series of poorly constructed shanties and lean-to's just north of the state capitol. Filled with gambling halls, saloons and houses of ill repute, it isn't a particularly pleasant area and one often left to the coloreds, and the Irish and Jewish immigrants. That Sunday morning, the streets were dotted with the presence of drunkards passed out from the previous night's festivities and even a few tottering ones who still managed their feet despite obvious impairment. None of them could provide any useful information in locating the man who shined the fixtures in The Doctor's Building.

Spying a colored woman of some resolve hanging her laundry out on the line on what was likely one of her few days off, I walked over to the makeshift fence that defined her own little tract of land. Her line was attached on one end to the corner of her shanty, on the other end it tied off to a rake handle stuck in a metal pipe. Everything in her small area was made up of cast-off items salvaged from other people's lives.

Asking after John, I was embarrassed that I didn't know his surname, and I was forced to identify him by the place of his employment. The woman was naturally suspicious of a white man on foot searching for a black man early on a Sunday morning. Had I been on horseback or in a carriage, I doubt that she would have offered me any information at all. However, she replied, "I think he live on the next street over. Ask over there 'bout 'im."

One street over was slightly rougher than that I had just left. Halfway down the block, I encountered some of the damned who lived in this corner of Hell. The three men seemed to materialize out of thin air from behind a nondescript assembly of boards and chicken wire meant to serve as a home for some poor family or even families. They sized me up quickly and two blocked my way going forward while the third obstructed the road behind me. Outnumbered and in no mood to fight, but realizing that there might be little choice, I attempted to bargain with them. The offer of four bits for information on John only served to pique their interest further and tipped my hand that I did indeed have money on my person.

They stalked slowly toward me, one shifting a long pine board from his left hand to his right. Another toted a pipe.

Given the choice, I was not sure which would be a worse fate, and in my panic, I began to threaten them. "I'm with the police, and you had best back off!"

It caused the man with the plank of wood to falter in his resolve, but he took his initiative back up again when his friend assured him.

"He ain't no copper. 'Sides, he ain't goin' to be tellin' nobody nuthin' once we done wid 'im."

Pride might have made a better man stand his ground and fight, but common sense urged me to make a run for it. My odds were best at getting past the single man behind me. Then I heard the sound of quick footfalls behind me as another person joined the fray.

"Mister Black!" The voice was winded, but it was a friendly beacon in this part of town. John stopped long enough to catch his breath only a couple of steps further from me than the other man. His hands were on his knees with his labored breathing. His galluses dangled loosely about his knees in his haste. "I'm glad I found you. Missus Jones told me you was looking for me." Then as if noticing the other men for the first time, he shouted, "Whatchall doin'? This man can have y'all lynched jes' for actin' like you might do sumthin'. Git on outta here 'fore he has ya'll all taken to jail."

The three dispersed grumbling at the quick end to their early morning exploit.

One threw the wooden plank to the ground and it clattered loudly in the quiet Sabbath morning. The one behind me simply vanished into the maze of shanties.

John came quickly to my side and took me by the arm and kept a wary eye on the remaining man holding the lead pipe.

The lead pipe stood his ground a few seconds longer until he was alone and outnumbered by John and me. And then he spat on the ground and stalked off.

John pointed back in the direction from which he had come. "C'mon. Les' go dis way." He quickly moved to guide me around the corner and out of Hell's Half Acre as fast as possible.

It wasn't in the direction of the dump, but I didn't argue the point.

Once we are clear of the more offensive shelters my eyes still darted side to side in the wake of the confrontation. "How did you know I was looking for you?"

"Missus Jones sent her boy runnin' fer me. Said she sent you to the next street over, but she thought you mighta gone the wrong way. She know it rough over there, so she sent him on ta git me."

Missus Jones might well have saved my life." I told him as we walked.

"Jes' might," he deadpanned.

Quite the odd couple, we traveled out Eighth and arrived a short time later at the point on the roadside where Samuels had disposed of Miss Nancy Pettigrew.

John gestured with both hands. "He lef' her here?"

I nodded. "She's most likely dead, but we haven't found the body."

He shook his head. I guess he figgered she been wid a colored man, he gonna treat her like she colored, and jes' toss her out side da road."

I pulled the hat from my head and ran my fingers through my hair. "I won't argue that point with you, John. But let's see what we can find and get out of here before the sun starts to stir the smell too much."

"Smells like Hell's Half Acre do sometimes." With that, he jumped down the embankment into the muddy ditchwater.

Together we trudged through the sodden ground at the bottom of the trench where Miss Nancy Pettigrew was last known to be. The water that covered my feet to the ankle was as cold as the trail.

The ground offered nothing new. It was covered in standing water that had grown fetid with the smell of the rotting wet garbage that surrounded the area. Still we were in search of something that must exist, there was only a question of where.

There was little possibility that the body could have moved from the trench in which I stood. It was deep and the mound of dirt on either side was imposing, especially for anyone so incapacitated as Nancy Pettigrew was purported to have been. Still, I thought that she might've been alive, and if so, that she might've crawled out from her makeshift grave. I sent John in one direction while I headed in another looking out into the brush along the ditch. The thicket was dense, but a short ways down, there was a break. Pushing the branches aside, I stepped through and into a different world, the sight of which was even more disturbing than that of the refuse heaps.

## ~ THE DOCTOR'S BUILDING ~

In the small opening was camped a conclave of beings that bear only a passing resemblance to the human race as society has come to know it. Their faces were dark, burned by the sun and dirty with grime. Their clothes were mismatched layers of indiscriminant men's, women's and children's clothing collected from the mounds of garbage cast off by society just as these people were. Their hair was unkempt and thick with grease from not bathing. They are known simply as the dump people. No one really knows, nor even cares exactly where they live other than to know that they are somewhere in the proximity of the refuse heap. What I spotted was the nomadic formation of a gypsy camp hidden away in the brush, only yards removed from the place where Samuels claimed to have disposed of the body.

A small fire smoldered under their makeshift tarp. In the middle of the gathering, various articles of well-worn clothing hung on the limbs of trees around the tiny colony. The filthy band of creatures was either unconcerned or unaware of my approach, and I was upon them before they had a chance to scatter or otherwise react, which they didn't do in any case.

My presence among them was unique. I myself was a mess having been foraging in the downpour in the muddy trench alongside the road, yet I was no comparison to them in all of their squalor. Here, I was the outcast in my waistcoat and newly soiled work boots. The troop was friendly enough offering me some of their soup and a place to sit, both of which I graciously declined, hygiene being a serious concern.

As I related the story, the tribe gathered closely around me cutting off what little breeze there might have been. They listened intently but cautiously.

"You with the police?" one asked.

I threw caution to the wind for fear of alienating them. It might be a trap to determine my viability as a target, but I denied any involvement with the authorities.

"Part of my team awaits me at roadside," I said indicating the general direction from which I had come and hoping that no one checked.

As I finished explaining, an elderly woman moved forward sweeping her arm to clear a path among the vagrants that were her companions. "We seen her. Bastard threw her out like yesterday's news. Figgered she was some high-priced whore got outta line," she paused and wiped her runny nose with her sleeve. "Ain't no way to treat a body no matter what they done. Ev'body deserves a bit of respect when they time comes," she growled looking as though her *time* was growing near, the wrinkles on her face accented by the grime that covered her face.

I swallowed hard. "So what happened to the body?"

"They's a man in town what takes care of our kind," she snarled.

"Really?" The surprise in my voice was poorly masked.

I drew a look of shame from the woman before she confessed the limits of his assistance, "'Course 'e don' bring that motorcar ambulance. 'E jus' brings is ole horse drawn one 'e ain't 'ad reason enough to git rid of yet. We sent somebodys a runnin' fer him and he come on out right away. He takes 'em over to the schools and they cut on 'em for practice then they give 'em a respectable funeral. Least they claim to. Who knows? Maybe one day one of our bodies 'll help 'em learn something.'" At that comment, the entire crew gave a muted round of laughter followed by hacking and wheezing coughs.

"Can you tell me where to find him?"

She obliged me with the name and address of an unfamiliar undertaker. Before I could begin my way back to the embankment, I found the woman clinging to my shirtsleeve, and in a pitiful plea, she told me the plight of her small clan and the cholera epidemic that had been sweeping the city and had wiped out fully half of their population. My first reaction was that this particular plague might be God's way of clearing out some of the lower echelons of society. Once my head cleared and I put aside my prejudices, I realized that this might be God calling on me to act. I hastily agreed to see what I could do for her and her friends before returning to the ditch where I left John. Though I searched for him, he was nowhere to be found, and I clawed my way back to the top of the embankment where I found him waiting.

He was crouched just beyond the lip of the road, his eyes darting back and forth along the roadside. He stood up when he saw me ad walked over to give me a hand up the final bit of the slope.

"I wasn't goin' to git in there wich ya', but I's watchin' ya' the whole time. If'n you'd needed me, I's there, but I didn't think them folks would want a black man wanderin' into their camp and all."

"That's twice you've gotten my back today, John. Looks like I owe you a couple of favors. But now, I've got something to work with. We need to get back and get changed." We set a brisk pace as we returned to the city, eager to put distance between us and the encounter.

Making short work of my clean up, I was quickly back on the trolley headed for the funeral director's place of business. Undertaking is a dreadful occupation made all the more unpleasant by the advent of the automobile, which causes horrendous mutilations. When someone is gravely injured in an accident, it is the mortician who responds with his ambulance. The living are couriered to a physician. If your life is in peril, it is best to hope for a skilled mortician who is able to distinguish the living from the gravely ill, and is honest and not past due on his rent. Otherwise one might find themselves the victim of an overzealous gravedigger, put out of their misery as a favor to the victim and their family as well as the funeral director himself.

Morticians make me especially uneasy. When I have to deal with them, it's in the line of some of my more unpleasant business. Further heightening my anxiety is the fact that I have never seen one seated. The entire profession seems populated by irritatingly slow moving men who always stand, tireless individuals who work all manner of hours handling the dead.

The man I met was pleasant enough in nature, even if unsettling. The bony fingers of his hands moved constantly, always busy at some task. He wrote. He tapped the table. He folded his handkerchief. Or he simply clasped his hands, but never for long before he set them to work again.

His calm manner coupled with my knowledge of his trade made me squeamish in his presence. He was amiable and proved to be of the honest variety of his profession.

He motioned me to follow and I trailed along behind him, his hatless, balding pate to me as he spoke. "Yes, I remember the girl. Sad state she was in at the time. Soiled unbelievably badly, like she had been rolling in the mud. Whoever had given up for dead and abandoned her certainly did so in a most coldhearted way."

I grabbed him by the shoulder and spun him around. "So, she was alive?"

He took a breath before answering, apparently accustomed to outbursts in his profession. "Not to the inexperienced eye," he cooed. "But I've seen many a body in my day." He drifted to the side, dug a fag out from his vest pocket and lit it. Drawing in deeply, his next words came in a long exhaled cloud of tobacco-laden smoke. "She hadn't passed on. No." He wagged a bony finger at me. "Close to it though. About as close as one can get without being gone."

"So what happened to her?" I held my hand out to him as if he might place the answer there.

He turned from me and began walking down the hallway again. "Took her to the hospital. They're the only ones could care for her properly. Wanted to take her to General, but she was so bad off, I went ahead and took her to the one nearest me when she started to convulse." He drew another breath of smoke before continuing. "Didn't think the poor thing would make it. From the looks of it, I might've been doing her a favor if she hadn't, but that's not really my place to decide, though there's times for sure that it would be a blessing. Folks who wouldn't have been able to recover no matter what – severe blows to the head, bleeding that won't stop. You know what I mean, I suppose."

"I suppose. But where did you take her?"

"Told you. The hospital."

"Yes, but which one?"

"Ah," he said realizing that he had not given the name, "The Women's Hospital."

"At Eighth and Union?" I almost screamed.

He turned and looked me dead in the eye. "It's the only Women's Hospital I know of."

He adjusted the white rose on his lapel. "I left her as a Jane Doe. The attending physician pegged her as a prostitute and refused her at first. I was missing other paying opportunities. So I got the doctor to take her anyway. It was easy to see that her case was one of dire need. That and a small payment convinced him to admit her."

Thanking the man profusely for his time and paying him more than the cost of the bribe spent on the doctor, I raced for the building across town, but only steps away from Samuels and my own offices one block up Polk Avenue from The Doctor's Building.

Out of breath from the run, I arrived at the red brick building standing alone at the top of the rise. Its interior retained the permanent smell of freely splashed disinfectant. Cold, white ceramic tile covered the floor and the walls up to chest height. Starched linens shrouded every gurney and bed in view and the crisp aprons of the nurses layered over their regular street clothes provided a pure white canvas on which any stain or untidiness was easily noted.

I located my contact, an old friend from medical school. He had always been a smart one, and someone who kept his head about him. He fit the mold of the medical professional perfectly.

He wore the same wire-frame glasses that I remembered from school, but had added a few pounds to his frame. He had lost a bit of hair on his head already at his relatively young age.

His glasses perched on the end of his nose, he greeted me with a smile, but when he saw my state, his look changed to one of concern. "Nathan, however are you? Are you alright? You aren't looking to well."

I was out of breath, but managed to speak, my hands on my hips. "Quite well. Good to see you. Sorry for the intrusion. I'm still looking for that girl I called you about."

He shook his head. "I already told you, there's no one—"

"She's here. An undertaker brought her in two weeks ago. Covered in mud. Left her as a Jane Doe."

His eyes popped open. "Well, that's an honest mistake. I didn't think she was the one you were searching for," he apologized. He had attended to her himself as a charity case, and she did not fit the profile I had given him. Yes, she was attractive, but I had described her as a strong and independent woman and an acquaintance of Beatrice, probably much in the same vein as my own love. The woman brought in that night did not fit that description. In retrospect, the mole on her chin he did remember, but could not recall it from my sketch given over the phone.

"Could it have been someone brought in on another night, by a different mortician?" he asked, and to which I gave him a firm negative response. Consumed by his own thoughts, he considered the options. "She must be the one since I don't recall anyone else being brought in under similar circumstances."

"Take me to her, please," I said. He motioned to the door, and we moved in lockstep down the hallway and up a flight of stairs.

All the while, I peppered him with questions about his patient.

"Is she alive?"

He placed a pencil in his pocket. "Yes, she is alive."

"Has she recovered?"

He walked faster than I could keep pace. "Yes, she's recovered quite well."

"Any ill effects from the trauma?"

"No, she didn't seem to have any ill effects as a result of the trauma she's endured."

As we reached the floor, he stopped at the door to the hall. "There are some things you should know, especially if you are seeing this girl," he said.

"I assure you that the relationship is purely professional. She's a missing person for whom I've been searching on behalf of a client for the better part of two weeks now," I told him.

Torn between his friendship with me and his professional obligation, he decided to run with friendship. "Nathan, let me tell you," he began. "This woman has endured a severe trauma. She was in a coma for two weeks as the result of an overdose."

"An overdose? I'm afraid I don't—"

He put up a hand to silence me. And then he put a hand on my shoulder. "Not only that, but she was assaulted as well, if I'm to believe—"

It felt as if I'd been punched in the stomach. "Assaulted?"

He held his hand up again.

"Nathan, I must tell you, our discussions became very frank as she realized the severity of her condition. She confided a great deal in me. I'm betraying that confidence to you as a friend, because I feel you need to know these things before you pursue this further. The assault apparently took place after the overdose. She claims not to have had relations with a man for several days prior to the affair."

I staggered at his words. "Are you certain—"

But he stopped me yet again.

"And, Nathan, I do hope for your sake that you are not seeing her as you say, but if you are, you should also know that she is with child. Still in her first trimester, but nevertheless with child. And the fetus appears to have survived the coma, though it may experience some ill effects. It'll be difficult to know until the child is born," he paused again waiting for my response, but I gave none awaiting the remainder of the information.

"Nathan, if I'm to believe her account, and I've no reason not to, and there's certainly nothing to be gained by her making this story up, the child is that of a black man whom she's been seeing."

He bit his lip with anxiety afraid that he had shattered my heart with the revelations, but determined to allow me to retain my honor in the situation. Silenced by the disclosure, my friend attempted to minister to me. "Nathan, you've demonstrated far better judgment when it comes to women. Why would you turn your back on Beatrice for such a trollop?"

My initial reaction was to take offense, not on behalf of myself, but on the part of Miss Pettigrew whom I had come to know through her acquaintances and of whom I had drawn, quite a different picture. Still

I stayed my protestations and motioned for him to lead on allowing his suspicions to run unchecked rather than be forced to offer more denials that would only fall on deaf ears.

He relaxed his shoulders ever so slightly as we walked and tried more familiar ground with me. "But Nathan, why on earth did you quit medicine? You were far and away the best in our class. You did so well in your studies. I simply cannot understand the path you've chosen."

I shrugged. "Perhaps it was a poor choice on my part, but I simply lacked the enthusiasm for it. It just wasn't for me, I suppose."

"It didn't have anything to do with —"

"No." I cut him off. "No, it had nothing at all to do with that."

The final few steps of our trek carried us to the end of the corridor in silence. Arriving at the ward, my friend stepped over and addressed the nurse. Taken aback, my friend gave the nurse the same look I had seen from dogs on hearing a high-pitched whistle. Keeping a professional distance, I was unable to hear the discourse even as it grew louder.

The friend waved me over, "My apologies. She's no longer here. Apparently, her personal physician arrived this morning and issued a discharge order for her. The order was eagerly received, and she's already checked out. Her physician even settled the bill."

And likely as not, Miss Nancy Pettigrew had fled not only the building, but the city as well.

"Her personal physician?" I inquired of the nurse.

"Yes, a nice older doctor. I've seen him here before, but I didn't handle the orders personally, so I didn't catch his name. I can look it up if need be."

"Yes, please. Thank you," I said.

I fidgeted while she retrieved the paperwork, but my friend had more, "One last thing Nathan. About this drug overdose, this addiction has led her to excess once. Over the past two weeks, she should have been able to get past the withdrawal. But there's no guarantee that she won't go back. If she does, look for the telltale signs – bluish lips and fingernails, pinpoint pupils, weak pulse, shallow breathing and muscle spasms. If you see anything like that, just know that she may be back on the morphine."

The word stopped me cold in my tracks, and my mouth hung wide open.

The physician nodded his head in silent confirmation.

A sudden rush of realization came over me. The feeling of having been made a fool flushed my face.

Not waiting for the nurse, I had already made the door by the time she returned with the file in her hand calling after me to ask if I wanted the physician's name or not.

# 26

Entering The Doctor's Building, I struggled to put together a rational string of events leading to this particular conclusion and fought at the same time to define a path by which it was false and there could be a positive outcome to the entire affair.

A light burned in Doc's office. The Mississippi Florentine glass diffused the glow enough to hide the images, but could not disguise its passage. My footsteps were heavy in the hallway announcing my approach. His door was open – ajar even. Taking the brass handle in hand and unsure of what to expect, I braced for anything. The lights were out in the reception area, and I passed quickly through, pushing past the swinging gate in the waist-high counter. A slice of light bled into the hall like a beacon directing me onward.

He sat, pen in hand, composing a letter. The desk lamp cast a bright, round beam that blotted out the remainder of the room in relative darkness. It threw its light on a page of stationary covered in writing in blue-black ink with which he was engrossed. His look was startled, but not surprised as if he had expected someone else. "Hello, Nathan," he said.

"Hello, Doc," was all I could muster.

"You're actually a bit earlier than I'd anticipated," he sighed. "It would seem that I've been party to a most unpleasant set of events, far darker than I'd ever imagined. I got caught up in that downward spiral of sin that the evangelists are always preaching about. It's scary how right they can be after the fact, and how wrong they are in the midst of battle."

"How did you get mixed up in all of this, Doc? How could you use me like that? How could you pretend to be a friend when you were nothing of the sort?"

"Of all that has happened, that wounds me the deepest, but I know you can't believe that right now. You can't put stock in anything I say, but from this point forward, I'll give you nothing but the truth." He gestured to the chair across his desk where so many of his patients had sat – recipients of both good and bad prognoses. "It's a long story, Nathan. Pull up a chair."

The seat was slightly warm as if recently occupied.

He took a deep breath and sat down at his desk, lowering his body into the chair. "I'm afraid I'm guilty of resorting to the same tactics as Samuels, engaging in errors of omission, and failing to provide you with all of the details of my background. You see, morphine has been a secret acquaintance of mine since the War Between the States," he began.

"When I was wounded by that stray rifle shot, I was fortunate that it merely grazed my spine, and I retained the use of my legs. However, the resulting pain was immense, and up to that point acquainted with such pain only as an observer, my suffering had been unbearable. I was given laudanum for the pain. That was my first personal introduction to the drug.

"As an assistant to the Union surgeons, I had access to it in sufficient supply, though the South had lacked it for their use. The quantity required for me to support my habit was unaccountable in the middle of a war where morphine was used as commonly as if it were water.

"At the end of the war, I suffered through terrible withdrawal, but managed to come clean of the drug. When it came time to select a career, I moved into the medical field and back within reach of the accursed elixir. Personal fortitude, if you will allow me that much, saw me through the next several years as I became a young practitioner.

"Years later, I was thrown from a horse late one night going to visit a sick patient. I hit the rock wall along the pike and landed on a stone mile marker. The fall aggravated my wound, and I found no relief. I carried morphine with me when I traveled, and in my haste to reach my patient, I dosed myself for the first time since the end of the war. It was the only thing that would allow me to get back on the horse and complete my journey.

"From that point on, I constantly resorted to the numbing of my senses to alleviate the pain in my back. Maintaining large amounts of morphine on hand is common in a medical building where so many procedures are performed in the doctor's office without benefit of hospitalization. The results were not telling for a time. My life continued to run its course and I maintained a steady, thriving practice.

"As I got older, manning the practice daily became increasingly a burden. The morphine made it possible to continue, but my body required larger and larger doses as its tolerance for the drug grew higher.

"Twice I overdosed by accident. The first time, I awoke in a morphine hangover in the comfort of my own home, late for the day's appointments, but none the worse for wear. I sent word to the office that I was sick. I went clean for almost four days after that, and then the withdrawal had set in driving me back to the drug cabinet.

"The next time I was less fortunate. I awakened to the sound of my nurse entering the office. She thought me asleep and suspected nothing other than that I was overworked. I was unable to make my appointed rounds that day for the lingering effects and left the office telling her that I had developed influenza the night before and had become so ill that I could not get myself home so I had stayed in the office.

"Yet my fight with the addiction was not so simple. Many a day I left the office in a morphine-induced stupor. Anyone who saw me simply assumed that I had been tippling a bit and no heed was given the matter. My trusty mare would see me home, if I could at least make it to the carriage.

"One night on the edge of a particularly strong dose, Miss Pettigrew happened upon me. Adopting the stance associated with a progressive woman's attitude, she had helped me struggle to my hansom. For that small favor and in the hope of keeping the matter quiet, I had insisted that she accept payment. A week later, she caught me in the same situation. Shortly thereafter, she began to lie in wait for me.

"Whether it was concern for an intoxicated surgeon or greed wasn't clear at first. Either way, she began to appear every night with an uncanny ability to detect my departure and when she missed me for one or two nights running, I fell into the habit of making payment for the missed nights and the favor of her silence.

"Determined to be free of the situation, one night I stayed late in the office. As I sat in the office waiting for dusk to fall, I heard the reception room door open. The soft steps proceeded down the hallway in the direction of my office. The door ajar, she leaned against the frame and gently pushed it open the rest of the way with her foot.

"From that point, things digressed rapidly. She began coming to my office to meet me rather than waiting for me to appear. It wasn't every night, but most nights. And each night, she refrained from the numbing compound of which I partook, watching in morbid fascination as I administered the dosage. I offered to her each time, but she maintained her resolve and steadfastly refused.

"One night she arrived at my office, ill-tempered and with a terrible headache from the day's work. I had already taken my measure for the day and was prepared to leave. She asked if I had any powders for a headache. I responded by asking about the severity of the pain in my trained manner. When she moaned in pain as a response, I simply moved to my cabinet and extracted a measure of the morphine drawing the plunger back to siphon the liquid."

He dabbed at his brow with a handkerchief, his hands trembled with the confession and took a sip of water before continuing.

"She didn't resist. The dosage was slight. Enough to dull the pain. Enough to relieve the suffering. Just a taste. An introduction, if you will.

"The next night she arrived early enough to catch me administering the drug. Bothered again by recurring headaches when I made the offer again, she didn't refuse. She watched intently as I prepared her syringe. As I brought it to her side, and swabbed her arm with an alcohol-imbibed cotton ball, she was critical of the amount noting that it was a fraction of mine. I explained how my long-term use of the drug had led me to this point and that a dosage for her in such an amount might be fatal. I explained how morphine dulled the pain, but that it also slowed the heart rate and made breathing more shallow leading to heart failure or respiratory arrest in an overdose. As I moved the needle toward her arm, she turned her head to avoid watching the steel point pierce the skin.

"Things went on in this manner for a matter of weeks stretching into months. She partook whenever she had a headache, which was fairly often. In fact, they became increasingly frequent, probably as a result of addiction setting in. Once, she requested a vial and syringe to take with her. I asked her how she would inject it when she couldn't even bear to watch, and the matter never came up again. But whenever I administered the drug, her thoughts and our discussion were consumed with its trappings, properties, uses, effects and the potential for overdose.

"During that time, I was making not only the payment, but also providing the drug. That combined with a series of other poor financial decisions left me heavily taxed. I was unable to retire and unable to go on working as I had. The added burden of Nancy became something that I just couldn't afford.

"I explained that fact to her one night as I administered a dosage for her. She was understanding. She offered to help me financially—

what little she might be able to. I was unaware of her embezzling, so I took it as the naïve thinking of a young girl. We parted company and the burden of the past few months was temporarily lifted, but from personal experience, I knew it would return.

"A few days later, she showed up on the doorstep of my home banging on the door in the early evening and causing a general ruckus in the neighbor that didn't go unnoticed. Clutching at her stomach in pain, her nose ran uncontrollably, and she wiped it with her sleeve in lieu of any other option than simply to allow it to flow.

"I hurried to the door, and ushered her in. Once inside, she first sought to cajole me into providing her with a dose of the opiate. She quickly resorted to begging me for a prescription. I declined, not wanting to provide any evidence of my wrongdoing in writing that might be traced back to me.

"In the full throws of withdrawal, she cursed me in words and phrases unfamiliar a mannered young woman, blaming me for her addiction and insisting that I give her a fix. I tried to deny having any in the house, but she knew that to be untrue and began demanding in a screaming rage. When I insisted that I had none, her ire rose to a tempestuous tirade of shouted insults and threats. Then she ran to the front door, yelling her intention to go screaming through the neighborhood and tell everything. At that, I relented, gave her a dose and sent her on her way.

"To her credit, she tried to wean herself from the drug, but her efforts never survived more than three or four days at a time. The scene repeated itself at my home twice more before I decided to remain steadfast in my refusals. When she showed up again, her entreaties and verbal abuse were fruitless in convincing me to give her a fix.

"Aware as I was of her unpredictable nature and unsure of her intentions to follow through with what she threatened, I still balked at getting the drug. What transpired during that time of withdrawal induced rage crossed the line. She pleaded with me. Pitifully at first, then increasingly insistent. Then as if sensing a weakness, she offered herself to me. I refused, but realized that she posed a very real threat to create a situation beyond control if she was willing to make an offer so extreme. I went to retrieve a vial and syringe from my bag in the study, and for the first time, I contemplated overdosing her and being rid of the situation for good. Unable to reconcile in my mind how that scenario might play out and coming to my ethical and moral sensibilities, I banished the thought.

"When I returned, Nancy was standing stark naked in the hallway her arms stretched out as if asking me to take her and dance. Taking her wrist into the pit of my arm and swabbing the joint of her arm, I injected the serum. As I did so, she leaned over and kissed my neck.

"I froze. Rather than risk making the wrong choice, I became a passive observer. When she pulled closer, I felt a stirring that had lain dormant for several years. Her hand pulled free of my arm and moved to the front of my pants. I wanted her, but embarrassed, I admitted that I could muster nothing. My extended use of the drug has rendered me impotent, and as much as I wanted to find pleasure, I was completely unable to participate. It was no fault of hers, though she perceived it to be in some way a shortcoming of her beauty or her charms, and she took great offense at the rebuff.

"She didn't appear again for the next two nights. One of those apparently was the evening when you met her, Nathan. A fair moment between some brutal ones. Then she appeared at my office in nearly the same state of withdrawal as she had been before. She demanded the drug. Demanded that I give her a vial and syringe and warned me not to try any of my tomfoolery. 'I won't be subjected to the embarrassment of that again,' she said before threatening to expose my every indiscretion.

"As I ushered her in to my office, I recognized the near collapse, and the threat it posed. I prepared a syringe for her and one for me as I had done before and placed them in my lab coat pocket. This time, when I reached for my pocket, and she averted her gaze, I switched the syringe and delivered my dosage to her.

"She went out almost immediately. Within minutes her heart rate slowed to a fraction of its normal pace. Her breathing became so shallow that I couldn't detect it. Had I held a mirror to her mouth, I might've known she still had some life in her. At that very moment, I don't know what I would've done. I might've even given her more, most assuredly killing her. Now with some distance on the entire affair, the thought of my actions keeps me awake at night wondering what could've been, and the answers don't comfort me." He took off his glasses and rubbed at his eyes with both fingers before replacing them.

"The deed done, I had no idea what to do next. Already in a stupor, but also in a panic, I took an extra dose to calm myself. It allowed me to collect my thoughts though in an admittedly clouded state. I waited until the offices were empty, then used her key and put her in her office. To the casual observer, it would look like heart failure.

"Taking her up via the stairwell, I deposited her body in her office, then went and pulled a ledger from her desk and opened it up to the final page of entries. I left her to be found in the morning. My own senses were so impaired by the morphine that I couldn't detect the faint signs of life that she may have exhibited.

"As for her assault, I point the finger squarely at Samuels. I'm simple incapable. She was left unattended in a locked office accessible only to him, and he was seen by Romeo removing her from the building and disposing of her at the trash heaps. Lord knows what may have happened to her there, but he's at fault in that regard," he said tapping his fingers stiffly on the desk to emphasize his denial.

There was precious little that I could offer Doc in his confession, but I absolved him on that count. I noted that the dump people who had found her included a woman with an oddly placed sense of dignity who had watched her body since the time it was placed amongst the garbage.

Relieved somewhat by the dismissal of one charge to be brought against him, he continued, "I waited for the other shoe to drop – for her body to be found in the office, for there to be an inquiry. None was made. No body was discovered. I panicked thinking that she might've regained consciousness and now lay in wait for me. After a few days, I determined that not to be the case as she would have already come for me in search of her much needed fix.

"Then a few days later, while eavesdropping on gossipy conversations, I got wind of something. I overheard my nurse talking with a receptionist in the building, your Beatrice, as it turns out. She said that her boyfriend was being brought in to look for the missing girl. His office was to be just around the corner."

"Two hours later, I staggered into your office. I think you know the rest." He took a deep breath and exhaled.

An awkward silence hung in the room daring one of us to speak. He stood and walked to the medicine cabinet. He opened it with his key, withdrew the witnessed confession of Samuels, and handed it to me. "You'll be wanting this. I'm just composing my own right now, if you'll allow me a moment to finish."

I steadied myself on the arms of the chair and forced myself to stand, "I guess I left the fox in charge of the henhouse." I took the letter from his grasp. "I have a phone call to make."

"I know," he replied.

"Can I trust you to stay put while I make it?"

"I've been here waiting for you all afternoon. Why would I leave now?" he hunched over the desk and picked up his fountain pen.

Walking to his receptionist's desk, I picked up the receiver and called for the police. The call took only a moment, but I lingered at the counter not wanting to face a dishonored friend.

Returning to the room, I found Doc slumped over his desk, a rubber hose bound around his arm and the syringe still protruding from the crook of his arm. My first reaction was to grab for the needle, but I quelled the instinct, realizing that it was too late the moment I had left the room.

Beneath his extended arm lay a page of stationary, the ink of the ornate script still wet and addressed to me:

*Dear Nathan,*

*By the time you read this, I will be gone. The favor of your friendship has been greatly appreciated in these twilight moments of mine. I trust that we have been afforded enough time for me to clarify everything. If not, please accept my apologies and rest assured that I had the best of intentions to do so.*

*Anything I tell you about Miss Pettigrew, I tell you in confidence. There is little need for her to be further disgraced.*

*On the subject of my dishonor, so be it. There is no one who will be harmed by it, only some colleagues who will be offended. Some may be disappointed.*

*This may be an awkward request for you, but please allow me a bit of dignity, more than I deserve, and do not share this note with the authorities. I have prepared a shorter statement for them that should cover the issues and provide sufficient clarification for you in your investigation to ensure that justice is done.*

Hastily scrawled at the end of the page apparently written immediately after I had left the room was a short postscript:

*The breath of the living is cheap, so I did not insist that our friendship was genuine. Please accept the words of a dying man and know it for what it is. My friendship is true, and my betrayal causes me far greater injury than you can imagine.*

*Doc*

Beneath the letter was another page written earlier, the ink already dry:

*To whom it may concern:*

*Let this clarify that I did provide undocumented treatment of Miss Nancy Pettigrew with morphine, did intentionally promote her addiction to the drug, and did subsequently attempt to kill her by means of an overdose.*

*After doing so, I then placed the body in her office using her key to gain access and left it there for discovery. Her subsequent mistreatment and abuse (of which I learned from a colleague) is not of my doing, but I am at fault for her condition which allowed it to occur.*

*There being no reason for me to deny the attempt to murder her, please accept this as fact and exhaust all efforts to bring any other culpable parties to justice.*

*In death,*
*Dr. Mortimeyer Breedlove,*
*M.D.*

I read and reread the notes until the police arrived. It didn't take them long, but it was enough for me to have been over the contents of the two pages repeatedly. On hearing the officers in the hallway, I quickly folded the page intended for me and stuck it in my jacket pocket to honor Doc's request.

I explained to the police about the case I had been working on but gave them precious little detail which annoyed them to no end. They asked questions for which I had no answers, and then they repeated the questions to get the same answers. They listened attentively and took copious notes while I spoke. They kept me far longer than necessary. But in the end, they honored my professional discretion, and based on my good personal standing with the department, they released me under my own recognizance with a stern warning to not leave town until the matter had been cleared up.

Somewhere in the wee hours of the morning, they rolled Doc's body out of his office, and a short time later, they escorted me home, dropping me off at the front door to my apartment building.

# 27

My senses were somewhat dulled by the affront they had endured over the course of the night. The arrival of the police, the subsequent questioning, my inability to provide answers, and the arrival of the undertaker to carry the body away were all a blur.

Opening the door to my apartment at four in the morning, it was in this condition that I entered. No longer aware of my surroundings and my mind reeling from the twist in this affair, some pieces remained unaccounted for, but not for long.

As the door closed behind me, a sense of incongruence rushed over me. Before I could process the inconsistency, the lamp turned on. Seated in my rocking chair was none other than the previously assumed dead—Miss Nancy Pettigrew. She was a gaunt specter of the beauty I had known. Feature for feature, she was exactly as described, soft-faced with milky, white skin and a firm jaw. But the paleness lent her an unhealthy look and her strong jaw stretched the skin around her skull. In the shadows of the light where she sat, her hair lost the chestnut coloring and faded to black. Her figure was thin from the ravages of the morphine overdose and the subsequent hospitalization, but still somehow underneath it all, her beauty and intensity managed to bleed through. Her presence was menacing in and of itself, and it was made all the more so by the derringer she held in her left hand and which I recognized from the dresser in her boarding house.

"Seeing as to how you let yourself into my apartment, I felt it my right to let myself into yours." The voice, gravelly as described, held the pistol with the barrel pointed loosely in my direction.

With her right hand, she motioned me to take a seat on the bed. Noticing my gaze fixed on the weapon, she warned me, "Let me assure you that I am quite good with this. I grew up on a farm with two brothers who taught me well. Don't make me prove it," and she indicated the bed again, this time with the barrel.

I doubted that she would fire within the confines of my apartment building and risk awakening the entire occupancy. But at the same time, I had come to realize that there was a great deal unexpected in this woman and a willingness to commit murder was not something that I cared to discover at this point. Resigning myself to a more cautious approach, I took the indicated place at the foot of the bed.

Sinking into the mattress, we stared for a few moments, each one sizing up the other. Unable to bear the silence and growing increasingly perturbed at being held hostage in my own apartment, I ventured to speak, "I've been looking for you. And when I finally find you, it's in my own room."

"You didn't find me, Mister Black. I found you," she stated flatly.

My pride again wounded by a strong woman, I sat in silence for a moment drinking in the details of the situation. I chided myself for letting her get the drop on me. I should have gone to her boarding house to intercept her rather than going to Doc's office first. The day's discoveries had me involved to the point of distraction, and it had not occurred to me that she might not immediately skip town. I tried an offhand remark to lighten the gravity of the situation. "That dress looks nice on you. I believe that's the one that I picked up."

She bowed her head to look down at the dress, "Yes, I believe it is. I wondered how it came to be there and suspected that you had picked it up, though I cannot fathom why you might have done so. However, that *is* part of the reason that I wore it." Then after a prolonged wait, she curled a lip and spoke, "Since you have taken your own sweet time getting here, Morti must have been true to his word and done as the poor fool intended."

"If you mean that he killed himself, then yes. However, I see no honor in his being true to a promise to kill himself. He betrayed me. Betrayed my trust," I spat, and tears began to well up in my eyes despite my attempts to hide them.

"The good Doctor betrayed us all. You, me, Samuels, that bastard! Before any of us, he betrayed himself."

Anger made her rigid in the chair, and she gripped the gun so tightly that her knuckles turned white. A few seconds passed, and her shoulders dropped, and the blood began to flow in her fingers again, as she wiggled the hand holding the gun.

She turned her head to the side, her fingers to her mouth and her brow furrowed. Her eyes moistened, and she heaved a few deep breaths stemming the flood of emotion behind a broken façade. If I was to take her by force, that was the time, but fatigue slowed my reactions, and I remained wary of the unexpected with her in my diminished state.

I motioned to the pistol. "Please don't shoot me by accident. I f I die intentionally at your hand, that's one thing. But to die as an accident would be most embarrassing."

She snuffled and cleared her nose, wiping it absentmindedly with the hand holding the revolver heedless of the added weight that it bore. I shall try to be as cautious as the situation permits."

Then she laid the gun in her lap but kept her grip on it. "How did you get involved in all of this?"

I put my hand to my mouth and coughed. "Fair enough. You have the gun, so I'll go first. Samuels hired me on. I don't remember the exact date. I do remember that it was the Monday following the day I met you. We spoke of Johnny Dodge."

"Ah yes, Johnny Dodge." She threw her head back and gave off a soft resigned laugh before turning her head and muttering to herself, "Samuels could play the odds and still lose every time."

"I'm afraid I don't understand," I rubbed my eyes and played dumb trying to draw out what may remain yet untold.

"Surely you know about his gambling?" I saw her mouth move, but her eyes were hidden in the shadows.

I nodded my head. "It seems to be quite a serious habit."

"Well, he was a lousy gambler. Always took the long odds trying to make up for the money he lost taking the last set of long odds. He has a terrible compulsion when it comes to wagering." She shook her head in disgust, "I tried to convince him to take the small stuff, but he still had to go for the big ones, not that Johnny Dodge's was big, mind you. But even taking the ones with good odds, he still missed. If I remember correctly, a sister in Memphis was to be the beneficiary." She picked at the arm of the chair with her fingernail.

"Elizabeth Dodge?" I recalled her name from the open letter written to the newspaper a few days prior.

"I believe so. The name sounds familiar at least. At any rate, that was one of ours." She held up a slender solitary finger.

"One of your what?"

"One of our policyholders..." realization creeping across her face, she looked me dead in the eye, "...in his scam."

"His scam?" I leaned forward at the first significant departure from what I already knew.

"Yes. His. 100 percent his idea. Of course, he couldn't execute it without me involved. He can't even add two plus two and have it come out the same each time. He claims that the numbers flip flop on him or something when he looks at them. He never even finished sixth grade. He lied in order to get the job. Had a fake diploma and everything. And since he couldn't do the books himself, especially with a bookkeeper looking over the figures every day, he blackmailed me into it once he found out about Romeo. Sure, I reaped the benefits as well, but nothing like the numbers he was taking out."

"Wait a second," I stopped her. "I need to understand all of this, if for no other reason than to keep Romeo out of it. Can you walk me through this from the beginning?"

She took a deep breath and laid the right hand over the left still holding the gun. "Pilchard Samuels is not the man you perceive him to be. He is a more despicable creature of tarnished character and ill intent. He hired me for my attractive figure and pretty face with the intention of pursuing me romantically. I'm not being arrogant, Mister Black, he's told me as much. Luckily, I saw through him fairly quickly and squashed his early advances."

"Samuels was not easily deterred. He began to follow me. I didn't realize it. At first, I just thought it ironic that we seemed to show up at many of the same places. Then it began to dawn on me what was going on. But generally, he had better things to do on Friday evenings in the Gentlemen's Quarter, so he suspended his stalking each weekend from the time when I boarded the train until I returned to work on the following Monday.

"He was determined to find a means by which to win me over. His luck turned on him, and he became desperate. And he followed me on the train. I didn't know it at the time, but he had a plan to bilk the insurance company to support his habits.

"But he couldn't find me on the train. As the train rolled closer to Louisville, he chanced on a sighting of me as Romeo was leaving my compartment. He hid in the vestibule and waited for Romeo to go back to his station. Then he knocked on my door. I thought it was Romeo, just coming back. When I opened the door, he pushed his way in while I was till in the act of adjusting my clothing. It was obvious what had been going on." She glared at me from the shadows daring me to pass judgment on the matter.

I did not oblige her, and I leaned back on the bed using my arms to support me.

She twisted a loose strand of hair around her finger and tucked the lock behind her ear. "He just grinned and said "Oh, but it does, my dear. It does. It concerns me greatly because I need some assistance, and I have just now found someone who can provide that very thing." I didn't know what he was talking about at the time.

"I thought at first that he intended to force himself on me, and I prepared to scream. It would have brought Romeo running, and Samuels would have been pulled off at the next stop.

She took a deep breath causing her chest to heave. "But he assured me that that was not his intent especially in light of his recent discovery that I was tainted more deeply than he might have ever imagined. Then he proposed a deal.

"In exchange for his silence, he wanted me to fix the books. With a bookkeeper in hand, he was ready to hatch his plot. He promised to make it worth my while, providing a small allowance of the take for me.

"Samuels began diverting policies. His agents turned them in and got credited by his books, but the company never saw those transactions. Over the course of a few months, the plan built up a core group of policyholders who submitted their payments each month to the post office box in the Arcade. I processed the payments, paid the commission due the sales agent and Samuels pocketed the rest giving me a token payment. It was an annuity with little risk. I tried to improve our odds, or at least defer the inevitable. I insisted that we pick healthy younger people from the new policies.

She heaved a deep sigh. "The plan was functional and practical—until one of those phony policyholders died—which eventually would happen. Samuels threw away his money at the gambling tables in the Gentlemen's Quarter. He even took a trip and lost everything he had on a riverboat at one point. His losing streak extended and he put down increasingly more in an attempt to win it back.

"I used my small take on extravagances like new clothes and trinkets. I wore store bought dresses, the finest garments and spent freely on perfumes and makeup. My appetite for the finer things grew, and I skimmed more off of the books. Samuels was ignorant of the entire process, so he was none the wiser. It just goes to show that women are equal or better."

I suppressed a small grin. "True. Women are often a man's equal. But there is no honor among thieves."

Her mouth hung open. "So you make me out to be a thief? Well, I suppose that's deserved."

I waved off her embarrassment. "I won't dwell on it. Is that all, or is there more?"

Her shoulders relaxed. "Much more. The diverted policies impacted the revenues for Samuels' territory. After a short time, he began to receive pressure from the home office to produce more sales. The phony policy holder scam had decreased sales over a period of months jeopardizing Samuels' position and threatening to expose his transgressions."

"We suspended new activity for a month having already established a steady recurring stream of income by that point. The income was sufficient and held Samuels for a while until recently, when his gambling habit fueled by indiscriminant tippling and whoring took a turn for the worse. His cash needs increased just as the funds began to plateau.

"No longer able to afford the women, he became increasingly aggressive and offensive in his suggestive manner with me and other women who surrounded him. I kept him at bay by citing Trinidad and all of his railroad family as my protectors. Still his leering glance permeated the office and nothing I could say stemmed his lewd remarks and open ogling."

She put a hand to her head. "Headaches plague me off and on. The pressure of the situation cultivated a headache the night that Breedlove first administered the morphine. The tension of the situation was lessened when the home office relented on its pressure to perform, and we began to issue phony policies again, but by then I had developed a taste for it. The morphine steadied my nerves and allowed me to continue on."

She rubbed her temples with the thumb and forefinger of her free right hand. "I could use some now."

I thought to jump then, but held on to some thread of a hope that things would turn out such that violence against a woman would not be necessary.

She replaced her hand in her lap and sat up straight. "Then a policy holder died. The sum of the payment was not as high as it could be—one hundred dollars, but the timing was poor and we were both forced to shell out of our own paychecks to meet the shortfall. In addition to that, Samuels' had no experience in the paperwork associated with paying a claim nor did he know the procedure to follow." We were flustered. We scrambled, worried that we would be discovered, but we managed to pay the claim.

"Shortly after that, Doc cut me off. Pardon me if I'm blunt, but around that same time, I missed my time of the month. At first, I blamed it on the addiction. I viewed his retraction as a blessing in disguise until the withdrawal set in. I was desperate for release from the withdrawal. Concerned that I might already be pregnant, I took the view that it was my body to do with as I pleased. And with a mulatto baby growing in my belly, my world was in ruins anyway.

"Then it got worse," she said. "Johnny Dodge was one of our policyholders that we had tapped to be part of our plan. When you told me about him, I went back in and told Samuels. We had to come up with the money to pay off the policy, and we simply didn't have it. We plotted all night on how to cover it. I was holding out on how much I had, but even that was not enough. That bastard fool Samuels went off that night and used his *gambling skills* to try and win it, but that only made matters worse. By the next morning, he had thrown away what little we had been able to scrounge up." Her voice trailed off. "It was all a house of cards."

"Our discussion that next day bordered on panicked as we tried to figure out how to establish sufficient funds for the policy. The stress of the situation coupled with Breedlove's denial of the drug resulted in a tremendous headache, and then the withdrawal began again. I sought him out that evening, and he overdosed me.

"I regained consciousness nearly two weeks later. The ordeal taxed my body so heavily that it took days to recover and regain some degree of strength lost during that time." Her strong resolve served her well – a lesser woman would not have fared so well, not even Beatrice, I fear. She thought long and hard about the situation, and how she might proceed.

"Breedlove found me and masqueraded as my personal physician. I hated the sight of him, but made a deal with him anyway. He signed me out just as he thought I might be found. I went to his office after he had released me to be sure that he followed through on his end of the deal. I found him there alone much the same way I had the first night I went to his office. As I walked in, he smiled and motioned me to the chair, the chair.

She ran the finger of her right hand along the barrel of the pistol. "He admitted his offense freely, and I offered to kill him where he sat. He replied by sliding a sheet of stationary across the table."

She showed it to me. It was a duplicate of the letter he had composed for the police.

She pointed at the page in my hand. "He asked in return that he be spared the last portion of his life that he might have a chance to meet with you to clear things up as a friend. I assume that he did so. After that, he was to subject himself to the same fate as that to which he had intended to oblige me."

I started to rise from the bed startling her and causing her to level the gun at me anew, "Sit down. You've already almost died once tonight. I wouldn't push your luck any more."

"How's that?" I asked.

"You showed up at Doc's office just as I was leaving," she said. "I had just opened the door when I heard your footsteps in the hall. I left it cracked so that you would come on in, then I hid behind it." She paused and stared, an expressionless poker face, "If you had looked behind that door, it would have been the last thing you ever did because you would have met with this gun." She shook the derringer at me.

Understanding crept upon me, as I realized that I had been Doc's appointment with fate, and while expected, he did not welcome it. It had come more quickly than he had anticipated.

Deciding to call her bluff now that I had the entire story, I rose, "My legs are falling asleep, and I am tired of sitting." When she didn't respond, I staggered on wobbly legs to the window. "I'll stand if you don't mind and watch the sun come up."

At the window, I saw that it was in fact twilight and that dawn was breaking over the city. Steadying myself with both hands against the wide casing of the window, I inquired simply to satisfy my curiosity, "Where did the name Boo come from?"

As I peeked back at her, a smile spread across her face, "First time I met him, he happened on me in my drawing room on the train. I hadn't shut the door all of the way and it fell open when he knocked. He scared me half to death. Every time after that, he called me 'Boo,' and it just kind of stuck between us."

Encouraged, I returned my gaze to the rising sun and ventured to press my luck. "Miss Pettigrew, with all that you have told me, you do appear justified in your actions."

A loud grumble gave voice to her skepticism.

"Granted," I continued, "there are certain things that happened early on for which there is a price to be paid. But you have killed no one. Your crime is not a capital offense. As a matter of fact, given that you are with child, I think that the court would grant you an unprecedented degree of leniency," I lied.

I heard her pick the gun up out of her lap. "I don't aim to find out."

I continued to stare out the window intentionally avoiding her gaze while I sought more solid arguments to win her over. "And what is to become of my illustrious employer, Pilchard Samuels?"

She shifted in the chair. "If he were a colored man, I'd just point my finger, and he'd be dead or in jail for what he did to me. As it is, it would be his word against mine and there's nothing to be gained by that." The chair creaked as she fidgeted in it. "Rest assured though, he will get exactly what he deserves one day, and until then he will live every moment of his insipid life in fear of the reprisal yet to come, constantly looking over his shoulder, unable to sleep, double checking the locks on his doors and jumping at every loud noise." She wiped spittle from the corner of her mouth with the back of her free hand. "He will never be allowed to outrun what he's done."

"So you intend to kill him?"

"He well deserves it, but far be it from me to decide the fate that the Lord intends for him. Better that he does it himself and keep my conscience clean of the matter." Her words cut bitterly. "I've already put him on notice of my return from the dead. And his superiors will be most anxious to speak with him when they receive my ledger. It was between the mattresses in my room, where I had put it every night. I left a copy at the office as well. Twice the work, but well worth it. It's a wonder that you didn't find it, sleeping right on top of it like you did."

Annoyed at having been outdone once more, but not wanting to agitate her, I shifted the focus of my question looking for a common ground. "You are a religious woman then?"

"Mister Black, you ask a lot of questions, but you hear more than most do when someone speaks. I imagine that serves you well in your line of work."

I turned my back to her once more. "Well Miss Pettigrew, I am growing tired of this little parlor game of yours. Here is what I think. You have no intention of killing Pilchard Samuels, and he must be high on the list of people whom you might consider killing. I, on the other hand, have done you no harm and may hold the key to your defense. I doubt you are going to shoot me. You've not killed anybody yet and there's no sense in starting now."

The chair stopped rocking.

I yawned. "A gunshot would awaken everybody in the building, and it would only make matters worse."

I heard a groan from the chair as she rose, but I stood steadfast at the window looking at the sun breaking over the city. A floorboard creaked, and I turned to find her upon me with the stealth of a cat, her eyes wide and her arm raised to strike me before I could react.

# 28

I awakened on the floor of my room. The sunlight had crept across the sky and beaded down brightly in my eyes. My head was sorely tender, both on the forehead where I had been struck and in the rear from where I had met the windowsill in my fall. The fault was mine for turning my back on a desperate woman.

It was already noon, and she was long since gone. Dizzy from the fresh wound, I drug myself to the sink and doused my face with water from my cupped hands trying to get my wits about me. The effect was only mildly effective, but it was enough to propel me out the door and onto a passing streetcar.

I rode into town, the haze nearly dropping me to my knees as I stepped off. The stop was only one block removed from the boarding house, but it was a journey that wore me to the bone. Pushing through the front gate, I rounded the corner of the house with reckless abandon headed for the outside entrance of Nancy Pettigrew's room.

The door was unlocked, and I staggered in, clearly unprepared for another confrontation even with the frail and embattled Miss Pettigrew, but I didn't expect to find her. The closet stood open, the valise gone. A considerable amount of clothing still hung in the closet, much of it practically new. The reading glasses were gone from the writing desk. Some of the perfume bottles appeared to be missing and the drawers had been hastily ransacked for their more promising items.

A small pile of clothing lay in the floor, the clothes she had worn the night before when she waylaid me in my own home. My strength failed me, and to avoid blacking out, I dropped to my knees. Kneeling there amongst the scattered pieces of clothing, I gathered them in my arms. The smell of her perfume lingered on the waist and the skirt. Her undergarments carried the aroma from being next to her skin. Unable to stay awake any longer, I collapsed on the floor. I regained consciousness in the fading light of the late afternoon some hours later, stiff and aching from the hard floor that was my resting place.

Still handicapped by my aching head, I made for the post office box. When I arrived and looked in, I found it emptied of the stack of letters from the previous visit. Disappointed, I staggered back to the boarding house letting myself once more into the room and passing out on the mattress.

The following morning dawned clear and pleasant, the sunlight landing on a single sheet of paper left on the desk, a hastily written note from Nancy dated from the previous day that I had not seen in my hindered state. It was to the landlady:

> *Thank you for the pleasure of the room over the past several months. It may come as little surprise that I am no longer in need of it. I will send a forwarding address. My cousin, Mr. Nathan Black, may come by to gather some final things. Please extend the courtesy of the room to him should he so desire it. I understand that he has already paid through the end of the month.*
>
> *Sincerely,*
> *Miss Nancy Pettigrew*

I knew better than to hold out hope for the forwarding address or ever seeing Nancy Pettigrew again.

Despite all that had transpired, I remained fascinated by the woman. I had seen her with the curtain drawn back, but somehow I managed to see past that. The aura that had surrounded her in my mind's eye had been enhanced instead of diminished with the knowledge of her flaw. Perhaps she was deeply flawed, perhaps more deeply than I thought, and perhaps beyond recovery. But still, her vision consumed my mind, and I wondered at what might have been.

Maybe the last blow to my head had completely undone my senses, made me irrational. But I thought of how I might have won her heart. I disregarded the penalty that she would no doubt be required to pay for her misdeeds, and I dismissed the issue of her addiction as a fleeting weakness that she would easily overcome. Her disregard for society and its boundaries was a youthful rebellion.

I would go with her to her family and be her beau. I would walk proudly down the street with her on my arm. I would help her fend off the demons of addiction. With me by her side, she would be different. My integrity and my determination would become hers. She would inherit those qualities from me. I would have claimed her.

But I would never know.

# Epilogue

After a lengthy discussion with the police and further explanations, the remainder of my day was shot, the fresh wound to my head driving me to bed early yet again. Awakening in my own apartment the following morning, the return to my usual morning ritual was a welcome event. I gathered the daily journals for a long morning of reviewing the news of the past few days. Broadsheet in hand and coffee at the ready, my first sip was warm and bittersweet, but it went untouched and subsequently cold after the first savory mouthful.

Tommy Rogers and his Nashville Vols managed to move on, much as their former teammate likely would have urged them to do. Out on the road on a hot evening, they had faced the in state rival Lookouts, an admirable adversary in third place in the Southern League. Only the tough New Orleans team boasted a better record.

That win put the Vols in a great position, but to win it in the fashion that they did made it that much sweeter. Tommy "Machine Gun" Rogers started the game retiring the first three sluggers one right after the other and continued on in that fashion, taking down his opponents as they came to the platter each time – three up, three down for seven consecutive innings.

In a flawless outing for the Gallatin Gunner, he attained the ultimate pinnacle afforded a baseball pitcher, a perfect game. The feat required the Herculean catches of two mates – Billy Lee and Gus Williams—whose contributions were deemed only slightly less impressive than the pitching of their leader.

Only two other pitchers have achieved the feat of the perfect game in modern times and the great Thomas "Shotgun" Rogers had added his name to the list. Unable to let history be forgotten, the reporter, Blinkey Horn, deemed it important to record that Tommy performed his feat and "Not a batter did he hit…" Journalists increasingly move about with neither culpability nor respect for good manners, unlike in the days of Grantland Rice.

But the news went cold like the coffee. This very morning's paper caught my eye and stopped the coffee from touching my lips again that day. A new and most unpleasant precedent had been set. Useful and a relatively new tool, electricity has become fairly prevalent. It makes its mark impressively along the streets in the form of lights and trolleys. Its mark on the home brings light and refrigeration, but it also has a dark side.

Like a handful of other states, Tennessee had figured out how to harness the tool to do its dirty work. According to the account in the newspaper, Julius Morgan had the distinction of being the first man electrocuted for a crime in the state of Tennessee. The event must have been more horrific than that relayed by the sterile reports. That he deserved punishment was of no debate. That he received such a severe penalty was the fate of a colored man living in a white man's world.

A few moments later, I was brought back to more current issues by a rapping at my door. A young man appeared there, an electric fan in one hand and a clipboard for me to sign in the other. I took the delivery and never went back to the news as I spent a few moments trying to determine the best placement for the fan to provide me with some small respite from the heat.

I had put off my next order of business nearly the entire morning. Now I grabbed my hat and pulled on my jacket intent on the obligation I had made of myself to Beatrice. It had been over a week since we had last spoken due to my preoccupation with the affair into which she had thrown me. It was nigh time that I made my true feelings for her known and took her hand in marriage. And I planned to meet her as she departed from work this evening.

I rode in on the trolley to Church Street and proceeded casually through the heart of the city's commerce, intent on visiting each of the jewelers before settling on doing business with one. At the corner of Church and Capitol Boulevard, the twenty-foot high clock atop a lamp post marks Stief's corner, the three story jewelry store of such reputation in the southeast. The street lamps are extinguished in the daylight, but the timepiece captured my attention and at 2:00 by its mark, it lured me to the storefront beneath the wrought-iron canopy suspended by four thick black iron chains. The recessed double doors admitted me to a cavernous room akin to that which Ali Baba must have experienced.

Glass counters on massive legs were filled with bracelets, rings, earrings, necklaces and other trinkets and formed a hollow rectangle of charms to entice the mind. A clerk waited on me from the middle of the counters ready to show me anything that I pleased. The complement of silver, china and other gifts lining the walls was impressive and one that I felt certain Beatrice would approve of. A stairwell in the back led to more upstairs, but I never made it that far, entranced by the wealth of options contained in the counters before me.

There were more choices than I might've hoped for, and the decision was a long and arduous one as I sought perfection within my price range. After poring over the choice of a ring, I settled on one that was simple, but elegant like Beatrice herself. I did not know the measurement of her finger, but they offered to size the ring accordingly if it was not exactly as she needed. Once I had decided, the purchase required that I forfeit virtually all of my savings including the check from Samuels. The clerk generously offered to hold the ring for my return. At the bank, I withdrew all that I had and cashed the check leaving little more than was sufficient to maintain an account. The entire experience took far longer than I intended, and by the time I concluded my transaction, it was the clock on the street that reminded me it was nearly 5:00, and I rushed to catch Beatrice before she departed her office for the day.

A new face greeted me as I entered the office where she worked. When I inquired after Miss Rose, she responded by asking as to my interest. On learning who I was, she instructed me to wait while she informed the doctor that I was here. Protesting that she need not interrupt him and wanting to forestall the inevitable meeting with him in the wake of Breedlove's death, I was left standing in the waiting room while she trundled off.

Her employer was vindictively glad to see me now that his colleague and my protector was gone. The severity of his enjoyment at my loss was distasteful at the least. A German friend once told me that such emotion is referred to as *Shadenfreude*. It literally translates to mean the malicious enjoyment of another's misfortune, but no English word accurately translates the level of spite intoned by that word in its native tongue.

However, his pleasure was only partly founded in the death of my ally. Casually wiping his hands on his smock, a dark streak staining the white coat, he informed me that Beatrice had resigned her position as of last Friday. Assuming that there was more to the story, I self inflicted the injury by asking him for a reason which he gladly supplied.

I hit the Polk Avenue stairs taking two at a time with reckless abandon.

My heart was pounding by the time I reached the gate to Beatrice's house where I was greeted once again by Beatrice's twelve-year-old sister dressed in her own Sunday best. We both looked dressed for an occasion, but she was consumed with playing hopscotch, holding her doll and tossing rocks into the appropriate squares drawn in chalk on the concrete in front of the house.

Seeing me, she quickly told me that which she was aware I wanted to know, "She's already gone."

Completely winded, my right side aching from the run, I was doubled over with my hands on my knees trying to catch my breath. "Where...is...she?" I managed.

"They left already." She didn't look up from her doll.

"Where?" I panted and leaned against the porch post.

"To the train station silly. Where else?"

Still not sufficiently recovered to run any more, she offered more details of the most recent events to which she had been party.

"I got to be in the wedding. I was the flower girl," she preened. "Caroline was the bridesmaid," she said offering up her accomplice. "Darren is really sweet to me. He brings me something every time he comes over. He got me this doll," she said holding up the same doll she had presented over a week ago for my inspection. "Daddy says he's going to save his business. He said that Bea should marry him. She cried about it a lot, but in the end, she said it would be good for Daddy's business." She continued to ramble on, "He has a car. Daddy says he's a bit of a jehu in it, but it's nice. I think it makes a lot of noise, and it stinks."

I was paced the front porch perplexed about what to do next.

The little girl droned on, "Beatrice said she saw him when she was out with you to the theatre the other night. She pretended to be sick and came home early to avoid having him see her out with you."

Her words stopped me in my tracks. "Damnation!" I spat.

The twelve-year-old's mouth and eyes flew wide open at the curse and her face blanched in horror.

I continued pacing on the porch my side aching still. "Sorry. I don't mean to offend."

"Daddy says you shouldn't say things like that—"

But I was no longer listening. I dragged myself to the gate and began with a more paced effort to make my way to the Union Station. Had her employer told me that she were leaving today I could have run to the terminal instead of her home, and had a chance of catching the train. As it was, the locomotive was due to depart any minute and my detour to her house had cost me precious moments in which I might have managed the train.

The closer I got, the more the fatigue tore at my limbs and deterred me from my goal until I found myself running into people on the street.

The steeple of the shrine of the railroad loomed ahead taunting me that it could be seen from this distance yet still be so far beyond my grasp. A block removed, I heard the shrill whistle of the departing train and was forced to pull up in admission of defeat.

I staggered the final block to the station and walked past to stand on the viaduct over the tracks on which the trains are carried to northern destinations. The train had finished backing up and the engine was beginning to pick up momentum traveling away. Where I stood, the train must pass directly beneath me. As it did, the plume of the locomotive chugged a filthy stack of smoke that covered the bridge and bathed me in the soot and ash of the iron monster.

Looking down on the tracks, I saw the cars roll past. For an instant, I thought that I saw her face in the window of one of the sleeping cars staring back at the station. In the next instant, I imagined that I saw Nancy Pettigrew's face looking warily back as well. Only then did it occur to me that Pettigrew might have chosen to wait and leave on the Wednesday-evening train bound for Chicago with Romeo rather than leaving on the previous day's train without him. Had I caught the train what would I have done? Beg Bea to marry me even though she already had married someone else? Had Pettigrew arrested or begged her to forsake her Romeo and stay with me?

Standing on the viaduct, it shook with the rumble of the iron procession on the tracks below. Enveloped in the fumes and smoke of the engine, my clothes were soiled, and I watched as the train pulled away from the station.

# Notes

A good-faith effort has been made to remain true to the timing of events and the existence of the businesses and people during the time period selected for this book. For the most part, the reader will find that while the main characters and the story are fictional, the facts and public events presented are entirely true and chronologically accurate. One notable exception is the existence of the business the Southern Turf. The Southern Turf remains one of the most colorful elements of the early 1900s in Nashville. Its demise ultimately came about in February 1916, approximately four months prior to the time period during which this story is based. There is no doubt that there were alternative gambling houses and saloons of which could be written, but none as well documented or as colorful as the Southern Turf. So in a fit of artistic license, I extended the life of the Southern Turf by a few months.

## PLACES AND THINGS

We are fortunate that some of the great places and artifacts mentioned still exist today, albeit often in different modes of business.

The Arcade is one of the earliest indoor malls in the country and is still in existence today serving the downtown community with the same type of businesses it has provided for almost a century—postal service, barbers, hairdressers, restaurants, clothiers, drugstores, optometrists, peanut shop, and more. There are recent rumblings that it may become a parking lot as so many of the great architectural examples of early Nashville. Let's hope that it does not come to pass.

Castner Knott, also known as Castner's, closed the downtown doors to its faithful customers in 1996. The company itself continued for a number of years with other locations in the city before being sold to Dillard's in 1998. The downtown building still stands today, the main floor as a Morton's Restaurant and the upper portion as offices. Serious consideration has been given to preserving the basic structure with a tasteful modern touch. When a façade added in the 1960-70 time period was removed, it was discovered that the building and its windows had been well-preserved and the original brickwork and windows remain on the restored structure today.

The Doctor's Building had three additional floors added to it in 1921. It still exists today fully renovated and in use as a general office building. My father, Jim Hendrick, and my mother's father, Leonard S. Sims, managed the building along with the adjacent Bennie Dillon Building and the Vendome from 1921 until the 1980s. My maternal grandfather was known as the "Bishop of Church Street," a tip of the hat to the ownership of the buildings by the Methodist Board of Missions for many years. The architectural details of the building are true to my memories as a boy spent growing up literally in every nook and cranny of that building and the recollections of my parents who likewise spent a good number of years there, my mother as a child with her father and my father as a summertime carpenter's apprentice and later as manager of the building.

The Southern Turf Hotel became the offices for *The Tennessean* newspaper in 1916. It had a series of less illustrious tenants before being beautifully restored for its current use by the law firm of Trauger, Ney, and Tuke.

Union Station stills stands today, an elegant luxury hotel in the heart of the city. Its train shed, an architectural artifact was demolished recently due to safety concerns and for the expansion of a parking area.

Sadly, many other places no longer exist.

Athletic Field or Sulphur Dell with its sloping outfield is gone. It is now part of the Tennessee Bicentennial Mall and a state employee parking lot. A historical marker and fountain designate the area where the ball field once stood.

Glendale Park fell victim to the automobile. Originally an attraction to encourage use of the local rail system, it was unable to accommodate the need for parking and the demise of the trolleys in the 1940s. It is now a residential area covered in homes built mostly in the 1950s. Remnants of the old park remain visible including the entrance steps in a residential backyard, the foundation for the lion's cage in the front yard of a local church and the bear cave crafted in a hillside.

Greenwood Park no longer exists. It is now primarily an industrial park. However, the cemetery associated with Preston Taylor and of the Greenwood name still exists today and is one of the few cemeteries with plots available in the vicinity of the city.

The Maxwell House Hotel was lost in a Christmas Day fire in 1967. The local offices for a national banking corporation are located on the site where the grand hotel once stood.

The Trolleys no longer run in Nashville, at least not on rails. A modern-day reproduction of the original trolleys complete with tires and fueled by diesel roams the streets as more of a novelty than the mode of transportation of its inspiration. The original trolleys were sold to Seoul, Korea where they greeted many a surprised soldier from Nashville during the Korean War.

The Vendome perished in flames in October 1967 as has been the fate of so many other great structures. The building had endured the transition from Vaudeville and opera to the moving pictures and into the modern-day motion picture era before its ultimate demise.

The Women's Hospital is long since gone, superceded by newer more modern facilities. An office building originally built for the American General Corporation and more recently used as a State Office Building has its footprint where the hospital once stood.

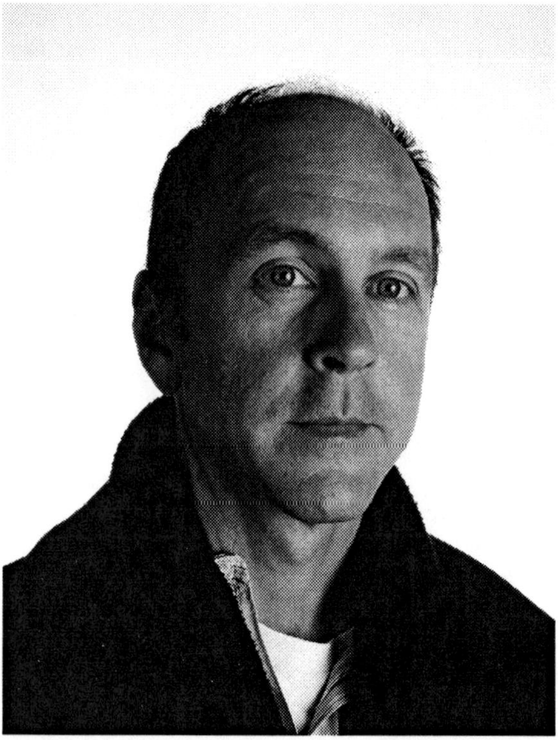

# About the Author

Robert grew up in Nashville. His early attempts at writing came in the form of illustrated comic books, and he even penned a song by age eight. He won the coveted Sam Davis Award for his historical chronicling of Sam Davis' life, but seeking acclaim for his work has never been a priority.

Unlike most of the wordsmiths in his native Nashville, he is not an aspiring songwriter who moved there from Canada or a farm somewhere in the Midwest. He is an author who claims the city as his home — a place where he grew up walking the city streets and learning the idiosyncrasies of the "Athens of the South" first hand.

He left his birthplace for a period of time to travel, work and study in faraway places like Australia, Germany and even Ohio and Alabama before returning to his home town for a professional career. Thrown into the high-tech world, he helped establish a local technology company before striking out on his own.

His fascination with a past age is evident in his obsession with historic architecture and his current business endeavor, a railroad service company. He loves to travel and spends his time chasing down railroad tracks in rural Tennessee towns that time has forgotten, riding his bicycle, restoring a 1920's bungalow and enjoying watching his children grow.

He graduated from Montgomery Bell Academy. From there, he spread his educational net wider and completed undergraduate studies at Auburn University and graduate studies at The Ohio State University. He also spent time at the Universities of Mannheim and Bonn in Germany.

The Doctor's Building is Robert's second novel. The first one — well, it was good practice.

Printed in the United States
67246LVS00003B/94-114